Hard Drive!

Hard Drive!
As the Disc Turns

Gordon Hughes

Gordon Hughes

2007

Hard Drive!

To my wife Shirley, who shared this journey.

Author's Preface

In 1980, Seagate Technology invented the first hard disc drive for personal computers, an invention that disrupted the world of computing. Seagate's innovators played their parts with courage and grace in the electronic computer revolution that began over fifty years ago with huge vacuum tube machines, far less powerful than today's PCs. The number of hard drives manufactured worldwide each year will pass one billion in a few years, for computers, printers, portable music players, video cameras, and TV recorders. Seagate is the largest drive maker today.

Craziness was commonplace in early Seagate for the company to survive, which its people called a "cowboy company." This would be impossible to capture in a simple documentary. Instead, this is the story of my adventure of a lifetime in research and engineering, expressing my admiration and respect for the founders of the company. Some may feel I have overstated their roles, but the original Seagate team that worked with them would agree that I haven't.

So, this is a fictional novel of craziness, excitement, and tears as Seagate first thrived, nearly died, survived and finally arrived dominant in drives. Thanks to those Seagators who participated in these adventures and thanks to those who gave me stories. Any mistakes are mine.

Glossary

Al	Seagate President and Chief Executive Officer
Bit	A unit of digital information, a single "0" or "1"
Byte	Eight bits, digital information that can represent one alphabetic character
Crash	Mechanical wear failure when a head fails to fly over a disc, instead making contact
Disc	User data bits are stored on disc magnetic surfaces, each bit on a nanoscopic spot of disc surface, magnetized north-south to store a "1" bit or south-north to store a "0" bit.
Doug	Seagate Chief Technology Officer "CTO"
Finis	Seagate hard drive inventor and Senior Vice President of Marketing
Gigabyte	One billion bytes, 1000 million bytes, 1000 megabytes
Head	A recording head writes and reads the bits on a disc surface, mounted on an air slider that flies millionths of an inch over a disc on an air cushion
Jim	Grenex Vice President of Technology
PC	IBM or IBM clone Personal computer
Stan	Doug's Vice President of Drive Engineering
Tom	Seagate's Vice President of drive manufacturing, later Seagate President

Prologue

Gordon and Shirley were flying from San Diego to San Jose, California, in their single engine Mooney airplane. It was night and they were in clouds, forced to fly on instruments. The plane's nose rose and dipped as they passed through the clouds, and the autopilot adjusted to keep them on their assigned altitude and air route. Gordon had just completed a trip to the University of California at San Diego, for computer hard disc maker Seagate Technology. Seagate and other computer data storage companies were founding a research and education center for their technology at UCSD. Gordon had represented Seagate.

"The engine sounds different," Shirley said.

Gordon had noticed an engine vibration. "It's misfiring," he said. "I'm checking into it." He scanned the engine instruments. They were all normal but the engine occasionally hiccupped roughly. He switched to the other gas tank. *Still rough*, he thought. The vibration was becoming more frequent and more severe.

Gordon recalled that his career at Seagate Technology had begun ten years earlier while piloting a small plane, and he wondered if it was now about to end in one.

He remembered that first flight to Seagate vividly.

I.

Meeting Seagate

In July 1982 Gordon landed his single engine airplane at Scotts Valley near Santa Cruz, California. Its airport lay in a valley closely ringed by forested mountains, requiring an awkward approach to land. One of the Apple Computer founders had recently crashed his small airplane there and the airport was about to be closed by the town fathers.

Gordon worked as a research engineer. He loved outdoor adventures, had climbed most of the tallest mountains in California, rafted through the Grand Canyon Colorado River rapids multiple times, and had taken powerboats far upstream into the rapids from Lake Mead. He wore glasses and had penetrating eyes that disturbed some people, eyes that seemed to see a little beyond surface appearances.

He had a Cal Tech Bachelor's degree in physics and doctorate in electrical engineering. He was fascinated with learning how the universe worked, and intellectually gifted just enough to go into research. This allowed him to avoid the tough realities of engineering products in the real world of unexpected technology failures and boom-bust business cycles, realities that researchers rarely see.

As Gordon taxied his plane to a parking spot he wondered how to get a taxicab in this rustic valley. He was meeting with Doug, the Chief Technology Officer of Seagate Technology, a high-tech startup company in Scotts Valley, a town on the seaward side of the San Francisco peninsula, westward from Silicon Valley near Santa Cruz. Gordon was interviewing for a technology job at Seagate because his research lab at Xerox had been closed in a budget crunch. He had worked in magnetic recording research at Xerox for 14 years, the technology used to store information on computer hard disc drives.

Gordon loved mathematics and never insulted its worker bees, the numbers, by writing out their names. Fourteen wasn't mathematical, 14 was.

"I'm Doug," said a tall distinguished looking man stepping from a Porsche 911 he had driven up to Gordon's parked plane. Doug was dressed casually but his car and clothes looked new and expensive. He was tall, as many leaders are, and carried himself with an erect military posture. He had dark hair and a neatly trimmed beard with traces of gray.

Gordon hoped his amazement didn't show. "Does the Seagate CTO often pick up job interviewees, sir?"

"Everyone at Seagate uses first names," Doug replied. "Titles get in the way of getting things done in a startup company like ours."

For the first time, Gordon noticed the unusual way Seagate people had of jumping to the final conclusion of a conversation, ignoring all intermediary discussion, like how Doug had known where and when to pick him up. Somehow they omitted the ordinary conventions of conversation to get to the end conclusions faster. They sometimes inserted "blah, blah, blah" in the middle to mark the omissions.

They drove in Doug's Porsche down Scotts Valley Boulevard, a straight country road passing through a sleepy town with occasional stores, some boarded up. The town had no traffic lights. A freeway bypassed the town, noisily occupying the valley center, luring most of the traffic and all of the tourists away from any exposure to local town businesses.

"The town fathers are encouraging high-tech companies to locate here," Doug explained, "to keep the town from decaying." Doug turned a corner at a farm feed store and they drove down a back road past weed-covered fields. The rural atmosphere suddenly vanished as they entered a newly paved street with high-tech industrial buildings on both sides. They might have been in Silicon Valley instead of Scotts Valley, and the buildings bore similarly obscure high-tech names. One building was marked "Seagate Technology." Doug parked and showed Gordon around the factory, the single building that housed all of Seagate in 1982.

"Our current manufacturing volume is 600 hard drives a day," Doug said, "for Apple II and IBM personal computers. The drives hold 5 megabytes of user data on two discs, 14 times more than the floppy disc drive they replace, and they access user data far faster. We're now designing 10 megabyte drives and we want you to help us raise their storage capacity higher."

Building 600 drives per day seemed impossible to Gordon because disc drives had always been built a few at a time, rather like airliners in Boeing factories.

"We built the first 'Disc II' drives for the Apple II by hand and sold them for $800 each. Now Apple pays us far less and we have to manufacture in large volume to make a decent profit."

"Can I see the drive test area?" Gordon asked, thinking that the true manufacturing volume would be clear there. They walked down a factory hall, passing windows that looked into a series of clean rooms filled with dozens of workers putting drives together, each dressed head to toe in a clean room white garment called a "bunny suit." The long hall terminated at the end of the drive assembly line, where Gordon saw sliding glass doors covering one entire wall of a large room filled with steel carts. Each cart held hundreds of disc drives on rack shelves made of steel rods, looking like barbeque grills. The drives and shelves had rectangular shapes, reminding Gordon of a Picasso Cubism sculpture. Red lights on the drives blinked busily on and off, accompanied by a soft cacophony of mechanical buzzing.

"This is our burn-in room, where we test each drive for several days at an elevated temperature to weed out infant failure drives. Their red LED activity lights come on whenever a drive is writing or reading data. Go ahead, stick your hand inside. The drives are sealed against contamination before they leave the assembly clean rooms." Doug was smiling, accustomed to visitors finding it difficult to believe so many disc drives could be running in a single room.

Gordon slid the glass door open a little and put his arm inside. *It must be over 100 degrees in there. The clicking from that many drives sounds like a swarm of crickets in Mormon desert heat*," he thought.

"The insides of the drives are even hotter from the heat of their spinning discs and motors," Doug said.

"What are those shoebox size machines with long plastic tubes poking into the drives? They look like hospital IV tubes."

"They're detectors for microscopic dust particles. NASA originally developed their technology to test clean rooms where space satellites are built. They give an alarm if they detect any dust or contamination particle larger than ten millionths of an inch. We use them to make sure new drives are running clean. Particles that get between a recording head and the disc surface it's flying over can cause the head to crash. The air slider skis that carry each head fly only 19 millionths of an inch above the disc surfaces.

"Actually, NASA particle counters aren't precise enough for our work and we've had to redesign them to detect much smaller particles than NASA allows. As a matter of fact, I'm looking to hire a clean room technologist—do you know one?"

"Yeah, I do. His name's Ron. I'll give him your number."

They walked out the rear door of the building, onto a parking lot. A row of tall trees stood on the far end of the lot, blocking some of the noise from the freeway just beyond. Gordon was surprised to see dozens more of the rack carts sitting in the parking lot, each covered with plastic wrap and filled with silent drives. He looked at Doug with a puzzled expression.

"We've outgrown our shipping room and we're using this parking lot as temporary space."

"Isn't Scotts Valley close to the San Andreas Fault?" Gordon asked, still wanting to test Doug's expertise. "Couldn't an earthquake be disastrous with all these drives on carts?"

"We've done an earthquake survey on Scotts Valley and the real risk is from the San Andreas Fault over the hill, far more dangerous for Silicon Valley than us.

"I'll show you the new campus we're building down the road," Doug continued. They walked back to his car and he drove them to the side road, plunging them back in the rural countryside. A minute later he was turning off Scotts Valley Boulevard onto a newly constructed side street with a shiny new sign naming it "Disc Drive." Gordon smiled at the pun as he saw it led to a Silicon Valley style industrial campus with two high-tech buildings under construction, each twice the size of the Seagate building they had just visited.

"That's pretty funny Doug, naming the street Disc Drive."

Doug smiled. "Ask Al about that."

Gordon guessed that having a little fun in disc drivery might be a Seagate cultural mantra. He liked the idea. They turned around and drove back onto Scotts Valley Boulevard, stopping a few blocks down at an empty mall building designed for six small retail businesses. They went inside and looked around, stopping in a corner office obviously intended for the boss. They sat down.

Doug said calmly, "Gordon, I want you to be our Director of Recording Technology. This building will house your lab while we build your permanent building next to the two new buildings you just saw on Disc Drive. You can buy whatever equipment you need and hire whomever you want for your group."

Gordon was taken aback by this Silicon Valley bottom-line directness. Doug reached into his coat pocket for an envelope. "This letter is your Seagate job offer showing your salary and your Seagate stock option." Gordon's eyes widened as he read the letter. The salary offer seemed shockingly high to a researcher like him. The stock option alone was a small fortune at Seagate's current stock price. It was a typical five-year option, to motivate him to work hard to make the company grow so the option would be worth more after several years, when he would be able to sell the first quarter of his Seagate shares.

"Also, we want you to work with Grenex, our new venture capital startup company that's developing a cobalt magnetic disc for future Seagate drives."

Gordon was intrigued, familiar from his Xerox research with high-tech cobalt magnetic recording discs that allowed more computer information to be stored on each disc. Cobalt discs could help Seagate greatly expand its business. His eyes lit up. "Doug, I've been working in computer data storage on cobalt recording discs for years! Before Xerox

I worked on cobalt discs up to four feet in diameter at Librascope in Glendale. After that I helped design twenty inch diameter cobalt disc drives at a company Xerox bought to get into computerized document processing." He left out an intermediary job he had had at an aerospace company, thinking it not relevant.

"Yes, I know," Doug replied in his composed manner. "The job offer letter also shows your Grenex stock option, priced at 5¢ per share."

Gordon felt his head spinning as he estimated what those shares would be worth if Grenex was successful and its stock rose to $50. He knew that most Silicon Valley high-tech companies were like a Fourth of July firework show. They soared high, then failed and vanished. Only a few became long-term success stories like Hewlett-Packard and Intel. But Gordon was thinking that even if Grenex failed, starting a new Seagate recording technology lab was his dream job. He could see that Seagate wasn't going to fail.

He didn't know that if Grenex did come close to failure, both his Seagate job and his entire career would be in peril. He didn't understand that life in a Silicon Valley high-tech startup company was like war. Long, high-stress job hours put heavy pressure on people's lives and health. Silicon Valley design teams had to survive through multiple cycles of new product designs; otherwise, technology "racial memory" could be lost. NASA space mission design teams were under similar high-tech stress, but disbanded after a single mission. Hard learned lessons were sometimes forgotten by new NASA teams and nearly two-thirds of Mars space probes had failed.

Words sprang from Gordon's lips without any command from his brain. "I like the job offer!"

"I want you to meet Al in Las Vegas next week," Doug said.

Gordon knew Al was Seagate's President and CEO, and had been on the IBM engineering team that invented the world's first disc drive in 1956. That first drive had weighed a ton, had 50 two-foot diameter discs, and stored only 5 megabytes: the same capacity as Seagate's first miniature disc drive. Al had later formed several Silicon Valley startup companies that manufactured disc drives in competition with IBM.

Al was an outstanding leader who inspired great loyalty in his team members. He didn't personally invent disc drive technology: not the 1956 IBM RAMAC disc drive, or the first floppy drive, or the first hard drive for personal computers.

Al's contribution was to make high performance, low cost drives available to the world. Early drives had been built a few at a time. Al built them by the millions.

His companies were run under strict ethics. This came from Al himself, who was honest to a fault. He once said, "I decided that I couldn't lie about anything, even though lying would make things better." Al's ethics had the virtue of being so simple that they were perfectly clear to every company employee. In ambiguous situations, they would simply ask themselves, "What would Al say?"

2.

Computers in Victorian England

Disc drives were the answer to a world dream a century and a half old, for fast storage and retrieval of computer programs and their data, a dream that began with the work of Ada, Countess of Lovelace in Victorian England. She developed the first computer programming concepts for Charles Babbage's 1820 *Difference Engine*, a mechanical computer.

A century and a half after Babbage, early personal computers like the 1978 Apple I were toys because they had no disc drive, and only a few hundred were sold.

The 1979 Apple II had the first PC floppy disc drive and millions were sold. One of Al's companies made Apple's floppy drives.

At the time Gordon joined Seagate, disc drive technology was about to simultaneously explode in performance, sophistication, nanotechnology, and affordability. Disc drive internal hardware and software technology were becoming as sophisticated as the computers they were installed in. Uses would explode for low cost, high capacity, high speed disc drives.

When Gordon's Xerox lab closed he had consulted for Apple Computer on a new floppy disc drive they were designing. He had bought a surplus Data General 800 minicomputer from his closing Xerox lab and ran it at home, doing magnetic recording designs for the new Apple floppy drive. As his own boss he quickly found that he overworked himself. He found himself running computer programs morning to night. The pay barely matched what he had made at Xerox, and he had no medical or other benefits. He told his friends, "I have the world's toughest boss: me." This Seagate job seemed like a dream to him.

As Gordon took off from the Scotts Valley airport to fly home, he wondered what he was in for. He had been born in L.A., had always worked at quiet research jobs in the L.A. area, had never lived in a city further away than Pasadena, and his girlfriend Shirley lived and worked in L.A. Shirley was a medical lab technician at the University of California at Los Angeles. She was a beautiful woman, five feet two inches tall, a slim brunette with nut-brown eyes that twinkled with fun and intelligence. When she smiled her face turned radiant, brightening the world around her like a sunrise over Hawaii. Tough as a Marine in matters of personal responsibility, she had an amazing sensitivity to people. When Gordon occasionally visited places they usually went to together, strangers would tell Gordon of her thoughtful kindnesses, like bringing lunch to a store clerk who had no relief worker to give him a noon break. Shirley saved her money as her father had taught her from his experience in the Great Depression. She had invested in apartment buildings and then a commercial mall.

Slim and outgoing, Shirley would poke her elbow in Gordon's ribs if she thought he was being too geeky or not listening to her. Gordon couldn't bear the thought of leaving her.

After he landed his plane back in L.A. he drove to Shirley's house in Sherman Oaks for dinner. She was a gourmet cook and as he walked in he wondered if she would make one of his favorite meals. Perhaps beef scaloppini, or pasta carbonara, or fajitas with chili rellenos she called "Mexican trout." They looked like breaded fish, fresh from the stream and ready to fry.

Gordon was about to explain his job interview when Charles, Shirley's tomcat, came into the room and began rubbing against his leg. Gordon thought Charles was the world's greatest. He was a large grey tomcat with white paws. Charles had a regal and serene bearing, was affectionate with people, and was a fearless hunter. He presumed anyone arriving at Shirley's house had come solely to pet him. When Gordon drove up to her house, Charles would often be sitting on her driveway, intently watching for rats in the ivy across the street. Once, as Gordon walked in, he had seen Charles suddenly leap up and race across the street into the ivy at fantastic speed, seizing a rat with his teeth.

He caught so many rats they made him ill. After that he left the rats at Shirley's door, expecting praise. The man living in the house across the street with the ivy became fond of Charles after rats stopped appearing in his basement. He began sneaking treats out to Charles at his hunting post on Shirley's driveway.

Mockingbirds sometimes dive-bombed Charles as he sat in the driveway. He totally ignored them as they chattered and flew past, an inch from his ear. One time, Gordon arrived to find a circle of mockingbird feathers around Charles' usual post on the driveway. *I wonder if I'll find a dead bird at the doorstep.*

On trash pickup days, Charles would occasionally encounter one of the clever coyotes that lived in the hills of Los Angeles. They checked neighborhood garbage cans for food and knew which day of the week the cans were put out. Like Charlie Brown in the Peanuts comic strip, Charles seemed able to distract potential enemies by starting a discussion. If a coyote did try to attack Charles, his backup was to jump onto Shirley's roof, first leaping onto the half-inch wide top rail of a fence, then balancing on its narrow edge as he prepared for his second leap to the rooftop.

"Honey, now that Charles and I have said hello properly, I'll tell you the big news. I have the job offer from IBM that you know about, and now this one from Seagate. All the disc drive companies in L.A. have folded and one way or another it looks like my job is moving to Silicon Valley."

"Well, I'll quit my job at UCLA and we'll move to Silicon Valley."

This act of faith melted Gordon's heart, and he suddenly knew how deeply he loved her and that he couldn't leave without her. His fear of marriage commitment evaporated at the thought of losing her. But he wondered how to find the courage to ask her to marry him. She had been a happily independent single lady all her life, enjoying trips with Gordon in airplanes and boats, large and small, to go traveling, water skiing, snow skiing, and river running. Gordon was quietly terrified. *What if she says no? Maybe she just enjoys traveling with me, not marrying me.*

Shirley began making dinner. Gordon watched, enjoying the way her slim figure moved.

Dinner turned out to be Steak Diane. They ate in silent enjoyment for a time. "Honey, I have an idea how to choose between the two jobs," he told her. "I'll call Robert. He's a buddy that worked at the IBM San Jose disc drive research division. He just started his own recording disc manufacturing company, Lanx. Robert's a brilliant recording theoretician. Get this; he owns a World War II halftrack, a tank-like vehicle he once drove to IBM, terrifying its management. They thought their parking lot would get torn up. His hobby is collecting large heavy machines. He told me, 'I wouldn't have driven the halftrack to IBM again even if my bosses hadn't objected. Driving over concrete streets caused a bunch of wear on my steel treads and I found out replacement treads cost thousands of dollars.'"

They finished and Gordon cleared the table and rinsed the dishes while Shirley put away leftovers.

The next morning, Gordon made a call. "Hi, Robert, I need some job advice. My Xerox lab closed and I have two Silicon Valley job offers. One's from IBM research."

"O.K.," Robert replied. "What's the other one?"

"It's an offer to start a recording technology research and engineering group at Seagate. I'd be doing recording designs for their new technology drives and helping them develop new recording heads and discs."

"Like the cobalt discs we're developing here at Lanx, Gordon?"

That guess was uncannily accurate. "I can't say, Robert. That's proprietary information."

"The IBM job sounds like the same kind of research position I had with them. They're good people and it's a smart and stable company, but..."

"But what, Robert?"

"Well, I think you'll like Seagate more because you'll have the personal reward of getting new technology into production. You'll be able to help design products that'll be used by people all over the world."

"Thanks. I appreciate the advice." Robert's words helped him realize how exciting Seagate could be. *And to think the IBM job was at the top of my list, until now.*

"Stop by Lanx the next time you're in the Valley," Robert said. "I'll show you our operation. You probably remember Susan, our disc magnetics technologist."

"Yes, I remember her," Gordon replied. He recalled a well endowed brunette with a magnetic sexual chemistry.

Gordon was one of five children, and had a twin brother who would have been a model son if Gordon hadn't frequently incited him into trouble.

Initially a normally social child, Gordon turned inward when he found he was last to be chosen in any school sport and wasn't attractive to girls. When he reached fifth grade he realized he was the shortest boy in his class and last to be chosen for a baseball team. His early interest in girls was crushed when he realized that being shorter mattered.

He turned to solitary interests like electronics, math, and physics.

Gordon spent his childhood studying electronics instead of learning social graces, like remembering people's names. He grew up unable to remember names of people he was introduced to. He thought intellectual skills were superior to such "people" skills. In his college years at Cal Tech, he and the other students had grown to normal heights, and many had similar childhood stories.

Gordon's father was a decent and honest lawyer of genteel manners from the U.S. South. He grew up with three brothers in Memphis, Tennessee. Brother John was a world famous Internist and Jim had written the standard text on pediatrics. Gordon had once flown his father to Memphis to visit them. They flew to Oklahoma City for fuel and lunch, arriving in Memphis that evening. They had gone to gatherings of the large Hughes family clan and seen the Memphis Belle, a Boeing B-17 bomber retired from World War II after somehow surviving 25 bombing missions. One weekend, the Hughes men drove to cabins they had at Bear Creek Lake in Arkansas. They boated around the lake on Jim's flat deck party barge to the tune of "Happy Days are Here Again." Jim played a flute, Uncle John a violin and the rest sang loudly on and off key. As they rounded bends in the heavily forested lake they startled fishermen in anchored bass boats. Back in the cabin they competed at horseshoes while drinking "weak and puny" cocktails, a fatal concoction they had invented long before.

The next morning Jim's boat motor wouldn't start. Gordon took it apart and cleaned gunk out of its gas lines. "You're rather clever at many things, Gordon," Uncle Jim said as he watched.

"If I pumped gas for a living, I'd feel stupid and worthless compared to the Memphis Hughes clan," Gordon replied.

Gordon's salvation was his tolerant and loving mother. Through her came his lifelong love of music from her piano playing of Debussy, and his love of philosophy through her college books. She worked in personnel for a department store in downtown L.A., and managed to successfully raise five kids, although Gordon was a great challenge.

She encouraged his science interests, once unwisely accepting the gift of a professional chemistry lab with gallon glass bottles of nitric and sulfuric acid. Gordon tried combining nitric acid and glycerin, hoping to make nitroglycerine. He was fortunately ignorant of the correct recipe. Throwing rocks at a pint bottle of his "nitro" in the back yard, the explosion could have killed him and destroyed part of the house. He also made gunpowder bombs, fortunately with similar lack of success.

His mother tolerated Gordon's misdeeds even though they made her home the first place city investigators came to when a fire had been lit on some nearby vacant lot. After a grammar school lock picking escapade, the principal bet his mother that Gordon would wind up in jail. Mother counter bet that Gordon would graduate from Cal Tech instead. It was Gordon's good fortune that his mother was active in school affairs and president of the PTA. When Gordon got in trouble, the principal called her first.

His behavior finally got him sent to a psychologist in downtown L.A. His mother drove him to the sessions and they had picnic lunches afterwards in MacArthur Park, throwing bread crumbs to the ducks. Gordon loved these outings and invented ways to keep them going. He taught himself to write backwards and upside down, which got him several more trips to the park. He practiced drawing a Buck Rodgers space battle with one starship destroying another by blaster rays. The therapist finally told his mother to just patiently wait until Gordon decided to grow up. Today's less forgiving society might have labeled him "autistic" or "attention deficit disorder" and sedated him.

The potential consequences of these foolish pranks ultimately penetrated Gordon's young mind. He finally realized his mother couldn't always protect him. If he was convicted of a crime when no longer a juvenile, he might be barred from the technology career he longed for. He decided to become law abiding. Like many boy children, he primarily needed to be taught the thin veneer of proper behavior to successfully live in modern society, to mask the human genetic wiring that had evolved for mankind to live in small villages where all adults were equally responsible for all children. A mark of any successful civilization was its ability to civilize young boys before they became criminal adults, by simply making it more rewarding to be honest.

As Gordon turned thirty, he was appalled to discover that people skills were far more important and complex than technology skills. Everyone seemed to have learned these skills except him. Although he struggled to catch up, he found that an adult couldn't learn social skills as easily as a child. He struggled unsuccessfully to memorize people's names as they were introduced. He carried photographs of people and wrote their names on the backs. Sometimes people asked for a copy of the photo, thanking him for his thoughtfulness and not suspecting his handicap. He wrote names of people down on scraps of paper, to memorize later ("Robert Planter/black hair/wears loud shirts/brilliant recording research for IBM/owns Bonanza airplane and World War II half track"). He put these scraps of paper in his shirt pockets, where they would usually be later lost in the laundry. He finally began a lifetime habit of writing names and descriptions in shirt pocket diaries, eventually amassing twenty years of tiny annual journals.

Gordon finally learned to translate the conventions of normal social conversation and mentally "compute" appropriate replies, although it felt like translating into a clumsy alien language from a foreign country. Gordon's social translations became automatic after a few years. Sometimes people even complimented him on remembering names of their family, not realizing he had just looked them up in his diary. The invention of email and hand-held PDA computers were godsends, to permanently record names, events, and dates. He could search his past contacts with someone, to remind him what he knew about the person and what to say.

Deep down, Gordon thought most people found him unexciting. As a conversation piece, he had started carrying around an Italian man's handbag he had bought on a trip to Venice, Italy. He found he could stuff it with many useful things: his wallet and check book, glasses case, magnifying glass, compass, and a miniature pepper mill that held samples of foreign pepper corns he collected for his exotic pepper hobby. Later, it also held his cell phone and PDA portable computer.

3.

A Scientist Gets Religion

One afternoon, Gordon was wondering why he looked at the world so differently, and suddenly realized that his viewpoint of life was completely abnormal. In a flash he saw the normal human viewpoint and realized that it was a deceptive distortion of a deeper reality. He had to understand what that meant and so he went for a walk to try to clear his head. Passing a church, he entered and sat in its empty and silent sanctuary. He needed a quiet place to think out his revelation and a church seemed appropriate, although he hadn't been in one for years.

Being a scientist, he set out to apply the scientific method using a simple hypothesis: if God is real, God can have no limits.

I need to throw out everything I believe about the universe and start over. Our world of ordinary experience emerges from an unlimited reality beyond that acts as the projector of the totally captivating movie we all live in. Its complexity and busy commotions constantly change to distract everyone from looking away from the screen. I'll call this deeper reality the Central Truth. It has limitless power to convince because it has none of the limitations of space and time.

Our space-time universe is limited to surface appearances that we interpret as physical objects separated by space and carried in a relentlessly flowing river of time. Now I see that the apparent future and past is really a dimensionless Unity of space in a timeless Now. Even science itself is mesmerized by its intricately detailed surface appearances, and deals only with concrete and repeatable surface 'facts.' Science believes in a past and a future consistent with experimental verification, but experiments are possible only in the Now moment of time we're perpetually imprisoned in. It's our only direct immediate experience. I must be seeing the mystery that people long to understand; that makes scientists search for a "grand unified theory of everything," that unites all reality into a single Unity.

The scientific method itself is a way to create new apparent reality, by assuming a hypothesis and working to make accepted reality depend on its validity, like Maxwell's laws of electromagnetic radiation require radio and x-

ray waves to exist because visible light waves exist. Scientists make hypotheses and try to "real-ize" them. New ideas have to hook into accepted truth or they get rejected. Like a jigsaw puzzle, new pieces have to fit with the others somewhere.

This Central Truth must be the common source of both science and religion. I remember rejecting the Sunday school religions Mom dragged me to, with their dumb pictures of God and Jesus as bearded white men wearing robes. Science and religion seem incompatible because science requires experimental demonstrations for proof of physical space-time hypotheses; religion only requires faith. Finding God may not require proof, but I think science's logic could be an invaluable guide. God's infinite acceptance and love must include all creatures, and God must somehow not mind any of mankind's games—peace, war, faith, atheism.

I remember the Buddhist Bhagavad-Gita book a grubby hippy handed me as I was passing through an airport once. It said that Truth could be realized not only through simple faith, but also through logic. A bloody cross or a shroud of Turin isn't necessary to find God and Jesus.

His enlightenment wrenched him away from the ordinary human world of space and time, bringing him reluctantly near the presence of a brilliantly white Being of total acceptance, who wordlessly offered him a choice between returning to the human world or rejoining the Central Truth that gave rise to all. Gordon chose to turn away from the Central Truth and continue his life on Earth, as most did that came to this place.

He faced a difficult mental task because his enlightened mind was now sensing the entire sea of human thoughts, like a radio simultaneously listening to all stations at the same time. A torrent of thoughts from all humanity nearly overwhelmed him, coming through the "sixth sense" shared in common by all life. Selfish, mean, and evil thoughts overpowered quieter kind and good thoughts.

After a difficult mental struggle, he managed to pass through the shadow of death that some called being "born again," and tune down the "Common Sense" radio that some called intuition, instinct, or gut feeling. *These other names are just euphemisms for this sense shared in common by all humans, a sense most people are reluctant to talk about. Admitting its existence would threaten their comfortable space-time movie world. Mankind fears to look too closely at the Common Sense, but the world's lower animals must comfortably use it to teach rules of social behavior to their young, rules too complex to be genetically coded; rules misnamed as "instincts." Mass riots and the shared madness of crowds must come through the Common Sense. The reason nursery rhymes persist for centuries is through children unconsciously sharing the Common Sense: "Ring around the rosy" from the 1665 London plague, ended only by the great Fire of London that destroyed the plague fleas and the rats they rode on.*

In returning from his enlightenment, Gordon could choose a single understanding to bring back to the ordinary world. He chose probability theory mathematics relevant to statistical pattern recognition. His insight was to allow pattern probabilities to have probabilities. It led to his best technical paper, published in the January 1968 issue of the *Transactions on Information Theory.*

4.

Pauling and Feynman: Charismatic Cal Tech Professors

Gordon had studied at Cal Tech at a unique time: when Richard Feynman and Linus Pauling were teaching. Feynman had not yet won his Nobel Prize in Physics for quantum electrodynamics. Pauling had his first Nobel for discovering the nature of the chemical bond. His second Nobel would be the Peace Prize for his successful public campaign to end nuclear bomb testing in the Earth's atmosphere.

Pauling almost earned a third Nobel, by nearly beating Watson and Crick to the discovery of the DNA double helix. Pauling was a pioneer in early DNA molecular structure research beginning in 1951, but the British had better microphotographs of DNA molecular crystallography. Pauling was unfortunately barred from traveling to England by unfounded accusations during the U.S. anticommunist panic. He missed seeing the British DNA photos and thereby missed sharing in the Nobel. Watson and Crick published first.

Cal Tech had only male undergraduate students in 1955 and Gordon was among equals in the freshman class. They were mostly white and Asian, with several blacks. It was an ego blow to be among students smarter than him, but he had expected that. He had read a *Time* magazine article extolling the brilliance of Cal Tech students, so he had spent the summer before studying the freshman textbooks. Some students drowned in Cal Tech's pressure cooker competition. Others pondered *Mad* magazine's motto "Potrezebe, it bounces." They all discussed mathematical questions like "Can you integrate that over all space?"

Pauling and Feynman were outstanding teachers who understood the nature of youngsters studying to become scientists. Feynman played bongo drums at student gatherings and talked of his lock picking days at Los Alamos during World War II atomic bomb development. Gordon and many other boys immediately bought piano wire and became expert lock pickers. During Pasadena rains they walked to class through campus underground steam tunnels, picking door locks to get in and out of class buildings.

Feynman's physics lectures awed all of them. He would say, "I wonder how lightning works and how powerful it is." Turning to the blackboard, he would think aloud on how clouds became electrically charged by winds, and write physics math equations on the board to calculate how many volts and amps were produced in a lightning strike. The boys thought he was coming up with ideas as he spoke, not realizing that the best teachers all have a certain amount of showmanship.

Gordon often attended Cal Tech's Wednesday night demonstration lectures. These were held weekly by the Physics Department on topics of general interest, and were open to the Pasadena public. One evening Feynman gave a public lecture on quantum mechanics, fascinating and captivating as always. After the lecture ended, Gordon walked out of the lecture hall behind two elderly Pasadena ladies with white hair. One was talking to the other. "I never realized how simple quantum mechanics was until Professor Feynman explained the subject."

That's wonderful, Gordon smiled in admiration.

Linus Pauling also employed showmanship in his weekly chemistry lectures, although Gordon didn't realize it until years later. Pauling would peer tolerantly over the top of his bifocal glasses at his audience of a hundred geeky boys, most wearing glasses and wearing a slide rule holsters on their belt.

Holding up a colorful crystal, Pauling had once said, "What is the size of the molecule that makes this beautiful lapis lazuli crystal, also called sapphire?" Taking a six-inch slide rule from his coat pocket, he had moved its slide back and forth and announced "12.1613 Angstroms."

Everyone used slide rules in those days and the boys knew they were only accurate to three digits: 12.1 could be read off but Pauling's six digits could not. They speculated among themselves on how Pauling did it, some guessing he could remember the entire number if the slide rule gave him the first three correct digits.

Gordon came closer to the truth. "Lattice constants are only measured to three digits. I looked up sapphire in the physics library and it's listed as 12.1 Angstroms."

The boys never quite figured out that Linus actually calculated the correct 12.1 Angstroms, but then added extra random digits to mystify his young audience, a bit of innocent but attention-holding showmanship similar to Feynman's.

Many Nobel Prize winners had similar showmanship talents. Less showmanship, less chance of a prize.

One day a fellow student in chemistry lab had asked Gordon, "Why are you dissolving iodine crystals in ammonium hydroxide?"

"I'm making nitrogen triiodide. Our weekly freshman chemistry lecture starts in an hour, and it's a guest lecturer from another school. I'm going to smear this wet powder on the blackboard sliding rails and the floor."

"Why do that?"

"Because when it dries it becomes a touch sensitive explosive, which will go off when the lecturer steps on it or moves the blackboards. There'll be a big bang and clouds of purple smoke."

An hour later, the guest lecturer had filled a blackboard with equations and threw it up with a flourish to get a fresh blackboard to write on, creating a tremendous boom and a cloud of purple smoke. He had stood absolutely still for the rest of the lecture, writing and erasing on one small section of one blackboard.

It never occurred to Gordon to even imagine doing this when Professor Pauling lectured.

After Gordon received his bachelor's degree from Cal Tech in physics, his mother took his diploma to his grammar school principal and collected on her bet. Gordon knew that without his mother and a few special school teachers and adults, he very well could have wound up in jail instead of Cal Tech.

He continued his studies at Cal Tech, doing his doctorate work in experimental electronic physics. But his professors found he broke lab equipment too often, and they advised him to turn to theoretic computer mathematics work for his dissertation.

To support himself while working on his PhD, he took a part time job at Librascope, a computer company in Glendale near L.A. Here he saw his first disc drives, built for Navy submarines. They only stored a few megabytes of data even though they were larger than refrigerators. He found that Librascope engineers designed new drives by scaling down the components of their last successful product. They scaled down the diameter of the recording head core; a small donut made of magnetic ceramic called ferrite, and scaled the copper wire coil wound through it. These heads recorded bits on a magnetic disc by sending current through the coil, and later read back the stored bits as small voltage pulses in the coil when disc magnetic bits passed under the head. He developed a mathematical theory to properly design new drives, allowing their performance to be predicted in advance.

This was the start of Gordon's career in disc drive research and design.

He applied his new theory to the latest product Librascope was designing and showed his results to its project manager. "You're telling me that my readback signals will be smaller than one millivolt? That's quite amazing to be able to predict that in advance. If you're correct, my drives won't meet their data readback bit error rate specs. But I have to allow for the possibility that your theory may be wrong because I have a very tight program schedule. What should I do?"

Gordon thought for a moment. "Double the size of the coil opening in your ferrite recording heads, so you'll be able to fit in double the number of wire turns you're now intending. There's no harm if I'm wrong. When you do see the small readback voltages I'm predicting, you can just double the number of turns to double the voltage. If you have to redesign the ferrite coil opening bigger to make the turns fit in, you'll have a four month project delay before your new larger ferrite heads can be manufactured and shipped to you." The manager agreed, and was glad that he had when Gordon was proved correct in the tragic month of November 1963.

5.

Keeping Nuclear Missiles Deadly

When Gordon finished his Cal Tech PhD in 1963 he took a job as a system analyst at Autonetics, an aerospace division of North American Aviation. He worked on the Minuteman missile program, the U.S. land-based intercontinental ballistic missile fleet. It had obsoleted earlier and better-known cryogenic liquid fueled ICBMs like Atlas and Thor, due to Minuteman's advanced integrated circuit computer, disc drive, inertial guidance gyros, and low-maintenance solid fuel rocket.

Gordon felt the work was his contribution to national defense during the Cold War, because he hadn't served in the military. He was in high school during the Korean War, and Cal Tech got him a draft deferment during the Vietnam War.

Minuteman missiles could reach Cold War targets up to 3000 miles away, with trajectories passing over the North Pole. For that reason their underground silo launch pads were built at Air Force bases in northern U.S. states. A Minuteman missile nose cone carried three reentry vehicles, each able to deliver a 1.2-megaton hydrogen bomb to an individual target.

With a thousand of these missiles ready to launch in minutes and obliterate Earth many many times over with hydrogen bombs having the explosive force of 3,600,000,000 tons of TNT, World War III was being deterred during the Cold War and indefinitely afterward.

Albert Einstein, who wrote the letter to President Franklin Roosevelt that started the World War II atomic bomb Manhattan Project, was once asked about World War III. He said "I know not with what weapons World War III will be fought, but World War IV will be fought with sticks and stones."

The Minuteman project was highly classified on a "need to know" basis, which had an unfortunate side effect of sometimes hiding problems in the program. Gordon found he could use the Common Sense to get a "big picture" view of the missile system and its project divisions, and he got a Top Secret clearance to help find problems hidden across "need to know" boundaries.

One of his early projects was analyzing the work of the Missile Reliability Department, which had hundreds of workers and occupied one entire Autonetics building. They analyzed field reliability failure reports from the thousand Minuteman missile silos. Gordon decided to research one of these failure reports, apparently submitted by a crusty field technician who had written, "The hydraulic actuators in your missiles all begin leaking oil after a year or two. I'm tired of wiping the hydraulic fluid up. Can't your engineers design anything that keeps working in my real world at the bottom of an 80-foot tall missile silo under a 100-ton blast door?"

Gordon looked at the signatures of the men in the Reliability Department who had handled this complaint. One man logged in the field reports, a second collected statistics on failure types, a third applied binomial probability math to the report data to prove the missiles were reliable, a fourth wrote memos summarizing the reliability, and a final man filed the memos away. Gordon slowly came to realize that these people had no function except to send pieces of paper to each other. He also figured that using binomial math was wrong and only served as techno-blabble.

He investigated where the original silo field reports actually came in and found a small engineering group that received them first. They assigned engineers and technicians to solve each problem and documented the results. The hundreds of workers in the Reliability Department were completely uninvolved in any of this actual work, and only received copies of final reports from the actual problem solvers. Gordon took this bizarre situation to the main program office. They smiled and told him, "That's not a surprising situation in government work. We call it a 'G-job.'"

Apparently Washington Pentagon brass couldn't believe that so small a reliability group could properly serve a missile program so critical to U.S. defense in the Cold War. Gordon wrote up his conclusions and sent them to the program office to officially record the situation. He was surprised to get a letter in return, promising the closure of the entire reliability division.

A few months later, Gordon stopped at the Minuteman reliability building out of curiosity. It was indeed closed and its hundreds of staff gone. He went to see the small engineering group that did the actual work fixing missile problems. Its boss told him, "Yeah, we noticed they were gone, but we never understood what they actually did for the company anyway. The building they were in was constructed to house the original Minuteman guidance design engineers. There was a lot of excitement in it years ago during the first test firings from Vandenberg Air Force Base up the coast. We monitored the missile telemetry here and there was a lot of cheering when a missile hit its target island in the South Pacific. The telemetry antenna they used is still up on the building roof."

Gordon was having lunch in his office one day with his boss and several other Autonetics researchers. The company offices were furnished with scarred desks and filing cabinets that North American Aviation had bought in a World War II business expansion, to save money by not buying new desks for Autonetics.

Gordon lit up a cigarette and noticed his boss was frowning. He had been smoking short unfiltered Lucky Strike cigarettes since graduate school at Cal Tech. Looking around, he noticed that no one else was smoking. *Everyone in this group has stopped smoking except me. What's the chance it might hurt my performance reviews?* He decided to use this idea as motivation to quit. He snuffed out his cigarette and threw the pack into a wastebasket.

"What brought that on?" his boss asked, smiling.

"Nobody else smokes in your group, and I'm going to use that fact as my motivation to quit."

"Good luck. You realize there'll be a betting pool on whether you'll hold out for a day, a week, or a month, don't you."

"I'll bet $500 on no more cigarettes for me ever." *I think that may be just enough motivation for me to quit.*

Changing the subject, Gordon asked Bill, "Why do you bring peanut butter and jelly sandwiches for lunch every day?" "Don't you ever get tired of them?"

Bill said, "I loved them when I was a kid but my mother wouldn't make them for all my school lunches. Now I can have them all the time. I'm making up for a lost childhood."

He took another bite, shook his head in delight, and remarked, "I hear they're promoting John to Chief Scientist. He says our department has barely the minimum number of PhD degree researchers the government requires, and he's threatening to take it below minimum by leaving, if they don't give him the title."

Gordon spoke up. "You know, I wonder if John actually has the Stanford physics doctorate he claims. He doesn't seem to even understand undergraduate physics when I talk to him."

"Hey! I'll check with Stanford!" exclaimed Bill. He picked up a phone, got the number of the Stanford Provost office, and dialed. After explaining his request and listening for a few minutes, he said, "You don't show John with any Stanford degree at all? He was an undergrad but dropped out in his sophomore year? I see. Thanks very much." Bill hung up the phone. "I'm taking this to our division president," he said, storming out the door.

"Bill sure seems steamed," Gordon observed.

The next day Gordon ran into Bill and asked, "What happened?"

"John's Chief Scientist promotion papers had gone up the management chain all the way to the company Board of Directors. When the president got my message he found nobody had checked John's references when he was hired. The president was so angry he fired the personnel vice president on the spot. It looks like John overheard me calling Stanford because he's skipped town. He sold his car to a friend and told her he was going to South America. I bet he gets a job down there as a Chief Scientist, using the same phony resume he used here. The man's a pathological liar!"

Gordon's next Minuteman project was studying the missile targeting accuracy. He learned there were periodic launches of missiles with dummy warheads from Vandenberg Air Force Base at Point Conception on the central California coast. Their target was Kwajalein Atoll in the South Pacific. It had been chosen because the missile flight was entirely over the Pacific Ocean, to not endanger anyone on land in case a missile failed. Minuteman was an autonomous intercontinental ballistic missile, whose onboard computer handled all of its guidance and targeting. Once launched, no ground radio signal could cancel its mission; neither friend nor foe could stop its flight. Only flight test missiles carried self-destruct devices that allowed radio commands to abort a flight from the ground.

Gordon had once seen a Minuteman test launch while standing in front of a Las Vegas casino. The missile contrail lit up the twilight sky in the west. He saw its first rocket stage separate after 60 seconds of flight and saw the white contrail it left get quickly twisted by stratosphere winds. *Wow!* A few months later, he had been surf fishing with his friend Red at Jalama Beach on the coast in front of Vandenberg. Both wore waders and Gordon had just cast his line with its large triangular weight that carried the lure beyond the surf line.

Red said, "Gordon, listen to that klaxon that just started blaring. I've heard it here before. It's the Minuteman missile final launch warning."

They were turning around to look just as a Minuteman launched from the base behind them. It was awesome to see a black rocket with a blinding tail of fire rise behind the golden California hills that separated the base from the seacoast. Its roar beat on their bodies and ears as the missile flew directly overhead, accelerating supersonically towards the southwest.

Gordon looked up the history of Minuteman flight test data, which showed the missile had remarkable accuracy in landing in the center of the Kwajalein Atoll lagoon. Everyone accepted that this accuracy would be valid for actual war launches, but the repetitive testing reminded Gordon of the way army artillery was ranged onto targets. He went to check his thinking with Bill.

"Bill, an artillery cannon crew will fire a round beyond their intended target and then a second round in front of it. By bracketing the target in between, they know that interpolating between the two miss distances will accurately aim their gun directly at the target. Then they issue the order 'fire for effect.'"

"You think the Vandenberg targeting people use past missile test data to get aiming corrections to drop the dummy warheads in the center of the Kwajalein Atoll lagoon?"

"That's what I'd do in their place, Bill. But Minuteman ICBMs in war silos have only a mathematical aim point for their Cold War targets. Their computers are programmed using geographic coordinates, the target's latitude and longitude taken from military maps. They have no way to correct any targeting errors."

"Gordon, write a memo to the Vandenberg flight test program office. Ask if they use ranging corrections developed over past test flights."

"O.K., I'll also ask for data on the accuracy of test missiles hitting the lagoon when they only use geographic map targeting information."

This question went beyond Top Secret and he didn't expect to receive any reply. But a few months later he heard that Minuteman managers were trying to arrange a missile test flight from one of the operational Minuteman silos in northern Montana. The flight path would take the missile directly over Seattle, and the city fathers were extremely worried about the possibility of the missile failing in flight and hitting the city.

Minuteman's flight trajectory computer program and targeting data were stored on a small disc drive in its missile nose cone computer. Those drives used perpendicular magnetic recording, forty years before commercial disc drives adopted it. The Minuteman guidance computer was the first complex electronic device designed using integrated circuit chips and was also the first mass use of multilayer printed circuit boards.

Like the Internet forty years later, integrated circuit chips were a world-changing technology that only the U.S. government could afford to develop. IC chips and multilayer PCBs were just out of development in the late 1950's and the U.S. government paid the heavy price for industry to learn how to make them at reasonable cost and high yield, for Minuteman. Initially only a few percent of production line IC chips worked. Chip makers struggled to bring their yield up, percentage point by point, by fanatic attention to details of cleanliness and purity of materials. The public supported the high cost because it was national defense in the Cold War.

As with earlier radical new technologies like automobiles and airplanes, ICs, PCBs, and disc drives finally became cheap decades later, allowing them to become ubiquitous in modern mass produced consumer electronic products.

The Rand Corporation was the first Cold War think tank, formed out of Douglas Aircraft in the 1950's. Rand quickly conceived the U.S. Mutual Assured Destruction "MAD" defense policy, which led to redesign of the Minuteman electronics to withstand radiation from hypothetical Cold War Soviet nuclear bombs exploding above their silos, called "pin down attacks."

The missile had been designed to accurately fly over 3000 miles and hit its target within a fraction of a mile, but couldn't launch if its silos were being continually bombarded by enemy nuclear bombs during a future World War III.

Minuteman ICs had been a great success until their resistance to nuclear radiation was checked. Testing showed that the IC chips would short out under the ionizing radiation and "latch up." This rendered them inoperable as long as electrical power remained applied. The irony was that the missile electronics would have been automatically radiation proof if it had been designed using the older vacuum tube technology obsoleted by transistors and integrated circuits.

After an initial panic in the program office, a system level fix was adopted which turned the missile electronics off for tens of microseconds to unlatch the ICs, and then back on to resume guidance. Later, an IC consultant arrived at the program office with a proposal to replace the chips with new semiconductor technology that wouldn't latch up. Gordon closely monitored his progress for any missile system implications.

One afternoon, Gordon was standing in the missile nose cone assembly factory with Bill, watching a lead box being installed around a shoebox-sized Minuteman guidance computer with its small disc drive. The box with the computer was about to be installed in a missile nose cone. The lead shielding was to prevent nuclear radiation from reaching the computer, but Gordon saw a problem as he watched a technician bolt down the box. The man was picking up a drill to make holes in the lead box for the computer's electronic cables to pass through.

"Bill, nuclear radiation will also go through those holes. Why isn't an engineer here to help him do it correctly? It would be simple to wrap the cables with lead foil sheathing."

"Gordon, these kinds of problems are caused by the 'need to know' security rules. Some radiation physicist thought up the lead box idea; some mechanical engineer was assigned to design the box without being told about the cables; and some manager thought that any technician would be able to bolt it down in the nose cone. The U.S. government had similar problems in the World War II Manhattan Project, when it prohibited Los Alamos physicists from inspecting the uranium purification factories in Oak Ridge, Tennessee. They might have had a 'dirty bomb' atomic explosion there if Cal Tech professor Richard Feynman hadn't convinced the army general in charge to let him inspect the factory."

"How do we get this problem fixed without violating those secrecy rules?"

"Let's walk over to the main administration building and talk with Captain Warren, the Air Force officer in our Minuteman program office. He's the key person keeping this whole program running successfully, and he's the only man who can 'bend' the secrecy rules to put the right people together and solve a problem like this."

"I've seen Captain Warren in meetings, Bill. He writes top secret information in a little dime-store notebook that he carries around with him. It would cost us our jobs if you or I did that without classifying every notebook page 'Top Secret' and registering it with the company documentation office."

They arrived at the captain's office and found him seated at an ordinary desk in an ordinary blue US Air Force uniform that bore few medals. He had no secretary and no staff. Captain Warren looked under thirty and Gordon thought him very young for such responsibility.

It only took only a few minutes for Gordon to explain the radiation shielding problem.

"Well, that's about par for the course," he said. "Don't concern yourselves about this any further. You've given me the necessary information and I'll see that it's taken care of."

"Thanks," Gordon replied. "I'm surprised the U.S. Air Force would make a single man like you responsible for such a critical missile program." Bill looked aghast at Gordon's directness.

"One reason I'm the local point man for Minuteman Air Force System Engineering is because I have a physics PhD from MIT," Captain Warren said. "The Air Force paid for my MIT degree and now I'm paying them back. A couple of years from now I'll be running a B-52 bomber wing for the Strategic Air Force, keeping nuclear weapons aloft 24 hours a day, just in case your Minuteman missiles fail to deter a Soviet attack."

"Glad we're on the same team," Gordon said, and turned to leave the office.

They walked back to their engineering building. "Bill, it's amazing that Captain Warren has such a modest rank for the single most critical person in the entire United States assuring Minuteman ICBM R&D success. America certainly can't wait for actual nuclear war to find out whether a complex system like Minuteman will actually work."

"That's why he mentioned the B-52 strategic bombers," Bill replied. "There's also the Polaris nuclear missile submarine fleet as another backup. So there are three independent deterrent forces."

"I wish the world needed zero deterrent forces," Gordon said.

Gordon's last Minuteman job was searching for overlooked missile electronics needing radiation hardening. Walking to the Minuteman documentation office one day, he asked the clerk for several schematic drawings, including the master drawing of the complete missile electronic system.

"I'll need to see your 'need to know,'" the clerk demanded.

Gordon wasn't sure how to answer her, but an idea came to mind.

"May I speak with your supervisor please?"

This produced a gracious lady with a southern accent, who quickly rounded up a stack of drawings, liberally stamped "Top Secret." He signed a dozen pink Top Secret document receipts for them, and carried them back to his office.

After a few days studying the drawings, he found an electronics box near the missile tail that hadn't been radiation tested. Its transistor circuitry controlled the carbon steering vanes in the exhaust of the solid fuel rocket. The guidance computer constantly compared the missile present position with the targeting trajectory stored on its disc drive, and sent correction signals to the box to steer the missile on course. The box had been overlooked because it had no IC's and was far from the nose cone where most of the electronics were. He went through detailed schematics of the missile tail circuit, so he could analyze its response to ionizing radiation. It consisted of a simple set of power transistors, resistors, and capacitors, quite similar to an ordinary DC-coupled audio amplifier. His analysis suggested a simple circuit change to avoid radiation latch up. He wrote the analysis up in a four page report that he took to the documentation office to have classified as Top Secret and distributed.

The remaining missile radiation problems were worked out over several expensive years and a little reprogramming of reality. Finally, everyone in the program basked in success and they called for a celebration.

Bill was eating a piece of a missile-shaped cake and chatting with Gordon, who was struggling with a strong urge to light up a cigarette. Six months had passed since his decision to quit and he still suffered.

"Gordon, this morning the IC consultant told the program office he had patents on his IC latch up fix and he demanded royalty payments from the U.S. government. Look over there at the program office table. See how glum they all look?"

Gordon never learned the outcome of the consultant's patent royalty demands, but was hopeful that national defense needs would prevail.

Autonetics lost a big government contract shortly thereafter. Gordon's Minuteman work was over, and he began to bid on and win small Air Force research contracts. They led to the technical paper he was proudest of, on probability theory mathematics for statistical pattern recognition, to allow computer identification of objects in aerial reconnaissance photographs.

He decided to quit aerospace one day after he overheard the

executive assistant to the Autonetics president saying, "We're so nearly broke we can hardly pay to light the parking lots at night."

The disc drive engineers Gordon had worked with at Librascope were now designing disc drives for Xerox in the L.A. suburb of El Segundo. The town hadn't been named after the "second gate" of the centuries-earlier Spanish land grant rancho in this area, as local romantics claimed, but rather after the town's Standard Oil refinery, the company's second California refinery. He happily rejoined the disc drive engineers in 1969, leaving the aerospace world of Top Secret clearances. He was relieved to be able to account for all of the secret documents he had checked out over the years, because he didn't want to find out what would happen if he couldn't.

The Xerox job had paid more and he was given a window office with handsome new furniture.

6.

An Electronics Manufacturing Nightmare

Gordon had done design engineering at Xerox on 20-inch diameter disc drives called "RADs" for random access disc. A RAD was similar to IBM's original RAMAC disc drive, which weighed a ton and was larger than two refrigerators placed back to back. RADs were half the size of RAMAC and stored 2.5 megabytes.

RADs had a transparent plastic window enclosing their two vertically oriented spinning discs. The two discs were aluminum platters electroplated with nickel, then polished smooth and plated with a magnetic cobalt alloy. It had 512 fixed heads, one for each data track. Modern disc drives have one head for each disc surface, moving on an air slider to access data on circular magnetic disc tracks. Having so many heads made RADs very expensive, but their data access was very fast because their heads were electronically selected and didn't have to mechanically move from track to track.

One afternoon Gordon had been watching a RAD under test in the factory. As he looked through the plastic cover at the spinning discs, one of the heads struck something on the disc and flew off its mounting spring. The debris was microscopically invisible but was carried around by the disc motion to the other heads. In seconds all the heads had crashed and everything had became obscured by a gray cloud of aluminum powder ground from its discs. The multi-horsepower RAD spin motor screamed as it ground to a halt. *That's awesome!*

A week later, Gordon had met with his boss Andy, Ken, and Jack. "I've been testing the RAD recording head ferrite we buy from the Ferroxcube Company in New York," announced Ken, a Xerox quality engineer who was tall, lean, and wore wire frame glasses. "Their latest ferrite coming in is electrically conductive."

Ferrite was the magnetic ceramic they used to make RAD recording heads. Ken was holding an engineering document specifying that their ferrite material needed to be electrically insulating.

"That'll cause serious RAD problems if it's conductive enough," Andy said. Andy was Gordon's boss, who had a habit of wearing loud Hawaiian shirts to work. "We wind copper wire coils directly on the ferrite heads. Ferrite edges are sharp and could cut through the wire insulation and short out the coils. We better test some heads electrically."

Gordon added, "Wait! Let's test at elevated temperature as well as room temperature. Thermal expansion of hot ferrite will aggravate any shorting."

A day later, they had established that almost all recently made heads shorted out at higher temperatures.

"Don't we test our RAD disc drives at high temperature?" Gordon asked.

"No," Jack replied. "We test only at room temperature. Apparently nobody thought high temperature testing was necessary. Maybe every RAD we shipped this year has heads that'll short out when they get hot. A million dollars worth of RAD drives may be about to fail. That could bankrupt our company."

"Hey, it's not quite that bad," Ken said. "I checked. It's just the last four months of production."

"That's bad enough. We need more information," Andy replied.

"Look at this graph in my magnetic materials physics book," Gordon said. "There should be less than 50% iron in the ferrite. It becomes electrically conductive if there's more than 50%. That could be what's happened at the Ferroxcube factory."

Chemical lab analysis of ferrite samples quickly showed that to be the situation.

Two days later, Gordon, Andy, and Jack boarded a DC-6 prop airplane and flew to New York City to visit Ferroxcube in the nearby town of Saugerties.

"Here's chemical analysis data on samples of the last four months of ferrite you shipped us," Jack told the Ferroxcube Company president at their meeting. He was a short bald man wearing a wrinkled navy blue suit. "Your ferrite is required to have less than 45% iron, but it actually has well over 50%."

"I don't know how that could have happened," the president replied. His eyes were moving evasively.

"We need to inspect the material handling area in your plant," Jack said.

"Where do you mean?" countered the president. "Exactly which building do you want to see?"

Gordon looked at Andy. They were being stonewalled. Andy shrugged.

"We'll come back tomorrow morning and tell you," Jack said as he stood up. They left the plant.

Driving to their hotel, Jack said, "He's a stubborn non-engineer man who has no idea of the technology behind the product he's making. I'll drop you off at the hotel. Don't expect to see me until tomorrow morning."

Jack rejoined them the next morning as Gordon and Andy were finishing breakfast.

"Let's go," Jack ordered. They were soon back in the Ferroxcube Company president's office.

"We need to see Room 5 in Building C," Jack stated plainly.

The president surrendered. "O.K., I'll take you there." Inside Building C they followed a trail of red and white powder on the floor to Room 5.

Gordon told them, "The red powder you see is the iron oxide that they mix with the white zinc oxide powder you see over there. The mixture is heated in a ceramic oven under pressure, to make ferrite in small bricks."

"Hello, Jake," the president said to a man standing inside Room 5. "Jake is the foreman here."

"Please show us where and how you mix the ferrite powders," Gordon said to him.

"Right here using this scale," the foreman answered, pointing to a white weighing scale, "by scooping the red and white powder onto it like this." He demonstrated.

"That's the same kind of scale that candy stores use to weight chocolate!" Gordon exclaimed. "It can't be accurate enough. And look! He's got more than 50% iron on the scale right now!"

"Well, we do that to make the ferrite pass its magnetic tests better," the foreman said.

"Do you test ferrite for electrical conductivity?"

"No, we don't test for that," the foreman admitted.

They walked back to the president's office in silence.

The Ferroxcube president looked beaten as Andy explained that half a million dollars worth of disc drives were about to short out, and that the matter would be settled in court.

As they drove back to the airport for their flight home, Gordon asked Jack, "How on Earth did you find out where to go to in that factory?"

"Well, last night I went to the bar closest to the plant. I bought beer for several people that work for Ferroxcube, and found a guy that worked in the material handling area. It was Jake, the foreman we just talked to, and he explained exactly what he did. All we had to do was get the president over there to witness it."

"Jack, I'm glad you didn't ask me to accompany you. Bars always make me want to smoke cigarettes. Smelling the smoke still makes me want to have one." A full year after quitting, cigarette smoke hadn't yet become unpleasant to Gordon.

Back at El Segundo the next day, they traced the shipping papers for the last four months of RAD drives. They found that half of the drives with the shorting heads had been shipped on one train to a computer company back east. The train had derailed and an insurance claim was being processed for the destroyed drives.

In the end, only $300,000 worth of drives had to be returned to the El Segundo factory to have their heads replaced. Their finance department was able to bank the railroad insurance proceeds months sooner than their customer would have paid his bill for the RADs, turning the loss into a slight gain.

One day Gordon had driven to San Diego to talk to a recording head manufacturer about ordering heads for his Xerox research work. Over lunch he had chatted with its president James, who was describing a radar system he had designed for his Bonanza single-engine airplane. "I've just sold manufacturing rights for the radar to RCA," he finished. "I celebrated by buying a new Porsche 911."

"Congratulations. I'm also thinking of buying a new car. My old Dodge Dart is in bad shape. I figure the payments on a new car will only cost me a couple of hundred bucks a month."

James knew Gordon had recently been divorced, and was at odds on how to occupy his spare time. "I have a different suggestion, Gordon. Keep your Dodge and use the money to take flying lessons instead."

"That's an interesting idea, James. I'll look into it." Back in El Segundo the next day, Gordon had found a flight instructor and took his first flying lesson at Hawthorne Airport. He was hooked as soon as he found how convenient travel by private plane was, and saw the many dials, gauges, and instruments airplanes had.

A few months later, Gordon's fellow Xerox worker Pete had asked him for help in a deal he had made. "I have a contract to automate a printed circuit board plant in Walden, New York. It's a side business, nothing to do with Xerox. We can make a pile of money from it."

"O.K. Pete," Gordon had said. "But here's the deal. You put up all the money for the equipment, and the travel to New York to install it."

Pete had process control documents describing how to operate the hydraulic presses that the Walden plant used to laminate sheets of epoxy and copper into blank circuit boards. The blanks were sold to electronics manufacturers who patterned the copper layers into printed circuits, using photographic projectors and chemical etching.

"I know the right process control microcomputer to buy," Gordon said. "It runs a simple 'Tiny Basic' computer language, and I'll program it using your Apple II. We'll use a RS-232 data cable to transfer the program to the microcomputer. The program will issue electronic commands to open and shut valves to do all the press operation steps, like closing a water drain, then turning on a hydraulic pump to raise the press cylinder."

After a month of programming and testing, Pete and Gordon took an airplane to New York. They checked the two computers as baggage. Pete wanted to complete the installation in a single weekend and be able to return to Xerox for work the next Monday.

After landing in New York, Gordon was watching through his plane window as the baggage unloaded. He saw the Apple II in its soft case start down the baggage conveyor belt and fall off halfway down, onto the concrete ramp. A rough looking baggage handler grabbed it and threw it onto a baggage cart.

"Not a good omen, Pete."

They picked up a rental car and began their drive to Walden after sunset, but became lost before they got out of New York City. "Pete, that sign means we're going the wrong way, heading for the Verrazano Narrows Bridge. Go over that bridge on your right, the one all lit up."

By sheer accident they drove over the Brooklyn Bridge, awash in light on its centennial anniversary. "It's an experience of a lifetime, Gordon!"

Late that night they pulled into a Walden motel and early Saturday morning they drove to the plant.

"Looks just like a New England water mill for grinding grain, Pete."

"That's exactly what it was for the last two centuries. When the mill became obsolete and was closed, a printed circuit company bought its big brick building cheaply, and cheaply hired the local people put out of work by the mill closing."

Inside the mill they met the plant engineer, a taciturn New England man. The mill had a single large open space inside, encircled by four brick walls reaching up to a high roof. The wooden axle of the original water wheel protruded through one wall. The axle had been sawed off to a short stub and a clock nailed to its cut off end. The mill floor was half filled with flat tables piled with copper and epoxy sheets, raw materials to make printed circuit board stock. Several massive hydraulic presses sat silently in the other half, patiently waiting to bond sheets together. The smell of hot machine oil lay heavy in the air.

A small observation room sat in the center of the plant, the size of a small office, with windows on its four sides. Pete installed the process control microcomputer in an electronics rack inside the room and Gordon asked the plant engineer to put the largest press through its normal manually controlled cycle.

This press was an immense steel machine nearly as high as the mill building. Its antique brass nameplate announced it was a 600 ton French Oil Press with a two foot diameter steel ram shaft.

It'll be cool to see this giant machine controlled by the little microcomputer.

"O.K., first we open this drain valve to release any water from condensed steam," the engineer explained.

Gordon saw this on the process control instruction and nodded.

"Then, we close this switch to start the air modulator pump, which makes air pressure to operate the hydraulic valves."

"But the air pump switch isn't called out in the document," Gordon objected.

"Well, there are several minor steps we didn't bother to put in."

Gordon realized he would have to add to the program using the Apple II, if it was still working after its fall at the airport. "There's very little memory space left in the microcontroller," he told Pete. *Well, I did expect a Pete adventure.*

Gordon inserted new code into the program using the Apple II keyboard and transferred the modified program to the microcontroller through the data cable. They scotch taped bits of paper to the air valves to verify that the microcomputer was correctly turning them on and off. When the microcomputer turned the valves on, air blew the bits of paper about, which they could observe through a window in the observation shed.

The microcomputer opened the water drain correctly when they tested the revised program. It started the air pump, and issued the air modulator command to open the hydraulic valves to raise the press cylinder. The correct air valve paper fluttered but then the program halted, waiting for the press to signal back that it had moved up to the top of its stroke and was ready to descend. The press neither moved up nor down.

They worked, reprogrammed, and retested all day Saturday and all through the night. Around 3am the microcontroller code had unsuccessfully sent its signals innumerable times and had been corrected endless times. Unknown to the men, steam pressure now rose slightly inside the press, clearing an internal water condensation blockage they didn't know existed.

Steam billowed and hissed when they next ran the program. Hydraulics whooshed and the massive ram shaft rose smoothly and powerfully up to the mill ceiling. Gordon jumped to his feet in surprise. Then the pump stubbornly sat at the top of its stroke, silently refusing to obey its next signal to descend.

Sunday morning dawned after an all night struggle with valves, wiring, and program code. To save memory space, Gordon had removed all the space characters from the Tiny Basic code, so instructions that had been readable, like:

"IF VALVE=3 AND STATUS=OPEN THEN STOP" became an inscrutable

"IFVALVE=3ANDSTATUS=OPENTHENSTOP."

By noon Sunday they still hadn't successfully completed a press cycle. The plant engineer glanced at the mill door. "That man coming in is our new president. Last week they fired the old president, the man who arranged to buy your press controller. This new man is determined to cut costs wherever he can."

"That's great news," Pete groaned.

Gordon sighed. *Thanks for not telling us. Lord save us from taciturn New England engineers.*

They showed the president how the computer worked, puffing the bits of paper on the air valves, while the giant press sat immobile and silent.

"The press isn't moving," the president observed.

Gordon and Pete were exhausted from working 36 hours without breaks, sleep, or meals. Pete wasn't thinking clearly when he smiled at the president and said, "With this new automation you'll be able to make scrap at ten times your normal rate."

Gordon turned off the computers. *That's the end of this adventure.*

Thrown out of the plant without their microcomputer and without payment, they got in their rental car to return to New York City for their flight back to L.A. Stopping for gas at a Walden gas station, Pete discovered he was out of money. Gordon had brought none because of his rule of not paying for Pete's adventures. The New York winter temperature was below freezing and rapidly getting colder as the sun set. Pete threw himself on the mercy of the station attendant, and New England rural charity got them enough gas to get back to the New York airport, but without any dinner.

Four months later, in the summer of 1974, Gordon and Pete had set out to fly Gordon's plane around Baja California, first flying south to the tip of Baja at Cabo San Lucas. They had landed on a dirt airstrip with a deserted thatch shelter and a nearby beach.

They had unrolled their sleeping bags under the airplane wings and gone to bed. Gordon woke hours later in the middle of the night, hearing the plink-plink of raindrops falling on aluminum wings. He smiled, comfortably warm and dry in his sleeping bag on the sand beneath one wing. He heard Pete muttering under the other wing, thrashing about and finally climbing into the back of the airplane. Its rear seat had been removed to make room for Gordon's 100cc Honda folding motorcycle. Gordon knew something was amiss because Pete's muttering sounded close to cursing, and Pete never swore.

As dawn broke the next day, Gordon woke in his sleeping bag on the sand to see a small native girl standing silently near the airplane. She wore a crude dress woven from cactus fiber and had an open innocent face untouched by any contact with gringo civilization or airplanes. She looked at him with wide eyes as if he was a god descended from the sky. She held an even smaller child by his hand. Behind the two trailed a procession of scrawny goats, pigs, and sheep, more or less tied together by crude ropes braided from the same fibers that made her simple dress. Gordon silently stared at this innocent primitive scene, neither wanting nor able to break the spell. The girl finally continued on her way with her little band to find water or food. Not a word had been spoken.

Gordon rolled over in his sleeping bag to watch the tiny procession depart, and saw a tranquil dawn scene of sea and rocky beach. A lone pelican was gliding over the sea surface. He saw it scanning the sea for its first fish of the day, wing tips hovering inches above the water. Still half-asleep, Gordon watched the bird suddenly stroke powerfully to climb steeply, whirl around in a barrel roll, somehow eyeball the exact spot on the sea its unsuspecting breakfast was under, and vertically dive into the sea with wings folded. Bobbing back to float on the surface with a fish in its mouth, it seemed to have an air of satisfaction.

Dawn clouds and ocean shallows wore hues of pink and scarlet as the sun rose from the sea. A tropic breeze swayed palm trees, bringing the scent of sea salt. Entranced, Gordon watched the shallows turning to aquamarines as the sun climbed up into the sky. Tiny sparkles glinted from the waves, like scattered diamonds. Gordon smiled, warmed as much by this peaceful scene as by his sleeping bag. He was nearly a thousand miles south of the U.S. and far from its perpetual busy clamor. He treasured this totally relaxed feeling of being "Baja-ed."

As he lay watching, Gordon heard a low penetrating "whoosh." It sounded like wind blowing through a cave. He sat upright and looked toward the sound, seeing only a smooth patch in the ocean swells, nothing more. A minute passed and then a large black whale broached above the sea surface, sunlight shining off its tail flukes. A spume of spray rose high in the air from the whale's blow hole and Gordon heard the cave wind sound again. The whale was so close to shore he could see grey spots on it, looking like barnacles on a ship bottom. It was a Pacific gray whale at the southern end of its annual migration from the Arctic north.

"Wake up and look, Pete!" Only mutters came from within the plane.

Gordon got up to see what Pete was doing. He looked very cramped in the plane's rear, with the motorcycle as bed partner.

"I was fine until the rain began last night, then I discovered I was in a low spot on the ground where rainwater collected. My sleeping bag got soaked so I moved inside."

"Let's put the bike together and go look for breakfast," Gordon said.

Baja roads were rutty dirt tracks in the 1970's and the motorcycle slipped and slid in the sand as they rode along, struggling to keep the bike upright. After fifteen minutes they reached the Palmyra Hotel down the coast. Parking the bike, they walked past palms and pools to the Palmyra restaurant. Sitting down at a table overlooking a lovely beach, they ate excellent huevos revueltos, Mexican scrambled eggs. Pete poured an entire bowl of hot salsa over his and asked the waitress for more.

As they were leaving she asked, "Numero del cuadro?" What was their room number? They weren't able to communicate that they weren't staying at the Palmyra and wanted to pay in cash. Pete finally stepped in, saying "Room 40" in bad Spanish, a room number they had passed walking in.

Gordon exclaimed, "Shame on us, Pete." "No hab-lo Espanol!" Pete replied in his broken Spanish accent. They left breakfast money on the table, over tipping the waitress, and left.

Continuing their erratic motorcycle journey down the sandy dirt road, they slipped and slid to the town of Cabo San Lucas. It was then a small sleepy village at the end of the thousand mile dirt road snaking down the length of Baja California.

Cabo appeared deserted, with a mangy dog sleeping in the middle of the dirt road. He was chewing on a bone stuck in the dirt. A white cruise ship was anchored outside the harbor and its shore boat was nearing the town wharf, about to land tourists. A few minutes later, a sea of tourists walked onto the dirt street, their vivid summer clothing colorfully clashing.

The town suddenly sprang to life as all the store shutters opened. The dog lazily got up and walked to a safer shady spot under a tree to lie back down. Pete and Gordon retreated to a restaurant and ordered lunch. Pete asked for an extra bowl of their hot salsa which he poured over his lunch.

"Aren't you worried about catching on fire, Pete?" Gordon asked.

After half an hour the tourists had bought all the souvenirs they wanted and had returned to the shore boat. The stores immediately shuttered as the boat left, and the town again appeared deserted. The mangy dog reappeared and retook its place lying in the middle of the road.

Back in L.A. a month later, Pete had announced he had a new project. "My buddy Gene found an opportunity to sell a 300 amp electrical surge protector to the U.S. Navy at Point Mugu. Let's build a prototype. They'll pay a bunch for it."

"O.K." Gordon had replied. "We'll need two inductors in series with the electric lines, and an AC capacitor across the lines. I'll choose their sizes to allow the 60 cycle AC electricity to pass through without loss, but stop any sudden electrical surge from passing through, like from lightning. The little bit of surge that gets through the inductors will be shorted out by the capacitor. A normal surge protector circuit is about 20 amps, so we need one 15 times more powerful." Looking at a table of copper wire sizes, he found that the electrical code required triple-zero size wire for a 300 amp circuit.

"Pete, to make the inductors we'll have to wind copper wire nearly half an inch in diameter around magnetic toroids." These were donuts cast from magnetic ceramic. "We may need Superman's strength to wind them."

The next weekend had found them in Gordon's garage checking a 300 amp electrical junction box they bought, some three inch diameter toroids, a spool of ooo copper wire that took both men to lift, and a roll of silver solder. "Regular solder will melt if we use it to join the copper wire to the junction box lug bolts," Gordon said. "We need silver solder to withstand the heat from 300 amps passing through."

The next day they took the finished junction box surge protector to a breezy hilltop in Topanga Canyon, where Pete knew a 350 amp arc welding power supply was located. They fastened the welder leads to the junction box lug bolts, shorted out the box output terminals and fired up the power supply to its full 350 amps. Walking a good distance away for safety, they waited for results. Their mothers would have recognized the scene from their childhoods. Apart from a loud hum from the power supply and from the junction box, all appeared well.

They sent the surge protector to Point Mugu with Gene, but they never heard back from the Navy. Neither box nor money returned. "I'm glad you paid for the parts, Pete," Gordon said.

Gordon's next side project was with Gene instead of Pete, and turned out better. Gene had found an aviation antenna company at Santa Monica Airport that wanted to modernize its airplane radio signal splitter circuits. These were small metal electronic boxes that allowed two airplane radios to share one antenna, avoiding the need to mount a second antenna on the airplane's exterior.

Gordon met with the company president, who took him to watch a woman making one of their splitters by soldering dozens of tiny resistors and capacitors into the small box. She was a stunningly beautiful Mexican woman with an overpowering sexual aura. Gordon's legs felt like Jell-O and he struggled to keep his composure. She smiled knowingly.

"I can replace all those electronic parts with two small toroids wound with coils," he told the president. They agreed on a consulting fee and Gordon started work on the project at home. After weeks of frustrated failure he finally realized that the design theory math he was using wasn't able to explain what was wrong. Theory said each radio was supposed to receive its electrical signals only from the antenna, but signals were also coming across from the other radio.

In desperation he connected test equipment to his experimental splitter circuit and began soldering randomly selected capacitors in random places in the circuit. After hours of trial and error he found that putting a very small capacitor in an illogical part of the circuitry miraculously made the splitter work. He ran more experiments to find out why and discovered that his magnetic toroids weren't the pure inductors his Cal Tech mathematics assumed. They had a little magnetic loss as well, that was cancelled out by the new capacitor. Gordon's lesson in experimental reality versus theory would be a valuable engineering lesson.

Several months later Gene called Gordon. "I want to take my new Russian lady friend Tatanya to Las Vegas, and I'll pay all the expenses if you'll fly us, including for you and your lady friend Shirley." Off they went, landing at McCarran Airport, parking at the private side, and taking a taxi to town.

"I want to see the Siegfried and Roy dinner show tonight," Tatanya imperiously demanded.

"I wonder how Gene is going to get tickets with only an hour's notice," Gordon asked Shirley. Half an hour later they were standing at the end of a long line of people holding Siegfried and Roy tickets and waiting for the showroom doors to open.

"Stay here," Gene said. "I know how to do this." Inserting twenty dollar bills between the fingers of his left hand, Gene walked to the head of the line and talked quietly with a doorman. In a minute Gene was waving them forward and they were admitted into the empty showroom to select any table they wanted. Gene's left hand was now empty. Gordon and Shirley looked at each other in awe of Gene's nerve and success. As they finished dinner in the now-full showroom they were even more awed when white tigers appeared by magic, walking between the dinner tables.

As they left the show, Gene walked with Tatanya. "We can go see Diana Ross tomorrow if you'd like."

"I want to see her tonight," Tatanya demanded. "Right now I'm going to look in the jewelry store in the lobby."

Gordon and Shirley waited for them, dropping quarters in a slot machine, which agreeably ate them.

"Do you know that slots are just ATM machines in reverse, Shirley? You can trust the machine like a bank, but to go in the opposite direction. Your cash is guaranteed to steadily go in instead of come out. Each Vegas slot takes in over $100,000 per year."

Tatanya reappeared, wearing a brilliant diamond pendant, with Gene in tow.

"Cost me $25,000," Gene whispered to Shirley.

Off they went in a taxi to see Diana Ross. The line at her showroom seemed even more impossibly longer, and a sign over its entrance proclaimed, "Welcome Western Beer Distributors to our Exclusive Show starring Diana Ross Queen of Motown."

Two well-oiled beer distributors were talking. "The California State Liquor Board is trying to break my monopoly on beer distribution in L.A. How do you handle the liquor board in your Nevada territory?"

The other man replied, "My company controls liquor distribution in the western half of Nevada, including Vegas. The board gives me exclusivity and even outlaws competition from any mail order liquor companies. If some state commission asks them to open up beer distribution to other companies, I tell them to say that retail liquor prices would go up without my economy of size. And it's amazingly easy to keep the board happy. I'll show you how I keep the Nevada Alcohol Board under my thumb. Do you see the man going into the showroom now? He's the liquor board chairman. It only costs me $5000 a year to keep him happy, including his Diana Ross ticket tonight."

There was a separate line for the general public, but Gordon could see that none of them were going to get in. Gene walked forward to the front of the line with a new green bush of twenty dollar bills growing from his hand and they were admitted. Diana sang beautifully with her Motown saxophone band.

In their last adventure, Gene and Gordon flew to Orlando in January 1986 on a contract Gene had with NASA. He sold them magnetic sensors that were molded into the solid rocket fuel propelling the two booster rockets that take NASA shuttles into space. Gene's sensors monitored the solid propellant burn rate. If any section of the rocket fuel burned much faster than another, the flame might reach the rocket casing and cause an explosion.

In the morning they met with a sensor manufacturing company in Orlando and decided to spend the afternoon visiting Cape Canaveral. They learned the shuttle Columbia was scheduled to be launched the next morning. Six previous launch attempts had been canceled for various technical reasons. They decided to get up the next day at 4am in hopes of seeing a launch.

And so they were standing with a small group of people on a sand spit a mile or so from the shuttle, in darkness before an approaching dawn. Columbia was on her launch pad illuminated by brilliant lights, her vents releasing clouds of vapor. As the countdown neared zero, Columbia's engines fired with a blinding light that made the illumination lights look feeble, and the shuttle rocked back on its launch pad, held down by mechanical locks while its engines stabilized.

An instant later the tremendous sound reached Gordon and slammed him backwards with physical force as the shuttle slowly rose into the blackness. A minute later it emerged high in the dawn sunlight far above and its booster tanks separated, trailing plumes as they dropped down and away from the shuttle, falling to the sea.

The experience was indescribably beyond any launch Gordon had ever seen on TV.

As they watched the shuttle climb out of sight they could not realize just how fortunate they were to have seen this particular shuttle launch. The next crowd of people standing on this sand spit a few weeks later would be watching the shuttle Challenger.

7.

If You Fail at Manufacturing,
Lose More Money Doing Research

The Xerox Company had bought the El Segundo business that made RAD disc drives, just before Gordon joined it to do RAD work, leaving the Minuteman aerospace company. Xerox allowed its new division to quickly become unprofitable and its manufacturing soon ceased. It had been a startup company and its key employees cashed in their stock options and quit as soon as the Xerox purchase money made it possible. Xerox employees at its headquarters in Rochester, New York called the purchase "the Xerox billion dollar mistake."

Gordon's work had then changed from RAD engineering to research work, at a L.A. branch of the fabled Xerox Palo Alto Research Center. His PARC lab fabricated the first professional-quality computer mouse for the PARC Alto computer that inspired the design of the Apple Macintosh, after Steve Jobs had been invited by PARC management to see its closely guarded network of Alto personal computers. PARC had designed a personal computer using the first IC RAM chips, each having only 1000 bits of memory. Alto introduced the first icons on a desktop screen, for easy launching of programs using a computer mouse. They had also invented Ethernet to hook Altos together in networks.

The PARC scientists had strenuously objected to showing their inventions to Steve Jobs, but their management may have given up hope of ever convincing Xerox to put their very expensive Alto into manufacturing. Apple redesigned the Alto innovations into their low cost Macintosh and the rest became Silicon Valley history.

After Xerox headquarters failed in manufacturing disc drives they had moved on to hire management consultants to send to their divisions. These concocted silly projects with hokey abbreviations, like TOTB for "Think Outside The Box."

In one Xerox TOTB assignment each researcher was ordered to spend the next weekend conceiving a totally original idea. Gordon ignored the TOTB weekend assignment, instead flying with Shirley to San Luis Obispo to visit her sister Donna and husband Elmer.

Elmer had picked them up at San Luis Obispo Airport and that afternoon they had sat in the doorway of Elmer's garage, drinking beer and watching a herd of Highway Patrol cows in the meadow below. These cows were black on top and white on the bottom, looking like California Highway Patrol police cars. Many had black on their bottoms as well and people called them "Oreo cookie cows."

Gordon noticed that a group of cows had just walked to a new grazing spot in the meadow. When they stopped they remained pointing in the same direction they had been walking. Grabbing a camera he snapped pictures of the parallel cows. Back at Xerox on Monday, he carefully wrote "north pole" and "south pole" labels on their heads and tails using a calligraphic pen, and titled the photos "Animal Magnetism." He handed it to his Xerox boss, telling him that he had invented a new method for magnetic recording.

That was the last said about the TOTB assignment.

When Gordon retold the parallel cow story in later years he was often given other aligned cow stories in return. Strangers told him Wyoming cows turned their hind quarters towards blizzard winds to shield their faces from cold, and cows in tropical climates turned their heads towards the sun to evaporate sweat. A British man on an Italian ski lift said that his farm calves had genetic white spots on their rear ends to give each following calf a mark to steer by. Their young could see the spots in deep brush and be able to follow.

Gordon had spent the next fourteen years doing disc drive research at Xerox, until a company budget crunch closed his lab. He was consulting for Apple Computer when he interviewed at Seagate for a new job.

8.

Detested Technologists Overrun Las Vegas

A week after Gordon first met Doug in Scotts Valley he flew his plane to Las Vegas to meet Al, Seagate's President. After landing, Gordon was led by a golf cart to a parking spot at Butler Aviation, on the private aircraft side of the airport. Butler's business was instant first-class service for business jet flyers. It was crowded with jets whose passengers received red carpet treatment because the jet owners bought thousands of dollars of jet fuel. Gordon's plane took only fifty dollars of aviation gas but he received similar first class treatment by parking with the rich people's jets, a little known secret of private airplane flying.

Gordon shut down his engine and got out to put his cockpit cover on. Standing on his wing he looked over the airport fence at the Las Vegas Strip, seeing gaudy wedding chapels and cheap motels. The only visible evidence of the gambling mecca was the modest sign of the Flamingo Hotel, said to have been built by the mobster Bugsy Siegel.

The "follow me" cart drove him to the Butler terminal and they offered their van to take him downtown. He was dropped off at the Golden Nugget Hotel just two hours after parking his car next to his airplane at Santa Monica Airport. Private airplane flying had fewer delays than airline flying and offered higher personal security with far less hassle. There were 8,000 airports in small towns and large cities in the U.S. and one was usually much closer to a flyer's destination than airline airports. There were only fifty airline airports in major cities that had usably convenient schedules.

Al was in Las Vegas for the COMDEX personal computer trade show. This annual show was already overflowing the Las Vegas Convention Center space and was the second largest annual convention in Las Vegas, attracting over 100,000 PC engineers, salesmen, and customers. Its size required COMDEX to build additional Convention Center exhibit buildings using its own money.

The COMDEX people were universally detested by the Vegas casinos and cab drivers because computer people didn't gamble much and were cheap tippers. The city was stuck with geeks for a week.

Gordon found Doug in the gambling casino of the Golden Nugget Hotel and the two walked over to introduce Gordon to Al. Al was at a crap table, down by $70,000 but looking unruffled. "I hear you're a technology genius, Gordon. What can I do to help you join us?"

Gordon knew he wasn't a genius, but he had one good instinct: to want to swim in the pool with the smarter fish. He didn't mind being a dumber fish in that pool. Curiosity and learning were Gordon's passions. He loved learning from people smarter than him and Seagate seemed like such a place. To him, "smarter" referred to pure intelligence; labels like race or sex were irrelevant. He was known at technical conferences for asking direct questions of speakers with faulty points of view, saying "I have a dumb question, because I don't understand why..." The more polite masses didn't directly confront such speakers.

Gordon was still dazed by the Seagate opportunity and could only think to ask Al for two things. "Could Seagate help me with selling my L.A. house and buying a new one and also allow me to fly my airplane on company business?"

"Of course you can fly your plane, if you promise not to ask me to fly with you," Al answered smiling.

Gordon smiled back, knowing from his own piloting experience that small airplane flying could be safe with frequent pilot recurrent training and proper airplane maintenance, the same way airline flying was made safe. Yearly retraining for emergencies was necessary to overcome the inherent fear of flying that even pilots had, arising from the reptilian instincts humans inherit from their caveman ancestors. He also knew that some small plane pilots trained only to minimum standards, flew minimally maintained small airplanes, and sometimes crashed. Airlines and business jets could afford the cost of safely training pilots and maintaining airplanes, but many individual small plane owners found it costly.

Al was quite correct about small airplane safety because the public had no way to distinguish the safe pilot majority from the less safe minority. They had no way to know a pilot's recent safety training or airplane maintenance except by flying on airlines. People's questions about small airplane flight safety were best answered by airplane insurance companies. Gordon's insurance cost him about the same as insuring a car of similar value.

Al turned. "Doug, set up a Seagate loan for Gordon's new house with the principal and interest forgiven after eight years." Gordon learned this was called a Silicon Valley "golden handcuff." It was nice to get the house loan, and he naively imagined working for Seagate forever.

In a final moment of panic, Gordon blurted out his real concern. "Sir, will a technology researcher like me really be welcome at a manufacturing company like Seagate?"

"Call me Al; please take this complementary ticket and go see our COMDEX exhibit and our customer's exhibits; and when can you begin working for us?"

Gordon decided that all Seagate people must know this trick of jumping over the middle of conversations to get to the conclusions faster, like Doug and Al. He resolved to learn how himself.

Leaving Al and Doug, he spent several hours walking through miles of aisles displaying COMDEX exhibits of computers, printers, disc drives, and software. He stopped at a booth labeled "Cow Ware."

"What's Cow Ware?" he asked the man in the booth.

"It's our PC program to help dairy farmers manage their herds of milk cows. The farmers input the breeding line and milk output of each cow, and the program computes which cows to breed and which to send to the glue factory."

"Thanks," Gordon said and walked on. *There'll be no end to the market for computers and disc drives if they get into every specialized occupation on Earth.*

Gordon started back to the airport, passing by Al again. Al was still at the crap table, now up by $100,000 but not looking any more excited than when he was down by $70,000. Smiling and shaking his head, Gordon joined the cab line outside the hotel. The cab took an hour to get him back to Butler Aviation and the taxi driver chatted with Gordon about the big crowds. Gordon thought he looked like an immigrant who had picked up an American street look. His long braided ponytail partly obscured his large gold earrings and the tattoo on the back of his neck. Gordon looked at the drivers Las Vegas license on the front seat back and saw a mug shot of the man without the hippie additions.

"COMDEX is the second biggest event we get in Las Vegas. Want to guess what's biggest?" the driver asked. Gordon had no idea.

"Every year in early December the Rodeo Grand Championships are held here. The crowds are so huge I just drive to the airport and shout at the taxi line, 'Anyone for the Golden Nugget, come get in.' My cab fills up in a wink. And I can get back to the airport fast to pick up for another hotel.

"A couple flew in to get married a few months after the last rodeo and they called my taxi phone to personally ask me to take them to a wedding chapel and be their best man. They had met as strangers in my cab at the rodeo the December before!" Gordon laughed.

Back in his airplane at McCarran Airport, Gordon radioed for his departure clearance and ground control instructed him to take taxiways Whiskey and Echo to runway 19 left. Pulling into the run-up area at 19L he heard a call over the radio. "Mooney at 19 Left, may our Gulfstream taxi by to take off before you, sir?"

Gordon saw a large business jet approaching down the taxiway. He knew the Gulfstream pilot's radio request was unnecessary because he had heard ground control clear the jet to taxi to the runway for immediate takeoff. It needed to take off first because it was the faster plane. The radio request was partly professional courtesy common in airplane radio communications to emphasize flight safety, and partly the Gulfstream pilot wanting to not surprise Gordon.

"Sir, it would be my pleasure if you taxied by without delay," Gordon radioed back, hinting to the Gulfstream pilot that he knew jets hated to wait on the ground burning fuel. Sitting with jet engines idling was expensive, rather like keeping a fire burning by feeding it hundred dollar bills. Such undertones were common because every radio transmission was tape recorded and could be reviewed by FAA regulators.

The Gulfstream looked almost as large as a Boeing jet as it taxied past Gordon's small plane and took off. Gordon was cleared for takeoff a few minutes later and he departed Las Vegas for the 75-minute flight back to Santa Monica Airport, flying an air route above the Las Vegas to L.A. highway.

Climbing to his cruise altitude, Gordon heard the radar controller talking to another plane. "Top Gun 21, contact Nellis Air Force Base, and I thank you for your service to our country." This wasn't standard aviation terminology and the words brought a lump to Gordon's throat. She repeated them to each military plane in turn as Gordon flew on.

A dark veil of night fell as he flew south over the Nevada and California desert. Thousands of stars began to fill the desert sky, far more than he ever saw in lighted cities. Passing Palmdale, Gordon saw a lambent glow beyond the mountains ahead. It permeated the sky far ahead of him although the terrain below remained pitch black.

Must be the lights of L.A, but I don't remember seeing them this far north before.

As Los Angeles came into view 15 minutes later, Gordon's eyes opened wide. L.A. was a dazzling sea of floating light that seemed to stretch forever He was soon flying over the San Fernando Valley and could see from Burbank to his east to the Ventura coastline far to his west, and far beyond Orange County to the south. Passing beyond the mountains he saw an arc of light snaking 100 miles east. It ended in a softly glowing island: Palm Springs. To the south, another arm of light curved along the seacoast beside the dark Pacific Ocean, to the glowing island of San Diego. Gordon was seeing over two hundred miles in every direction. There was no sensation of speed in the still night air and not the slightest bump to hint he was even moving. Gordon looked at his groundspeed and saw the plane was ticking off 250 mph over the ground. *I could never explain this experience to anyone except a pilot.*

Pilots were sometimes asked why they fly by polite people who omit the rest of the question in their minds: "Since there can be danger." Few pilots were able to describe their experiences above the ordinary flat world humans lived their lives on. Occasionally, pilots try by writing spiritual or allegorical books, like Richard Bach's *Jonathon Livingston Seagull* or Saint-Exupery's *Little Prince.*

9.

Let's Get Married!

Flying home after meeting Al at COMDEX in Las Vegas, Gordon landed at Santa Monica Airport, fueled the airplane and taxied to his parking spot. He got in his car to drive to Shirley's house. *Well, I'll want to ask Shirley to marry me, but I don't think I have the nerve. What if she says no?*

He walked in, scratched Charles behind his ears, kissed Shirley, and was rewarded with her brilliant smile. She handed him a scotch and soda, parked him on a kitchen stool, and began making pasta carbonara, one of his favorite sinfully delicious Shirley dinners.

He told her the Las Vegas story but didn't have the nerve to bring up the subject of their new life up north. Shirley said nothing about it either. Gordon knew she wanted to talk about it because she always carefully planned any travel.

After several days of private agony, he went to a drug store and bought a greeting card, wrote on it "I Love You, Shirley! Please Marry Me!" and handed it to her. He thought this was a logical solution to his tied tongue.

"Well, that's an unusual way to propose," she said, pausing long enough to terrify him. "Let's get married!"

Gordon felt several tons of unnoticed weight disappear off his shoulders and he kissed her. "I'll have to sell my share in this plane." His partner in the plane was Ted, a Xerox electronic engineer. Ted was muscular, liked to bike and hike, and to compose silly songs. Ted was skilled with tools and had a complete workshop, with lathe, band saw, and hydraulic press. Gordon's skills extended only to drill press and welding. Ted and Gordon had taken their two power boats up the Colorado River from Lake Mead and into the Grand Canyon over many summers, with occasional spectacular boat breakdowns and one boat lost in the rapids. Ted's workshop repair facilities were invaluable.

Preparing to move north to join Seagate, Gordon put his share of the plane up for sale and started looking for a faster airplane. He decided on a Mooney retractable, manufactured since the 1950's in Kerrville, Texas near San Antonio, and nicknamed "pocket rockets." He bought a turbocharged model that could fly at 231 mph over a thousand miles at 24,000 feet altitude.

Gordon and Shirley planned a honeymoon in the northern Italy Dolomite Mountains, but he remembered that Al and Doug wanted him to start work quickly at Seagate, so he selected technologists to hire for his new Seagate group from his closed Xerox research lab. He knew Kermit was most important because he was their recording experimentalist. Technology discoveries were made in labs, not by theory people doing math at office desks.

Kermit was lean and wiry and looked like a cross between an intellectual and a hippy. His casual street manner concealed a deep intelligence. One of the Xerox researchers had originally met Kermit at the Santa Monica Muscle Beach where he played chess day after day. Kermit needed very little money to live but was nearly broke at the time, making him agreeable to work for Xerox. His motorcycle had broken down next to a parked car with a "For Sale" sign and he had spent most of his money buying the car. He had abandoned the motorcycle where it died. There seemed to be no women anywhere in Kermit's life and he wouldn't answer any questions about them.

Kermit was a hands-on engineer. He wired up experimental electronic circuits in three-dimensional rat's nest patterns instead of the orderly printed circuit boards favored by most electronic engineers. He had no college degree but knew more practical engineering than most with one. Whenever Kermit said, "Come look! I've found something interesting in the lab," Gordon knew a significant discovery could be forthcoming.

So Kermit was the first engineer that Gordon flew to Scotts Valley to visit Seagate. Before landing at Scotts Valley Airport, he flew him over the Santa Cruz sequoia forests that look like battle formations of green soldiers marching down to coastal cliffs. He correctly figured that Kermit would be hooked into wanting to live in this lovely area. Doug gave Kermit the plant tour and made him a handsome salary offer. Kermit accepted.

Gordon repeated this trip over the next few weeks with Rob, Jack, and Sam.

Rob was a careful, detail-oriented electronics engineer, a valuable addition to any design group. Doug made him an excellent offer, but

Rob asked, "Will Seagate sell my home in L.A., pay for my moving expenses, and give me a loan for a new house in Scotts Valley?"

Gordon told him he was lucky to get rid of his L.A. house since it was on unstable land that sank a bit in every heavy rainstorm. "Don't buy another house in a flood plain, Rob," Gordon kidded.

Rob was a confirmed bachelor who dated a girlfriend only until she began dropping hints about marriage. This meant a new girlfriend every year or so. Rob had two children from a failed marriage that he was raising as a single father. He rotated home duties in engineer fashion: one person cooking, one washing dishes, the third cleaning house. Rob rotated his family through his list of a dozen dinner recipes, in strict numerical order.

Jack had a powerful frame and an army sergeant-like appearance, with a deep gruff voice that concealed a heart of gold. He had worked on large disc drives for many years with Gordon at Librascope and at Xerox, and was the best manufacturing engineer Gordon knew. Jack's talent was solving practical manufacturing problems.

Stationed in Germany in the U.S. Army after the Korean War, Jack had once heard base gossip about a tank that had burned up due to faulty maintenance. Jack had gone to see the base commander. "Sir, I can replace that tank, and I can do it without officially scrapping out the burned out tank."

"Sergeant, I'd like to see the magic trick that avoids scrapping it. Make it so." The commander was thinking that officially replacing the tank would make an expensive hit on his budget, and the resulting investigation would put a blemish on his peacetime service record. Jack was fully aware of this, of course. Jack began to process hundreds of paper forms for scrapped tank parts through Army Headquarters, each form to get credit for one individual part in the burned tank. Parts replacement costs didn't come out of the base budget.

A month later he asked the commander to accompany him to a local German rail yard. A railroad flatcar sat alone on a side rail line, carrying a bulky object covered by a tarp. Pulling off the tarp, the commander was astounded to see a new tank.

"That's the replacement for the burned tank? How did you do it?"

"I have a buddy in Headquarters maintenance that processed my paperwork to get credit for the most expensive scrap parts from the old tank. The total was enough for this replacement tank; part costs always add up to more than the price for a new machine. May I have your authorization to requisition a tank transporter to move it to the base?"

"Jack, after making a burned up army tank disappear and a new tank reappear, I'll sign anything you hand me. And I'm promoting you; as of now you report directly to me."

Sam was devoted to their Xerox lab, always thinking of ways to improve the lab or to help its people work together. When he heard the lab would be closed down he quit in anger and moved to Bremerton, Washington, taking a job driving a Snap-On truck and selling tools to mechanics around the city. He wasn't very successful at sales and was happy to join Seagate.

In late 1982 the four of them sat around the kitchen table in Gordon's L.A. home, writing out an electronics equipment list for their new Seagate lab, including a $120,000 DEC VAX 750 minicomputer. Although word processors were a rarity in 1982, Gordon's VAX had advanced features for its day, including a report writing program. Gordon intended to use it to compose engineering memos and then type them out on its central control terminal, to be xeroxed for distribution. After they finished and the group left, Gordon sat alone at the table, going over the list which added up to over $500,000.

Heavy rains during the previous week had finally eased up a few hours earlier and a warm sun began to peek through the clouds. Gordon saw movement out of the corner of his eye and looked up through the kitchen window, across the canyon he lived in. He was quick enough to see the start of a torrential landslide of mud and plants as an entire waterlogged hillside avalanched down onto the house below.

The landscape began its fall as a single intact piece; all its plants and trees moving together, breaking up as it hit the back yard of the house below. It instantly filled up its swimming pool, pushing the pool water ahead of it into the rear of the house. The mud followed the water inside.

If it isn't forest fire season in L.A., it's flood and mudslide season. After calling the fire department he walked over to the house, found no one home, turned off its electricity to prevent a fire, and returned to finish the list of people to hire and equipment to buy.

Gordon and Shirley got married and flew to Italy to spend their honeymoon skiing. They met an Italian group of skiing friends in the Dolomite Mountains, and joined them for ski mountaineering over the top of a mountain range and down the opposite mountain side, through the Val Mesdi, the "Valley of the Midday Sun." The trip began by taking a cable tram up to the mountain top. Fifty other skiers in the tram turned down the mountain on regular ski runs, and their group turned uphill to hike to the summit in their ski boots, skis over shoulders. After a hot climb through deep snow to the mountain top, the group put their skis on to pole over the flat summit towards the Val Mesdi.

After a kilometer of poling over the flat summit block, Gordon saw a narrow opening at its vertical cliff edge. He looked down a steep chute. It ended in rocks hundreds of meters below and then opened into a less steep valley filled with powder snow. *I know I'm going down this one way or another. It's a kilometer back to the top of the tram, all uphill. I may as well just start down now.* Shirley watched him vanish down the chute.

The chute was very steep but had excellent packed snow and was quite manageable. Gordon skied down far enough to be out of the way of the others, and stopped.

He heard a cry above him. One of the Italian women was sliding down on her back, quickly picking up speed. The Italian expedition leader skied across the chute, grabbed her as he passed, and stopped. She was laughing as he picked her up onto her feet.

The group reached the valley and tried to ski its deep powder. Shirley handled the powder with ease while Gordon struggled to stay upright. At last they emerged in the valley below, back among the ordinary ski crowd.

10.

Starting at Seagate

After returning to L.A. from Italy, Gordon drove his car north, filled with clothes, bedding, lamps, books, cook ware, and a TV set. He moved into a small rental house in the forested San Lorenzo Valley, in the mountains east of Santa Cruz.

The next morning he drove to the Seagate building in Scotts Valley that Doug had given him to set up his new lab. His drive was along a scenic road winding through redwood groves. It was quite a bit more pleasant than his L.A. freeway drive to Xerox in El Segundo had been. He parked at his new lab, noticing its address was on a side street, Quién Sabe Road. He smiled as he recalled that "Quién Sabe" was Spanish for "who knows," because he had no idea where or what his new job would lead to.

When he got home that night he found things had been moved in his absence. He also smelled pipe smoke.

"I think there's a ghost in this house," he told Shirley over the phone that evening. Suddenly, a noisy motor started up in the kitchen. "Hey! Hang on while I check that noise out, honey."

Setting down the phone he went into the kitchen and found the stove hood fan running. He turned its switch off. Picking up the living room phone again, he said, "It was the kitchen hood fan. It couldn't have turned itself on. I'm going to try an experiment tomorrow to see if the ghost can go through walls or not." He said goodbye, hung up, poured himself a scotch, and began making Shirley's breaded chicken recipe for dinner. He had a dozen of her recipes written down in engineer fashion. His recipes not only described the ingredients and quantities, but also how to slice and cook them and how to find them in a grocery store.

He called Shirley the next evening. "Last night I put a metal rod in the track of the glass door to the back yard. It can't be jimmied open any more. When I got home today nothing was disturbed in the house, not even some sewing thread I scotch taped across several doors. But the sliding glass door has been pulled back a bit to hit the metal rod. I left it fully closed. So much for the ghost. More like a nosy neighbor.

"Honey, I've learned something really important about looking for a home for us up here in the Santa Cruz Mountains. Ignore houses like this one, deep in a valley and surrounded by trees. The sun comes up late and sets early because of the mountains towering over the San Lorenzo Valley, so I never see the sun. A sure sign is moss growing on roof shingles, like this place."

When Shirley began house hunting she found this could be detected in "home for sale" advertisements by phrases like "nestled in the woods."

After a month, Gordon moved out of the woods and rented a sunny "Mother-in-law" garage apartment on a Scotts Valley hilltop, a code name for an apartment illegally built over a garage. It was just a few blocks from his new lab on Quién Sabe Road.

His new Seagate group arrived one by one over the next few weeks. Shirley stayed back in L.A. to sell her house, leaving Gordon with little to do in his spare time, of which he only had little anyway.

One evening Kermit took Gordon to a Zen Buddhist meditation in Santa Cruz. Kermit was a devotee of Alan Watts, an illumination dispensing Guru. They drove to the Santa Cruz mission, one of the California missions built by Spanish Friars in the eighteenth and nineteenth centuries. It was still an active Catholic church, as were many of the missions up and down the California coast. Parking their car next to adobe barracks where Indian "converts" slept after their daily forced labor on mission farms, they walked to a nondescript house, were led into a bare room, and silently instructed to sit on cushions facing a wall like seven other strangers were. They sat in Lotus position and hummed a mantra, "Om Mane Padme Hum." Gordon tried to focus on the sound as instructed but the aches in his legs kept intruding.

A beatific enlightened master arrived after an hour and dreamily smiled at them for a while. After another endless interval they heard a distracting commotion at the entrance. When Zen finally ended they learned it was a drugged-up hippy girl looking for a crash pad. Gordon found the Zen experience boring and non-illuminating. His leg muscles hurt from sitting so long in the Lotus position.

II.

A Common Sense Radio

After Zen, Kermit invited Gordon up for a drink and they drove to his Santa Cruz apartment. It was clean and neat, and without any trace of female presence. Brewing herbal coffee in a pot on his stove, Kermit said, "I think Buddhist meditation gives an illuminating insight into God, from a scientific point of view. Don't you agree?" In the background, Kermit's Hi Fi was softly playing Erik Satie's piano work *Barefoot Dances.*

"Sort of like becoming One with your inner geek?" Gordon wryly replied. "I personally appreciate God when I see our universe as God's movie that humanity shares through the Common Sense, the unconscious communication we all silently use to decide on how the universe behaves."

Kermit took a sip of tea and raised a single eyebrow, "That's an awful strange concept to swallow in one gulp. Is this movie universe your own idea, Gordon?"

"Nope. More than two thousand years ago in ancient Greece, Plato's book *The Republic* called our human condition 'The Cave.' He described our reality as hypnotic projections of images on the wall of a dark cave, wherein all humanity was confined to prevent them from seeking to experience the sun outside the cave. Plato said anyone breaking the hypnosis and finding their way outside into the sunlight would become terrified and desperately seek to return to the dark, fearful of ever speaking of his experience. Over the ages, many humans have sought and found that same Central Truth, from Plato's Greece to our modern world, but anyone who speaks of it has failed to follow the rules of the Cave and is considered weird and perhaps insane. Some call it the 'collective unconscious.'"

"Gordon, are you saying that all humanity is just a mesmerized audience in God's theater, watching a totally engrossing movie that God creates and directs? Sort of like the 'Force' in the Star Wars movie?"

"The Truth is always accessible but widely ignored.

"Maybe I can describe it better as a computer game. We're video game players, totally fixated by the action on the screen, irritated if anyone distracts us. We don't want to think or talk about anything but the game. To believe in the game we ignore the many unlikely coincidences necessary for our space-time universe to exist and support life, the impossibly many curious constructs in the movie.

"Scientists can see our universe is artificial, but all their attempts to study why fail to be reproducible by other scientists. Humanity senses any attempt by science to directly reveal the objective Truth of God, through their collective but unconscious Common Sense, and they unconsciously shift reality a bit to make any such science irreproducible."

Kermit squirmed uncomfortably. "It's true that the universe seems artificially constructed. Quantum mechanics has twenty arbitrary parameters that scientists can't predict from any theory; they have to be measured by experiment. If some were larger or smaller by just a few percent, no life would exist."

Then his face brightened. "Listen, Gordon! Science has come a long way since Plato's day. Today's string theory physics could be a scientific version of Plato's Cave. It says our four-dimensional space-time universe is projected from a hidden multiverse of ten dimensions or more. We see only a 3D space-time projection, just as Plato said."

"The string universe could be the projector of Plato's Cave all right. But ten dimensions would be just a bigger but still finite universe. It might be a step closer to the Central Truth, but adding any fixed number of additional dimensions just takes you to another more complex illusion. Limiting God to ten dimensions or any other definite number is a foolish attempt to restrict God. Quantum field theory scientists have a much better picture of our universe, with well-established physics and a long history of experimental confirmation. They study the Metaverse, the collection of all possible universes, including ours. Their Metaverse has an unrestricted number of dimensions, and allows our past and future time dimensions. It doesn't try to restrict God."

A soft breeze stirred Kermit's window curtains, carrying a hint of the nearby sea. Gordon saw a box of audio cassette tapes sitting on Kermit's coffee table, labeled "Alan Watts Radio Talks." *Looks like Kermit recorded all of them.*

"I recently read an article about your enlightenment guru, Alan Watts. It said he died an alcoholic."

"Don't judge Watts' work by his alcoholism, Gordon. He often gave his best enlightenment lectures while drunk. Many religions use drugs to see God."

Gordon looked unconvinced.

Kermit scowled. "Your concept of a shared common sense or collective unconscious seems fuzzy to me. Can you turn your idea into a concrete, testable hypothesis that the scientific method can be applied to, with mathematics to test its validity?"

"You don't ask much, do you? O.K., here goes. My description of the Common Sense seems rather like radio transmission, doesn't it? You know, science doesn't explain exactly *what* radio is. It's content with mathematics that only *predicts how* radio waves behave. Suppose science made the Common Sense similarly commonplace and reliably usable, using special 'radio' transmitters and receivers."

"Was that pun intended, Gordon? Surely humanity wouldn't permit directly exposing this Common Sense of yours, if it exists. Why would this quantum radio work any better than the 'quantum telepathy' method people call 'intuition'?"

"Because intuition can't be scientifically investigated without treading into the forbidden territory underlying our space-time universe. People accept technology solutions like radio transmission because they're limited and not threatening.

"My idea would be to create a new 'radio' technology to allow practical use of intuition. Instead of directly revealing the Common Sense, the new 'radio' would make it dependably useful, and somehow without the threat of making people's secret thoughts readable by others. The objective would be to 'discover' or 'invent' a new radio that accesses the Common Sense. You would turn its 'on' knob, tune it to a 'channel,' and receive or transmit by thought alone.

"Imagine using such a 'radio' to mentally control artificial arms or legs, enable sight for the blind, hearing for the deaf, to run your computer without having to type on a stupid keyboard, to signal for help in an emergency anywhere in the world, or for an infinitely fast and free Internet, available anywhere."

Kermit noticed Gordon was panting a bit from his effort to explain. "You're serious, aren't you?"

"I'm only asking you to accept it as a scientific hypothesis, to be verified or rejected by the usual experimental methods. If someone did prove the idea correct they might win a Nobel Prize and get rich."

Kermit rubbed his head. "I admit it's rather intriguing to try analyzing God using the scientific method. So how would someone go about inventing such a radio?"

"I think the way to begin is to adopt a fundamental logical rule that if God exists, God can have no limits. Any restriction on God is false. We can't say that God is limited to exist only in some other place called 'heaven,' somewhere other than here and now. Our universe must be a true aspect of God even if it's a limited one. Ask yourself how space and time must appear to God under that 'no limits' rule. God's 'Space' has to be a single Unity that somehow allows the apparently separated objects we see. And you and I have to be limited aspects of God, actually within God's single Unity of space and time. We're made in God's image, as it were. Our relentlessly flowing river of time would be just a restricted view of God's eternal 'Now.' Our universe and all its history since the Big Bang would really be just one of infinitely many ways of viewing the Unity."

"And where does that lead to?" Kermit asked skeptically.

"Please be patient and keep an open mind! I'm getting there! Quantum mechanics shows that time and space are digital, not continuous. Science long ago established that there's a minimum quantum size of space, and a minimum quantum step of time.

"Here's the hypothesis: our entire space-time universe is recreated 'between' each quantum time step, and its 'new' space can't change from its 'old' by more than the minimum possible quantum space size. Humanity mutually agrees on the changes that will occur in each new moment, through the Common Sense.

Kermit looked doubtful.

"I know this seems crazy. Quantum mechanics always seems crazy. But it's been repeatedly proven correct for a century now. It requires every quantum event to have an observer, and that an observation collapses the probability choices of how any event *could* occur, into its single *actual* occurrence. Like whether an atom moves one way and not another. Doesn't it seem crazy that quantum mechanics says observers are necessary for our universe to exist? And physicists can't explain exactly what or who the observers are. This new hypothesis explains the quantum observer craziness by proposing that all humanity makes the event choices for each time step. We're all observers, agreeing on the universe's jump events by using the Common Sense."

"So who were the observers before any humans existed, during the fourteen billion years after the Big Bang began our universe?"

"Remember our hypothesis, Kermit! Only the 'Now' moment really exists in time. The past we imagine only has to be consistent with our Now. The same goes for the future. Only the Now really exists.

Physical experiments are only possible in the present moment, though the apparent past and future can help test scientific theories.

"Getting back to the main idea, we don't see the infinitesimal jumps because they're so small, and because we humans focus on the space and time moments themselves, not on the jumps between moments. It's sort of like music. Musicians know that the intervals between notes are critical but they go unnoticed by the audience unless played wrong."

"That's all quite an extraordinary leap beyond proven physics, Gordon."

"You're right. Carl Sagan said, 'Extraordinary claims require extraordinary proof.' So let's take a baby step first, a step that physicists could agree with. Here it is. Take the minimum space quantum that science experimentally measures; that's the Planck length in meters. Divide it by the minimum time quantum in seconds. That'll give you a speed in meters per second. The 'baby step' hypothesis is that speed will turn out to be the speed of light, and that'll explain why nothing can move faster than the speed of light, the basis of Einstein's theory of relativity. When the 'baby step' is studied in mathematical detail, other fundamental physics laws may also naturally emerge, along with the light speed limit.

"After this 'baby step' is verified, the rest of the hypothesis will seem less extraordinary. The Common Sense will be seen to have no speed-of-light limit because all humanity shares in the mutual recreation of the 'new' space by 'knowing' every detail of the past moments. It operates in the jumps between moments, or maybe it *is* the jumps.

"I've simplified the picture a bit by skipping some quantum probability math, to make the point that once physicists see the relationship between time and space quanta and light speed they'll naturally be eager to explore the physics of the jumps. Once scientists accept how the Einstein light speed limit arises naturally from the quantum nature of our changing universe, they'll start developing math to describe the Common Sense; then use that math to set up laboratory experiments to characterize the jumps; and finally extend the math to look for 'quantum radio' technology that can instantly transmit and receive information."

"That's crazy enough all right, Gordon. But you said 'experiments to characterize the jumps.' Don't you first need experiments to prove there *are* jumps?"

"No, that's another accepted fact of quantum mechanics. Every physicist can calculate how an observer knowing the outcome probabilities of an *individual* potential event sees them collapse into a single concrete existence in the next time jump. They only need to go a step further to consider that *all* events in our universe recur simultaneously in each successive time step.

"And quantum mechanics already indicates that the Common Sense is faster than light speed. Two nearby quantum particles can become 'entangled' by quantum events, and both particles can later instantaneously and simultaneously change even when they're far apart. Likewise, when people interact intimately as they do in a family, their quantum states can become entangled. That can allow instant knowledge of what's happening, even when they're far apart."

"Come on, Gordon. Quantum entanglement is proven physics only for small groups of subatomic particles."

"Aren't we humans just larger bunches of those particles? A group of particles makes up the collective events each of us calls our life; our bodies moving through space, lungs breathing, brain thinking, and so on. Mothers can become entangled with their children and husbands as they live together, and later sense their condition even when they're far apart. That's how woman's intuition works, according to our hypothesis."

Kermit thought for a moment and then raised another objection. "O.K., I see where you're going with this, but the quantum math describing how the entire universe jumps to its next new moment would be indescribably complex. There's too many billions of billions of equations to solve. Is there any concrete hope that your hypothesis could lead to solvable mathematics?"

"You're right, quantum probability math describing how our entire universe collapses into its next space existence would be far more complex than the math describing individual quantum events.

"But the 'baby step' discoveries will encourage scientists to attack the math difficulties, perhaps by computing effects from far-away objects using statistical math to average them in groups. Most of the objects in the universe don't change at all between jumps, so their math is simple, and it's almost as simple for the many events that keep changing in the same way, like Earth rotating and stars shining. Their probability of different event outcomes is small enough that simple perturbation math may work."

"And because the laws of physics must be obeyed, they make the math simpler by decreasing the number of quantum possibilities?"

"Right. They're Common Sense consensus rules for jump behavior in the Now moment of our universe. Sort of a mutually agreed upon norm for our universe.

"Anyway, for a Common Sense 'radio' we only need detailed math to describe just two of the billions of billions of events. The first is to add an information transmission event to the group of quantum events that constitute the sender's next time jump. The second is to add a reception event to the receiver's.

"I'm saying that the Common Sense 'quantum radio' is so specific an idea that its quantum math should be simple enough to solve. Even if that simplified math requires supercomputers to solve, they're readily available. Or maybe you could simplify the math by beginning at the subatomic level with two small groups of particles. Their quantum collapse into the next moment could involve the observer of each group sharing or influencing part of the probability collapse of the other."

"Why not just directly invent such a radio and avoid the difficult math entirely. Edison didn't need math to make his inventions. The universe makes the jumps all by itself, all the time. Just look for a technology way for a radio."

"Well, O.K., but you'd need to be an inventor ingenious enough to come up with the right experimental idea to test and develop."

They shared a comfortable silence for a time, both thinking over the hypothesis.

Finally Gordon said, "Look Kermit, I'm not intending an attack by science on religion here. Science aims to improve human existence by creating and uncovering practical principles of our space-time universe. Science focuses on advances in our physical world; in health, energy, medicine, agriculture, and quality of life. It researches the 'how' of scientific law; more directly usable than religion's metaphysics of 'why.' Science can't study ideas unless they can be tested in our universe, but that doesn't mean scientists can't personally appreciate God. They just leave the elusive 'why' to religion. There isn't any real conflict between science and religion except when spiritual believers claim supremacy over science, like in Creationism or Intelligent Design."

Kermit replied, "People like Creationists can believe anything they want because they never demand real world proof. Creationism is no less fanciful than any other imaginable theory. Claiming the Earth has a Biblical age of twelve thousand years instead of science's 4.5 billion has no more claim to truth than believing the Earth is one minute old and all memories earlier than a minute ago are illusions. All claims like that are just mental games if there's no way to prove or disprove them.

"There's a crucially important problem in teaching Creationism in schools in place of science, Gordon. People who deeply care about the education of children must insist that kids be first taught the scientific method. Its judgment skills will serve them throughout their lives. After they learn it, they can be taught Darwinism, Intelligent Design, and Creationism, for practice in applying the scientific method.

"If America stops teaching its children science and technology, the U.S. will be doomed to a third world future. Asian countries won't stop teaching their children to become scientists and engineers, and Asia may come to dominate the world's economy, as technology innovation and manufacturing move there from America."

"Amen, Kermit."

12.

House Hunting in the Countryside

Shirley drove up from L.A. to Santa Cruz several times to look for their new home, but it was Gordon who found it. Their requirements were that the house be single level, 7 to 15 miles from the California coast, and have a sunny view. Both native Californians, they knew that further than 15 miles from the coast meant no marine air to moderate summer heat and winter cold. Less than 7 miles meant the house would be under the gray gloom of coastal stratus clouds many days. Shirley was strictly a sunlight lady.

Gordon's apartment landlady let him know of such a house for sale by a member of her church, in the small town of Boulder Creek twenty minutes up a scenic road winding through San Lorenzo Valley redwood groves. Valley towns like Boulder Creek were summer vacation homes until the 1960s. Their owners had to permanently occupy them after the San Francisco hippy era faded because many hippies moved into the valley, breaking into vacant homes to live in them. Boulder Creek's single movie theater closed when hippies began using it as a refuge from winter cold. Normal citizens avoided the theater because of the bath-phobic hippies.

The valley had been a popular vacation area before the hippies moved in. Big Bend was nearby, California's first redwood forest park. Hollywood stars like Bing Crosby had stayed in the valley's Brookdale Lodge, famous for a mountain creek running merrily but noisily through its dining room. Now the lodge was only famous for its ghosts. Brookdale would thrive again in some future era, when history and charm in a redwood forest near San Francisco demanded it.

Gordon and Shirley drove to see the house, which had been for sale for five years. Shirley brought Charles, since he had to approve any new home. As they drove into Boulder Creek they passed one market, one video rental store, one pizza restaurant, and then Boulder Creek itself, gurgling beneath a small wooden road bridge. The entire town was only a few blocks long. They drove up a steep hill and found themselves in the nicest neighborhood they had seen in the entire valley. The road continued up a steep driveway to the house for sale.

They knocked on its door and a grandmother-looking lady answered. She began to greet them, but her husband standing beside her immediately interrupted, blurting out, "The price for this house is non-negotiable. I listed it with a real estate agent five years ago but now I'm selling it myself. Agents are crooks who charge commissions too big." Charles looked up at the man patiently.

In the house tour they saw its living room was stuffed with massive black furniture. *That stuff would look better in an ancient European castle.* Red velvet wallpaper and garish green carpets glared out here and there around the gloomy furniture.

Gordon whispered to Shirley, "It looks like a San Francisco bordello. Or maybe a stage set for a ghouls and monsters TV show."

"Sssh," she said smiling. Charles politely inspected the decorating scheme without comment, looking left and right as he followed them down a long central hall.

The guest bath was a stark black room, the walls around its bathtub tiled with cheap gold veined glass squares that Gordon had seen long before in discount decorating stores. They walked to the end of the hall and into the master bedroom. It stretched across the entire end of the house. Gordon checked its bathroom. *Whew, not stark black.* He looked at its "surprise shower," as he would soon come to call it.

The house had a redwood deck on its long side, facing the San Lorenzo Valley. They walked along it and leaned on its railing to look down the valley.

"This will be the view out your kitchen window, Shirley. Isn't it beautiful?" That earned him one of her five thousand watt smiles.

The pad for the house had been bulldozed out of a sandstone mountain, giving it a stunning view of the redwood forest groves stretching down the San Lorenzo Valley as it wound towards Santa Cruz and the sea. The sandstone cliff behind the house bore bulldozer blade marks. The cliff was topped by more forest, nearly encircling a large redwood water tank above.

This tank belonged to the San Lorenzo Valley water company and Gordon would soon discover that the water pump filling it from the valley below often failed. The highest elevation house in the neighborhood would be first to discover the failure and this was that house. Gordon would often learn of the failure in mornings when he was in the "surprise shower," all soaped up with no water to rinse. The water company had wired the pump back to their Boulder Creek office over local telephone company lines. This put high voltage on the telephone lines which gave telephone maintenance people shocks. They disconnected the illegal pump wires whenever they found them and the tank would begin to empty.

Gordon would soon learn this was typical of life in the rural, laidback, hippy San Lorenzo Valley, where the usual number of operating headlights on a car was one instead of two. The only political battles in the valley occurred at valley water company district meetings, often over company truck access to their water system pipes and tanks. The local hippies came to the meetings wearing overalls and Mother Hubbard dresses, acting tough and demanding to be paid for water company access over private roads they considered theirs, though they had neither built the roads nor owned them nor maintained them. Some were phony hippies, actually wealthy lawyers living in mansions in the mountains, illegally built without county permits. They came disguised in hippy clothes, but this was a small valley and the locals knew them by name. "Aren't you Mr. Cheatham, the lawyer who threatens county inspectors with a shotgun when they come to your house to write you up for building code violations?"

The water company usually won these arguments using Robert's Rules of Order techniques, by tabling or overruling hippy demands. Houses had no water meters because it was common for the valley to receive over a hundred inches of rain a year. During one such year, California was experiencing a drought and everyone in the state had to ration water by not watering lawns and gardens or washing cars. Except for the San Lorenzo Valley, which had unlimited water in its reservoirs until December, when a sudden cold snap froze the water company's uninsulated pipes, breaking them open and creating an instant water shortage.

Gordon and Shirley decided to buy it. "I'll make you an offer on your house," Gordon told its owner.

"I won't accept a penny less than my asking price."

Gordon figured the man's finances must be tighter than his because he had the house loan from Seagate.

The man's wife intervened. "Now, dear, don't be so stubborn."

Gordon offered a token $1,000 below the man's asking price, asked him to pay for a septic tank inspection, and they left. They stopped at a local real estate office to arrange for an appraisal and an earthquake inspection. When the appraisal came, he saw the house was worth considerably more than what the owner was asking. *I wonder if I should tell the man he's asking too little. Hmn. Nah, he's too bad tempered.*

A local geologist surveyed the house for Gordon. "It has several excellent features going for it: massive rain gutters, good water drainage, and this site. The valley can get five inches of rain a day, but this house will never flood up on its hill. Looks like a bulldozer carved this site out of solid sandstone. The rock is geologically 40 million years old and it's survived intact all that time. All of Santa Cruz County is close to the San Andreas Fault, where it runs up the east side of these mountains through Los Gatos and under Stanford University, but this house sitting up here on solid rock will be safest from earthquakes."

A week later, the owner accepted Gordon's offer but refused the inspection, saying that he didn't know where the septic tank was located. Gordon decided to try dousing to find the house septic system. He cut and bent ordinary wire coat hangers into L-shaped iron rods and dipped their ends into a toilet bowl. This "told" the rods what they were looking for. *I wonder if fishermen do the same when they choose their bait and cast it into the water. They always know what kind of fish they're after, but how do the fish know which hook to go to?*

Gordon walked the front yard and driveway, holding one rod in each hand, their long sides pointing horizontally forward. The rods twisted backwards in his hands as he walked over the leach field pipes, apparently buried underneath the asphalt driveway. He decided the septic system itself was inaccessible unless he hired heavy equipment to plow up the driveway and remove a massive stand of Juniper bushes planted in front of the house.

Gordon didn't care that dousing was unscientific. He saw it as interesting and thought the scientific method might possibly explain it some day by some new principle. The scientific method required keeping an open mind while gathering all possible data for testing a hypothesis, never prematurely throwing one out as nonsense.

When Gordon met his new neighbors lower down on the hill, they told him that it wasn't advisable to disturb the "monster" that lived in their septic tanks. The "monster" was fussy, and needed to be fed a special yeast pill every week. If its demands were ignored, the leach lines would clog and the tank would have to be drained every year by a honey bucket truck. This made sense to Gordon, liking the neighbor's monster story. They also told him that winter rains often felled forest trees, bring down electric lines and causing power outages.

13.

A Silicon Valley Startup Company

In 1980, Seagate began manufacturing disc drives in Scotts Valley. The town was named after Hiram Scott who jumped ship in Monterey Bay in 1850, bought the valley, and became rich and then broke during the California gold rush. The Seagate founders liked the area and Seagate was one of the first Silicon Valley companies to locate in Scotts Valley.

Finis was Seagate's Senior Vice President of Marketing, the man who invented the original concept of shrinking computer hard disc drive technology to fit in a PC, replacing a floppy disc drive. He first drew his idea on a cocktail napkin at a Silicon Valley bar. Finis went from unknown engineer to famous small drive architect, becoming yet another Silicon Valley legend.

A likable man of graceful manner, Finis was remarkably trusted by Seagate customers. Although he became wealthy from his contributions to Seagate's success, he was approachable by everyone. He personally wrote articles for trade magazines to promote Seagate disc drive products, articles he could easily have ordered his marketing people to write.

Al was Seagate President and CEO. At an earlier job at Memorex he had championed an open-technology business model of manufacturing IBM compatible disc drives. He had sold drives with the same performance as IBM's at 15% lower price and he encouraged other drive makers to do the same. The competitive markets he formed were his key to high market volumes at lower prices. Al had later built another mass market at a second company he started, for the 5.25-inch floppy disc drive used in Apple II and IBM PCs. Al was forced out of that company over disagreements with its board of directors. Before he started Seagate he had run commercial fishing boats and a restaurant in Santa Cruz. Al's reputation for entrepreneurship and simple honesty gave him a remarkable charisma. He was an ideal person for president, whose reputation could attract investors with startup money.

He and Finis brought in Doug as Chief Technology Officer, and brought in Tom from a low-cost PC manufacturer to run manufacturing. Tom had a reputation of terrifying people, even men physically larger than him, never taking "can't" as a answer to a company problem. He was famous for once jumping on top of a marketing executive's desk who wouldn't respond to Tom's orders, kicking everything off the terrified man's desk except the picture of his wife, and then asking, "Do I have your attention now?" Everyone at Seagate knew the story. They had all heard about the hand grenade that sat on Tom's desk, nobody certain whether it was live or not.

Doug ran Seagate's engineering department, with Stan as his top Vice President of Drive Engineering. Gordon found Stan to be a brilliant technology manager with an instinctive ability to distinguish technical facts from hopeful fiction. He was also a decent and simply nice guy. But Stan would not tolerate clumsy or lazy engineering.

Marc was Doug's engineering staff assistant. Al had apparently hired Marc as an errand runner for upper management, with duties like finding new Seagate building sites in Scotts Valley. He seemed to have unusual influence with Al, having worked at Al's last two startup companies. Marc was a thin man with a sharp face, eyes that never quite directly looked into yours, and tobacco stained fingers. He was shrewd about people but ignorant of engineering. Gordon soon found him to be a devious manipulator of people. Marc was innocent of any skill or knowledge of disc drive technology or of Gordon's magnetic recording work, and in his ignorance he would do his best to make Gordon's life hell.

The Seagate founders had initially tried to get their startup money from venture capital companies. That was unsuccessful until Al got an investment from Norm, president of the Dysan Company. Norm's computer industry experience allowed him to see the major business opportunity Al and Finis were offering, an opportunity that no venture capital company was able to see. Dysan was a manufacturer of standard 8 and 14 inch diameter magnetic recording discs. Norm supplied money and equipment, as well as Seagate's first 5.25-inch recording discs. Norm also offered a low disc price along with his investment in Seagate stock. Seagate was more than happy to accept.

Using Norm's money the Seagate founders were able to build a development lab and later get an investment from TVC, a venture capital fund. They began to design and build the first PC hard disc drive by leasing a building in Scotts Valley and hiring Ed, a mechanical engineer who always wore white shirts and dress slacks, a dress code obsoleted by earlier Silicon Valley startup companies. Doug designed the electronics, Ed the mechanics, and their wives helped assemble prototype drives. Tom was impressed by how quick and easy the technology seemed.

One evening they left the plant with three drives running overnight in test.

When they returned the next day they found that two drives had broken their track motor drive belts and the third drive was singing.

"It sounds like a tuning fork," Doug said. "What do you suppose is making that singing sound?"

Ed put his ear close to the drive, and then turned the disc drive upside down. Picking up a screwdriver from a workbench, he put its handle to his ear and touched the blade to various spots on the drive case.

"This screwdriver 'stethoscope' tells me the ground spring is vibrating." This spring was a small rectangle of thin stainless steel with one end screwed to the metal case of the disc drive and the other end touching the end of the rotating shaft of the disc spin motor. It bled off static electricity that spinning discs might build up, like a person moving over a rug.

"Watch," said Ed as he pressed his finger on the spring to change its friction on the rotating motor shaft. The singing stopped. "Let me experiment with this. I'll find the right spring force and position adjustment so they don't sing.

"Now we need to put the two track motor belts under a microscope to see why they broke," Ed said. These belts were made of thin stainless steel and were wrapped around the drive shaft of a track motor. Track motor rotation moved the heads from one disc data track to another. "I'll run over the hill to Silicon Valley and rent a microscope."

At the time, Seagate only owned a few soldering irons, some assembly tools, one desktop test computer, and one oscilloscope (bought used).

When Ed returned with the microscope he carefully examined the broken belts. "They fatigued from the continuous overnight bending and unbending around the track motor shaft, as it rotated back and forth moving the heads. I think the breaks begin as cracks at the belt edges because the stainless steel they're cut from is too thick and the edges aren't smooth enough. That tells me enough to know how to fix the belt design."

After resolving a series of these design problems, Tom began to plan for volume production. One morning, Ed came to work and found a note from Tom: "I just placed an order for 10,000 of these."

Ed looked at the drawing under Tom's note on his drafting board, for the aluminum casting that would be the case of the new drive. *MY GOD! My case design is nowhere near finished yet! Tom's rush to get production started will bankrupt us!* Ed's stomach twisted in pain and he didn't notice that Tom's note was attached to a page from a parts catalog of standard steel washers, and 10,000 of them would cost only $100. *I'm going to leave Seagate just as soon as my stock option is far enough into the money.*

In these initial years, when Seagate needed additional workbenches, desks, or chairs, Doug would drive his old pickup truck to Dysan and load up. They bought discs from other suppliers as well as Dysan, so they could continue drive production if any one supplier ran into manufacturing problems.

14.

Grenex Advanced Cobalt Discs

Seagate began drive production using common industry "brown paint" discs, which IBM had invented for its first disc drive in 1956. Brown paint was sprayed on polished flat aluminum platters that had been "cookie cutter" cut from aluminum sheets about 1/5 of an inch thick. The pigment in ordinary brown paint was iron oxide, magnetic rust, which could be magnetized by a recording head to store bits. Recorded magnetic bits created magnetic fields just above the paint surface, fields that a read head could sense as it flew over bit locations.

Al, Finis, and Doug had a long range objective for Seagate to develop and make its own high-tech discs. Seagate got financing for a cobalt disc startup company named Grenex, from the TVC venture capital firm. TVC expected to ultimately make many millions of dollars off the Grenex stock it received. TVC was more than willing to put up the funding based on Seagate's original disc drive business success.

Part of Seagate's contribution to the Grenex venture was hiring Gordon and his group to help Grenex develop discs that could allow Seagate drives to store more data than its competitors using brown paint discs. Letting TVC money pay for disc development allowed Seagate to continue investing its own profits in low-cost high-volume drive manufacturing factories, critical to its continued business success. Gordon and his engineers got Grenex stock options, along with the new people hired to run Grenex. Besides working on Grenex cobalt discs, Gordon's group would develop advanced recording heads and electronics for future Seagate drives.

"Doug, I've studied the Grenex proposal to TVC." Gordon was sitting in Doug's office one morning. "There are far too many risks in it. Grenex's proposing much more than a normal cobalt recording disc. Their proposal for an advanced perpendicular recording cobalt disc will require Seagate to develop entirely new perpendicular recording heads and electronics to use their discs in our drives. If we attempt to use our present recording heads and electronics with that kind of perpendicular recording cobalt disc, they won't store any more data than the brown paint discs we're now using."

He handed Doug a technical memo he had written and printed on his VAX. "Here's my mathematical analysis proving what I just said. Seagate has no way either to buy or manufacture such heads today. We'll have head R&D and production capability sometime in the future, but not soon enough.

"That's just one of five distinct risks, any two of which could cause Grenex to run through all the TVC money before finding ways around them. There's more than enough risk in bringing any new technology disc to high volume production. Simultaneous new disc, new head, and new electronics are far too dangerous. "

"So what's your solution?" Doug responded. With Silicon Valley optimism, he assumed that if Gordon knew the problems he also had figured out the solutions.

"I can design cobalt disc magnetics compatible with our head and electronic drive technology that will still be double-density: let us store twice as much data on each disc. The mathematical analysis I just handed you shows we can make double density drives using our present heads and electronics if we just scale down the head dimensions and fly height. But the discs won't be perpendicular magnetic."

"TVC demanded an advanced perpendicular technology proposal," Doug replied. Gordon realized Doug was asking if he had a business solution as well as a technical one. Gordon knew technology venture capital firms had a peculiar blindness. They forgot they were business and finance experts, not technology experts.

"Doug, I know we have to go with an advanced perpendicular technology proposal for TVC, but I want to work out a backup plan with Grenex that'll insure we're certain to get a usable double-density cobalt disc. Let's call it our 'mystery' cobalt disc. It'll give us a backup if the advanced disc technology fails. I've been talking with Jim, Grenex's new VP of technology, on how to do that within the TVC contract limitations."

"O.K. Gordon, go ahead with your plan." Doug trusted his people without unnecessarily interrogating them on details. That would only happen if Grenex was failing.

"Moving on, what's your opinion of Grenex's proposal to use sputtering to manufacture their cobalt discs?"

Sputtering was a way to spray cobalt atoms in a vacuum system containing a bit of electrified Argon gas, to coat aluminum disc platters with cobalt metal films a few millionths of an inch thick.

"Doug, we used cobalt electroplating in my past work. That would be the least risk. The DC magnetron sputtering systems Grenex proposes to build are based on an existing commercial design that's successful but isn't production oriented. Successfully designing sputtering machines to produce thousands of good discs per day is higher risk than electroplating, but I believe sputtering has a far longer range future. The biggest problem Grenex will face is production engineering their sputtering process, and their people do have a good technology background for that. Of course, there will be the inevitable unexpected problems that come with any new technology. Even electroplating would have many of them."

"Then sputtering is the decision," Doug decided. "Seagate is in this for the long term."

The Grenex advanced cobalt disc proposal was approved by TVC and Grenex established a small development lab in the Silicon Valley town of Sunnyvale. Its president was Earl, who had previously run a sputtering technology company but had no experience making magnetic recording discs.

Gordon met with him. "Earl, I know several consultants with magnetic disc manufacturing experience, willing to work with you."

"Please give me their names," Earl said in his deep basso voice. "Several people have already called me wanting to consult."

Grenex began hiring consultants to advise them on which machines to buy to electroplate aluminum platters with hard nickel; machines to polish the nickel platings smooth, so heads could fly without hitting asperity bumps higher than 8 millionths of an inch; disc cleaning machines; sputtering machines to add the cobalt metal films; and dip coating machines to put a lubricant layer a few atoms thick on top of the cobalt films.

The lubricant helped heads slide smoothly as they took off and landed, when disc rotation started and stopped in drives. The consultants brought valuable advice but also consulted for Grenex competitors, acting as honey bees taking Grenex's best technology innovations to its competitors; to his friend Robert's Lanx company and several other startups racing to be first to develop production capability for cobalt disc manufacturing. Of course the honey bees flew in the opposite direction as well, bringing competitor's secrets back to Grenex.

15.

Industrial Espionage at Malone's Bar

Seagate's founders liked to stop by Malone's Bar after work. This was a bar and restaurant down Scotts Valley Boulevard, near Gordon's lab on Quién Sabe road. Malone's was a working class place offering nothing special except its convenient location. As Seagate grew, new employees also began stopping by Malone's for a beer after work.

The Seagate crowd had a habit of continuing the day's business discussions over drinks at Malone's. One night Carter, a Malone's regular, walked over to talk to Doug. Gordon was standing nearby, and noticed that Carter was dressed neatly in a brown suit. *He's can't be an engineer, dressing that well.*

"I work in marketing for your competitor Tandon, and I overhear everything you say every night. May I give you a bit of advice? Don't discuss business at Malone's."

The Tandon Company competed with Seagate by having its drive salesmen follow Seagate salesmen around to customers, to offer similar drives at slightly lower prices. Tandon was loosing its customers over drive reliability problems and the company was about to close its doors.

Gordon heard Doug thank Carter and then quietly say something else he couldn't make out. A week later, Gordon ran across Carter working in the Seagate marketing department.

"Well, well, Carter," Gordon said. "Welcome to Seagate. Did Doug hire you that same night at Malone's?"

"Glad to be working with you, Gordon. Doug told me that night he was going to recommend me to Finis because honest salesmen are as rare as unicorns. Al says they're even rarer." They both laughed.

Gordon was sitting at a table in Malone's another evening talking with Jim, the Grenex Vice President of Technology. He was a lean, well-mannered man, with an English accent.

"Jim, do you agree the TVC plan is risky and it will be wise to have a backup plan to manufacture double-density cobalt discs that can be used with Seagate's present recording head and electronic technology?"

"I do agree Gordon, but how can we develop such a backup disc under the TVC contract? It specifically calls for an advanced perpendicular cobalt disc."

"Jim, we'll need very few resources for this backup disc work. Sputtering cobalt films onto nickel-plated aluminum platters is known technology, so all the risks will be in the production manufacturing details like polishing and cleaning the platters with atomic-scale perfection. Those details will take a lot of hard work but it won't matter what cobalt alloy we use, so let's work them with the advanced alloy just as the contract says." Those "manufacturing details" would turn out to be dozens of technology problems they would battle for several years.

"We'll just spend a little time on the side developing what I'll call a 'mystery' cobalt disc alloy. I'll give you the magnetic parameters to look for. That'll probably be about 600 oersted longitudinal coercivity and 3 microinch-tesla magnetic thickness. I think you can get those magnetic properties by just adjusting the cobalt-chrome alloy composition you'll be developing for the TVC advanced cobalt disc."

"O.K. Gordon, that's a good backup plan. I'll buy you a beer on it."

Gordon nodded, glancing beyond Jim and seeing Marc, Doug's staff assistant, standing at the bar. Marc was at Malone's most evenings, often drinking so much that a taxi had to be called to take him to a local motel for the night. Driving over Highway 17 to his home in Silicon Valley was dangerous enough in the daytime when sober.

Highway 17 was the main highway running from San Jose in Silicon Valley to Santa Cruz. It followed the route of the slow train that had taken people to Santa Cruz beaches a century earlier. Its narrow, twisty mountain curves over the forested San Francisco peninsula had been straightened and widened in an attempt to modernize a two-lane country road into a four-lane freeway. This was only partially successful, resulting in a faster road that reduced travel time, but at higher speeds that caused more fatal car accidents. One particular blind curve was a frequent accident scene and cars arriving after an accident couldn't see it in time to stop. Five to ten car pileups resulted, ending only when the last wrecked car was stopped far enough back to be visible from the straightaway leading to the curve. The curve was so dangerous that a permanent electric sign had been installed before it. Police officers switched the sign on to illuminate "Danger—Automobile Wreck ahead." The highway had no on-ramps and accidents also happened to cars entering from side roads.

A concrete barrier had been finally erected down the center line of the road. Cars now hit the barrier instead of head-on traffic, increasing the number of car accidents to one a day but reducing the number of fatalities.

One of Gordon's engineers lived in San Jose and drove his Ferrari at high speeds over 17 twice each day, ignoring the dangers. Gordon had once noticed a "Semper Fi" sticker on his rear window and asked him, "Where did you serve?"

"Oh, I never was a Marine, Gordon. The sticker is there to reduce the number of speeding tickets I get on 17." He paused, watching Gordon look confused. "A lot of Highway Patrol officers are ex-Marines and they all respect the Corps. Most of them ignore my speeding. When they do try to catch me I accelerate to 140 mph and outrun them to a side road to hide."

One morning that engineer came to work looking disheveled. "My Ferrari was run into as I came over the hill on Highway 17," he told Gordon. "My gas gauge was low and I got worried about running out of gas, so I stopped to turn around and go back to Los Gatos. A car ran into me and the car behind ran into him.

"You stopped in the middle of a freeway?" Gordon was astounded by his carelessness. "You need to act a lot more sensibly if you expect to live much longer. What happened to the other drivers?"

"One car went off the road into the forest."

"Did the police come? Could he be still lying down there?"

"I don't know and I don't care. And I expect Seagate to pay for my car."

Gordon picked up the phone and called the highway patrol. "Have you been notified of an accident an hour ago on westbound Highway 17? Yes? There was a third car involved. Have you found it? No? Please look for it off the road in the forest."

Although Highway 17 was a danger to drivers it brought Gordon an indirect benefit. Santa Cruz residents didn't like to drive to work every day over 17 to Silicon Valley, which allowed Gordon to hire smarter secretaries than Seagate's pay scale could otherwise attract.

A week later, Gordon called the engineer into his office. "Apparently you sent a demand to Seagate's finance department that Seagate pay for your wrecked Ferrari. I received a memo from them today. They denied your claim of course. You weren't on company time nor on company business."

16.

Bike Crash at the Tree Circus

Gordon was coasting on his bike down the gentle slope of Disc Drive one summer morning, past the abandoned Scotts Valley Tree Circus. This old tourist attraction dated from when Scotts Valley was a rural tourist town on the road from San Jose to Santa Cruz beaches. Its trees had been trained to grow into fantastic shapes like waterfalls, birdcages, and braids. Closed for years, it was now overgrown with underbrush, its bizarre trees still visible. Gordon gazed dreamily at the forest scenery as he coasted along with his feet off the bike pedals, his mind in idle, enjoying the warm sun dappling through the tree leaves and shining on the green sequoia forest marching up the mountains beyond the valley floor. It was a picture postcard California day.

Suddenly Gordon's front wheel twisted sideways in a road rut and he flew forward over the handlebars, flipped in mid-air, and landed heavily on one shoulder on the street, upside down. Dazed, he crawled to the side of Disc Drive, his white shirt torn and bloody. His shoulder moved unnaturally and he wondered how seriously injured he was.

He crawled onto the curb in his bloody white shirt, woozy and wondering how to get help. A minute later, Marc drove by in his BMW. He stopped, rolled down a window, and sneered disdainfully. Gordon dizzily looked up at him. "Faking it again, Gordon?" Marc rolled his window back up and drove off without another word.

That ass Marc didn't even offer to call for help. Guess I'll have to somehow get back up the street and look for somebody. Fortunately, Doug's secretary had seen Gordon's bike crash from her office window and she called his lab. Sam answered. "Gordon's had a bike accident a little way down Disc Drive from your building. I can see him from Doug's office window. He's sitting on the curb and there's blood on his shirt."

A minute later Gordon saw Sam's ratty old pickup truck swing down the street. "Get in, Gordon. I'll put your bike in the back and we'll go to the hospital. What happened?"

Gordon explained his dumb accident as Sam drove him to the local Santa Cruz hospital. An emergency room doctor x-rayed his shoulder, examined him, and put his arm in a sling. "Your shoulder ligaments are torn, but they should heal in a few weeks."

Gordon saw a pay telephone in the hospital lobby as he and Sam walked out, and he stopped to call his secretary. "I won't be able to fly my own plane to Santa Monica today. Please get me on a PSA flight this afternoon, from San Jose to L.A. Give them my credit card number and tell them I'll pick up the ticket at the airport. Please get me a rental car too. Make a return reservation, but leave the date open."

Shirley wasn't happy when he arrived back in L.A. that evening with his arm in a sling. The purpose of his trip had been to help her pack up her house to move north to Boulder Creek.

"I don't trust a rural Santa Cruz hospital to make a proper diagnosis," she said, and immediately took him to see Doctor Bruce, an orthopedic surgeon. He was the son of her Sherman Oaks neighbor, the one who admired Charles Cat for his rat catching skills.

Bruce x-rayed the shoulder. "Your torn shoulder ligaments won't heal unless you have an immediate operation. That Santa Cruz doctor should have known that an ACP ligament separation of a centimeter will never heal by itself. Shirley, drive him to St. John's Hospital in Santa Monica. I'll call and make the arrangements."

Two long days later Gordon was recuperating from the operation with a Kevlar band now inside his shoulder holding the ligaments together. He felt like a horse had kicked him.

Shirley visited, exhausted from packing her house.

"You waited two days to visit me!" Gordon said.

"If you weren't in a hospital bed I'd poke you in the nose," she replied as she kissed him.

A month later they had moved into their Boulder Creek house and Shirley began to remodel it into a livable home. Gordon bought a five kilowatt generator to cope with the San Lorenzo Valley power outages his new neighbor had warned him about. He rewired the power company main electric line so he could easily switch his home to the generator in his garage. He found that five kilowatts was just enough to run a refrigerator, a freezer, den and kitchen lights, and a TV set.

Shirley contracted with a Santa Cruz company to replace the garish green wall to wall carpeting in the house, asking them why they thought an eyeball estimation of the square feet required was sufficient instead of measuring the actual rooms to be carpeted. Impatiently, the salesman wrote on his bid, "carpet entire house."

When she showed the bid to Gordon he said, "They certainly do things casually in Santa Cruz County. Does their bid mean they intend to carpet the concrete garage floor as well?"

The next day Shirley and her sister set out to pull the red bordello wallpaper off the living room walls so a painter could be brought in. As they steamed the wallpaper off, carpet installers arrived to begin rolling and nailing.

"Say, look here," one said to the other several hours later. "We're on our last roll and there's another two rooms to go." They called the carpet salesman. He told Shirley, "You need to authorize payment for more carpet."

Unfortunately the man had exceeded Shirley's tolerance limit. "Nothing doing," she replied. "I asked you to measure, not estimate. You refused and gave us a written bid to 'carpet entire house' for a fixed price."

After letting him sweat on the phone a few minutes, she continued. "I'll split the difference with you. I neither asked nor wanted the bathrooms carpeted. A water spill would ruin the carpet. So you only need to add enough additional carpet for the master bedroom...at the original price we agreed."

"Well O.K.," the salesman said, knowing when he was beaten.

After Shirley finished remodeling she showed the house to a real estate agent who had helped in her house search. "I brought many buyers to see this house five years ago when it was listed with our real estate office. Every woman who saw it threw up her hands and walked out, saying it would be impossible to turn into a home. How much did you pay for it, if I may ask? Really, that little? The sellers were foolish to avoid a commission by not using a broker. I would have got them 15% more for the house, after my commission."

17.

If You Build a Better Mousetrap the World Will Imitate It

*Seagate was fat with cash in late 1982, from the success of its initial ST-*406 and ST-506 disc drive products. The company had wisely started business as a low-cost high-volume manufacturer by scaling down existing drive components. This avoided the deadly risks common in inventing and developing new technology, risks that cause many technology startup companies to fail or run out of money.

Seagate's immediate success came partly from this low technology risk, but also because Al made the disc drive electronic and mechanical specifications publicly available and freely usable by his competitors. He was starting another open technology drive marketplace, as he had first done at Memorex with 14-inch drives.

This business model of standardized open technology has been called a political, marketing, and motivational activity, not actual technology. But the model can be key to widespread product sales success, as when VHS captured the TV video tape recorder market from the superior video quality but patented Sony Betamax. Customers liked standardized open technology businesses that no single company could dominate. Gordon felt a technology product benefiting many people was superior to a higher tech one used only by few.

Al's model was to establish open technology businesses in computer storage. IBM, originally a closed technology company, later adopted the open technology model and captured the PC market from the closed technology Apple Macintosh.

Seagate knew this open model brought a competitive vulnerability. It was in a parts assembly business, buying standard heads, discs, and integrated circuit chips from component suppliers that originally sold them to large disc drive manufacturers like IBM. Any other startup drive company could buy recording heads and discs from the same outside vendors Seagate used. Fifty disc drive competitors sprang up almost instantly, including H.P., Maxtor, Quantum, AMC, Tandon, Miniscribe, Atasi, and Texas Instruments. Some soon failed due to higher manufacturing costs or reliability problems. Others went broke when one of the large PC manufacturers became their dominant customer and later took its business elsewhere.

Al knew that to win this business market contest, Seagate needed to become an innovator of new technology that its competitors couldn't match. Recording discs were one such opportunity, and so Seagate started Grenex to make high-tech cobalt film discs.

Seagate's competitors Atasi and Rhodime turned to lawsuits after they failed to compete in manufacturing, a "sue if you can't sell" business model. One Rhodime lawsuit claimed to have patented the *size* of the recording disc, which should have been impossible under U.S. patent law. It was as ridiculous as trying to patent the length of a pencil, in a world filled with pencils of differing lengths.

Low profit margins made commodity technology products widely available to the public, but they also made paying patent royalties financially unworkable. The result was that Thomas Jefferson's U.S. patent system could harm modern open technology industries instead of helping them. In the multi-billion dollar disc drive industry, patents were mainly useful only for defense against infringement lawsuits. They didn't help technology progress in the way Jefferson had intended.

Predatory lawyers quickly detected Seagate's profits and attacked. Lee, a self-styled "King of Torts," brought multiple lawsuits. One of his suits claimed Seagate had illegally conspired to make its stock go up, another to make its stock go down. Reports reached the SEC that Lee was paying people to buy Seagate shares and become puppet plaintiffs for each lawsuit, by illegally offering to split settlement winnings with them. Only Seagate stockholders could legally bring such suits; lawyers couldn't offer them money to do so.

Lee expected Seagate's liability insurance company to settle each suit for a few million dollars, to avoid the risk and expense of going to trial. At one point Lee had four simultaneous suits pending against Seagate. Al put a full-page ad in a U.S. business magazine: "Enough is enough. Are securities lawyers holding your company ransom? Send me your business card." Lee sent Al his own card, marked "Dear Al: more is coming." This angered Al to the point that he counter sued Lee and won. Lee's crowning humiliation was when the court ordered him to pay Al's legal expenses in the lawsuit.

18.

Local Politics Wins in Small Rural Towns

By the time Gordon arrived to work at Seagate, the company was building headquarters and engineering buildings on its new campus, on the access road that Al named "Disc Drive." Finis had a green Carrara marble bathroom built in his office suite, and Al did the same. Doug built a smaller one, saying he wanted the building space to be used for engineering. Others thought it demonstrated the relative importance of engineering versus manufacturing in Seagate's early culture. At that time, only 3.5% of Seagate's revenue was spent on engineering, nearly four times less than most other high-tech companies. That helped Seagate aggressively compete on drive prices.

Al wanted his new headquarters building to have address number "1" so IBM would have to write him at number 1 Disc Drive. He spelled the street name "Disc" for a little fun as well, because IBM spelled it "disk." Al knew that Silicon Valley startup companies demanded intense hard work and long hours. Everyone had to cooperate to solve inevitable, frequent, unexpected technology and business problems, in alternating boom and bust business cycles. He knew people could burn out if they didn't have some fun while working.

But Al lost out against small town politics. The Scotts Valley town council turned down Al's address request. Although Seagate was the largest business and biggest taxpayer in Scotts Valley, Seagate's headquarters became "#920 Disc Drive." Political power in this rural town lay with its local businessmen, not its largest employer.

When Gordon came on board, Seagate employees were faced with long traffic delays driving home after work because there was no traffic signal to get out of Disc Drive onto Scotts Valley Boulevard. Al offered to pay the town to install a signal; they finally agreed to allow only a stop sign.

This was more than simple small town local favoritism. Several city council members owned much of the land in Scotts Valley, and they feared Seagate's fast growing size would give it too much power.

Gordon started his new Recording Technology Department in the Quién Sabe building that Doug had shown him on his first visit. Stern had been hired to work for Gordon and run Seagate's new Head Lab. Stern was an expert on recording head engineering and had immigrated to Silicon Valley from Germany. Stern loved California sun more than his native Munich snow and rain. He was more comfortable with German autocratic management methods than with Silicon Valley startup company culture. He was tall and had a formal German manner, like a minister to a Bavarian Lord.

Stern was given half of the Quién Sabe ground floor for the Head Lab he was setting up. It would need heavy machines to fabricate R&D samples of new recording heads for engineering testing of new Seagate drive designs. Stern was accustomed to German polishing machines, so they installed massive AC power converters to produce German 50 cycle AC from American 60 cycle.

Seagate's purchasing people were desperate to see Gordon. Doug had taken the equipment list Gordon's new group had put together in his L.A. kitchen, and had ordered Seagate's purchasing department to get the lab equipment delivered before Gordon arrived for work. Oscilloscopes, signal generators, logic analyzers, soldering machines, chemicals, microscopes and clean benches had arrived, but the DEC VAX minicomputer order needed more information.

Gordon soon found that Quién Sabe had no working telephones and no US mail delivery and was unable to find out why. That was *his* introduction to a small town. It took two weeks to get the mail and telephone working properly, with liberal use of, "Please give me your name" and "Please let me talk to your supervisor."

Things began looking up after several months. Gordon's DEC VAX 750 computer arrived and filled one of the offices. The VAX had two 14-inch disc drives, each two feet wide and three feet deep. It didn't have the new miniature Seagate drives because DEC thought they were toys for personal computers and not suitable for serious computing. That error was one of DEC's fatal mistakes as a company, because low cost PCs with Seagate's new disruptive technology disc drives were growing in performance and market popularity and would soon obsolesce DEC's minicomputers with their old big drives. DEC didn't appreciate that early automobiles were also toys compared to horses pulling wagons, and early airplanes were toys compared to trains.

Gordon now had Kermit, Rob, Sam, Jack, and Stern on board, and Stern had hired two women as head lab technicians. Gordon had hired Beverly as secretary.

Things were finally running smoothly when one day Stern stopped Gordon in the hall. "Gordon, you must immediately rule on a problem with my engineer Tony."

"Wie gehts, Stern?" Gordon replied, hoping his poor German would inject a little lightness.

"You must immediately discipline my new engineer Tony." Gordon was baffled by Stern's insistence and didn't want to make any sudden decision that might prove unwise.

He pointed at a maintenance lady watering the potted plant outside his office door. "That lady will make the discipline decision, Stern."

A bewildered look came over Stern. "But what would a plant watering lady know about recording head engineering work?"

"She knows everything, Stern. As you can plainly see, she's the 'Plant Manager.'"

Stern bent in laughter and took his first step onto the Seagate Way.

Gordon continued, "So what's the problem with Tony?"

"He's insubordinate and won't follow orders."

"O.K., I'll talk to him. Ask him to come to my office." Stern left.

A minute later, Gordon saw Tony walking in his office door. "Close the door and sit down, Tony. Are you getting settled into Seagate O.K.?" Tony nodded noncommittally but said nothing. He was a young engineer who was small and spoke little.

"What's going on between you and Stern?"

"He gives me orders on every detail of my work. He insists I do things his way and he won't listen to any suggestions of mine."

Seagate's culture required Gordon to know the details of his engineer's projects as well as they did. This made it easy for him to ask a series of specific questions on the projects Tony was working on. He took notes as Tony explained his ideas versus Stern's for each project.

In fifteen minutes Gordon had two pages full of notes. "O.K. Tony, let's go over these engineering decisions on your five projects. On three of them, Stern was right and you were wrong. The other two were tossups. Either your idea or Stern's idea would have worked on those two. Do you want details on the reasons?" Tony shrugged noncommittally.

"Here's my decision. Stern is your boss. That means he's authorized to give you specific 'marching orders,' as we call them at Seagate. I'm not going to overrule him unless he's wrong, or unless you or someone else has a better idea. I think what you really don't like is Stern's autocratic German management style. It's different from American management, but you're going to have to put up with it or leave Seagate. Which do you choose?"

Tony thought for a while. His engineering job at Seagate paid well, and if he stayed for three years his stock option should be valuable. "I'll follow Stern's orders, Gordon. But I won't like it."

"O.K., but don't let open disagreement happen again. If you think Stern is making a serious mistake come see me. But don't bring me any more disagreements where he's right instead of you." Tony left the office looking frustrated.

Stern was still a German citizen and Seagate had offered to sponsor his U.S. permanent residency application. Gordon and Stern arranged to meet with Polly, a Silicon Valley immigration lawyer. She told them, "Stern, the temporary U.S. work visa you now have works against us. You got it directly from Germany and although you could apply for permanent residency based on it, the U.S. immigration quota from Germany means it'll take years.

"Write the German government and ask them to apply for a Canadian temporary work visa for you. The Canadians admit every immigrant that applies, on the naïve theory that they're populating the millions of square miles of uninhabited territory in their far north. The U.S. and Canadian governments accommodate each other, and you can apply for a U.S. work visa from Canada even though you're a German citizen. You'll have to go to Vancouver to apply for it, but only for a few days."

Stern followed this unexpected advice, and a year later received his permanent U.S. residency, with Gordon vouching that Stern was making valuable contributions to the U.S economy as a Seagate engineer.

In this way America welcomed another European immigrant to its shores. Stern would return the honor by making important contributions to America's disc drive technology, and thereby to the computer revolution that was transforming America's commerce and culture. The American melting pot was still in action. The USA would wither if it ever ends.

19.

Space Wars

Gordon and Stern designed recording heads and sliders for new Seagate drives. Sliders were about 1/4-inch in size and had a miniature pair of ceramic skis designed to fly on a cushion of air over a disc surface, without touching. Gordon used the VAX to design these small rectangular air sliders, to fly tens of millionths of an inch over spinning discs. The head was fabricated on the rear of the slider. Its size was rapidly becoming microscopic. Stern built prototype heads and sliders for engineering drive testing. Gordon also used the VAX to design head and disc magnetics for new drives, so heads would reliably write data bits on the magnetic discs and read them back without errors.

Seagate contracted with Japanese companies to build heads and sliders in production volume. They were assembled into finished recording heads by bonding flexure springs to slider backs. Flexures were miniature flexible steel arms, triangles whose narrow end attached to the air slider part of the head that flew over a disc surface. Its wider end attached to the track motor that moved a flying head between inner and outer tracks on a disc. (This triangular spring can be seen on the book cover; the slider is at the right with only the copper wire coil of the head visible.)

Seagate was planning to build a new engineering building that Gordon's group was to move into, and he called a meeting to plan their new space.

"These are the building plans. Notice how the offices are laid out along the building outer walls and the interior is all lab space we can customize. We'll build our clean lab here, the head lab here, the microscopy lab there, and we'll put our wet chemical clean bench in this interior hall."

The group planned their lab layouts in detail; grabbing as much space in the building as possible in an instinctive game they called "Space

Wars." Gordon took the corner office with the best forest view, a large executive office with heavy steel earthquake braces running diagonally from floor to ceiling across its two large windows. He ordered an executive oak desk with a secretarial typing extension to hold his DEC VAX minicomputer display terminal, a large oak conference table for his office center, and a long oak credenza to put along one window wall for his Apple Macintosh and laser printer. In a few years a Sun desktop workstation with a Seagate drive would be sitting on the credenza; more powerful, far less expensive, and far less hungry for power and air conditioning than the VAX.

"Stern, you take this other corner office." Gordon grabbed a regular office for his VAX in spite of Doug's edict that "offices were to be used for people and not for labs." He doubled its air conditioning flow to cool the computer and installed high school gymnasium soundproofing panels on its office walls to absorb noise from its cooling fans.

"Dr. Gordon, there's a man with a big crane here to see you," the receptionist in their new building told him over the phone. Gordon bicycled from Quién Sabe over to the rear of their new building, which would be ready to occupy as soon as its heavy equipment was installed. He had hired a crane and rigging company to lift a four ton electromagnet from a shipping crate sitting in the parking lot behind the building, up to the second story and into a lab where he had installed a special load spreading platform to keep the magnet from breaking through the floor. The electromagnet was part of an instrument that measured magnetic properties of recording discs. In spite of the magnet's massive size and weight, its measurement chamber was only large enough to accept test samples a quarter inch in size. These were cut from the recording discs being measured.

When he arrived at the rear of the building the electromagnet was high in the air, swinging on a chain that hung from a massive yellow crane. The magnet was painted the usual red color. A rope was pulling the magnet horizontally toward the building. Gordon saw a man standing on the second floor pulling the rope through an exterior loading door high up, using a hand-operated winch.

Gordon instantly realized they were trying the old trick that it was harder to get permission to do something unusual than to get forgiveness afterwards. They had carefully timed their phone call to Gordon but he had arrived a little too quickly on his bike.

Suddenly there was a loud cracking sound and the horizontal rope shot out of the building, carrying a piece of wood the size of a railroad tie.

Freed, the electromagnet swung in a red arc away from the building and began to tilt the crane off its wide-spread steel feet. Gordon watched helplessly with eyes wide, awaiting the inevitable. *Will the magnet keep going, fall over onto the freeway traffic, destroy itself and kill some drivers, or will it swing back and bash a hole in the building?* The electromagnet swung to the far end of its arc, beyond the parking lot fence, and hung over the freeway for an endless moment, with two feet of the crane tipped off the ground at a dangerous angle. Cars sped by under the magnet. After a seeming eternity the magnet decided to return. As it began its swing back towards the building, an orange-shirted man on the ground threw a steel hook at it. The hook caught on the chain just above the magnet and the man grabbed a rope tied to the hook.

Snubbing the rope around a parking lot lamp post, the man slowed the magnet just enough so it didn't quite make it back all the way to hit the building. After a tense minute of back and forth swinging and the lamp post bending, the magnet finally returned to vertical rest hanging from the crane. The crane was tilted, the two feet it had pivoted on having dug through the asphalt parking lot.

The man introduced himself as the job foreman. Gordon looked steadily at him. "You lucked out this time, but you can't move that magnet into the building that way anyway. Even if you had succeeded in pulling it through that second floor loading dock by that rope, its 4-ton weight would exceed the building floor load limit as you moved it down the hall to the lab. It could break through the hall floor before you got it on my load spreading platform. Let's find a different way."

He and the crane supervisor walked into the building and up to the second floor loading dock. Gordon saw that the winch pulling the rope into the building had been connected to a large wood post laid on the hall floor, across the door of the loading dock. It had been braced against the door frame and the pull force had destroyed the frame. Gordon had watched the building being built and knew that although the door jamb looked solid, it was only sheet rock over thin metal framing.

The riggers finally decided to remove one of the large outside windows in the second floor lab the magnet was destined for, and brought in an even taller crane to lift the magnet directly through the window frame.

They soon had it hanging just above its platform, held by the yellow crane arm sticking through the window. The red magnet was at a twisted angle to the square platform it would sit on to spread its weight over a large floor area. It was too massive and heavy to rotate into alignment with the platform before or after they set it down. Gordon watched them lay a dozen iron water pipes in parallel lines on the platform, and then carefully set the magnet down onto the pipes. Two hefty men picked up two other pipes to rotate the magnet into alignment using the pipes as roller bearings Then they hooked the crane back up to the magnet, raised it an inch to remove the pipes, and set the magnet back down in its proper position.

"That was cleverly done," Gordon said.

The foreman replied, "You learn many tricks in the crane and rigging business."

"How much are you charging Seagate for the job?"

"Our original bid was $5,000. We didn't count on needing a second crane and more time, so we'll lose money on this job."

Gordon thought for a moment. "Send me a $5,000 invoice and a second invoice for the overage, and I'll see that both get paid. I was impressed you had a rope and hook ready to save my electromagnet and my building. I wonder if anyone in the cars driving on the freeway saw the magnet as it nearly fell on them."

Electricians arrived to connect the electromagnet to the high voltage power lines it needed to operate, and plumbers connected water pipes for its cooling. It needed so much electrical power that the magnet would overheat without water circulating inside it.

The next day, Gordon and Ron were standing in the nearly complete building looking at the building plans. Ron was the clean room expert Gordon had hired from Xerox at Doug's request, to help Seagate build its drives in dust-free and contamination-free clean rooms, to prevent head crashes. Tom called Ron his "Mr. Clean."

Ron was tall, lanky and lean. He wore western clothes and reminded Gordon of Will Rogers, whose motto was "I never met a man I didn't like." Ron had recently been given the biggest motorcycle Harley Davidson made as a reward for a clean room design he had consulted on prior to joining Seagate. He was about to ride it in the annual Barstow to Las Vegas motorcycle race across the Mojave Desert. Gordon considered motorcycles somewhat dangerous vehicles, although many older bikers drove sensibly and never seemed to have accidents. *Rather like private airplanes,* he thought. *They can be flown safely or not.*

Ron's wife had recently divorced him because of his long work hours and frequent trips away from home, common to Silicon Valley marriages. He had bought a sports car in a color Gordon called "resale red." It was so low slung that Ron had to carry a wooden ramp in its trunk to get over driveways without scraping pavement.

"Ron, we want to turn this large interior lab into a clean room for recording measurements. It has to be temperature controlled within one degree. Any more variation and thermal expansion will misalign our recording test instruments by too many millionths of an inch. The room also has to be shielded against all radio signals to prevent interference with our delicate electronic recording measurements."

"O.K, Gordon. I'll design you a clean room with special sealed wall board, HEPA air filters, and copper screens in the walls and floor. I'll get an electromagnetically shielded copper door for the room, which will cost about $50,000. We'll ground the screening to a long copper rod that we'll bury in the earth outside the building."

When the room was finished a month later, they found that the air conditioning ducts into the lab allowed radio signals in as well as air, so they soldered copper screens across the air ducts. That was almost good enough, but then they found microvolt AM and FM radio signals sneaking in through the electrical power grounding required by the building code. They solved this by cutting the electrical ground as soon as the building inspector signed the work off and left. Their earth grounding made the wiring just as safe.

Gordon took them all to the Shadow Brook Inn in nearby Capitola for a dinner celebrating their lab completion. The Inn sat at the edge of a brook deep down inside a forested canyon, reached by a quaint funicular cable car. They raised their glasses in a toast, everyone thinking their clean room construction was over, once and for all.

Gordon hung a large portrait in his new office the day they moved into their new engineering building. It showed a B-17 bomber squadron in flight on August 15, 1945, returning from a World War II bombing mission over Wiesbaden, Germany. It was a Keith Ferris watercolor print of a Smithsonian mural. Stern looked at it oddly every time he came into Gordon's office. After several weeks of this, Gordon asked Stern what he thought of the painting.

"Well," Stern slowly replied, "I was a small child living with my family in Wiesbaden during that bombing raid in 1945, and my grandfather was killed by the bombs that day."

A long pause followed. "I think I'll take the picture home, Stern."

Gordon's group moved into its new offices and labs. Stern hired additional female technicians for head design R&D, to wind tiny coils of copper wire over ferrite head cores, using microscopes to be able to see the wires. They used a politically incorrect hiring interview question to check an applicant's ability for such fine work: "Do you sew?"

Stern and Gordon now had primary engineering responsibility for recording head and disc design, test, and purchase. They shared responsibility with Paul, the manager of Stan's head and disc product engineering group, responsible for keeping outside head and disc suppliers in sustained high volume production. Gordon and Stern became involved in Paul's production technology issues only when unusual problems arose, which occurred more frequently than any of the three liked.

Seagate bought its high volume production heads from the Japanese companies Panasonic and TDK. Rudi was the account manager for TDK, whom Gordon had known from his Xerox days. Rudi had patiently had TDK fabricate research heads for Gordon at Xerox, even though no production orders followed. Rudi's patience paid off when Gordon moved to Seagate and had engineering responsibility for millions of heads per year that TDK sold to them. Gordon knew he could trust Rudi to follow through on quality and schedule issues.

Gordon was also working with Grenex on the new cobalt disc manufacturing technology. Weekly meetings were held at the new Grenex R&D lab over the hill in Sunnyvale. After one of the meetings, Gordon was talking to a visiting salesman of disc cleaning equipment.

"Your company Hobart made my home dishwasher," Gordon remarked.

"Hobart makes washing machines for many purposes," the salesman replied. "I sold a couple of commercial dishwashers a few years ago to your company president, Al. He bought them to clean glassware at a bar he was running in Santa Cruz." Gordon and the man had a good laugh over Al's unusual career before starting Seagate.

Gordon gave papers and talks at disc drive industry conferences, to promote the performance and reliability of cobalt discs. He demonstrated their superior magnetic technology that could double disc data storage capacity over the brown paint discs everyone had always used since the original IBM RAMAC drive. People had questions on cobalt disc durability, their resistance to wear as head sliders contacted disc surfaces during disc spin up and spin down, and on potentially higher corrosion dangers in using cobalt metal instead of paint.

In one talk Gordon showed a picture of a massive disc drive made for the US Navy by Librascope in Glendale, California.

"This picture is a new Librascope drive, made 15 years ago. The next picture shows an old drive returning to America on an aircraft carrier deck. Notice that its exterior aluminum case has turned green from sea air corrosion. But the three-foot diameter discs inside were protected by the outer case. The drive still worked when cleaned up and tested for resale. Only its external multi-horsepower spin motor had to be replaced. Here's the drive's picture when it was resold to the Pacific Telephone Company. They used these drives for fast data access to recorded voice messages, like 'That phone number has been changed, the new number is...'"

He visited Apple Computer to advise them on using Seagate drives in their Macs. He remembered consulting for them two years earlier. The Apple floppy disc drive he had done recording designs for had failed and the project had been cancelled. Only echoes of the project remained: the lingering lawsuits and legal fees engendered by disagreements between important executives.

Although one of Apple's founders had made crucial design contributions to the original PC floppy drive developed at one of Al's previous startup companies, Apple's core competency was in computer technology for consumers, as its better known founder first showed with the Apple II, then the Macintosh, then Pixar computer animation, and later iPod music player computers. The iPod design was so clever that many users weren't aware they had bought a tiny computer with a hard disc drive inside, or that the music files they had paid for were carefully protected against losing their iPod or its hard disc crashing. Apple capitalized on its Macintosh design and marketing expertise in skillfully putting a hard drive into their iPod. It sold sensationally into a consumer market where other electronic music players had failed because they used disc drives improperly, running the battery down too fast or occasionally crashing and losing their consumers' recorded songs.

20.

To Drain a Swamp, First Fight off its Alligators

Soon after Gordon arrived at Seagate, he became engulfed in intense engineering problem solving. Totally unexpected manufacturing problems suddenly arrived and the engineers had to solve them. Everyone just dropped their normal tasks to jump on a new problem as a team. They all knew that if they failed, the company might fail. This real-world engineering was totally foreign to Gordon's orderly research experience. Technology researchers like Gordon shied away from the disorderly and difficult realities in engineering for volume manufacturing of new technology, and they rarely experienced real world engineering.

Silicon Valley companies hired researchers like Gordon, made them directly responsible for engineering new technology, and gave them generous stock options to motivate them to face the difficult realities. They no longer had time for research but they could hire researchers as they moved up the management ladder. The stock options could be large enough for a researcher-turned-engineer-turned-manager to become financially rather comfortable.

In Gordon's first months at Seagate, he felt like an outsider on production head and disc problems because of his lack of manufacturing experience. After watching several problems being solved, Gordon sensed this team spirit, paused to think about it, thought *why not, a*nd joined in wholeheartedly. His outsider feelings evaporated when he was confronted with a production panic that Doug ordered him to personally solve.

He was summoned to Doug's office one day.

"Gordon, new drives in the factory are suddenly reading back stored data incorrectly. The factory says the heads are bad. We have to ship good drives to IBM in volume within a week and Seagate will be in a serious financial problem if we can't find and fix the problem."

Doug was speaking in a calm and persuasive voice, delivering what Gordon came to call "Marine Corps marching orders." Doug and Tom had been Marines in the Vietnam War and they flew an immense U.S. Marine battalion flag over Al's headquarters building on Marine Corps birthdays.

Gordon walked back to his office. *Well, it's my problem this time. What if Stern and I can't fix it that fast?*

"Stern, I need you to move into the factory. Find out what's wrong and tell me whatever you need. We have to find and fix the problem in three days or less. Update me twice a day and when you find anything new."

Stern left to pack and Gordon called Camille at Seagate's factory. A strikingly well-endowed blond, she had originally been hired as a Seagate drive assembler. Camille had a powerful sexual aura that radiated like a nuclear fireball, always turning Gordon's legs to Jell-O. Gordon thought the personality traits of power and sex were often related. His example was Margaret Thatcher, the British Prime Minister.

Camille had rapidly risen to manufacturing line supervisor, with a reputation for instantly firing fellow female workers over small perceived mistakes. Camille admired and imitated Tom's take-no-hostages management style. She had picked up Seagate's "Marine Corps management" culture in her first few weeks.

"Camille, I'm sending you an engineer. Can you help him analyze the head problem and run special batches of drive builds to try out fixes?"

"Sure. Anything for you honey," came silkily over the phone. Gordon was fortunately sitting down.

Gordon next phoned Paul. Head production problems were Paul's responsibility and Doug had put Gordon in Paul's territory. But Gordon knew Paul was an excellent Seagator, without a selfish bone in his body. Seagate came first, Paul and his people second.

"Paul, Doug ordered Stern and me to immediately step in to solve the bad head problem. What do you think and what do you know about what's going on?"

"I heard about this a day ago and was just about to ask you for help. Drive final test yields suddenly dropped drastically and the final test equipment calls the failures 'excessive data playback errors.' The factory people haven't a clue what's going on. Please use me and my engineers any way we can help."

"I'll do that, Paul. I've sent Stern to the factory. I think the problem isn't in my head and disc recording design because drive yields have been excellent up to now. Something's gone wrong in the factory. Wait until Stern and I get some ideas on what it might be. It's dangerous for us to make any guesses until we get facts from the place where the problem is happening. Without facts we'll just go in circles."

Stern called the next morning. "The factory managers were overjoyed to see me. They'd been guessing what was wrong, desperately trying random fixes, and none worked. Tom has them all terrified of failing. Camille put me in charge when I told them I came to conduct an engineering investigation. I thought she was going to kiss me!"

Gordon felt a pang of jealousy. "Well, it's a relief they accepted our marching orders without a struggle. Production people are often unsympathetic with engineers sent to their factory."

"It helped that Paul called their head of production, Gordon. The man told me Tom was putting heavy pressure on them, and Paul called him to offer any help you and I need. Paul specifically backed us."

Stern told Gordon what he had learned so far. "I used one of the low power binocular microscopes that the factory women use to wind head coils, and I quickly found that slider skis and heads are being ground up inside the drives. The head damage first causes the data readback errors, but the sliders are starting to crash as well."

"Crashing" meant the two slider skis weren't properly flying on a cushion of air. Instead they were hitting disc surfaces and wearing out, like skiing over rocks.

"Gordon, I looked at many heads under the low power microscope, and the skis look chipped and rough as if sandpapered. I also see metallic looking particles on the skis. But where could they come from? All drive components are cleaned before being assembled into drives inside the factory clean rooms."

Gordon thought a moment. "Stern, I think the metal particles are doing the sandpapering. Get a high power microscope somewhere and look closer at the particles on the heads using high magnification. Also use it to look at the surfaces of new discs and new heads, as well as those from failed drives."

"Good ideas, Gordon. I'll ask Camille to help me find a microscope and collect a sample of parts to look at. I'll call you back in 2.35 hours."

Gordon smiled. German engineers like Stern were famous for their precision, but this conversational use of impossibly exact numbers like 2.35 hours was because of a story Gordon had told him. He had told Stern about his student days at Cal Tech, watching impossibly precise calculations by double Nobel Prize winner Linus Pauling on his six-inch slide rule. *A little technology showmanship is good for occasional relief while working hard.*

Gordon's phone rang two hours and twenty-one minutes later. He knew Stern had timed it precisely.

"Camille rushed out and grabbed the best microscope in town. Tom has been calling the factory twice a day to push them. And yes, there are microscopic metal particles on discs from crashed drives as well as on the head skis. The particles all look like the same metal. They're not magnetic; I tried bringing a magnet near them on the microscope stage. Abrasive metal particles are somehow getting on disc surfaces and causing head crashes when drives start running for the first time. The factory missed them because they're too small to be seen without a microscope."

Gordon scratched his head, seeing a gestalt mental image of the entire drive assembly process. Inside the case of a sealed drive were a spin motor spindle and two discs, held apart by an aluminum spacer ring, so two of the four heads could fit between the discs. Another head flew on the bottom surface of the bottom disc, and the fourth head flew on the top surface of the top disc. An aluminum carriage held the four heads together in a unit, properly positioned to fly on the discs. It was called an E-block because it looked like a capital letter E with the head flexure springs fastened to horizontal bars of the E. He expanded his mental image, adding the production processes of the vendors who made the drive parts.

"What did you find on new discs and new heads?"

"They're clean. I don't see any particles on them at all."

"Stern, since the particles only appear when a drive is assembled they must be coming in on one of the aluminum parts; the case, the E block, or maybe the spacer ring. Put on latex gloves and wash several discs from crashed drives with pure alcohol. Collect the washings in a clean glass bottle. Keep washing crashed discs into the bottle until you have enough particles for scientific analysis. Let some of the alcohol evaporate if the bottle gets too full. Then take it to Surface Sciences Lab.

"The particles are probably aluminum. They can't be steel since your magnet doesn't pick them up. Paul and I will check the engineering drawings of every aluminum part inside the drive. When Surface Sciences analyzes their metal alloy we'll know where they're coming from."

Surface Sciences Lab was an example of a little known secret of why Silicon Valley was uniquely suited for high-tech electronics development and manufacturing. Silicon Valley companies needed local cottage industry shops like Surface Sciences Lab, which had specialists trained in scientific analysis of manufacturing problems, using optical and electron microscopes, and chemical analysis. Hollywood was another example of a concentrated industry with cottage industries for the movie business; shops renting specialty items like props, old cars, and high speed cameras.

Stern called a few hours later. "SSL found the particles are 4031 aluminum alloy and that there's oil on them, probably machining oil. I'm going back to the factory to put every aluminum part that goes inside drives under the microscope. That will take me until tomorrow morning. Meanwhile, you check the blueprints for parts using 4031 aluminum. Incidentally, Surface Sciences didn't have an open Seagate purchase order to use and I had to give them my personal credit card."

"Attaboy, Stern! If we had tried to put a purchase order though Marc he would have 'lost it' again and made us sweat for a month."

"Why does he act so stupidly? This problem is costing Seagate millions!"

Just then, Gordon noticed Marc standing in his office, closing the door behind him. "I'll call you later," he said and hung up the phone.

"Tell me what you're doing on the head problem, Gordon. The factory is still shut down and it's cost Seagate over a million dollars while you sit at your desk doing nothing."

Gordon instantly realized that Marc would use anything negative he said as ammunition against him, and Marc would try to take credit for anything positive. *Even worse, Marc's technology ignorance could mislead Tom, Al, and Doug, perhaps stopping our progress on a solution. Marc can't and won't contribute to solving this head crash problem. I have to somehow keep him from interfering.*

"We think the problem isn't the heads. I expect to know more by tomorrow afternoon." Gordon's statement was incomplete but not untrue.

Marc growled. "That's bull, Gordon. The factory says it's the heads."

Gordon leaned back in his office chair and looked calmly at Marc. He put on a poker face and said nothing. Marc finally stormed out of the office.

Gordon picked up his phone and dialed.

After one ring he heard "Doug." Al, Doug, and Tom answered their own phones using their first names. Although they had secretaries and administrative assistants, they didn't want intermediaries coming between them and people working on critical Seagate issues. Every Seagate manager followed their example.

"Doug, we've narrowed the drive read error problem down to one of two possible sources. The problem's caused by heads getting chewed up when drives first start up in final test, causing the data read errors. Stern sees small non-magnetic metal particles on heads and discs from failed drives, using low-magnification optical microscopy. They're not present on new discs or new heads that haven't been built into drives. So they're coming from the drive assembly process. Surface Sciences emission spectroscopy analysis identifies them as 4031 aluminum. The only possible 4031-alloy parts inside the drives are the E-blocks and the disc spacer rings, blah, blah, blah." Gordon finished before Marc had time to walk across the street and upstairs to Doug's office.

"Thanks. Keep me informed," Doug replied, and was hanging up as Marc walked in his door.

"Doug, Gordon is sitting on his can, doing nothing to solve the factory shutdown. I'm going to fire him."

An unreadable look came over Doug's face, and he thought a long moment before quietly replying, "Don't do that, Marc. I'll handle Gordon. Don't take any action concerning him without my approval first."

"Yes, sir," Marc replied, looking confused.

Meanwhile, Gordon had walked out of his office and down to the first floor Engineering Documentation Library. "Please let me look at the drawings for the drive case, disc spacer rings, and E-block bodies." That was every aluminum part inside the drive. "Oh, and please let me also see the drive master build drawing." That drawing would remind him of any aluminum parts he might have missed. He was verifying what he had just told Doug from memory. It was a repeat of his Minuteman experience, of finding an overlooked electronics box near the exhaust end of the rocket.

He confirmed that only spacer rings and E-blocks were made from 4031 aluminum alloy, walked back upstairs, and called Stern at the factory.

"Stern, check E-blocks and spacer rings for the particles."

"O.K., I'll check new parts and also old parts out of crashed drives."

Gordon got another phone call from Stern early the next morning. "E-blocks from crashed drives are all clean, but I see similar looking particles on spacer rings from crashed drives. New spacer rings also have the particles. I washed a bunch of rings and put the particles under the microscope. They look identical to the particles from crashed head skis."

Spacer rings needed to be washed and handled in a clean room after machining, to remove stray machining particles and oil, but this was well known and had never been a problem.

"Well, Stern, this is turning into a Sherlock Holmes detective mystery. The game's afoot, Watson—I mean Stern! Find the supplier that manufactured those spacer rings and call me again after you personally inspect his machining and cleaning processes."

Stern and Camille went to the factory purchasing department to talk to the spacer ring buyer. He told them, "I recently began buying from a new cheaper spacer ring supplier. I canceled the previous supplier because he was charging 0.3 cents more." The man appeared proud of himself.

An outraged look came over Camille's face. It was her "I'm about to fire you" look. "Give me the address of the new supplier and phone him that we're on our way to immediately inspect his factory."

Camille and Stern drove to the new spacer ring supplier's factory. They found the company was machining spacer rings in a dirty World War II Quonset hut with no clean room at all. The company owner told them, "The Seagate buyer insisted I give him a price so low it wouldn't cover clean room removal of machining particles and oil off the spacer rings. He asked me if my other customers had clean room requirements on the machined parts I sell to them. My other customers use these kinds of parts on automobiles or lawn mowers or kid's wagons, so I said no. He sent me this letter."

Stern read the letter. "It authorizes no clean room, all right. A buyer wouldn't know that microscopic aluminum machining particles can grind up and crash disc drive heads. He ignored the company rule that engineering has to approve any parts vendor change."

Stern immediately called Gordon and updated him.

"We're saved, Stern! In less than three days! I'll take it from here." Gordon only had to ask Doug and Tom to insist that the factory return to using the original engineering-approved ring supplier. Gordon later heard from Camille that the buyer so proud of saving $3 per thousand spacer rings had been fired for costing Seagate nearly a million dollars in scrapped drives and lost business.

As Gordon thought through this experience he realized it wasn't really engineering at all. It was technology forensics. He finally understood the old cartoon that showed two engineers standing knee deep in a swamp. Its caption read, "We were ordered to drain the swamp. Who knew we'd have to fight off alligators first?"

Gordon thought hard. *How on Earth can Seagate keep solving unexpected problems like these? There'll certainly be many more of them. We need Sherlock Holmes detectives who can do scientific analysis with rigid objectivity. In manufacturing problems like this one, it's critical to gather failure data at the place and time where the problem happens, and not make any advance guesses about possible causes. The real causes will be total surprises, and advance speculation will only lead in useless directions. Sir Arthur Conan Doyle made this exact point in several of the Sherlock Holmes stories he wrote in the 1880's and 1890's. This time the factory jumped to the wrong conclusion that recording heads were to blame because drives were incorrectly reading stored bits. The actual cause was a completely different drive component, dirty disc spacer rings.*

Seagate wasn't the first company to manufacture disc drives. Gordon asked around Silicon Valley and was soon able to learn that he needed to hire scientifically trained drive forensics people. He found these "alligator" problems were common to every industry providing products and services to the public; from photographic film, to airlines, to criminal forensics. In contrast to police crime labs where forensics analyzed people crimes, drive forensics analyzed evidence bearing silent witness to "crimes" against disc drives.

A month later, Seagate was running smoothly under its normal 70-hour work week pressures. Stern walked into Gordon's office. "I have a problem with Pam, one of my head lab ladies. She's sick too often. It's delaying my head lab delivery schedules for new test heads to the drive design engineering groups. Should we fire her?"

"Who's her closest friend in your lab?"

"Tina, I think."

"Let me work on it."

Later that day, Gordon asked Tina to stop by his office. "Tina, can you tell me why Pam's sick so often? Maybe we can help her."

"A month ago Pam decided she had to become a hard-core vegetarian, a vegan, and now she eats no dairy foods at all. The rest of us are worried about her health."

Gordon knew that dairy foods carried essential amino acids. "Perhaps I can talk her into becoming a lacto vegetarian, Tina."

"You'll have to be tough. She's convinced she has to be vegan."

The next day, Gordon asked Pam to come to his office. She stepped through his door, looking nervous.

Gordon took a deep breath and steeled himself. "Pam, you're having too many sick days. If you can't improve your health, Seagate may have to let you go." Her eyes darted back and forth, making Gordon feel guilty. But he soldiered on. "I have a suggestion how you can be sick less, if you do want to keep your job."

"Please tell me. I really do want to feel better and not be sick so often."

"Pam, your strict vegetarian diet is endangering your health. *Please* become a lacto vegetarian. Do it for the lab girls and for me. Adding dairy foods to your diet will give you safe levels of vitamin B12, potassium, and calcium. Look here. I got these two books for you, *The Compleat Vege Cookbook* and *Laurel's Kitchen*. Please promise me you'll carefully read and follow them, and that you'll come see me every week and tell me how you're doing."

A week later, he heard a cheerful Pam bragging to her head lab friends about her new lacto diet. Gordon smiled. *A person taking credit for an idea is a person sold on that idea.* He made a note to add this to a memo he was writing called the "*The Seagate Way,*" on Seagate's company culture.

21.

Trading Old Technology Secrets for New

Gordon stopped by Malone's bar one evening after work. He wanted to ask Al a question. He saw him at the bar talking with Tom and Doug, and walked over.

"Al, I've been invited to participate in the Lake Arrowhead Workshop on magnetic recording technology. They invite eighteen leading technologists in our industry to meet at a remote location east of L.A. I can learn a lot about new technology our competitors are developing to use in their disc drives. But I'll have to do some horse trading. They know we're working on cobalt discs for higher capacity drives. I want to trade a few old secrets about cobalt discs, a few things they'll soon learn for themselves anyway. What do you say?"

"That's O.K. Gordon," Al replied in his deep gravelly voice. "Use your own judgment. Our business is all about getting drive technology into manufacturing and products onto the factory shipping dock before the competition can, not about hiding research on drive designing. Technology secrets never last longer than a few months anyway because engineers quit and take jobs with competitors. The consultants every company hires are just like bees, flitting from company to company, spreading secrets around in exchange for money instead of honey."

Gordon knew that Al was quite correct. Even if competitors somehow got Grenex's confidential process documents for making cobalt discs, they would still have to struggle through years of difficult problem solving just as Grenex was doing, to get high factory yield.

A month later, Gordon flew his airplane to Cable Airport near Claremont, California. The workshop attendees were meeting at Harvey Mudd College in Claremont for lunch and then bus to Lake Arrowhead in the mountains east of L.A. As he tied down his Mooney at Cable, he saw a Grumman Tiger plane landing. This would be Mike, a well known technologist from IBM.

Gordon watched as Mike's plane made its final approach. His eyes widened as he saw Mike wasn't flaring to raise its nose before touching down. He watched in trepidation as the plane slammed its nose wheel hard onto the runway and bounced back up into the air. He expected Mike to add power to keep the plane from stalling in the air and hitting even harder on the second bounce, but he heard no sound from its engine as the plane seemed to hang in the air twenty feet above the runway, time standing still. Then the laws of gravity and aerodynamics took hold and the plane slammed into the ground, collapsing its nose wheel and skidding forward on its nose to a graceless stop. Gordon ran to the plane along with three men that had been talking in a nearby hanger. The plane sat on the runway with its nose on the ground, its propeller bent into a pretzel, its main wheels sticking its tail high in the air.

"Are you O.K. Mike?"

"Sure," Mike replied, sitting in the cockpit as casually as if he made landings like this every day. The men pushed down on the airplane's tail to raise its nose, and rolled it off the runway on its main wheels.

Mike asked, "Are any of you aircraft mechanics?"

"Yes," one replied. "I run Cable Aviation out of that hanger over there."

"Can you repair my plane?" Mike asked.

"I sure can," the mechanic answered. "When do you want it finished?"

"Can it be finished when I return in three days to fly home?"

"No problem. Give me the number for your insurance company and I'll take care of that too."

Gordon thought this was far too easy for an airplane accident, but it did illustrate an important point: airplane accidents on the ground are usually far more survivable than those that happen in the air.

These Arrowhead workshops always began with a tutorial talk by an expert on some data storage topic currently in the news. This year a semiconductor engineer named Boris had been invited to talk on whether or when semiconductor flash memory would replace hard disc drives. Boris had never been to an Arrowhead workshop, but had been told to be controversial. In his talk he claimed flash memory would rapidly progress from its several-megabyte initial products; that chips with 128 megabytes capacity were about to be announced; and flash would reach one-gigabyte chips in the next fifteen years.

Gordon asked, "Is the unit of product cost in higher flash capacity the price of adding an additional flash chip? In a disc drive the cost unit is one more disc and two more heads."

"Yes, that's correct. In volume the cost of one flash chip could drop to $20."

"Boris, one disc and two heads today cost $15 and they store half a gigabyte. A minimum capacity single-chip 1/8 gigabyte flash storage device like you're predicting will be cheaper than a minimum cost $120 drive with its single disc storing 1/2 gigabyte, because a drive has to have mechanisms and control circuitry. But a four-disc drive will store 2 gigabytes today and cost $165, compared to a flash device with 16 chips costing $320. I think flash could take the single-disc entry-level disc market away but how can it take the high-capacity drive market?"

Another disc technologist chimed in. "And it's not reasonable to compare today's real disc drive cost against your future $20 flash. When your gigabyte flash chips appear fifteen years from now, disc capacities should reach 100 to 200 gigabytes per disc. On top of that, disc drives allow unlimited fast writing of data. Flash chips have to be erased and then written, by a high-energy hot-electron process that physically damages the flash bit cells and makes writing slow. It takes seconds instead of the milliseconds discs take. Don't your flash bits wear out after only 50,000 writes?"

"Yes, but we'll improve that. And we have ideas to speed up writing."

Gordon said, "You don't need flash chips to allow more than 50,000 writes, Boris. Data storage customers ignore limitations like those write problems. They rarely even read manufacturer specifications. Unless flash devices actually fail and eat a user's stored data, you'll be O.K. I think few users will do that many writes. They won't notice the long write times because you'll use DRAM memory chips to cache user data just like disc drives do, right?"

"That's correct. We also spread the writes over the whole chip, so no bit cells get written more often than others."

The next speaker gave a talk that claimed the new CD-ROM optical compact disc drives just coming on the market would become very cheap, would become rewritable, and would make magnetic disc drives obsolete. The man was very convincing, and one IBM engineer spoke up at the end of the talk. "Will we have a few years left for magnetic drives so I get a chance to retire before we all get fired?" They all laughed, but their concern was visible.

Another technologist objected. "There're other important factors beyond the low cost of a CD drive.

"The optical head for a CD drive is a complex assembly of tiny lenses and motors," she contended. "There's only space and parts cost budget for one head in an optical drive, so they can only have one disc surface storing data. Magnetic drives can have eight or more discs storing data on sixteen surfaces. And that delicate optical head can't move as fast from track to track as our smaller and lower cost magnetic heads.

"There may be more data tracks on an optical disc today, but they can't put CD tracks any closer together without using laser light of shorter wavelength. That's a hard optical physics limit that doesn't apply to magnetic disc drives, which will have more tracks per magnetic disc than a CD within the next few years. In the future, magnetic discs will hold far more data than optical discs. CD drives will certainly have a place in computers but they won't kill magnetic drives."

Heated arguments broke out among audience members, typical of Arrowhead workshops.

The next talk was by a research scientist named Peter. He showed results from an experiment he had done on magnetic recording head corrosion by city smog.

"Disc drives have to work anywhere, even in smoggy Los Angeles. People put PCs with disc drives everywhere, including factories with corrosive atmospheres.

"I made up a chamber filled with typical city smog, using sulfur and chlorine gasses. Here's what your recording heads looked like after a month's exposure to normal smog levels."

The projector screen showed a picture of hundreds of heads that had fallen apart into pieces. The lead-filled bonding glass that held the head pieces together, which everyone considered far superior to ordinary adhesives, had corroded and failed.

The room became totally silent, every technologist imagining how many billions of these glass-bonded recording heads were inside drives all over the world.

"Now let me show you another experiment, where we put entire drives into the smog chamber." The screen now showed a drive with a heavily corroded exterior. Its aluminum case had turned green.

"The Titanic must look like that, sitting on the floor of the Atlantic," Gordon remarked.

"But not quite so bad inside," the speaker said, showing a microscope picture of the recording heads inside the drive "The heads are fine. All disc drives are sealed to keep dirt from entering and interfering with head flight over disc surfaces, and it appears that those seals make corrosive gases condense on the exterior or interior of the aluminum drive case before they can get to the heads."

There was an audible sigh from the workshop attendees. "We're very lucky," one said.

"The bullet missed us," added another.

Gordon scratched his chin. *I think I'll hire this science guy Peter.*

"Let's organize today's hike," said John, the workshop moderator. Arrowhead workshop sessions were staggered to open up several hour hiking time slots over noon each day. "Who wants to climb Marie Louise Peak?" Many hands went up, including Gordon's.

They drove to the trail head for the hike, along rough fire roads snaking through forest groves separated by areas of open land. John brought a handheld GPS along, the first one most of them had seen. They used it with a topographic map to find the closest fire road to the trail head; then they started hiking up a stream bed that allowed passage through the dense California chaparral underbrush. This oily hillside brush was common in California and was a major reason for the state's notorious reputation for wildfires. They could see a peak far off in the distance.

"I see ducks up ahead. We must be on the trail," John called out. "Ducks" were piles of three rocks on a boulder to mark a trail, placed unnaturally to convey their human origin. They climbed towards the ducks, with Gordon in the middle of the group, rolling up his sleeves as the exertion heated him up.

Boris was a heavy man and brought up the rear. At one point Gordon saw a duck in a shallow wash leading off to his left, but John had continued straight ahead. Gordon followed the group, remembering the mountaineering safety rule of always staying together. A half hour later they had lost the trail completely and were still far below the peak. Gordon's arms were bleeding from cuts caused by struggling through the chaparral. Finally they reached the rock face of the summit block, found a way to climb up, and sat down to relax on the rocky summit of Marie Louise. John studied his GPS while others ate sack lunches or took photos.

"You can see the entire Antelope Valley from here," Gordon said. "That town to the north is Apple Valley. There's a Roy Rogers museum there. His horse Trigger is stuffed and mounted on a display stand, and his dog Bullet is mounted on another. There's a third empty stand that some say is meant for his wife Dale Evans, Ha Ha! Over to the west is the Cajon Pass where the Santa Fe Trail led pioneers into California, and where Mormons came through a century and a half ago to found San Bernardino. To the northwest, you can see the Sierra Nevada, California's tallest mountain range. Just to the east is Deep Canyon, cut by the Mojave River, and the Pacific Crest Trail that stretches from Mexico to Canada."

John was still fiddling with his GPS.

Gordon said, "Where's Boris? It's been a while since I last saw him far back, trailing us."

John looked up, fished in his backpack and pulled out a hand-held two-way radio. "I gave Boris one of these radios; I'll try calling him. John on the peak calling Boris in the brush, come back Boris, 10-4?" Only static replied.

After fruitless calling on the radio for five minutes, they discussed the situation. "Well, I guess we have to go look for him," John concluded. They started down, found the correct trail down the ducked wash this time, and hiked down to their car, periodically calling out by voice and radio.

"Well he's not at the car," John said. "If he walked back on the road we'll find him by driving the car. Let's drive further along this road first in case he got turned around." They drove far enough to overtake any walker, then turned around and drove back to the conference center.

Boris was still missing when the afternoon session started. When they found his baggage still in his room John called the local forest rangers. He was still missing the next day when sessions resumed. "I'll call his work office," John told the solemn group. "They can notify his family." He went downstairs to call as the next talk began.

Ten minutes later, John returned with a frown on his face. The speaker stopped.

John walked to the speaker's lectern. "When I called his office, Boris himself answered. I was flabbergasted. He asked me what I wanted, like nothing happened. When I told him search and rescue teams have been hunting for him since yesterday, he just said, 'Why?' He told me he knew nothing about the disc drive topics we're discussing, he got tired of Arrowhead, and so he hitchhiked back down the mountain to the airport to catch a plane home. I asked him why he left his luggage and he said, 'Oh. I forgot it. Send it to me.'"

The group looked at each other, speechless. This was an unimaginable Guinness world record of geekness.

"What about the radio you loaned him?" Gordon asked. "It must have cost you over a hundred dollars."

"He said he got tired of carrying it so he dropped it somewhere on the mountain. And it cost nearly $500."

A month later Gordon had indeed hired Peter, to lead and help build Seagate's first science analysis lab. The two quickly began ordering every scientific instrument that might be useful in failure analysis of drive problems, no matter what its intended scientific use or its cost. They soon had a scanning electron microscope, ultraviolet and infrared spectrophotometers, atomic absorption spectroscopy, a gas chromatograph, wet chemical benches, and a number of microscopes. Peter built one of his smog chambers to test Grenex discs for corrosion resistance. Peter and Gordon hired technicians Mary, Karen, and Martin as analysts, and they quickly had a complete science lab up and running.

They soon built an extensive reference library of contamination chemical signatures. They could identify the individual signatures of Ponds or Jergens face cream on a crashed disc, and know that a female assembler had touched the disc after scratching her forehead with her latex clean room glove. Potassium residue indicated fingerprint oil left by touching a disc or recording head with an ungloved finger.

Peter was a research metallurgist and Gordon thought he would learn Seagate culture faster if he took him to one of Tom's daily hands-on manufacturing meetings. Every Seagate manager understood the job details of every worker reporting to him and that day Tom was going over drive shipping schedules with his manufacturing team. It wasn't surprising that a Seagate founder was scheduling drive shipment details; this hands-on culture made for a fast and nimble high-tech company. In the same spirit, Gordon had taken a Seagate class that trained drive assembly workers. Although he fumbled and lost several miniscule screws that fastened track motor steel belts onto track motor shafts, he passed the class by assembling drives at least half as fast as a production worker could. His graduation certificate as "Seagate Approved Drive Assembler" was proudly displayed on his office wall for newly hired employees to see.

Peter and Gordon sat down on a couch in a corner of Tom's conference room. Tom and his manufacturing managers were seated around an oak conference table. The opposite wall was a single floor to ceiling window, overlooking Scotts Valley green hills and forests.

Tom was speaking. "Kathy, you're telling me we're still shipping ST-412 drives from Scotts Valley to IBM Florida for tests; then we're paying to ship them back here to verify the Florida test results?" He had begun in a calm voice, which was slowly rising. "Direct shipments to IBM's sales warehouses were scheduled to begin two months ago. Isn't that right?" Tom's eyes were burning into Kathy's. She was turning white with fear and was swallowing quickly. Her mouth appeared paralyzed. "Tell me what this is costing Seagate!" His voice was now a roar.

Kathy looked like a death row convict walking down the last mile, headed for the execution chamber.

"It's about $50,000 a day."

Tom's voice rose to a crescendo. **"FIFTY THOUSAND DOLLARS! YOU'RE FIRED!"** The other managers seated around Tom's conference table were carefully trying to keep neutral expressions on their faces, instead looking like embarrassed school children. Tom was now genially smiling at them, like a teacher successfully concluding a lesson.

Gordon realized how stupid he had been to bring a meek scientist to one of Tom's daily meetings, which were well known for this kind of intensity. Peter was trembling as they slunk out the door behind a dejected Kathy. "Do you think he was really serious about firing her?" Peter asked.

"Of course not," Gordon quickly said.

22.

Disasters are Business as Usual

Several additional production panics occurred in 1984 in addition to the dirty spacer ring crash crisis. At end year Gordon was stunned when *enormous profits* were announced and Seagate stock was split! He finally fully grasped what it took to run a successful Silicon Valley high-tech startup company. Disasters were business as usual.

"We're earning our stock options," Gordon told his people. He was hinting they should stay the course at Seagate, work to make Seagate stock and their stock options go up, and not accept competitor job offers at attractive salary increases. These offers came from the many job recruiter "headhunters" hovering about Silicon Valley. Doug had classified the company phone book as a Top Secret document because of them, telling his employees that giving phone numbers to a headhunter was a company violation subject to termination.

Gordon had asked Steve about this. He was the headhunter who had arranged Gordon's original Seagate job interview, billing Seagate a fee of 20% of Gordon's annual salary. Steve occasionally called with other job offers and Gordon had once asked him, "How do you get Seagate phone numbers?"

Steve had laughed and said, "I have the current Seagate phonebook and I'll read you the publication I.D. and date to prove it. I only had to walk into a Seagate building, charm the receptionist, and give her $20."

Silicon Valley startup companies were high stress jobs; most companies failed in ten years or less; and stock options were the primary motivation they had to get and keep skilled people, to reward their loyalty.

This golden age of American entrepreneurship was ending because Federal government accountants were forcing companies to use theoretical mathematical research formulas to value stock options, to expense their mathematical value as losses on company financial books.

These phantom losses remained even if a company later went broke and its stock became worthless. The Black-Scholes mathematical formulas that the accountants were requiring were originally derived for short term pricing of stock derivative investments, not for valuing startup company stock options. The mathematics had validity for older stable companies with a history of years of steady stock price increases or declines. But they weren't valid for Silicon Valley startup companies, which often blossomed like a fireworks display for a few years, suffered through competitive business cycles, and ultimately failed. Accountants were arithmeticians, not statistical mathematicians, and did not understand they needed to allow companies to test whether their financial history met the mathematical assumptions the Black-Scholes theory was based on.

Gordon's stock options became worth a tidy sum in 1985, and he figured that Seagate's stock price was at a high point in the disc drive business cycle. After such a good year, Seagate and its competitors would increase production and begin an oversupply bust cycle.

Gordon talked to several stock brokerages, asking about exercising a portion of his options and selling the quarter of his stock permitted by the option terms. He knew nothing about the stock market but one brokerage offered a poorer price than others, so Gordon asked about sales commissions. He was told their commission was higher because they were not a "market maker" in Seagate stock. That seemed an important clue.

Gordon called the Seagate investor relations person and asked her which brokerages were market makers in company stock. Calling up one located nearby in Carmel, he was transferred to a broker named Skip. "I'm looking for a broker I can stay with for the long term. I know nothing about investing and just want to park my Seagate option sale funds in a something safe while I learn what to invest in over the long term."

"Gordon," Skip said, "our firm is a market maker for Seagate which eliminates one level of commissions. I'll handle your sale, get you the preferred commission rate we give our best customers, and I'll recommend California Municipal Bonds for you to invest the money in, for the time being. I can get you 6% interest bonds, free of federal and state taxes, equivalent to about 10% interest before taxes. Muni bonds are safer than money under your mattress because California has to maintain investment grade credit ratings on them. If they didn't, institutional investors would be required to sell them, big investors like retirement plans and banks."

Gordon was convinced. "O.K. Skip, I'll send you the paperwork."

Gordon had lucked out. Skip had a long career in brokering and knew how to get and keep his customers. Gordon grew fond of Muni bonds. They were simple to understand and as dull as dishwater, so they occupied little of his time. Good returns were possible by buying lower rated bonds. Even higher risk Muni bonds were safer than nearly all stocks. From time to time Skip would call Gordon with advance warning of a problem with some bond he held and they would sell before the news became widespread and its price dropped. Gordon earned 7.5% tax free on bonds that funded the construction of a Southern California Northrop B-2 bomber factory. Its interest rate was higher than other bonds because the plant was scheduled to close five years after Gordon bought the bonds. But Skip knew that the bonding authority had accrued reserve funds to make all interest payments after the plant closed. In 1987, Muni yields rose to nine percent, three times more than bank savings account interest after taxes.

Gordon and Skip did their investing over the phone. It was fifteen years before they met. Gordon and Shirley bet each other what Skip would look like. Gordon guessed football player and Shirley guessed accountant with green eyeshades. Gordon won.

One night at Malone's, Gordon mentioned to Al that he had spent some of his stock option money. Al had become concerned and had said, "Gordon, invest that money for your retirement, don't just spend it."

"I know you're right, Al. But I've always wanted a $3000 Questar telescope." Al smiled his approval of the modest amount, and Gordon didn't add that he was also buying improvements for his Mooney airplane. He was adding speed brakes, an intercooler, an automatic turbo controller, a pulse light system for collision avoidance, and tuned fuel injectors. He bought Shirley an expensive diamond ring and a Rolex watch with diamonds encircling its dial. Gordon was actually only spending some of the tax free income from his Muni bonds, not his principal.

These were heady days for Seagate stock option holders. Doug bought a $500 bottle of wine at a Napa auction. "It was bottled in my birth year," he told Gordon. Al now owned two Lear jets, Tom had a King Air twin turboprop plane, and Doug bought a Rockwell Commander turboprop. Doug once sent it and his two pilots to Oregon to pick up a Maine coon cat for his wife. Gordon figured that that was probably a $25,000 cat.

23.

Opera and Bugs Bunny in the Morning

To handle Seagate job stress Gordon developed a habit of beginning each day in as calm and peaceful a mood as possible. In his mornings at home, he watched Bugs Bunny cartoons with the TV sound off, while listening to Puccini opera recordings on his Hi Fi. His favorite music would switch from *La Boheme* one day, to *Tosca* the next, to the Eagles *Hotel California*, then to Maria Callas singing *Turandot*.

Gordon had fallen in love with opera late one summer Sunday during his Cal Tech days, while driving home after climbing Mount Whitney. That Friday afternoon he and his Cal Tech pal Hardy had driven up the Owens Valley to Whitney Portal in the California Sierra Nevada, above the town of Lone Pine. Hardy was a big man of few words, who had begun his graduate study at Cal Tech the same year Gordon arrived as a freshman. Gordon and Hardy shared an office at school. He thought Hardy was far smarter than him. Hardy was exceptional at solving Scientific American magazine mathematical puzzles. Gordon was closer to earning his PhD than Hardy, having discovered that the most important step was deciding to get it and get out.

Saturday, they climbed to the base of the Whitney cliffs at East Face Lake. On the way, they passed a mountaineer with ropes and rock climbing hardware hanging all over his body. A metal cup hung from his belt, embossed "Sierra Club." He glanced at Gordon's casual hiking clothes with scorn and spoke in clipped sentences only to Hardy. "You might get mountain training for this kid with you, and someday he could apply to the Sierra Club for membership. We take only a few of those that apply."

This reminded Gordon of Groucho Marx's remark, "I don't want to belong to any club that will accept me as a member."

Gordon's stomach was aching when they arrived at East Face Lake to camp. He had unwisely eaten a heavy breakfast that morning and then spent the entire day hiking with his blood going to his legs instead of his digestion. They set up their tiny camp by the small lake, which had ice floating in it. Hardy fired up his Primus gasoline stove and cooked their freeze-dried dinner. Gordon ate little. Darkness fell and they turned in.

Gordon awoke in total darkness hours later, sensing something was desperately wrong, but he couldn't figure out what. It seemed to take forever before he realized he was utterly freezing. His old sleeping bag that had served him well in Southern California Boy Scout camping was totally inadequate for the Sierra high country. He shivered and struggled, putting on all the clothing he had brought. He finally warmed up after donning two pairs of pants, two shirts, two pairs of socks, his parka, and climbing back inside his bag. After minutes of shivering he luxuriated in warmness, watching countless piercingly sharp stars in the black sky above their high altitude wilderness camp. He fell into sleep watching meteorites streak past madly twinkling stars in the cold unstable air above him.

Sunday morning he felt O.K. They ate a light breakfast before starting to climb the sheer rock face of Mount Whitney. The Fresh Air Traverse was the first challenge on this East Face route, so-called because it was a narrow ledge on a cliff wall with no handholds, barely a foot and a half wide and sloping dangerously towards the cliff edge. Gordon faced the cliff wall and carefully sidestepped along the ledge. Only the friction of his boots kept him from sliding off the ledge into thin air. Hardy belayed him with a rope tied around Gordon's waist.

Once across, Gordon took a position behind a boulder above the traverse, to belay Hardy's crossing. *I hope I can hold him if he happens to fall.* Hardy was hidden from view by the boulder.

"Damn," Hardy's voice echoed off the cliffs. Gordon braced for a big yank but was still nearly pulled off the mountain when Hardy fell to the end of the rope.

"Hardy! My God! Are you all right?" He heard only silence. A massive weight hung on the rope, so Gordon knew Hardy was still attached, but he might have been knocked unconscious after hitting the cliff. Hardy was twice Gordon's weight and there was no way Gordon could pull him up if he was unconscious.

Finally he heard Hardy's voice shouting, "I'm O.K! I'll climb back up the rope as soon as I get my breath back!"

Quickly enough, Hardy climbed the rope and joined Gordon, both breathing heavily behind the boulder.

"I'm sure glad not to fall all the way down that thousand foot cliff!"

"I never could have hauled you up if you were knocked out," Gordon replied.

The remainder of the climb was the most exhilarating of all Gordon's mountain climbing days. They climbed the Grand Staircase, whose steps were taller than people, then traversed the Exfoliation Slabs with the Owens Valley and White Mountains spread out before them.

Finally, Gordon started up the last chimney, a three foot wide vertical crack in the rock. He braced his back against one side, pushed with his legs against the other, and climbed like a spider. After a while, Hardy heard muttering from an invisible Gordon retreating back down the chimney. "I started up the obvious way but you can't get out the top of it unless you start with your back on the other side of the chimney."

At the top of the chimney, they reached the summit to find a hundred hikers that had walked up the 11-mile trail from the road end at Whitney Portal.

"Where did you guys come from?" one of the hikers asked. They were all sitting on rocks and looking exhausted.

"Up the east face cliff," Gordon replied, not aware that he was wearing an expression like the Sierra Club superman they had met earlier on the trail.

Hardy and Gordon rested a while and wrote their names into the summit register book.

"Look here, Hardy. There's an entry from a helicopter pilot who landed on all the 14,000 foot Sierra peaks in one day. Here's another entry from some joker who signed himself in as Superman."

They returned down the mountain on the Mountaineers Route, making great leaps down its debris slope of small loose rocks called scree. They arrived back at East Face Lake in a quarter of the time it had taken them to climb up, and hiked down to their car as darkness fell. They drove down Whitney Portal Road to Lone Pine, where they stopped to buy quarts of chocolate milk to drink as they continued south down the Owens Valley towards home.

As they drove back to Cal Tech that Sunday night, Gordon listened on the car radio as Maria Callas sang Verdi's opera *Aida*. Tears came in his fatigue as he fell into the story of a young princess coping with her slavery as a prisoner of war.

Opera forever after filled a private place in his mind, like his flying. It gave him hiding places for his ego, helping him promote his ideas at Seagate, which always went best if he let others take credit. "Success has many fathers," his former Xerox boss Andy liked to say, "but failure is an orphan."

24.

Real Estate Wars

Seagate's business success required expanding into more buildings in Scotts Valley. Borland Computer, a software company, was also expanding in the valley and an undeclared real estate war sprang up between the two. Doug's weekly engineering manager meetings became exciting when real estate war news displaced the latest disc drive technology alligator problem.

"Meet Alice," Doug announced at one of his meetings. A well-dressed and attractive lady was seated next to Doug. "She's been a commercial real estate broker here in Scotts Valley long enough to know the details of every property in town that Seagate might want to buy, build on, or lease. We've hired her as a full-time employee to manage our expansion in Scotts Valley." He paused, waiting patiently as his engineers struggled to understand this property business, so foreign to their technology jobs. "We've tried unsuccessfully to buy or move the trailer park that separates our manufacturing, headquarters, and engineering buildings. We need a professional on our side. That's Alice.

"Alice, meet my engineering managers. They normally worry about getting new products designed and into manufacturing, but I'm sure they'll be interested in what you can do for Seagate's real estate in Scotts Valley."

Alice was a handsome woman, looking forty-ish, and carried herself with the professional but relaxed bearing often seen in women that succeed in traditionally male careers, like Britain's Prime Minister Margaret Thatcher. Alice was leaning back in her chair with her arm on Doug's conference table, looking completely relaxed and totally capable. Gordon thought her legs looked sexy.

"A pleasure to meet you gentlemen," she said. "Let's get right to the heart of the challenges Seagate must meet to expand in Scotts Valley.

You may be surprised to learn that only a few men control everything in this valley." Eyes widened with interest and heads reared back in surprise.

"Less than five years ago, Scotts Valley was just a wide spot in the road to Santa Cruz, with some tourist traffic business. When the freeway was built most of the tourist traffic dried up. One man owned almost all of the land between Scotts Valley Boulevard and the freeway. Another owned most of the rest. These two men joined with several developers sitting on the city council and got the council to vote to open the town to industrial development.

"The Santa Cruz city and county governments are dominated by environmentalists who've long resisted any industrial development in the city and county. So this Scotts Valley 'inner circle' of a few men were in a unique position to make a lot of money off their 'island' of Scotts Valley city land, by encouraging industrial development here. Seagate's buildings are on some of their land and Borland Computer's are as well.

"It may also surprise you to hear that this 'inner circle' fears Seagate's rapidly increasing size; that they were behind the city council denial a year ago of Al's offer to pay for the first traffic signal on Scotts Valley Boulevard; and they were behind the vote last month denying your purchase of the land the trailer park sits on." There were murmurings of astonishment around the table. Many engineers never imagine what it takes to make the attractive industrial campuses they work in. "They even denied Al's request that his headquarters building have the address '#1 Disc Drive.'"

"Seagate is the largest business employer in Scotts Valley by far," she continued. "It's entitled to have legitimate influence on the town and on its council. But the 'inner circle' wants to maintain their power for profit, and they intend to do so by playing Seagate off against Borland. However, they don't pay attention to the details of Scotts Valley real estate like I do. I know every real estate secret in this valley and I intend to use them to get you the land you need, on fair terms at and fair prices.

"Borland has just made its first real estate move by buying the building across the freeway that Seagate now occupies under lease, the building you're using for engineering overflow space." Heads nodded in understanding. "Borland intends to use only a fraction of the building and they expect us to continue using our current space and paying them rent all the rest of this year, until they're ready to take over the entire building themselves. At that time they intend to give us an eviction notice. But they don't know I hear about every real estate transaction in Scotts Valley."

Alice saw their blank stares of incomprehension, smiled, and continued. "A week ago I gave Borland legal notice that we're immediately vacating the entire building. I wrote the original lease for that building several years ago and I put a clause in it giving a lessee the right to cancel its lease if the building was sold. That lessee is us. The Borland real estate manager was quite unhappy when I told him."

"But where will we put our overflow groups that are now in that building?" one manager asked.

"I've purchased an office building that's walking distance from our campus here, directly across Scotts Valley Boulevard. Borland has been leasing it as its headquarters. I wrote its original building deed when the 'inner circle' built it. I put a clause in its deed that if the building was sold, the new owner could cancel all of its leases. Borland's real estate manager was even unhappier this morning when I gave him an eviction notice. They must vacate both of those buildings by the end of this month."

"There's more than one building?" an engineer asked.

"The deed includes a second building behind the first, and also a third building that's under a long term lease to a medical group."

"You mean Seagate owns the 'Doc in a Box' building across the street from here? My wife takes our kids there!"

Alice continued, "I've told the medical group that we're willing to let their lease stand at the same rate. They were relieved we weren't going to increase their rent. In exchange, they're giving Seagate a discount rate on employee annual physicals. Al pointed out that this will take less employee time than driving across the mountains to the Palo Alto clinic Seagate has been using for physicals. If Borland takes us to court over being evicted from their headquarters, our case will be helped by how we treat this medical clinic."

Gordon was extremely impressed with Alice. "You beat Borland twice in a single week, and made them vacate their own headquarters with their tails between their legs! What'll happen to their real estate manager?"

"I hear he's now looking for a job at Scotts Valley residential real estate offices. Every commercial real estate firm turned him down." The room was silent with admiration. Alice looked rather pleased.

Seagate soon moved its engineering overflow from across the freeway into Borland's former headquarters building across the street. Now, Seagate people could easily walk between all their buildings.

This saved driving a mile down Scotts Valley Boulevard to get across the freeway, and then another mile drive back to the overflow building. Borland was forced to hurriedly lease a new headquarters building. It was at a poor location remote from the building they had bought across the freeway, which sat empty for several years.

25.

There Are Free Meals

Seagate's founders ran an open company and regularly held offsite employee meetings to discuss company plans and progress. Its leaders held these all-hands meetings to give their employees complete company status information. They knew employees could make the best decisions regarding their own work, but only if they were made aware of all company information. Every employee was given stock options for personal motivation, even secretaries and assembly workers. Seagate also gave bonuses and profit sharing. Those could add up to an extra five weeks of pay in a good year. These meetings were held in nice places and sometimes in grand ones like the Santa Cruz Cocoanut Grove. These open company meetings served their team purpose well when Seagate was a growing company, although not in bad times when layoffs were imminent.

Gordon had listened to Al, Doug, and Tom talk about Seagate's present and future products, finances, and customers in one of these meetings, as he enjoyed a filet of beef Benedict dinner.

Doug's weekly engineering manager meetings were also based on open company culture. He told his engineers everything, good news and bad, and held back no upper management secrets unless required by corporate law. Properly motivated, his engineers would do a better job by themselves than if he gave orders from above. This also meant that when an engineering crisis occurred, the engineer responsible would be expected to step forward and solve it, going to see Doug, Al or Tom only if upper management help was needed in applying the solution. "Open company" seemed exceedingly intelligent to Gordon.

Gordon had once asked Doug how they had come up with this 'open company' management method. Doug had answered, "When we started Seagate, we decided to throw out every management method we hated in every earlier company we worked for. We use first names instead of titles, and allow everyone to know everything, because information becomes power when an organization grows to have many layers of managers that only talk to their direct employees and to their bosses. Each layer instinctively protects itself by hiding operational problems from its boss, and by keeping management information from lower-level workers.

"The problem's most apparent in government, like in President Jack Kennedy's Cuban Bay of Pigs failure. Kennedy learned from that disaster to reach down into the military chain of command in the later Cuban Missile Crisis. He and his brother Robert reached the aircraft commander that would give the actual commands to fire weapons. Kennedy talked to him directly, keeping Russia from putting nuclear missiles in Cuba without starting a war."

Doug also organized a series of lectures for employees that he called the "Seagate Institute of Technology." He invited technology innovators at Seagate to speak on their work, calling them "brag" sessions. Gordon gave lectures on recording technology. His quizzes asked questions like "How can our ST-277 drive store 60 megabytes per disc using the same head and disc magnetic design as the 40 megabyte ST-251? Discuss the benefits and limitations of its (2,7) recording code compared to the modified frequency modulation code."

He gave easier quizzes to non-engineers. These classes were for business people Tom occasionally sent over to learn what the company actually did to make money. "How many heads and discs does a ST-251 drive have?" Gordon used Macintosh graphics to print "Certificate of Disc Drive Excellence" awards for "A" students.

He also began awarding "Cruelty to Disc Drives Award" Mac posters to engineers who abused drive technology, such as running drives outside clean benches with their covers off, unprotected from airborne dirt that could cause a head crash. "Cruelty" award certificates became prized and framed ones began showing up on engineer office walls. Gordon awarded one to the disc drive mechanical shock tester inventor even though it was a necessary test for new drive models. A test drive was strapped to one end of a foot long metal beam, hinged at the other end so it could be positioned vertically and let fall, like a pole vaulter falling from the top of his jump over the pole to the padded ground below. Only the disc drive under test fell and hit a hard metal block. The goal was for the drive to be able to survive the mechanical shock and still be able to operate afterwards. This tested whether a drive in a laptop computer would survive if its user dropped the computer onto a concrete floor. Gordon couldn't understand why people would think disc drives should survive such abuse when they were higher precision instruments than the expensive cameras nobody expected to survive such falls.

Seagate held annual company picnics in parks around Santa Cruz, with mandatory attendance and dunk tank rules for vice presidents and above. Beginning with Tom, VPs climbed onto a platform above a dunk tank so employees and their kids could throw balls at a target and see if they could hit the lever that dumped the manager into the water.

26.

Disc Drive Research Universities

Gordon and Shirley drove from their home to San Jose Airport with Charles in the back seat. The cat liked flying far better than driving and he especially hated the many turns on their mountain roads that threw him from side to side in the car. They parked next to the Mooney and loaded their baggage into the plane. Gordon was headed for San Diego as Seagate's representative on a committee of computer disc and tape storage companies. They were establishing a research center at the University of California at San Diego, to educate students in drive engineering and to research future drive technologies. They brought Charles along to take to a recommended vet in San Diego.

The tower radioed Gordon his FAA assigned route, southeast over the California central valley, over Bakersfield and Gorman, then over L.A. and down the coast to San Diego. Gordon radioed acceptance of the clearance and ran through his three preflight checklists; basic aircraft checks, programming the route clearance into his two GPS navigators, and setting up his flight instruments. He selected a navigation map on one of his GPS display screens and a traffic watch screen in the other. These TV-like displays showed moving maps with airports, navigation points, ground terrain elevation, nearby airplane traffic for collision avoidance, and storm locations up to 200 miles away. Its map display was currently showing the taxiways and runways at San Jose Airport, with Gordon's plane in its parking spot.

Airplane midair collisions were rare and usually occurred near airports, where planes congregate. The three dimensions of the sky made it very unlikely for two planes to be in the same place and altitude at the same time. *Collisions in flight are extremely rare, but it's still reassuring to have an electronic traffic warning system.* If its computer predicted that another plane was going to come within several miles and near his altitude in the next few minutes, a yellow warning would flash on the traffic display showing its position and altitude. An electronic voice would announce, "Traffic" in his earphones. The female voice had a precise British accent, and Gordon jokingly told friends it must have been recorded by Cathy, the British announcer on the TV show *Junkyard Wars*.

Gordon recalled simpler days when he had first begun piloting airplanes, before glass-cockpit airline jet electronics started percolating down to small airplanes. He and Shirley had once flown an earlier plane from Central California to San Diego to begin a Mexican vacation. The plane had the simple communication and navigation radios of its day. They had left in late afternoon because of work schedules and were flying in darkness an hour later. As they continued south, Gordon's peripheral vision suddenly caught a very close strobe light flashing from the blind direction behind him. Turning his head he saw another plane only seconds from a collision. A near miss was especially unlikely over the unpopulated California region they were flying over in the night, but Gordon had no time to speculate or even think about moving the controls to take evasive action.

His heart leaped into his throat. A split second later the other plane had passed very close over him and was sailing away to his left, its wingtip and tail lights flashing. He had heard its engine as it passed, meaning it had been only yards away. He looked over at Shirley and gratefully saw she was asleep. *Phew, that's the first time another plane ever came within two miles of mine. He was looking straight at me but I bet he never saw me because he never changed course.*

They passed over L.A. an hour later, its lights looking brighter and warmer than usual. *Life looks brighter if you've just come close to falling ten thousand feet to your death.*

Low clouds slipped beneath them as they neared San Diego. City lights began casting lambent glows through the thickening cloud layer below. Occasional bright city lights projected circular blobs of luminosity up into the dark cloud tops, looking like shining white chrysanthemums dreamily floating beneath the surface of a pond.

"Where are we," Shirley said, waking up.

"About ten minutes from landing. Look at the city lights. They're painting a lovely scene on the cloud tops below us."

The next morning Gordon had checked the airplane, preparing to fly to warmer Mexican climes. He had smiled when he caught himself foolishly looking for scrape marks on the cabin roof.

Three hours later they were flying above a lush green Mexican countryside, weaving around castle turrets made of air; towers of brilliant white clouds climbing high into the sky above their plane.

As Gordon weaved among them he recalled the words of a lady pilot writing about flying among similar cloud formations in a P-38 World War II fighter aircraft: "If I die right now, at least I will have known what it is to be alive."

Gordon's attention snapped back to the present when San Jose Airport's ground controller radioed his taxi instructions. He taxied, was cleared for takeoff, and changed radio frequency to Bay Approach Control as he climbed. Bay gave him a heading to intercept his assigned route. The sky was a cloudless blue as they climbed to 23,000 feet. Charles was looking out the back window, paws on the window sill.

The customary California northwest trade winds gave them a tailwind and his instruments predicted his 200 mph groundspeed would get him to San Diego two hours after takeoff. Richard Henry Dana had written of these trade winds 150 years earlier in *Two Years before the Mast*, when they slowed his sail up the California coast.

"We'll land at Lindbergh about 11am, Shirley."

Bay Approach handed Gordon off to the long range radar control center. Gordon set the new frequency into his radio and keyed his transmitter, "Oakland Center, Mooney three one golf hotel is level at flight level 230."

"Roger, 31 golf hotel," the center acknowledged.

A moment later, an airline pilot on the same frequency asked, "Three one golf hotel, what kind of Mooney are you that can cruise at 23,000 feet?"

"It's a turbo Mooney 231," Gordon replied, feeling fortunate to live in the U.S. where ordinary citizens were permitted such experiences.

Gordon started his descent for landing after passing L.A. It took 100 miles to get down to landing altitude at San Diego from 23,000 feet, going 230 mph in the descent. He landed at Lindbergh and parked between two business jets at Jim's Air, on the private side of the airport. In five minutes they were in a taxi.

At UCSD he met with members of other companies on the search committee. Denis from IBM summarized their progress. "Together, we've visited the semiconductor industry's research centers and universities to see how they function, and we've talked to Stanford, Berkeley, and UCSD about starting a research center on their campus for information storage technology. I'll ask James to now make the case for selecting UCSD."

James rose and said, "UCSD is just beginning its rise to engineering excellence and is eager for us to build our research center here. They'll let us endow four chaired professorships. Of the three universities we talked to, UCSD will best welcome and value us, and make us an integral part of their campus. I suggest we call it the Center for Magnetic Recording Research, CMRR." The committee unanimously agreed, and they moved on to discuss soliciting industrial sponsor donations, and searching for the four chaired professors. They agreed that these had to have proper technology qualifications as well as university academic stature.

That evening Gordon and Shirley flew home from San Diego. It was night and they were in clouds, flying on instruments and autopilot. "The engine sounds different," Shirley said.

"It's misfiring," he replied. He had noticed an engine vibration, which was slowly becoming more frequent and more severe. Minutes later it was shaking the entire plane.

"Ask the radar controller for help," Shirley suggested.

"Honey, I'll let him know we have a problem, but he can't fix our misfiring engine. We'll have to diagnose and deal with the problem ourselves. Right now, the military training base at Camp Pendleton is below us. If the engine quits completely we can try to land on the coast freeway. We can't see it in the darkness and clouds, but look at the moving map on the GPS. That green line on the screen marked 'U.S. I-5' is the freeway. If the engine quits we can follow the GPS map and land on it. But it will be dangerous. There may be power lines crossing the road and there will be cars to avoid. Instead, we're going to fly to the nearest airport with an instrument landing system. That'll be much safer, if the engine gives us that much time."

Gordon keyed his radio transmitter, "Coast Approach, Mooney three one golf hotel will likely request a precautionary landing in a few minutes: rough engine."

The radar controller responded instantly, "Roger, one golf hotel, suggest Orange County Airport 30 miles ahead. Say how many souls on board, your remaining fuel, and whether you are declaring an emergency."

"Roger, Coast. Stand by please."

Going through his engine emergency checklist, Gordon found that the engine ran smoothly on its left ignition magneto alone but was extremely rough on the right one. He left the ignition on left magneto only, instead of its normal setting with both magnetos on.

"Tell me you're not going to fly all the way to San Jose on one magneto," Shirley demanded.

"Wouldn't think of it," Gordon said. He keyed his transmitter. "Coast, we're two people, six hours fuel, and we're running O.K. on one mag. We request expedited handling to the airport but we're not declaring an emergency."

"Roger, one golf hotel, fly heading 320 degrees, vector to Orange County Airport."

They were soon flying over Orange County, southeast of Los Angeles. They would be able to land visually once they descended beneath the clouds and were able to see the runway lights. Ordinarily, Gordon would have made a full instrument approach because darkness and clouds reduce safety margins for visual flight. But that would take him beyond gliding range back to the airport if his engine failed completely. With an untrustworthy engine the safest course was to stay close to the airport and make an abbreviated instrument approach, descending below the clouds to find the runway lights.

"One golf hotel, expect Runway 19 Left. Follow the Boeing 737 on final for 19 Right." Between clouds, Gordon saw the 737 passing by at a lower altitude.

"One golf hotel has the 737 in sight," he radioed the controller.

"Follow him, you're cleared for visual approach to 19 Left, and switch now to tower frequency. Good luck, sir."

"Thanks for your help, Coast," Gordon replied, as he descended between the clouds. He couldn't see any airport lights, but his GPS showed him exactly how far the airport runway was and the rate of descent he needed to land on its threshold. He wouldn't be able to see the runway itself until he got below the clouds. He carefully reminded himself, *Focus! Getting fixated on minor emergencies turns them into big ones. Ignore everything except flying the plane. Our safety depends on my focus now.*

He carefully scanned his instruments as he mentally ran his emergency landing checklist. *Fly the plane, gear down, flaps down, prop high rpm, best-glide approach airspeed, missed approach plan, passenger briefing.* "Check your seat belt and harness, Shirley." He could now see the lights of Runway 19 Left and the 737 landing on 19 Right.

Landing the Mooney was an anticlimax, but as he turned off the runway Gordon saw five fire trucks parked beside the taxiway. Their red and white lights were flashing like July 4th fireworks, ready to roll if he had crashed and burned.

Taxiing to parking he said, "Honey, those fire trucks mean they decided we were an emergency. Bet you airport officials will be waiting to talk to us when we park."

"But we didn't declare an emergency and we made a normal landing," Shirley protested. Gordon just smiled. Parking and shutting down the plane, they walked into a small general aviation terminal. Charles stayed in the plane, curling up on the back seat.

A man with a clipboard was standing inside. "I'd appreciate you filling out this accident report form, sir."

"Of course," Gordon replied. "But would you mind if I strike out the word 'accident' and replace it with the word 'incident'? I'd like to keep this low key since only a precautionary landing occurred. The FAA regulations call this situation only an incident, not an accident." He started filling out the form without waiting for approval, and handed the completed form back to the man, who left.

Turning to the man behind the terminal counter, Gordon asked, "Can you call a mechanic for us and suggest a hotel to stay tonight?"

"I'll do both."

A half hour later, a mechanic had removed the engine cowling from the plane and unbolted the right magneto. "Look at this," he said, showing Gordon the magneto with its end cap off. "Its electrical breaker points came loose and got chopped up by the rotor shaft. I'm surprised it didn't just go dead instead of misfiring. I'll order you another magneto and the plane will be ready for you by noon."

"Thanks," Gordon replied, and walked back into the terminal.

The man at the counter said, "I got you a room at a hotel just across the street from here. It's very nice and they have a great restaurant that serves filet mignon steak kebob on skewers. It's half the price of their regular filet steak dinner and there's just as much filet."

They went back to their plane to get the luggage they had used in San Diego. Shirley tucked Charles under her arm and they walked across the street to the hotel. They registered for a room and told the clerk, "We're unintentional tourists. Our private plane had an engine problem flying to San Jose, and we landed here to get it fixed."

"In that case, I'm pleased to tell you that you qualify for our 'stranded passenger' policy. The room will be half-price, and please accept these coupons for half-off on any dinner in our restaurant."

"I like your hotel already," Gordon replied smiling. They took their bags and Charles to their room and went to the hotel restaurant. Silverware on the tables sparkled from the many lights in a massive chandelier overhead. They sat by a window with a view of the airplane takeoffs across the street.

Shirley summed up their adventure. "This turned out to be another small airplane 'accidental tourist' stop. Remember the delightful unplanned stops we made to avoid weather in Guanajuato, Mexico, and Jerome, Arizona?" They both laughed.

"What did the San Diego vet say about Charles?" Gordon asked, as he speared a bell pepper off the kebob skewer with his fork.

"Well, he gave me some medicine, but Charles is sixteen and getting frail from old age. He stopped going outdoors a while back. Remember when we had Kermit over for dinner, and he ran up the cliff in his sandals?"

"Yeah. Kermit said he found mountain lion paw prints in the forest above our home. Charles was smart to stop going outdoors."

A minute later, Gordon's attempt at putting up a brave front for Shirley collapsed, and he dropped his head to his hands at the thought of losing his close friend Charles. Seeing him, Shirley was also near tears. They both deeply cared for Charles Cat. They finished their meal in silence.

The next morning Gordon picked up his room phone and called his secretary Jan. He told her he was delayed in returning.

"Was something wrong with your plane?" Jan asked.

Gordon quickly invented a white lie. "Just the nuisance of finding it had a flat tire last night when we wanted to leave San Diego, and all the airport mechanic shops were closed for the day." If he told her what actually happened, the story would be blown up into an exaggerated tale of airplane danger and spread around Seagate. That was the last thing he wanted.

After breakfast Shirley and Gordon walked down the street to a shopping mall to look at fancy clothes and high priced jewelry. "Cheap at half the price," Gordon observed. Shirley smiled.

Their plane was ready at noon and they filed a flight plan back home. Their Mooney returned to its normal faithful behavior.

They flew over L.A. on their way back north and then over Gorman Pass. They saw several thousand giant yellow umbrellas planted in the ground below, covering the entire Gorman area south of Bakersfield. It was Christos's "Umbrellas," an ephemeral art project that planted 25-foot diameter umbrellas in the U.S. and Japan, and lasted only 18 days.

Back at Seagate the next morning, Gordon found a message from another university. The Dean of the Engineering Department at the University of California at Santa Cruz was inviting local industries to meet and advise the university on the relevance of its engineering programs.

Gordon drove to their meeting a week later. The UCSC campus was scattered around a redwood forest, its buildings tucked here and there, nestled between tree groves.

He listened to their engineering school presentations. They had good departments in computer engineering, math, and astronomy.

When they asked for audience questions, Gordon raised his hand.

"Every spring we Seagate managers get job applications from graduating students all over the world. There are so many resumes that we can only briefly scan them to select applicants to invite in for interviews. I get applications from your students but I've never been able to interview any of them. It's because no grades are shown, no GPA. I understand you use a pass/no pass system instead of letter grades to build student self-esteem, but that doesn't give me any way to select students strong in math and engineering for Seagate jobs."

The faculty looked at each other. The dean finally said, "We do understand that student grades are important to getting jobs and we'll add your voice to an ongoing discussion here about grades. Meanwhile, let me say that we have a code for the text that teachers put into the pass/no pass grades. We can decode the text and tell you what the letter grade would have been."

Gordon said nothing more. He had made his point.

A year later, Gordon would return to San Diego in Al's Learjet for the dedication of the Center for Magnetic Recording Research at UCSD. A picture would be taken of Al and other computer data storage industry presidents, each holding a golden shovel to turn the first earth for the new campus research building that their companies had paid for. By that time, Gordon had also sold Seagate on sponsoring a second major university research and education center at Carnegie Mellon University in Pittsburgh.

27.

It's the Taxes, Stupid

Technology companies must continuously progress to make better products at lower prices, or they begin to stagnate. Their customers were the winners. Technology business competition had been led by the U.S. for over a century, and had raised people's living standards over the world. Recently, the U.S. technology lead had begun to be shared with Japan, then Singapore, Korea, Thailand, and China.

Gordon was on one of his visits to the new Center for Magnetic Recording Research at U.C. San Diego. He went to the Faculty Club for lunch, and a professor sitting at his table noticed the name badge he was wearing.

"You're from Seagate Technology, the computer hard disc drive company? We've been studying the hard drive manufacturing business in our economics department. May I ask a few questions on why your industry moved its manufacturing to Asia?"

"Sure. Ask away," Gordon replied, reaching for a pink "Sweet N' Low" from the sugar tray, because they dissolved faster in his iced tea.

"It's obvious you moved offshore because hard drives are a low-profit commodity business and Asian wages are significantly lower than in the U.S. I'd like to ask you about some of the details."

"Actually, low Asian wages weren't the reason at all. The Singapore government thought the same way when they set out to court U.S. drive manufacturers. They came to us first because we're the largest independent drive maker in the world. When their government agency A*Star proposed that idea we told them there's only 45 minutes of assembly labor cost in a disc drive. Lower Asian labor rates would only save a couple of dollars per drive over U.S. wages. That's not enough leverage to overcome the Asian logistics problems. Technology and maintenance for our manufacturing line machines would have to be flown in from the U.S., for example."

The professor was looking rather stunned. "Then why did you move to Asia?"

Gordon smiled and took a sip of his tea. "The Singaporeans knew that commodity electronics industries are under heavy profitability pressures, just as you say, and they came back to talk with us again after they figured out that U.S taxes are a much more significant financial burden than U.S. labor rates.

"Singapore convinced Seagate to move its factory there by giving it a tax haven that eliminated all Singapore taxes and thereby eliminated almost all U.S taxes. Do you understand the tax economics here?"

"No, we study business globalization economics, not taxation policy."

Gordon wondered why global competition through tax policy was rarely openly studied or discussed by economists like this professor.

What would U.S. citizens say if they knew that the tax policies of their own government were forcing their U.S. auto, steel, and computer manufacturing jobs offshore to Asia?

"Here's how tax economics goes. U.S. companies that make products offshore and import them to the U.S. pay U.S. corporate taxes only on value they add in the U.S., like markups on U.S. distribution and sales costs. That's international tax law. But domestic companies manufacturing products inside the U.S. are taxed on their total profits. Commodity electronics companies are doing well if they make 20% net profit, and U.S. federal and state corporate income taxes of almost 40% on goods manufactured here cuts their profits significantly enough to make them noncompetitive against a foreign competitor with a tax haven.

"Here's a different example. Western Digital, one of our electronic chip component suppliers, was making 45% profit on its chip sales to us. We started making our own chips to lower their cost. Western Digital responded by going into disc drive manufacturing, buying the closed Tandon disc drive factory. That was a gutsy move because Western Digital would have to learn how to solve difficult technology manufacturing problems just as we did. I discovered they were forming their own science lab when several of my lab analysts took jobs there. Today, that kind of high-tech mass-market competition means that none of our component suppliers can make more than 20% profit, just as we can't.

"Singapore offered additional incentives. A*Star offered to help Seagate build its first plant and to supply highly educated workers at those low wages. They showed us the excellent educational standards in

Singapore, including the many available graduates from their National University. It's unfortunate but true that many of Seagate's U.S. workers at the time were less educated than the Singaporeans.

"So, Seagate became the first disc drive company to move its manufacturing to Asia, giving us significantly higher after-tax profits than our competitors. A*Star correctly figured this would force all the other drive companies offshore as well, to survive. As soon as Seagate began fabricating recording heads and assembling drives in Singapore, A*Star quickly toured the other U.S. disc drive manufacturers, enticing them to also come to Singapore, based on Seagate's example of successful high-tech manufacturing at tax-free costs they couldn't match in the U.S.

"Every American disc drive company moved to Asia, and high-tech manufacturing companies continue to move there. The Asian tax havens were supposed to be temporary, but they still exist. The U.S. tax pressure moving U.S. jobs to Asia was noted in a few remarks by Alan Greenspan, the former head of the U.S. Federal Reserve Board. But most federal officials and economists say nothing."

Gordon personally thought the international spread of technology brought worldwide benefits overall. *Globalization of technology manufacturing brings better jobs and higher living standards to ordinary people all over the world. In all Earth's history of foreign colonization, wars, and trade, technology manufacturing has most raised the living standards of ordinary people. It's painful for lower skilled workers in richer nations, though. Their jobs leave their country and they can't afford to raise a family on the high cost of living.*

The professor was silent for a minute and then said, "Some U.S. politicians call for full taxation of all global profits made by U.S. headquartered firms. They say that would prevent more American jobs from going offshore."

"So they say, but foreign companies can't be taxed that way by the U.S. Again, that's international law. If firms like Seagate were taxed more than they are now, lower foreign company taxes would drive prices so low that U.S. companies would be forced to go completely offshore or go out of business. An American capital flight would ensue and many more American jobs would leave the U.S., far more than the 15% experts estimate today.

"Please study what I'm saying in your economics department. You'll find that U.S. laws do say we must use our untaxed offshore profits to offset our offshore drive manufacturing costs, and that our profits are taxable in the U.S if we bring them back home. But that's only a paper accounting detail. Every couple of years the U.S. tax authorities object to our accounting and a negotiation alters our tax amounts slightly. The changes are never enough to return manufacturing to America. But they never force American companies to become completely foreign companies either.

"In the long run, globalization might evolve to help instead of hurt U.S. lower skilled workers. Their job security and pay could improve if the international economic community encouraged all nations to set consistent tax policies and globally follow them. The U.S. automobile industry is an example of a commodity industry that has long struggled to make money against global competition. Today, foreign auto companies like BMW, Mercedes, Toyota, Honda and Subaru manufacture cars in the U.S. using U.S. workers. The commodity electronics industry could follow the same path."

Seagate's first Singapore jobs were lower paid assembly work. Manufacturing may have gone to Asia for tax advantages, but Doug and Al felt that Seagate should increase its job opportunities for the people in host countries like Singapore. Critically important, Asia had high educational standards and excellent universities. Doug wanted to bring engineering jobs to these countries as well.

The Asian people needed training in high-tech engineering for this, so Doug started an offshore "Seagate Institute of Technology," which brought Asian employees to the U.S. as interns. After spending a year or so training in the U.S., they returned to their home countries with engineering design skills and to jobs with higher pay.

Jet air cargo was an important factor in the global spread of electronic manufacturing, just as freight transport by steamship a century earlier had made heavy manufacturing global. Seagate soon came to control a third of Singapore air cargo traffic, giving it priority over its Singapore competitors. Tom could ship drives quickly by air when demand was high. When drive sales slowed he shipped them by sea from Singapore's tariff free port. "Storing drives on ships in transit," he said, "costs less than air freight and adds no U.S. inventory cost to store them. To delay is to win."

Seagate also started a division in Ireland to do drive component manufacturing in Europe. It wasn't initially successful, ironic because magnetic recording had been invented by a Dane in Europe in 1898, and exhibited at the Paris Exposition in 1900 as the first telephone answering machine. The British had made major early inventions in digital magnetic recording, but no longer manufactured products.

But when Ireland's religious strife finally eased, high tech manufacturing began to blossom there. Irish tech industries grew increasingly successful, leading to higher living standards that increased pressures for peace.

28.

A Two Airplane Family

Shirley and Gordon's L.A. friends stopped by to visit them in their first year in Boulder Creek, but few returned for a second visit. Boulder Creek was too far from civilization. Aside from a few neighbors, there wasn't much to do in the valley for city folks like them. Gordon suggested Shirley get interested in some activity over the hill in the Bay Area.

"Let's enroll you in a weekend course in airplane piloting at Concord Airport. It's intended for spouses of pilots, to teach them how to fly and land a plane if the pilot becomes incapacitated." Gordon's plot was to get Shirley started on earning her pilot license. From their ski trips together he knew she loved taking lessons, but he also knew if he confessed his plot she might think she couldn't successfully complete pilot training.

He had mentioned the idea in an offhand way a year before and she had turned it down. She had said, "If I started taking flying lessons I know I could never learn to land the Mooney, and even if I did I could never imagine soloing any airplane, or passing the pilot written test, much less the flying test."

Gordon signed her up for the weekend course in airplane piloting. They flew the Mooney to Concord Airport and took a room at the airport hotel. Gordon met with the flight instructor who would teach Shirley how to fly the Mooney. He was Bill, a FAA-licensed flight instructor from San Diego who owned a Mooney himself.

"Bill, I'll tell you what I'm up to but please don't tell Shirley. Here's the deal. Don't spend time teaching her how to tune radios or navigate. Just teach her takeoffs and landings. Teach her to make successful landings. If you can do that I can convince her to start her pilot training."

"O.K. Gordon, that'll be no problem. I'm sure she'll do fine."

Gordon sat by the hotel pool during the weekend, listening on a hand-held radio tuned to the airport tower. Late Sunday afternoon he heard her call the tower to request another landing and he picked up binoculars to try and spot her. She landed the plane perfectly. As darkness approached an hour later, she taxied back into the airplane parking area near where Gordon sat. Her radiant smile lit the way.

Shirley began her flight lessons a week later with a flight instructor at the local Watsonville Airport, in the smallest Cessna, the 152. Gordon's initial flight training decades earlier in L.A. had been in a similar Cessna 152. She soloed without difficulty, passed her private pilot written test with a perfect score, and got her license. She took Mooney transition lessons and qualified for her "complex airplane" FAA license endorsement. Gordon thought they were finished, and they alternated piloting the Mooney on trips together.

Shirley began suggesting they visit various nearby airports with used Cessna 172 airplanes for sale. She wanted to be able to fly while Gordon was at work and she thought the Mooney was too complex a plane to safely fly without him on board. Gordon dutifully inspected each Cessna 172, pointing out its particular faults. "This one is too old; that one was used as a training plane and its engine is nearly worn out; this one has poor radios..."

One day he discovered that his detailed descriptions of specific airplane flaws had been a mistake, when he finished attending a workshop at the Center for Magnetic Recording Research at the University of California at San Diego. At the workshop he had learned about an IBM breakthrough in digital data read channels, called maximum likelihood bit detection. Bits could be packed closer together on discs using the new technology, allowing higher data capacity at the same drive manufacturing cost. Data read channel chips already had complex circuitry and changing the bit detection circuitry hardly added a penny to the chip cost. These lectures would be pivotal in alerting Seagate to this new technology in time to design competitive products using it. Maximum likelihood bit reading technology would quickly become used in all drives.

Carrying their luggage out to their Mooney to fly back to San Jose after the workshop, he saw Shirley and her Concord flight instructor Bill standing next to a Cessna 172 parked nearby. She proceeded to demonstrate that this 172 was free of every fault Gordon had found in other 172s. She held up a purchase contract. Trapped, he nodded that it was O.K. to sign it and buy the plane.

They became a two-plane family. Shirley earned her instrument rating in it to the universal praise of Gordon and her friends. She joined the woman's flying group, the 99's founded by Amelia Earhart. That gave her many new friends, who flew to a different airport every month for lunch.

29.

Stamping Springs

Gordon and Stern were called into Tom's office one morning.
"Now that we're assembling our recording heads in Singapore, their cost has dropped so low that their flexures are their most expensive component," Tom told them.

"You engineers have qualified only a single vendor in Minnesota to make our flexures, and they refuse to drop the price below $3.00 each. That's more than half the cost of a finished head now. I've hired Smithy's company in Silicon Valley to design and build a pilot production line for us so we can make flexures ourselves. I want you two to make sure Smithy's line will qualify for drive production."

"That's clear, Tom," Gordon replied. "We'll have Smithy install the line downstairs in my engineering building where we can monitor it closely. Stern and I will go visit his company today."

They drove over Highway 17 to Smithy's plant in Silicon Valley, and met with him to discuss how to proceed. Gordon made one demand. "You're talking about using personal computers to control your production line. I must insist you use professional process control computers, not consumer PCs. Professional computers can withstand electrical power surges that will crash or kill a consumer PC." He was remembering the 600 ton stamping press job with Pete in Walden, New York.

Driving back to Seagate, Gordon said, "Stern, this may turn out to be our 'Project from Hell.'"

"What do you mean?"

"You'll see soon enough." Gordon craned his neck to the right to see a little further around a curve that they were approaching, a frequent multiple-pileup accident scene.

A few months later, Smithy's men installed their flexure manufacturing machines on the first floor of Gordon's engineering building. Paper thin stainless steel sheets a yard square were fed into one machine to be cut into hundreds of tiny triangular steel pieces, which were stamped into final shape by the next machine. They were spot welded to smaller flexure pieces by a third machine and the completed flexures were heated and measured by a final machine until their spring force was precisely correct.

Gordon watched the installation with Smithy and Stern. "I see your process control computers came in boxes with pictures of a happy family looking at the computer under their Christmas tree. You ignored my request not to use consumer PCs."

Smithy levelly replied, "I take my orders from Tom, not you."

"If you don't want advice from us, I'll say only this. You and Tom better pray for your line to work. It's certainly not going to without a miracle." As Gordon left, he noticed that Smithy had set up a temporary office near his line, directly beneath Gordon's magnet upstairs. *Should I tell him a four ton magnet is hanging over his head?*

Gordon didn't need to go downstairs often to check Smithy's progress as he tried to make his line operational over the following weeks. In his office upstairs, Gordon could hear its cutting machine make a "poketa" sound as each sheet was cut into flexure triangles. He would hear "poketa, poketa, poketa" for a few minutes, and then a "queep" sound as the machine jammed or its computer crashed. There would be silence for a time as Smithy's engineers cleared the jam, made adjustments, and he would finally hear another sequence of "poketa, poketa, poketa, poketa, queep." The sounds reminded Gordon of the complex and unreliable machine in the *New Yorker Magazine* 1942 story by James Thurber, "The Secret Life of Walter Mitty."

A month went by and Tom became impatient, ordering Gordon and Stern back to his office "I want you two to personally fix Smithy's flexure line and make it work. And I won't accept failure." Stern blanched. He knew it was far too late for any simple fixes for the multiple problems Smithy had designed into his machines.

"O.K. Tom," Gordon replied, "but please don't wait until we get it working. Call our Minnesota flexure vender and invite them to come here to discuss price. Show them the line with its process control instructions posted on the building walls. Stern and I will be using extra thin steel sheets on the line to diagnose the technical problems and the machines won't be jamming while they're here. I bet they'll immediately drop their $3.00 price by half to make it uneconomical for you to put your flexure line into volume production. They won't know that Smithy's process can't actually make head flexures."

Tom smiled. "I'll do just that."

Gordon and Stern walked back to their building. Gordon said, "Do you realize that I just rescued both of us from a fatal trap? Smithy will get paid for his flexure line whether it works or not. Tom only made a handshake deal with him. He let Smithy write up the purchase contract. You and I had no opportunity to write Seagate engineering approval requirements into the contract. It only specifies delivery of the machines to Scotts Valley. Remember we sent Smithy an acceptance spec and asked him to sign it? He sent it back with a handwritten note: 'No thanks.' Smithy has been trying to make his line work, but he'll insist on payment even if it doesn't. We'll get the blame for its failure, not Smithy."

"But that junky production line will never make flexures in volume! Smithy designed those machines that jam so often, Gordon, we didn't! We'd have to start over from scratch!"

"Unfortunately, none of that matters. When Tom put us under marching orders to make the line work, we became responsible for the project, not Smithy. Once its failure becomes undeniable, Doug might not be able to prevent Tom from firing us.

"You remember the Silicon Valley 'Project from Hell' story, don't you? An ignorant manager starts an impossible project and orders his engineers to succeed at it or be fired. The engineers know it's going to fail, and carefully plan to get themselves reassigned one week before the milestone demonstration to the company president. The project gets reassigned to you and you get the full blame for a failed project you only worked on one week. Well, this would have been our 'Project from Hell.' Smithy would walk away with the money and you and I might get fired."

"But Smithy shouldn't get paid for junk machines that'll never work and we shouldn't get the blame!"

"Stern, even if they did work, Seagate will never use them to manufacture flexures. It's far more cost effective to buy our flexures from outside vendors."

"That's only true if Tom can keep lowering flexure prices, but how can he do that? This whole project got started because we have only one flexure vendor."

"Let's give ourselves an assignment, Stern. You and I will qualify a second flexure vendor by the end of this year. We'll second-source a high volume flexure, one that has been in our production drives the longest. That will be the easiest, lowest-tech flexure for another company to make. And let's qualify an Asian company with lower costs than our

Minnesota flexure friends. Second-sourcing a high volume flexure in Asia will give Tom the lowest possible price."

"So we'll only use our Minnesota vendor for new high-tech drive flexures? And Tom will accept their higher cost because he can sell those drives at higher prices?"

"That's right, Stern. Tom will never admit that any higher cost part is O.K., but he'll accept it because he can keep pressuring Minnesota on price, with a second supplier breathing down their necks."

And so it turned out that a failed flexure pilot production line got Tom what he really wanted: flexures for $1.75 and heading down.

30.

Factory Failures Help New Product Design

Gordon was musing on how pleasantly quiet his office was, now that the "poketa, poketa, queep" noise was gone from the background. The quiet was broken only by the buzz of occasional scouts from a wasp hive hanging on the outside wall of his office. They had found an opening into the roof and into his office but he was reluctant to ask to have the nest removed because the hive was outdoors in its natural element where it belonged.

"Gordon, I just got back from Singapore and I found something you need to know," said Ron "Mr. Clean," sticking his head into Gordon's office.

"I just got back from checking the Singapore clean rooms I installed three months ago, and I found all their air flow fans had been turned off because the breezes bothered the drive assemblers. Incredible! I fixed the fans and taught their managers how important they were.

"But what I came to tell you is that I discovered their managers are hiding the truth about their production yield losses and their scrapped parts, from Seagate's U.S. executives. They put their scrap in a special room and they plaster over its door when visitors from Seagate U.S. show up, like Tom. The door looks like a wall and visitors don't know anything is there. Inside the door is a stark, plain, windowless room, filled wall to wall and floor to ceiling with scrap motors, scrap heads, and scrap drives."

Gordon immediately realized this was a critical problem that Seagate had to quickly fix because Silicon Valley companies often used a unique and risky method to get new products to market faster than their competitors: *simultaneous product design and manufacturing.*

Seagate was dominated by a manufacturing culture and often attempted to build new drives before its engineers were finished testing their design. Tom liked to say, "Seagate production workers sitting in the factory are being paid by the hour so they may as well be assembling low yield drives as not working at all. If too few drives work I can call in Doug's engineers to find and fix the problems."

Normal technology companies had their engineers first design a new product and initially test their design by building small quantities of drives using hand assembly. After the design was finalized, manufacturing tooled up to manufacture the product. A pilot line manufacturing process was tested for yield at low volume and then slowly ramped to full scale production at high volume.

Silicon Valley people disdainfully called that slow and careful method the "East Coast way" and often attempted to perform all these steps simultaneously. Tom called it "simultaneous product manufacturing, sales, and revenue." He never included the engineering design process unless to remark that "engineers are just profit delayers."

This method carried risk of expensive failure, of course. If thousands of drives per day were manufactured and many failed their final tests, millions of dollars of scrap drives could rapidly be produced.

Why take such expensive risks? Because the first company to market a drive with higher data storage capacity and higher data access speed could set a higher sales price. It had no competition at that point. When a second manufacturer also achieved volume on a similar product, price competition immediately dropped both companies' profits below levels necessary to finance R&D of their next drive product. Even a few months of being first-to-volume could produce significant profits, because product lifetimes were less than a year.

Of course, a product manufacturing ramp to high volume could simply fail. Seagate would then abandon that drive model and have its engineers completely focus on design work for their next drive. Meanwhile, their successful competitor's engineers would be occupied with fixing their own alligator production problems instead of designing their next drive, and they might miss the next product marketing window. Seagate might be able to take that window instead.

This risky process also reduced the number of competing companies because few were willing to take such expensive risks, particularly East Coast and Asian companies. As Doug put it, "Fear, uncertainty, and doubt are our friend 'FUD.' Technology chaos and FUD keep the big Japanese companies from competing with us. Otherwise, they'd use their profits from selling cars and televisions to make drives that compete with ours, even if they lost money on them. FUD keeps everyone on a level playing field."

Seagate's "cowboy company" production ramps could only succeed through exceptional management skill, in both technology and in business. Doug's engineering vice president Stan was critical. He had an uncanny sense of precisely what the chances of failure would be if he prematurely put a new design into production.

Stan also knew when his engineers were beyond the point where pilot line testing of a hundred drives per day was no longer effective in exposing hidden design flaws. He knew when only high volume builds could force remaining latent problems to surface. Even sensible "East Coast" production ramps carried some risk of failure, from unforeseen manufacturing or business problems.

To beat the competition, Stan and Doug made risk decisions to ramp production up to thousands of drives a day if they were certain that production final test had 100% effective screens to prevent any drive from shipping to a customer if it had any possible reliability problems.

A critical reason Seagate usually succeeded at simultaneous product design and manufacturing was that Stan required his engineers to design a new higher performance disc drive by making the fewest possible changes to a high volume product already in production, thereby minimizing technology risk. This wouldn't have been accepted at a normal engineering-dominated technology company because engineers enjoy designing and redesigning. Seagate had to accept the price of only allowing incremental technology developments, not breakthroughs.

Watching this in action, Gordon saw several critical factors. Valuable design lessons were quickly learned from the failed drives. Design problems could be found and corrected faster than with the East Coast method, which could leave them hidden until production finally ramped. Burning up to a million dollars a month manufacturing drives that failed final test also produced extreme pressure to try extreme solutions, which somehow worked more often than chance should have allowed. In Gordon's aerospace job on Minuteman ICBMs, he had seen people under pressure sometimes cheating around the edges of reality, bending the laws of space and time a bit to shift problems to make them solvable, providing outsiders didn't watch too closely.

Silicon Valley didn't invent the idea of simultaneous product design and manufacturing. One historic American government project had been so urgent that it simultaneously ran research, engineering, and production: the mammoth World War II Manhattan Project that created the first atomic bombs.

Gordon was discussing a new drive design with Paul and several engineers from Paul's head and disc product engineering group. "We've only got a month to get this design finalized before Tom gets on my boss Stan's case," Paul said, concluding the meeting. "Let's not waste time doing this the East Coast way."

Gordon and Paul were chatting after the meeting ended. "Did you know that the East Coast way actually refers to DEC?" Gordon asked.

DEC was the Digital Equipment Corporation, the Massachusetts company that first mass produced minicomputers. Their man-size minicomputers replaced the original room-size mainframe computers, just as minicomputers would be replaced in time by PCs. DEC was a textbook business success of an engineering-culture technology company, headed by the legendary Ken Olsen and Gordon Bell.

Gordon continued, "DEC's culture was engineering dominated, the opposite of our manufacturing culture. DEC had a company culture of flat-out blunt arguments among its technology managers. Olsen encouraged and participated in those arguments. Their culture encouraged intense discussions on running a technology business, and for anyone complaining about a problem to take responsibility for solving it. That's where Seagate gets the similar technology-honest culture we have here. The difference is that engineering ruled DEC and manufacturing rules here. DEC engineers were in charge, not its manufacturing people."

"It's not quite the same, Gordon. Our CEO Al never raises his voice. Doug doesn't either."

"What about Tom? Look how well bellowing works for him. And Al won't tolerate a closed mind or an untruth, the same as the DEC founders." Both of them knew that beneath Al's gentleman manners was a layer of steel.

Seagate's time-to-market-volume culture rejected the DEC rational engineering business model as obsolete, but it kept DEC's technology-honest management model. Seagate's company culture was to also squarely face technology problems with stubborn honesty. Its founders knew that technology worked or failed according to scientific laws which couldn't be begged, ignored, bought off, or denied away.

Gordon called this culture the Seagate Way, and told newly hired engineers that the difficult problems they faced also made their jobs necessary, and because the problems were factual they could always be ultimately solved. Unlike politics where everything was a matter of opinion, no amount of denial would allow exceptions to the laws of physics.

Paul thought for a few moments and said, "I think the big difference between DEC and Seagate is we have aggressive competition in our business. When DEC introduced its first minicomputers it had no competitors, and it dominated the few that later arose. We have to move far faster than DEC did or our competition would kill us. That's why we reject the East Coast way."

"I think you're right, Paul. It's too bad this pattern of business model successions in the history of computer technology is so little understood. When major computer business innovators like IBM's T.J Watson, DEC's Olsen and Bell, and our Al leave the scene, a lot of history leaves with them. Books are written only on one leader or another, or they puzzle over why disruptive companies like DEC and Seagate could possibly fail over a trivial technology shift like a disc size reduction.

"DEC's engineering-consensus culture ultimately became their undoing. They reverse-engineered IBM 14-inch disc drives for minicomputer data storage, like we later miniaturized them for PCs. Those 14-inch drives were just the right size to fit in the frames of DEC's minicomputer products, and they knew it would be crazy to make drives with smaller discs because they store less data. Customers want to store more data, not less. But when PCs began as smaller computers sized for desktops, there was only enough space for the 5.25-inch floppy disc drives first mass produced for the Apple II. Our first hard disc had to be the same size as the floppy it replaced. That's where its 5.25-inch disc diameter comes from. When PCs evolved into serious computers and became wildly popular, DEC's highly successful VAX minicomputers were doomed. DEC was unable to adapt to the disruptive new PC technology and the company faded and died, its minicomputers becoming museum exhibits. "

"So why couldn't they just shift to make 5.25-inch drives and PCs, Gordon?"

"They were unable to adapt to the PC technology shift because the original toy-like PCs initially made no business sense either to DEC or to its customers. They were trapped in their minicomputer business model and ignored the Apple II and IBM PC business. Meanwhile, a new chain of customers, drive component suppliers, and salesmen grew in the lower cost PC market. The sales part of this chain is a critical factor that's usually ignored. A DEC salesman making a handsome commission on a $150,000 VAX sale isn't interested in working very hard to sell $500 PCs.

"When PCs grew powerful and DEC's customers suddenly shifted to buy them, it was too late for DEC to shift with them. The new PC market players dominated their low cost supplier, sales, and customer chain, just as DEC dominated its minicomputer business chain. Business researchers have studied these technology disruptions but don't seem to have seen that the shifts from 14-inch to 5.25-inch to 3.5-inch discs were merely signals that a new computer market had evolved which needed the next smaller disc size. These were business market disruptions, not company technology disruptions."

Seagate had become the new Cinderella in a half-century succession of disc drive technology companies, by fitting the glass slipper of the newest computer business market. Barreling into the computer marketplace then dominated by soon-ugly sisters like DEC, Seagate's drive sales soared along with its stock. Seagate would soon face a challenge equal to DEC's: to change its corporate culture from high volume and low cost manufacturing, to also emphasize high-tech R&D. It would also have to face the next disc size reduction.

Gordon and Ron both realized the Singapore secret scrap room could be fatal.

"Gordon, you have engineering responsibility for Seagate's heads, and letting Singapore managers hide drive yield failures due to head problems will prevent Seagate from fixing them."

"Ron, our Singapore production managers are Chinese, and I think maybe they aren't aware of simultaneous product design and manufacturing. Perhaps they believe they'll be blamed for the scrap parts. The obvious solution is to put some experienced Silicon Valley production managers in the Singapore plants. But there's a hitch. Singapore manufacturing reports directly to Tom. I have no direct authority."

That left Gordon with no choice but to go to Tom with the problem. Gordon feared the possible consequences as he walked across the Seagate campus to Tom's office. He had no desire to be yelled at.

Gordon walked in a fugue past the flag poles, fountain, and reflecting pond in front of Seagate's headquarters building at #920 Disc Drive. He barely noticed the Marine Corp battalion flag flying on one pole, a little below the American flag on another pole but above the California flag on the third pole. A pool sweeper was cleaning the fountain with a water vacuum. "Who gets the coins?" he mindlessly asked the sweeper as he walked by.

"Why, I get them...but I do grant wishes," the sweeper instantly replied.

Gordon brightened, figuring he could tell Tom that story before giving him the bad news.

He walked into Tom's corner office. Tom had recently been promoted to company president, Al remaining as CEO.

"Come on in, Gordon. Pour yourself a cup of coffee and sit down."

After telling Tom the pool sweeper story and explaining why Tom needed to send U.S. manufacturing managers permanently to Singapore, Tom was still smiling. Gordon relaxed. *Whew! It worked!*

Tom's phone rang. It was a Seagate marketing vice president calling from Korea.

The man's voice boomed from Tom's speaker phone. "BIG drive sales prospects here, Tom!" He named several Korean companies and then said "Goodbye!"

"Wait," Tom replied. "There's something else you need to say before you end a phone call to your company president."

"What's that?" boomed from the speaker phone.

"You need to ask to be transferred to the order desk so you can deliver the orders for the actual drives you have sold in Korea." All three laughed because marketing handles strategic planning; the sales department handles actual drive orders. But Gordon could see that behind Tom's laughter he wasn't looking happy at all. *Tom may know about some Seagate financial difficulty that he can't tell the rest of us about.*

Tom soon found several excellent U.S. production managers willing to move to Singapore as expatriates. Within a few months they became trusted friends and allies of the Singaporeans and the cultural problems vanished. Tom became so pleased with his success in Singapore that he opened another recording head assembly operation in Manila. This Philippine factory wasn't quite as successful as in Singapore. The factory building was leased from one of Ferdinand Marcos' cronies, a man who also controlled Seagate's Manila banking. Most everything went through Marcos or his cronies in those days.

Stern came into Gordon's office one day with news that Seagate had to send a second payroll deposit to pay its Manila workers that week, after the crony disappeared with the first deposit. He had apparently used it to flee the country, following Marcos.

31.

The Seagate Way

Gordon wanted to teach the "teamwork or die" philosophy to new engineers he hired, and he wrote a short memo that he printed on his VAX minicomputer, titled "The Seagate Way:"

THE SEAGATE WAY

The following is a collection of Seagate attitude and corporate culture that I sometimes give to new employees, to help acclimatize them. No attempt is made to give individual credit for them (see topics below: "Success has many fathers", and "Sneak around behind someone").

OPEN COMPANY

All employees should try to keep up with what's going on; what the products and projects are; and what the corporate "marching orders" are.

Each professional is entitled to know the "why" of his job. He is entitled to ask questions of anyone necessary, including the president. We all help run Seagate together.

It's better to take a small chance of loosing some secrecy by talking together, than to isolate Seagate into small non-communicating groups.

However, follow reasonable security precautions; mark and treat confidential documents as such; destroy them with the shredders; erase blackboards with sensitive information; and use the Project and Customer code names.

Communicate the literal unembellished facts to technical and management people; and do so as courteously as possible. Examples:

problem "bad news" is told best when told with a hint of how to overcome the problem. No grousing and complaining for its own sake; only to get necessary corrective action. Be specific and detailed.

Sneak around behind someone's back...and when he isn't looking... do him a favor. Help him in some way. If discovered, give someone else the credit.

On not getting credit for a good idea: remember that "Success has many fathers, but failure is an orphan". For example, a common way someone "signs up" for an idea is to become its father. That's why successful ideas have so many fathers. If most of us in act in these ways, even if some others don't, they may finally "sign up" also.

Corollary—The 'Perceived Fairness' Doctrine: everyone is willing to work hard doing their share of making Seagate run: management, professionals and support people together. This includes working overtime and some weekend days. Conversely, professionals working overtime expect their time to be necessary to the bottom line. This works best if they are allowed to know the facts and the business issues involved.

SMARTEST PERSON WINS
We are all confident enough of our own intelligence to encourage and accept advice and information from anyone: Engineer, manager, secretary, president, janitor. They all have their tales to tell.

No single group has the corner on "wisdom and virtue." Other groups do not operate out of "ignorance and malice." Beware of unconscious habits that might give others this impression (adopt a mental attitude that everyone has something worthwhile to say). Corollary—Eagles, but turkeys too: We are so smart that we can (courteously) do "smartest person wins" in the real world; where people are imperfect (even eagles are turkeys sometimes).

Any persons' activity benefits from a "design review", and so we seek and are openly willing to discuss our methods, data, and rationale with others. The smartest person has the numbers and the data. Someone who has only opinions is not, unless he can find legitimate fault with the numbers.

A person who resists requests for a design review, or who hides behind generalities or secrecy is not the "smartest person." If that person is thereby preventing the solution to design or production problems, he is not an adequate Seagate employee.

THINK SMALL
Presume you are personally running Seagate and it's your money. This is a truism of course, but that simply means that it is true. Spend when it helps reliable, low cost drives ship to customers; and watch pennies, too. Bargain with vendors, and give purchasing enough leeway to bargain. Borrow things. Share equipment. Buy from the local hardware store.

Do not make the reverse error of not spending money when it is correct to spend.

Minimize meetings and their attendance: the opposite of "meeting" is "working."

HANDS-ON PEOPLE
Professionals, including managers, can and do operate virtually all the instruments in their department. They know the technical details; they know the basics of the products we make. They know the current development and production disc drives, their components, and their virtues and problems in detail and on sight.

DON'T JUST STAND THERE, DO SOMETHING ("The Marines")
Seagate makes decisions—redesigns drives—recovers from problems: within days, using whatever information is available. If the information is negative enough, or the decisions are wrong enough, projects are stopped or cancelled.

Professionals foresee design and manufacturing problems far enough in advance to carry out any required long-term R&D; active design and manufacturing projects cannot wait for it.

People who merely react to immediate problems rather than foreseeing them, cannot reasonably ask for an R&D program to solve the problems (see "Smartest Person Wins," above).

SIMULTANEOUS ENGINEERING AND PRODUCTION
A corollary to Pareto's law (that the last 20% of any project takes 80% of the time and resources): when a Seagate drive is 80% designed and passes DVT, the last 80% of the design engineering process takes place on the production line.

Production parts-people-processes-problems are different from those in an engineering lab. Vendors redesign the parts and tooling, when ramping up into quantity production. Customers will discover problems in drive qualification programs.

Corollary: when a drive leaves the "customer evaluation" stage, production screens must be certain to catch bad drives, or drives must be sequestered until reliability and engineering analysis proves they are of shippable quality.

32.

Genetic DNA Recording Discs

"Gordon, please stop by my office when convenient," Finis asked over the phone. "I'd like you to analyze a new recording disc technology." Gordon walked across Disc Drive to Finis' office, passing the flagpoles and reflecting pond in front of the Seagate headquarters building. There was no pool sweeper this time, just a scattering of small coins in the water. Only the American and California flags were flying.

"I've had a call from Genentech, Gordon. They're suggesting we talk to them about a new recording media using bacteriorhodopsin. I'm not a scientist like you, but they tell me it's a biological material that the human eye uses to turn light into electrical pulses on the optic nerve."

"Of course, Finis. I'll visit them and give you a report." The next day, Gordon drove to Genentech's campus just south of San Francisco. He met a manager named Alan who walked him through the plant. Gordon saw massive cylindrical stainless steel vats.

"I thought I'd only see test tube size samples of pharmaceutical stuff like Interferon."

Alan laughed. "We think big here, Gordon. Those are vats of synthetic whey. When we start large scale manufacturing next year, we'll revolutionize the dairy business." Gordon was intrigued and impressed. If he had thought a little more deeply he might have bought Genentech stock and made a pile of money.

"I'm wondering where you do the recombinant DNA research, Alan. You know, the sealed labs with air lock doors, so mutant DNA can't escape and start a San Francisco epidemic."

Alan laughed again. "You're looking at it on these lab benches all around you. The worry-wart scientists and politicians have it all wrong. There's no risk in recombinant DNA research."

"I hope you're right," Gordon replied. A movie image of Godzilla destroying a city flashed in his mind.

They spent the next hour in a conference room with Genentech researchers explaining how bacteriorhodopsin might be used to store computer data, replacing the magnetic recording discs the drive industry had always used. "Have you ever looked at the salt flats at the south end of San Francisco bay, as you take off in an airplane from San Jose?"

Gordon replied, "Yeah. Some of them are very colorful, purple or yellow."

"Bacteriorhodopsin makes those colors. Its molecule can be twisted by an incoming light beam into either of two shapes, which reflect light as two different colors, purple or yellow. One color state could represent a zero binary bit and the other a one bit. It's optical recording instead of magnetic. We have a large scale process to coat disc platters with bacteriorhodopsin, which could replace the magnetic brown paint you now use."

They spent the rest of the hour discussing how to make and use optical light beams to write and read bits, and then Alan said, "Let's stop. It's time for our regular Friday party."

The group walked to the company cafeteria where a party was in full swing, complete with wine and beer. Gordon looked at his watch and saw it was only 3 pm. He had never known any company that allowed liquor on its premises during working hours.

At the party room Alan had to raise his voice for Gordon to hear him over the many laughing conversations. "We have this party every Friday to reward our employees for voluntarily working 70 hour weeks. Of course, it helps that they all know they'll someday make a load of money from their stock options. A lot of Silicon Valley startup companies have Friday parties like this."

Gordon sent Finis and Doug a technical memo on Seagate's prospects in using these optical discs. With the knowledge he had gained at the Arrowhead Workshop, he was able to demonstrate that optical recording was limited by the wavelength of the light beams. Magnetic recording on cobalt discs would allow continued increases in data capacity per disc without any such light physics limitations. Bits on magnetic discs would soon become far smaller than bits on optical discs, allowing a hundred times more data to be stored on each magnetic disc. He explained that future optical disc drives would be unlikely to use bacteriorhodopsin media because it would be more expensive than inorganic alternatives, and the molecules might switch colors inadvertently.

33.

Victory in the Real Estate War

Borland Computer was well respected by the world's computer software community, first because of the company's popular Turbo Pascal and C++ programming languages; later because of the war Borland CEO Philippe Kahn fought for programmers' rights and open standards. Lotus 1-2-3 had established spreadsheet software as a popular data calculation tool for PCs, and Lotus had sued Borland over its Quattro Pro spreadsheet package. Borland's open standards approach won in court against Lotus' proprietary development approach. Computer users everywhere cheered Borland. It also became loved for its "no hassle" software license that allowed its customers to install Borland software on unlimited numbers of computers, provided they used only one at a time. The company was seen as being on the side of the individual programmer, and Borland's software products were considered elegant, fast and bug-free.

The Scotts Valley real estate war between Borland and Seagate finally came to an end with Borland capitulating. Borland bought Santa's Village at the far end of Scotts Valley. This was a defunct old tourist stop that used to have Santa and Mrs. Claus, elves and gnomes, and a baby animal petting zoo. It had become outdated and had closed.

Borland set out to build itself a new campus there, constructing a colossal high-rise headquarters building. Gordon figured such hubris would court disaster sooner or later. Hubris was an ancient Greek belief that when a man strived to imitate the Gods they would soon strike him down.

Soon enough, Borland was hit by a business cycle downturn that caused a revenue shortfall. A major portion of Borland's business was selling software to improve the functionality of Microsoft Windows, database software in particular. Borland floundered after Microsoft took aim at it and went after the Windows database business itself. Microsoft built Borland's features into its own software products.

Borland ran out of money and credit before completing its new campus. Its charismatic founder Philippe Kahn left the company. Famous for playing his saxophone at Borland parties while wearing a Roman toga, he had even recorded and produced music CDs at company expense, distributing them to Borland customers. Kahn was one of Al's favorite examples of the importance of having fun in Silicon Valley high pressure companies.

Philippe Kahn left Borland but he had only temporarily stumbled. He soon reappeared with a new successful startup company, Starfish Software. He built that one up and sold it to Motorola. Then he founded LightSurf to exploit his invention of the cell phone camera.

Borland finally finished its headquarters high rise and found a new successful business software model, although it took many years.

34.

Mega-bricks and the CIA Lady

When Gordon had flown Kermit over the Santa Cruz sequoia forests on Kermit's first visit to Seagate, Kermit had indeed become hooked on the area. As soon as he moved to Santa Cruz he began a habit of taking weekend hikes through the forests. He especially enjoyed the stands of old-growth redwood, Douglas fir, and tan oak redwoods in Big Basin Redwoods State Park and the Henry Cowell redwood grove. He had taken Gordon on several of these hikes. Gordon's favorite began at Henry Cowell state park and followed the abandoned railroad line that had taken redwood trees timbered a century before, from the San Lorenzo Valley to Santa Cruz to ship. The line had continued to run as a tourist train until a major winter storm washed it out.

"So where did you hike to last weekend, Kermit?" Gordon and Kermit were standing in the lobby of the main engineering building waiting for a visitor to arrive.

"I drove to Roaring Camp and hiked down the tracks of the old logging railroad, through the redwood groves to Santa Cruz. I had an ice cream cone at the boardwalk and then hiked back to my car."

"Did you see any banana slugs?" Gordon teased. These tiny yellow worms were the mascot of the nearby University of California at Santa Cruz, whose athletes wore T-shirts labeled "Fighting Banana Slugs" and "Banana Slugs-No Known Predators."

"Sure. There's always a few hiding under bushes."

"What's that in the display case, Kermit?" The glass exhibit case in the lobby normally contained examples of Seagate's drives.

"It looks like a plain red brick wrapped in shipping paper."

"That's exactly what it is, Gordon. It's a Mega-brick disc drive from the MiniScribe Company."

Gordon knew MiniScribe had been a Seagate competitor in Longmont, Colorado. It had gone bankrupt in the last big disc drive business bust after loosing a large contract to supply drives to IBM.

"I remember they were being pressured by Q. T. Wiles to ship products so they could book sales revenue. He was a turnaround man their venture capital company asked them to hire, and he was pushing them by phone from his home in L.A. He blundered by not going to MiniScribe in person. When MiniScribe told him that drives couldn't be shipped because the company was going bankrupt and its drive design engineers had been laid off, Wiles insisted they ship anyway."

"That's right, Gordon. He wasn't there to personally watch them so they followed his orders by wrapping and shipping bricks. Their accountants booked revenue the company would never receive. Wiles was later prosecuted and convicted of securities fraud. This display is one of those historic write-only Mega-brick drives!"

Calling it a "write-only" drive was an engineer's takeoff joke on "read-only" CD-ROM drives: if you could never read any data stored in a Mega-brick drive, it didn't matter that data was never written in it. Laughing, Gordon thought about the many ways startup companies could fail, and that Seagate's continued survival and success was due to Al and Doug's culture of blunt technology honesty as much as its smart people.

An hour later they finished with the visitor, and Gordon walked back to his office for an appointment he had with the U.S. Central Intelligence Agency. His secretary soon escorted in a formal looking woman wearing a tailored gray business suit and flat black shoes. Her hair was done up in a severely formal bun. She stood in front of Gordon's desk and handed him her business card. Gordon wondered what she would look like with her hair down.

"Please have a seat. Would you like a cup of coffee or a soft drink? No?" Gordon got up from his desk to sit opposite her at the conference table in the middle of his office.

"When you called to make an appointment you said you were with the CIA, but your card says you work for a business supply company and there's no address or phone number on it."

Ignoring his questions, the woman said, "I've come to interview you on Seagate's global operations." Gordon remembered that CIA people were extremely secretive. They collected information but little came out without a "need-to-know." CIA information was one-way: everything came in but little went out.

"I'm afraid I won't be able to discuss Seagate's global operations without knowing the purpose."

She took a book the size of a telephone directory out of her briefcase and handed it to Gordon. He saw it was a guidebook of facts about the world's countries; their population, geography, politics and economies.

"The U.S. Congress finds these yearly guidebooks one of our Agency's most valuable products."

Gordon looked over the book and asked, "So there's no classified information in here?"

"Our Agency employs 50,000 people to scan the world's newspapers and daily communications. You would be surprised how many hidden operations can be pieced together from unclassified bits of information."

I wonder if the CIA still has any old-fashioned secret agents and spies, but I suppose I better not ask her. He had noticed the capital letter in her voice whenever she referred to her Agency.

"Couldn't your Agency just contract with commercial newspaper clipping companies to do that?" Gordon was wondering what U.S. taxpayers might think of the cost if they knew about the army of clippers instead of spies.

"Perhaps, but government employment offers us better salaries and benefits than if we worked for private companies."

She proceeded to ask Gordon questions about Seagate's operations in Singapore, Manila, and Japan. An hour later, she had never once said "CIA."

As Gordon walked her back to the building lobby, he asked, "Please send me a copy of the report you write on Seagate."

"That report will be classified, but you can get a copy of our yearly guidebook directly from the Government Printing Office." Gordon could only shake his head in wonder as he walked back to his office after she left. *People in Washington, D.C. sure live in a different universe than the rest of us Americans.*

He later read that only a few percent of CIA employees were covert spies, far outnumbered by the 50,000 news clippers.

35.

Finis Invents Another Smaller Disc Drive

Finis left Seagate in early 1985, beginning intermittent departures of its founders. He now owned a four-engine Lockheed Jet Star business aircraft and an eponymous business at San Jose Airport to park it at. Al owned a Learjet (only two jet engines!), and also parked it there. Gordon's Mooney airplane was parked there as well, making him a smaller-fish Finis tenant. He wanted to get a hanger at the airport but the waiting list was 20 years long.

Finis doubled Al's airplane parking rent after leaving Seagate. (Successful business leaders love competitive games.) Al countered by buying an airplane business at Monterey Airport and moving his Lear there, even though the deal required him to take on several other planes and several extra pilot employees he didn't need. Loosing Al's rent money hurt profits in Finis' airport business, but it was normal for wealthy men with jet airplanes and jet businesses to make little or no profit. They liked the tax deductions. One of the Apple Computer founders had earlier established an aviation business like Finis', A.C. Markkula with his ACM Aviation that served business jets at the same airport. Al soon had two jets at Monterey and an 18-hole miniature golf course on his Pebble Beach estate.

After leaving Seagate, Finis demonstrated a rare ability to actually *be* rich. In Gordon's practical engineering way of thinking, company founders weren't really rich while still working the long hours necessary to keep their employee's morale high. Billions of dollars of paper wealth wasn't real money without the time, ability, and talent to actually *spend* the money. Bill Gates was an example of unspent wealth while he was the active president of Microsoft. When he left day-to-day management he demonstrated a remarkable talent to be a rich man funding charities with uncommon wisdom.

Finis sailed his fishing yacht in Baja California with boatloads of beautiful people, was prominently seen on sports TV channels, and playing in Senior Golf tournaments.

In 1986 Finis started a new disc drive company in Longmont, Colorado, hiring the laid-off Miniscribe engineering team, a team that quickly became famous for faster-better-cheaper drive models He set out to market smaller 3.5-inch hard drives that his new engineering team had designed. These became the first successful 3.5-inch drives and marked the beginning of the decline and end of 5.25-inch drives. Although PCs were all built to hold 5.25-inch drives and CD and DVD optical drives are still 5.25-inch, Finis was able to market his 3.5-inch drives because of the trust major PC manufacturers like Compaq Computer had in him. As in Seagate's founding, Finis was unable to get venture capital financing until after the knowledgeable leader of Compaq Computer had invested money in Finis' new company.

Drive technology has always flowed in a continuous slow tide of decreasing disc size, for both business and technology reasons. Future higher data capacities at higher data access speeds favored the smaller 3.5-inch drives and by 1986 they allowed enough storage capacity for most customers.

Finis had an uncanny instinct for the timing of this tide and his 3.5-inch disc drive was quickly successful, initially selling 90% of his drives to Compaq.

Although Seagate had earlier designed and built 3.5-inch drives, it had failed to market them successfully, like DEC's failure to sell PCs to its VAX customer base. But Al knew how to overcome this failure, if he waited a while.

Gordon interviewed for a job with Finis, flying to Jeffco Airport north of Denver. He stayed at the Boulderado, a historic 1909 hotel from Colorado's past, its golden age of mining and railroading wealth. Its lobby was graced by a gilded inlaid ceiling and an elaborate chandelier.

He drove to Finis' plant the next morning to meet with John, its Chief Technology Officer.

"You're with Seagate?"

"That's right, John. I do their head and disc designs which we hope the competition won't be able to buy from their component supply companies."

John answered, "I like to say that companies like ours buy parts to make drives, Quantum hires the Japanese to make their drives, and Seagate makes drives from dirt. But we all somehow survive in the marketplace competition."

"That's a good one! And Seagate is the company run by Marines.

Did you know Seagate flies a Marine Corps flag at their headquarters?"
They both laughed.

"Gordon, I have a theory I call the 'quantum mechanics of disc drive manufacturing.' It makes unsold parts and drives go bad if they languish in factory inventory too long."

Gordon laughed. "That's because they go obsolete so quickly. Drive companies have to move inventory fast, before their models get outperformed by newer ones, and the old ones become unprofitable to build and sell."

John introduced Gordon to his amazingly small and effective drive design team. His disc spin motor design team was a single man with a magnifier lens attached to his glasses frame. He looked like an old-world watchmaker. Dozens of small glass dishes sat on his workbench, holding tiny motors and their parts: miniature bearings, coils, tiny magnets, and Lilliputian motor housings. His bench was half covered in felt, so accidentally dropped parts wouldn't bounce away and be lost.

He and John had recently invented a way to lower the cost of spin motors by eliminating their rotary position sensor. They found a way to electronically sense the motor rotary angle, information the drive electronics needed to energize the proper motor coils to make the motors spin discs in the correct counterclockwise direction. Seagate had a division of engineers designing its own motors.

Their recording engineer Lou took Gordon to lunch. "Yes, Finis does have an outstanding drive design group but it's still tough work, no different than any other high tech company. We just finished a new drive design. You know the team's excitement when a new drive operates successfully for the first time? It's sitting on a workbench with dozens of wires attached, monitoring it with oscilloscopes and digital logic analyzers, displaying details of its internal operations. Everyone cheers when its heads finally begin correctly seeking from track to track. Skyscraper and bridge builders must get that same feeling when they complete a new structure that benefits people; the feeling that makes them fly American flags on top. Well, I found myself bored when our latest new drive first ran last week. I'm going to find some way to get out of this rat race to work on long range stuff."

Gordon peered at him over his steak sandwich. "Lou, you know perfectly well that your company would have to be as big as Seagate before that'd be possible. And Seagate itself has no long-range research division."

"Yeah, I know," Lou sighed. A year later, Gordon heard that Lou was running a two-man research lab for Finis, in a small beach town north of San Diego, California. Gordon smiled at the news because Lou was an avid surfer but had been a thousand miles from the ocean in Longmont.

36.

Tiny Bumps and Tuning Forks

"I need you to immediately fly to the IBM plant in Rochester, Minnesota." Gordon was in Doug's office, no longer surprised by sudden summonses to receive Marine marching orders. "The IBM people say they're going to prove to you that discs in the drives we sell them have asperities above glide height. They're concerned our drives will crash in their PCs. Find the problem, verify it, and figure out what we should do about it. I'll send more engineers to help you, if you need them."

After a recording disc was manufactured, three special heads were flown over it. The first was a burnish head that polished the finished disc surfaces. This head had sharp edges on its slider skis to strike and chop off any disc asperity bumps high enough to hit a ski. Next, a glide head was flown over the disc surfaces, flying lower than any normal disc drive head. A disc was rejected if the glide head hit any asperities. An electronic crystal was bonded to glide heads to detect them, producing an electronic pulse when a disc asperity was high enough to hit the glide head skis.

The third and final test was a special head that recorded magnetic bits everywhere on the disc surfaces and then read them back to make sure all data locations on the disc recorded correctly. That test also checked whether the burnish and glide processes had removed any magnetic film fragments from the discs, leaving nonmagnetic bit-sized holes. A few of these bit flaws were acceptable because drives were designed with extra locations to store user data, so drives could replace defective locations with good ones. It would be impossibly expensive to manufacture perfect discs without a single defective bit in all its thousands of billions of bit locations.

The final flaw marking of each individual disc was done by its drive in manufacturing final test, during hours of drive reliability testing. Bits needed to be repeatedly written and read in every location, to find every possible disc flaw. An atomic-size scratch might cause a bit error only when a bit was accidentally written exactly on top of it, but not a few nanometers on either side.

Gordon remembered that IBM had been objecting to Seagate's disc glide testing for some time, but without giving any details that Seagate could act on. Instead, IBM had assigned its senior manager Ralph to monitor Seagate engineering meetings. Ralph believed his assignment was to scowl during these meetings and occasionally erupt in incomprehensibly irate tirades. Ralph had been on the original IBM disc drive team and was now very old, with a tendency to fall asleep during meetings. The Seagate engineers would snicker and try to make progress while Ralph slept, occasionally snoring loudly. Someone would wave his hands, point at Ralph, and break up the group by whispering, "I just saw him breathe in a fly!"

"O.K., Doug. I'm on it." Gordon instantly knew this was a serious problem and there was no point in doubting, stalling, or objecting to the situation. He always accepted reality and prepared to directly deal with it. He walked back to his office, thinking that this would prevent him from attending the upcoming international magnetics conference in Minneapolis. *I'll fly my Mooney to Rochester instead. The cross country aviation charts I bought will cover going to Rochester as well.*

A moment later he stopped thinking about engineering and travel details, as the magnitude of the business situation hit him. *What if IBM's right about our disc asperities and thousands of our drives in the field are about to crash? What if our disc manufacturers can't modify their processes to find and eliminate those asperities?*

He took off at 6am the next day from San Jose Airport and landed at Rochester Airport at 6pm. He took a taxi to the Kahler Hotel downtown and checked into his room. Gordon was surprised to find medication supplies in its bathroom. His taxi had driven past the Mayo Clinic to get to the hotel and he supposed long-term patients with chronic diseases might stay in nearby hotels. He had seen electric outlets for cars in the outdoor parking lots, and the hotel map showed underground tunnels going to the Mayo. *It must get mighty cold here when winter arrives a few months from now.*

He had a cocktail and dinner in the hotel bar and went to bed. Awaking in darkness, he looked at a clock and saw it was 3am. *What woke me?* The answer came a few moments later when he heard a loud groan from the next room. *Good grief, I'm in a hospital outpatient ward!* He went to the bathroom to stuff Kleenex in his ears. *I'll move to a different hotel if this IBM business takes longer than tomorrow.*

The next morning Gordon had breakfast with an engineering manager from the IBM plant, and they got in his car to drive to his plant north of Rochester. After they left the city, Gordon saw they were passing vast farm fields. All were empty except for stubble left from the last corn harvest. They passed occasional intersections with dirt farm roads between the fields. Some intersections had a lone tree or two with nearly bare limbs and a few leaves defying the approaching winter.

"In a month or two this'll all be white with snow and temperatures will drop as low as fifty below zero."

"That explains the electric outlets in the parking lots."

"Yup," the man said. "We put electric block heaters in our car engines to keep them from freezing."

"I'm a native Californian," Gordon replied. "We're terrified by climate like that."

The man smiled. "And in the seasons when it isn't fifty below we have thunderstorms instead. Are you wondering why anyone stays here? Many of our youngsters don't. They leave as soon as they grow up."

The view remained unchanged as they drove in the direction of Minneapolis, far to the north. The fields of harvested corn stubble stretched to infinity in every direction, as far as the eye could see. The dim sun low in the sky made the overall scene remind Gordon of a Stephen King novel. To break the silence as they drove on, Gordon remarked, "The horizon looks so far away it almost seems like the entire Earth must be flat."

"Gordon, Charles Fort started the Flat Earth Society a long time ago on American plains just like these. He told everyone it was obvious the Earth wasn't a round ball because anyone could see with their own eyes that it was flat. They were looking at flat country plains like you see here. You may appreciate that life on these plains has a certain sameness that could bore and depress many people. They need diversions like *Prairie Home Companion* on the radio, with Garrison Keeler and his Lake Woebegone stories.

"Fort's Flat Earth Society gave them something to talk about and was a great success. It still exists today. When Fort became an old man, he decided to confess he had made up the flat Earth story. Speaking before an audience of hundreds of Flat Earthers, he told them it was all a hoax he had made up because he was bored by plains monotony and he figured others were as well. Fort explained he had invented the idea because he wanted to give plains people something interesting in their lives.

"There was absolute silence in the room when he finished his talk. Then a roar of disapproval rose from his audience. He was utterly disbelieved and expelled from the society he founded. The Flat Earth Society today doesn't credit him for discovering the Earth is flat. Can you guess what they think is underneath the flat Earth?"

"No. Do they think the Earth is a giant flat rock in space, like the flying magnetic island in Gulliver's Travels?"

The man laughed. "They claim that flying saucers hide beneath Earth's flat under side, and that all the moon landings in the U.S. space program were hoaxes. I don't know why people don't fall off the edge of the Earth, and they don't say."

Gordon's head was shaking in wonder. He was smiling, liking the story.

"Well, I might have been interested in joining that society myself." Gordon was thinking of an incident during his college days.

"We Cal Tech students had heard about a night meeting of flying saucer fans in the 29 Palms desert a few hours drive east of the university. A bunch of us gathered fireworks, steel wire and tools, and we set out by car for the desert. We parked where we saw a roadside sign for the UFO meeting, and we crept in the darkness towards a bonfire surrounded by about fifty people.

"A woman was speaking. 'When I awoke in space, I found I had been taken while sleeping in my bed, and I was inside a gem-studded spaceship flying to Mars!'

"The woman was loud enough to cover up the little noise we would be making, and I took one end of a spool of wire and quietly tied it to a low rock, staying far enough from the fire to remain unseen. The other guys fastened the opposite end of the wire to a rock high above the ground, first threading the wire through eyelets they had taped to a firework cone called a 'shower of sparks.'

"As the woman described fields of diamonds she saw on Mars, we ignited the firework and let it start sliding down the wire. In the dark you couldn't tell whether it was large or small as it slid down the invisible wire, gaily throwing out sparks of white and blue.

"The lady shrieked, 'Look! There's the spaceship I traveled to Mars in!' Every eye turned to look at the sliding fireball; every voice exclaiming at the same time. I saw one silent man looking glumly down at the bonfire and I figured he was the UFO meeting organizer. Maybe he was thinking about his lost profits after his audience discovered that a flying saucer could be just a six-inch long fireworks sparkler sliding down a wire."

The IBM man laughed at Gordon's story as the Rochester highway continued endlessly on, straight as an arrow. At last, Gordon saw a square building in the distance, isolated and solitary among the fields. It was the IBM plant.

The man explained, "It's here because IBM got a tax break to provide jobs for our local young people. Some of them stay and work here instead of leaving to take jobs in Minneapolis."

They parked and entered a lobby where Gordon was given a visitor's badge. "This will badge you into the lab you will be working in." Gordon found out what that meant as they walked through the plant, the manager sliding his badge through card readers that unlocked doors between different plant areas. As they passed through an IBM minicomputer manufacturing area, Gordon saw they were still using old 14-inch diameter IBM disc drives. *Those will soon become dinosaurs and be replaced by Seagate's disruptive technology 5.25-inch drives.*

They descended stairs to a basement lab door marked "Clean Room. Approved Apparel Mandatory."

"Gordon, inside this clean room is an instrument they want you to study. They tell me it's highly secret and proprietary IBM technology that they aren't allowed to explain to outsiders. They're concerned that Seagate is not glide testing its discs correctly, and our company reputation is on the line if our personal computers fail because your drives crash inside them. IBM management hasn't authorized disclosure of this proprietary information to you, but the Rochester boss here says to just let you look at it without any explanation. They want you to experiment with this instrument by yourself, but to respect their proprietary rights. You can use the phone inside to call your engineering people back in Scotts Valley, and your badge will also get you into the bathroom and back. I'll be back to fetch you this afternoon."

Gordon thought this was strange behavior, as he donned clean room apparel over his street clothes. He put on a white one-piece bunny suit, mouth and nose mask, head bonnet, latex gloves, and slippers. Entering the clean room outer airlock, he closed its door behind him and stepped on a sticky foot pad that removed floor dirt from his slippers. He glanced at a water purification monitor on the wall of the airlock. Its display read, "Water resistivity 100 megohm-cm" and "Bacteria level below 1 ppm." Gordon smiled, remembering how surprised he had been to learn that bacteria were a problem in absolutely pure water systems. Ron "Mr. Clean" had told him that chlorine was one of the gasses removed to make pure water, making the water not only prone to bacteria growth, but also slightly corrosive.

Outgoing air blew any remaining dust off his bunny suit as he opened the inner airlock door of the clean room and entered. Clean room air pressure was kept a little higher than outside air so contaminants would be blown out instead of in. He heard air handler fans keeping the temperature constant and he saw copper window screens covering their air ducts to keep radio signals out. That meant that this was a recording test lab and heads would be flying on discs in the open clean room environment without the contamination protection they normally got by being sealed inside disc drives.

The airlock closed behind him and Gordon found himself alone in a silent white basement lab with no windows. The lab contained several workbenches, stools, and a desk. Bright fluorescent lighting gave it the ambience of a deserted hospital.

On one side of the lab he saw a spin stand instrument on which a 5.25-inch brown disc was mounted horizontally and spinning. A head was also mounted to the instrument and its slider was flying on the disc. The small slider was black and rectangular, about 1/4-inch in size. He looked closer and verified it was a Winchester head like Seagate used in its production drives. Winchester had been an IBM code name for an older 14-inch disc drive technology that Seagate had miniaturized to make its first 5.25-inch drive.

Picking up a magnifying glass he found on the bench, Gordon saw a glide head electronic crystal bonded to the top of the head, the side away from the spinning disc. He held his breath as he brought his face close to the spinning disc, to avoid contaminating it with moisture through his mouth and nose mask.

Looks like normal glide head technology. An oscilloscope was connected to an electronic circuit board to display electrical pulses from the crystal when a disc asperity hit the head. Each microscopic hit caused the head to microscopically shake, producing a glide hit electrical pulse from the piezoelectric crystal. He slowly twisted a micrometer on the spin stand with his gloved hand, moving the head from the outer track radius of the disc to the inner track near the spinning hub. The oscilloscope showed him many tracks on the disc that produced glide hit pulses every time the disc rotated the same spot under the head.

He found the head could be left at a track radius with glide hit asperities and the hit position pulses never changed. *That's unusual. A head normally knocks the asperity off, or wears it down enough for the hit to go away, or the head crashes. Permanent glide hits, but no wear or crashes,* he carefully concluded, as he meticulously examined the workbench area around the glide tester. He saw a standard Seagate drive, the model sold to IBM for its PCs. One of its discs and one of its heads had been removed from the Seagate drive, presumably the pair now mounted on the glide tester.

Closely examining the instrumentation connected to the oscilloscope, he saw an electronic high pass filter instrument, set to pass only glide pulse frequencies in the ultrasonic range far above audible audio sound frequencies. It rejected all lower frequencies. A tall bookshelf sat on the floor nearby, holding several plastic canisters of recording discs and a manual labeled *Clean Room Procedures* sitting next to a textbook titled *Ceramics*. He picked it up. It was a textbook on the scientific properties of ceramics. *Textbooks aren't normally found in clean rooms,* he noted.

The asperity pulses had an unfamiliar shape on the oscilloscope, like an electronic signature of a bell ringing, but at an ultrasonic frequency ten times higher that any ear could hear. *This frequency is far above anything I've ever seen used in glide testing. Hmm. The production glide testers our disc vendors like Normad use would completely filter out and reject this 200 kilohertz ultrasonic ringing frequency. They wouldn't see these asperities at all and would pass these discs as O.K.*

He carefully took data on the hits, keeping an open mind on the underlying causes, although the Common Sense told him that "like a bell ringing" was an important clue. Gordon was quite experienced at disc drive forensics by now and knew that any premature guessing would obscure and delay the real lessons to be learned. The truth was almost always a complete surprise.

Gordon measured the exact ringing frequency from the oscilloscope screen. Remembering that high pass circuits could electronically change pulses and make them appear to have a bell-ringing shape, he took the filter out of the circuit and again looked at the glide hit pulses on the scope. They were fuzzy and unclear now, but he still saw the same bell-ringing pulse shape now that he knew to look for it.

He stopped the spin stand and removed the head and disc from their spin stand mounts. Picking up a magnifying glass from a workbench, he checked the disc part number stamped on bare aluminum in the disc clamping area near its center mounting hole. It was from the Normad disc manufacturing company. *That's the primary disc manufacturer we use for these drives.*

Carefully picking up a pencil to scratch his chin, he wondered what Sherlock Holmes would do next. He knew if he scratched his head with a finger it would contaminate the latex glove he wore.

The head appeared to be a normal Seagate production head flying on a normal Seagate production disc. It should be flying higher than any glide head would fly and there shouldn't be any asperity hits. He picked up the head. Examining it with the magnifying glass, he saw the expected Seagate configuration of its flexure and tiny steel mounting base, and verified it appeared unaltered to his eye. He didn't have instrumentation in this lab to verify that it was flying at the correct height, but he knew the IBM engineers wouldn't try to fool him with tricks. This was just a random head from a random Seagate drive. *I'm beginning to see why they're concerned.*

Gordon arranged the clues in his mind and then walked over to sit at the desk to do some Sherlock Holmes deductive thinking. *Something has to be mechanically vibrating for the crystal to produce a ringing electrical pulse. But what could it be? What could ring or vibrate in a recording head at an ultrasonic frequency? Maybe it's the springiness of the cushion of air between the head and disc, mechanically resonating with the mass of the slider body...*

No, I know that hydrodynamic frequency. It's only tens of kilohertz. It comes out of the Reynolds equation that my VAX head flight computer program solves...

Maybe it's the head flexure spring mechanically resonating...

No, flexures vibrate at about 3 kilohertz. That's even lower in frequency. Hmm.

The lab was completely still and motionless. Faint flickers came from ceiling florescent lights and quiet sighs from air handler fans. A single man sat at a desk, dressed in white from head to toe, hunched over a pad of paper, brow knitted in concentration, his mind somewhere off in space.

He drew a cartoon picture of the 1/4-inch long rectangular head slider, and drew a cartoon hammer representing a disc asperity hitting the front of the head. He realized that the asperity "hammer" would cause a mechanical shock pulse in the slider. *Like a hammer hitting a brick and making a 'clink' sound. The mechanical stress pulse could bend the slider and make it ring like a tuning fork. It would have microscopically small amplitude, but electronic glide crystals are very sensitive. I could calculate the ringing frequency to verify if that's what's happening.* He wrote down a formula he remembered from one of his Cal Tech physics courses, to calculate the mechanical vibration resonant frequency of a solid body.

Winchester heads are made of ferrite, a hot-pressed ceramic material. So I need the mass density and bulk elasticity spring modulus of a dense ceramic.

Eyes widening, he remembered the ceramics textbook sitting in the bookcase. *Aha! So that's why that textbook is in a clean room! The game's afoot, Watson!*

He opened the book and looked up the data for his equation. He needed only an approximate calculation of the resonant frequency to confirm that the ceramic slider was acoustically ringing like a tiny bell. He would compare the calculated frequency to the 200 kilohertz ringing frequency he had measured on the scope. Exact precision wasn't necessary. If he could manage to follow the trail of evidence to the correct conclusion, avoiding all the many possible false trails, others would fill in the exact details later. He only needed to find the correct concept, the actual physics of what was happening.

Gordon calculated the theoretical ringing frequency of a ceramic brick 1/4 inch in its longest dimension. Comparing it to the ringing frequency from the scope, he saw they were the same.

Picking up the lab telephone, he called Rob back in Scotts Valley. "Rob, look up the circuit diagram for the Normad production glide testers and tell me the filter frequency they use for their asperity detection circuit."

"Can't this wait? I'm still working on the last assignment you gave me." Rob sounded frustrated and upset.

Gordon sighed. Good engineers needed time to properly analyze their project assignments, carry them out, and validate their results. Silicon Valley engineers' talents could be blunted if harried managers rushed them from task to task in "firefighting" work, never allowing them to finish their last hurried assignment before the next. Even worse was sending engineers to the factory for too long, to solve production problems. Forcing them to solve factory problems by trial and error, innocent of any scientific rationale, could turn them into production-minded people, because sometimes random trial and error worked.

"No, Rob," Gordon explained patiently, "this is a major problem with IBM, one of Seagate's major customers. Please just drop what you're working on and go look up the filter frequency."

A few minutes later, Rob returned to the phone. "Gordon, they're 14 kilohertz low pass filters."

"Here's what I need you to do, Rob. Get a glide tester from Ken in Quality Control. Use Doug's authority if you need to. Put it in a flow bench in our clean lab. Redesign its electronic filter to have a cutoff frequency of about 150 kilohertz high pass instead of 14 kilohertz low pass. The asperity hit pulses you're trying to detect are slider body resonances up at 200 kilohertz. Make the cutoff frequency high enough to filter out all low frequency signals, but low enough to not reject any slider body resonance signal. I estimate slider frequencies vary plus-or-minus 15% at most. Change the circuit in as simple a way as you can, so all the Normad production glide testers can be quickly modified the same way. Have Jack get you several canisters of production discs from Normad, glide test them with the old low pass filter, and then again with the new high pass filter. Choose one of the head lab ladies, and tell Stern I asked you to train her to do the testing for you. Verify that you see the same kind of test data I'm seeing here. I'll fax you my data now and I'll be back tomorrow night."

There was silence on the line for several seconds. Then Rob's professionalism kicked in. "I've got it, Gordon. I'll begin immediately." There was a pause. "There's something I should tell you, Gordon. Marc's been snooping around. He asked me where you were."

"Doug knows where I am; he sent me here. Tony may just be looking for an excuse to dock my pay again."

"But we're salaried engineers. He can't legally dock our pay, can he?"

"He did exactly that a couple of months ago, when I gave a talk at a Santa Clara University conference on the advantages of cobalt discs. He docked me a day's pay even though my talk was to show disc drive customers why they should buy drives with Seagate's new cobalt discs."

"Why does he pull that kind of crap? Why do you put up with it? Did you complain to Doug or Al?"

"Marc says California labor laws allow it, salaried or no. I really don't know what makes him tick. He seems to be fixated on the idea that Doug respects me more than him. He's trying to run me down in Doug's and Al's eyes, trying to get his own score up. You know, for bonus and stock option awards. It'll only get worse if you say anything to him. He may turn on you as well." Rob had no response and Gordon hung up.

Gordon felt tired as he called the IBM manager's office and asked him to set up an immediate meeting with their glide test engineers. He left the clean room, reversing the order of air locks and bunny suit clothing. Ten minutes later he was in a conference room filled with IBM people. They introduced themselves.

He looked around the room. "I'd like to congratulate you on making a major advance in glide test technology. It's genuine genius. I know how sensitive you must be on your new ultrasonic slider body resonance glide technology and I promise to respect your secrets. But I need to tell you what Seagate plans to do about the situation and I'm hoping for your advice and concurrence. Who's your expert that conceived the glide test stand instrumentation downstairs?"

The IBM manager said, "Cerese sitting on your left is our chief glide scientist at IBM." Cerese was a trim attractive lady, at the moment looking rather reserved and formal. Gordon easily sensed a deep intelligence behind her reserve.

Gordon turned to her. "Please check my data from your tester, and then I'll tell you the plan I'm proposing." They discussed the data sheets and he continued. "Seagate is going to have all its disc suppliers modify their glide testers beginning with our major supplier Normad. One of my engineers is now redesigning Normad's glide circuits to be 150 kilohertz high pass, instead of their current 14 kilohertz low pass. Does anyone have comments so far?"

Gordon paused until he saw a small encouraging nod from Cerese. He smiled at her. "We'll adjust the Normad glide hit electronics sensitivity so all asperities are detected on glide test discs I'm asking you to select here, for me to take back to Scotts Valley. Additionally, when Normad has the new glide test working to our and your satisfaction, I will then require them to lower their glide head fly height from eight microinches to six, to give IBM extra glide safety margin below the lowest recording head flight in our drives."

One of the IBM men looked up. "Does that mean Seagate admits it's been gliding too high on all the discs in your drives that IBM bought in the past?" Gordon thought for a moment. This man was a "company lawyer," a derogatory term referring to people who interpreted any technological progress as an admission that all earlier technology was faulty. *Guys like him only impede progress; the world would be better off without them.*

"Cerese has doubtless already given you the answer to that question. Let's let her be the expert on it. What I'm saying is that Seagate will unilaterally change its glide technology and lower its glide height because I can see that you're honestly uncomfortable with our present glide testing." There were nods all around the table.

Cerese smiled as if she and Gordon were sharing some unspoken secret. Gordon knew the "secret" was simple honesty and integrity among engineering professionals. Gordon had no legitimate option other than trusting her. She had the ultrasonic glide test experience, he didn't. Cerese would make certain that proper glide test discs would be selected, not discs impossible for Normad to manufacture. He had no more desire to risk millions of customer drives crashing than IBM did. Seagate had to accept the risks involved.

Such risks have to be taken for technology to progress or it will begin to stagnate and die, like buggy whips, mechanical adding machines, and minicomputers. This time it was Gordon's turn to make the risk call. Uncountable thousands of engineering risk calls like this had been made during the half-century of disc drive technology evolution. The result had been drives that stored tens of millions of times more bits on each square inch of disc surface than the original IBM Ramac drive in 1956. That had been far more progress, far faster, and for far longer, than Moore's Law of semiconductor chip transistor count doubling every 18 months.

Engineering progress like this was as old as human civilization itself; in fact it was a key enabler of great nations. Engineering progress allowed their great works to outlive their civilizations: the Egyptian pyramids; the Roman Coliseum, roads, and aqueducts; the Great Wall of China.

Like his anonymous predecessors in past disc drive progress, Gordon knew there would be no recognition for his work here; only the possibility of punishment if the new glide technology failed or significantly dropped Normad's yield of usable discs. There was no possibility of reward. It was reward enough for Gordon to have this opportunity to make a genuine contribution to real commercial technology, to improve products that people worldwide valued highly enough to spend their own money to buy.

He considered it unnecessary to tell the IBM people that he had asked Jack to check the drop in glide height with Normad before he left for Rochester. Normad could accommodate the lower glide height without unduly impacting their disc production. Earlier that day he had run tests in the IBM lab downstairs with the disc spinning slower, causing the head to fly lower. The ultrasonic asperities had been burnished away by the lower flying head. When he spun the back disc to full speed they were gone. Gordon was reasonably certain the asperities were weak and hair-like. Normad could likely burnish them off once they were able to detect them with Cerese's ultrasonic glide.

As the meeting broke up, Cerese and Gordon shook hands. "Please publish your ultrasonic glide work," he said. "Our industry needs to understand and adopt your technology."

"It's not likely I'll be allowed to publish any papers on my research. It's too valuable to my company for our management to permit it to become public."

Suddenly, a beautiful smile evaporated her reserved manner. "I want to let you know something. You just saved our management from having to make a decision that could have endangered their careers here."

"What decision was that?"

"Our company bosses had ruled that ultrasonic glide technology was highly proprietary. No other company is aware of it. We all figured you would come out of our lab with questions about it, and we warned our bosses that we would need their permission to explain the physics to you, so Seagate could see how critical this glide technology is for disc reliability. They faced having to authorize explaining the physics to you, against the company ruling that they couldn't. It was disc reliability versus violating company rules. They could lose either way.

"But you came out of the lab with more than questions. You figured out and proved the physics yourself, and you immediately wanted to talk about a corrective action plan. That's absolutely amazing. Does everyone at Seagate jump to the solution of a problem like that and ignore all the en route discussions?"

"Well, I learned that trick from Al and our CTO Doug. It's handy in a startup company."

"I also have to admit that we thought Seagate had only engineers working for them, not any scientists."

"I'm more like a cross between a scientist and an engineer, Cerese."

She shook her head. "We were dead wrong! How did you figure the physics out so quickly? I've been working on it for two years!"

How could I explain Sherlock Holmes technology forensics to a research scientist; the importance of a ceramics textbook that didn't belong in a clean room?

"Well, you did all the inventing and hard work, Cerese. I only had to figure out what you did."

Gordon said goodbye and left with the IBM manager for the drive back to Rochester. The man smiled wryly. "I hope the new glide testing goes as you say. We would have taken weeks or months to agree on a plan like the one you just made up on the spot. But it's a sound plan and I'll have the glide test discs we agreed on finished and delivered to your hotel tonight."

That reminded Gordon that East Coast people thought Minnesota was in the American west. *It seems very East Coast here to me; the same*

patient and slow engineering-dominated "East Coast" ways that Silicon Valley
scorns.

He was back in the air the next morning, flying west. When he got home that night, Shirley kissed him, fixed him a single malt scotch and water, and made pineapple chicken for dinner. He told her the story about Charles Fort being kicked out of the Flat Earth Society he invented.

Shirley replied, "Well, I've just thought up an invention of my own!"

"What is it?"

"I've invented a name for a new personal deodorant for athletes like race car drivers. It'll be called 'Pit Stop'!"

"Pit Stop? That's a good one!" he chuckled.

As they ate she said, "I'm worried about Charles. He's hardly eating."

"Charles is nearly seventeen, right? Have you taken him to a vet?"

"I'm taking him tomorrow." They looked at each other, both distressed.

When Gordon arrived at Seagate the next morning, he found Rob sleeping in a chair in his office. He sat down in a second chair and reviewed the asperity data he had taken at IBM, waiting for Rob to stir. Minutes later, Doug walked by on one of his occasional walking tours through his engineering buildings.

"Why are you sitting here instead of in the big office I built for you?"

"Sit here with Rob and me, Doug. You'll want to hear how the IBM disc glide problem is getting resolved." Doug and Gordon sat, waiting for Rob to wake.

"Oh, you're back," Rob said groggily. "I must have fallen asleep some time after 4am. That's the last time I remember looking at my watch. I've been duplicating your asperity measurements here using a new circuit I designed, one we can add to the Normad disc glide testers."

Rob compared his data with Gordon's. They agreed.

Rob continued, "We'll use the IBM glide test discs you brought to set the tester sensitivity. Stan has his engineering pilot production line modifying a dozen Normad glide tester circuit boards."

Gordon replied, "O.K. Rob. I'll ask Jack to set up a meeting at Normad this afternoon. You start documenting everything in complete detail. There's always a chance that some coincidental production failure may occur at Normad and shut down their disc line at the same time we introduce ultrasonic glide. We'll want to be sure that ultrasonic glide can't be made a scapegoat to explain some unrelated production failure to Tom."

Doug smiled. He was thinking back to when he had hired Gordon. His cardinal rule for hiring people had worked once again. Just look for smart people with good attitudes. Pay less attention to what their last boss said about them.

"Gordon, you and your group have done your usual outstanding job for Seagate. We should thank Xerox for its years of investment in your disc drive technology research. It's like the Apple Macintosh that commercialized Xerox research in personal computer design. You've helped Seagate commercialize Xerox research in disc drives."

37.

When the CEO Names Your Cat

Gordon drove to Santa Cruz after work one evening, for an all-hands employee dinner meeting at the Cocoanut Grove resort. Driving through Santa Cruz, he passed over the San Lorenzo River near its mouth at the sea and saw the river mouth was choked with waterlogged logs from centuries-old timber cutting in the San Lorenzo Valley. The winter's first big storm had dropped ten inches the day before, washing old logs from the forest into the river, its swollen current carrying them downstream and onto the beach. Dozens of people were on the beach with chain saws, cutting up trees for firewood.

Santa Cruz was the original California Surf City where Hawaiian princes introduced long board surfing into America. The historic Cocoanut Grove resort sat comfortably next to a century-old boardwalk, the home of the most famous and historic wooden roller coaster in California. Gordon thought this seashore scene showed the finest aspects of California.

Gordon found Al, Doug, and Marc in the lounge of Cocoanut Grove, waiting to start the meeting.

He ordered a drink, sat down next to Al and said, "Charles was a once in a lifetime cat, the greatest cat in the world."

Charles Cat had died in his sleep a week earlier, seventeen years of age. Gordon and Shirley had grieved as they brought out their pictures of Charles, remembering their many years with him.

"Charles chose to live with us for seventeen years and I want to name our new kitten after him, but Shirley insists on a different name."

"Gordon," Al said in his deep gravelly voice, "name the cat Winchester." Gordon was taken aback. Winchester was the IBM codename for the disc drive technology that Seagate had miniaturized to make its first 5.25-inch drive. But Shirley wouldn't know that.

"When your company CEO names your cat, that's it," Pat said smiling. She was Al's Executive Administrator.

Gordon thought quickly. "That's a great name, Al! I'll tell Shirley that when the cat behaves she can say 'Good boy Winney!' And when it misbehaves, she can say, 'WINCHESTER! STOP THAT!'"

Everybody laughed, Gordon as well. It's always good when the Chief is smiling.

Doug asked Gordon, "Have all your engineers visited Seagate's plants in Singapore?"

This was one of Doug's ways of keeping his engineers educated on Seagate's primary mission of high-technology low-cost manufacturing.

"Well, Doug, I haven't been there myself."

Doug turned to Marc who was now looking defensive.

"Gordon is scheduled to visit Singapore next month," Marc snapped. Gordon was going to an international magnetics conference in Tokyo where he would stay in an expensive but micro-size hotel room, so small that sitting on its tiny bed he could reach out and touch every wall, even the bathroom shower door. When the conference ended he would fly to Singapore to visit the Seagate factory, and stay in a luxury hotel suite whose bath was larger than his entire Tokyo room, at a third of its price.

It was time for the "all-hands" employee meeting to start. Gordon walked with Al out of the lounge.

Al said, "Gordon, I remember our first meeting years ago in Las Vegas when you asked me if a researcher like you would be welcome at a manufacturing company like Seagate. You've survived and thrived in our cowboy company. What do you think now?"

Gordon shook his head. "It's been the technology adventure of my lifetime, Al. I feel very fortunate to have joined the company and I'm thinking of writing a book on my experiences at Seagate. Not sure exactly what'll be in it, but I do know the title."

"What's that?" asked Al, who tolerated Gordon's puns.

"I'll call it *As the Disc Turns*." Al dropped his head in laughter.

This Cocoanut Grove all-hands employee meeting was no expense barred, typical of early Seagate. It began with a free bar followed by a choice of steak or lobster dinner with wine. Many in the dining room were dressed in slacks and white shirts, some in suits, a few in Levis and T-shirts. As they sat in the dining room, laughter and conversation rose, as did smoke from the cigarettes many people held. The dining room glass roof opened occasionally to let the smoke rise out, closing before cold sea air filled the room. Gordon finished his coffee and asked a passing waiter for a refill. As the waiter began pouring he was startled to see brown liquid filling the cup. He glanced at the coffee pouring out of his pot to confirm it was still black. Rob was watching and said, "Why do you put cream and sugar in first instead of last like everyone else."

"My coffee stirs itself that way and stays hot because I don't have to put a cold spoon in it." As a fellow engineer, Rob understood the thermodynamics but thought Miss Manners wouldn't approve.

Al rose to speak first in the employee meeting following dinner. He was wearing a sports shirt with his usual nametag in these meetings, declaring him "Zookeeper." If asked why he didn't wear a tie, Al would say, "All the tie's going to do is cut off the flow of blood to your brain."

"Success is fragile and I want to remind everyone of that because we've just gone through several quarters of business success, beating our drive competitors on the loading dock where products ship and profits happen. So put your hearts into getting our new drives smoothly and quickly into high volume production. As Thomas Edison said, 'Genius is one percent inspiration and ninety-nine percent perspiration.' I also encourage all you engineers to continue your work on Seagate's other most important task, developing new drive technology.

"Now I want to talk about your personal lives instead of your Seagate lives. Please save a part of your life to enjoy yourself. Don't spend every waking hour at Seagate, or thinking about Seagate. And remember how precious your personal reputations are. Nothing can replace the loss of personal ethics and integrity."

Everyone knew the company way to make an ethical decision was to ask, "What would Al say?"

Tom was next, speaking about needing everyone's help in helping Seagate succeed.

"In our jobs it's O.K. if only fifty percent of our decisions are correct, even if the other half are mistakes. Avoiding or postponing decisions is the biggest mistake you can make.

"Let me tell you my own last big mistake. You engineers work hard because you believe in your work, but our drive salesmen are snakes who have to be spoon fed with rewards. Our last sales contest awarded Bermuda cruises to the top ten salesmen selling the most disc drives, with cruise tickets for their wives as well. I sent letters to the winners' wives after the cruise, congratulating them on their husbands' award and asking if they enjoyed the trip.

"Why was that a mistake? Because I got letters and phone calls from a lot of those wives asking, 'What cruise? I don't know anything about any cruise.'" Laughter slowly filled the room, as the younger engineers also figured it out. "For the next sales contest the first prize will be a Ferrari Testarossa." Everyone cheered.

At the end of Tom's talk, a new engineer held up his hand. "Does Seagate have a company song?"

Tom was taken aback for a second but quickly answered, "Well, I don't know the tune but the lyrics are 'Build, build, build, sell, sell, sell, money, money, money!" The engineer looked surprised as everyone else laughed. He may have wondered why "design, design, design" wasn't in the lyrics, if he was too new to know that Tom regarded engineers as mere delayers of production. He liked to say, "Manufacturing makes money, engineers cost money. When Harry Truman was president, Marines cost $5000 a year and saved the USA. Today, engineers cost $120,000 per year and delay production."

Gordon nodded in understanding. *Tom is certainly not an engineer. Engineers always want to perfect their designs by elaborate testing, but the Seagate culture often produces reliable drives faster. Tom's right, on early starts for volume manufacturing of new products. There's a price, however. Only incremental engineering progress is likely; real breakthroughs have to come from other companies and they often cost Seagate heavily.*

As the meeting broke up, Al stood at the door handing out notepads and glass paperweights with the Seagate motto KISS, "Keep it Simple, Stupid." He was also offering autographed copies of a cookbook titled *Fandango* he had authored from his days running a restaurant in Santa Cruz before starting Seagate. He had "Ernest for President" T-shirts on display. These were for a public campaign of Al's protesting the lack of ethics in politics. Al was promoting his dog Ernest as a congressional candidate in the next election, telling people that Ernest was absolutely loyal and honest and would never accept the bribes politicians called "contributions." Al's high water mark in politics was helping to get legislation passed outlawing frivolous lawsuits. But Al failed to get Ernest on the ballot.

Gordon's own political viewpoint had become less conservative as he grew older. He had joined the Libertarian Party when he first began working, reasoning that everyone should take care of themselves. In later years he grew to see that America's free enterprise system needed guidance by laws, and that the wealthy should help the less fortunate. They could freely choose to pay taxes or donate to charities. One of Gordon's favorites was the Salvation Army because of their quiet dedication to helping disaster victims and the poor. Their administrators worked for little pay, unlike larger charities that paid their leaders millions of donated dollars, while paying advertising agencies to solicit more public donations.

He didn't feel his own viewpoint was any more worthy than more liberal or more conservative viewpoints of other Americans. *Most so-called liberals live in large cities on America's coasts. Unlike small towns, big city people get isolated in separate special interest groups, hardly knowing what their next door neighbors think. News media, law courts, and the Congress are concentrated in large cities like New York and Washington, DC, and they naturally focus on matters important to their own liberal interest groups. I think they would more accurately be called elitists than liberals. They rarely think about middle class Americans whose jobs have gone overseas or been taken by illegal immigrants. Or why the Boy Scouts have a moral code, or about low income American seniors living on Social Security checks they worked a lifetime to earn, but denied access to government assisted low-cost housing because Washington gave the housing to favored foreign refugees instead.*

Gordon drove home from the all-hands meeting and told Shirley that Al had named her cat Winchester. She smiled at men's games and said, "I hope Winchester grows up dignified enough to fit his name. This morning I saw him jump onto the back of the couch and then fall off backwards onto the floor. He peeked around the back of the couch, looking warily at me to see if I saw his graceless fall. He turned his head away shamefully with his eyes shut."

"Cats don't feel shame, Shirley." She smiled.

The next morning was Saturday, and at 5am Gordon was out on their house deck adjusting a camera tripod. It was November 1985 and he wanted to photograph Halley's Comet. Astronomy was one of Gordon's hobbies. He searched the sky looking for the comet, scanning in small sky patches the way he looked for star constellations. But he couldn't see Halley's anywhere. Finally he stopped, shivering and disappointed in the cold night air. Ready to give up, he took a last look at the entire sky, seeing the countless stars piercing the black curtain of night.

Suddenly there it was, the comet head high in the sky, its tail stretching diagonally across most of the heavens. *Wow!* It was impossible to miss once his perspective was big enough to see the comet. It was quite visible above the few lights in rural San Lorenzo Valley. Gordon changed his 50mm camera lens for a wider 35mm lens and kneeled down next to the tripod to take pictures.

As dawn slowly arrived, Gordon saw that fog had silently crept up the valley in the night. The top of the fog layer was below their house and he looked down on a formless white undercast hiding their green redwood forest view below.

Over morning coffee, Shirley said, "We need to hire someone to saw down the tree on top of the cliff. I've made a deal with a crane operator to take the trunk away for free after we get someone to saw it down."

Gordon replied, "I thought you were going to ask the San Lorenzo Valley Water Company to split their $300 crane cost with us when they replace their redwood neighborhood water tank on the cliff above us. I'm hoping the new tank will end my 'surprise showers.'"

"When I called the water company they were still mad we wouldn't let them bring their two-ton truck up our fragile driveway carrying their new water tank. They refused to consider sharing the crane so I called the crane operator. He said that he would charge them the full price and take away our tree for free."

"I'll cut it down today," Gordon said. *I don't need to call a professional tree cutter. I can climb the cliff and then climb the tree carrying my chain saw. I'll cut the tree so it falls in the driveway thirty feet below and misses the house.* He had bought his first gasoline chain saw after moving to Boulder Creek and enjoyed sawing stuff for Shirley. "I'm a skilled 'brown thumb' gardener," he told friends.

An hour later he climbed up the cliff with the chain saw, then up the tree. Pulling the chain saw up the tree by a rope tied to its handle, he fired it up, cut a V notch in the tree to set which way it would fall, and then made a final back cut nearly through the tree. The tree started creaking. It was ready to break. Shutting off the chain saw, he lowered it back down the cliff on its rope. *I'll finish this with a hand saw.* When the tree finally started to fall, he dropped the hand saw and held tightly onto the tree trunk. The trunk whiplashed violently, nearly throwing him off as the tree fell down the cliff and onto the driveway. *Last time I'll try that crazy idea.*

A few hours later the tree had been cleaned up and the crane had arrived to hoist the new water company tank to the top of the cliff from a truck at the bottom of their driveway. It then turned to pick up the sawed-off tree trunk pieces and drop them at the foot of the driveway. Shirley kept several trunk pieces for firewood.

Later that day, he saw the valley fog had silently departed, but fog still tentatively poked over the coastal mountain passes to the sea, looking like white hands combing forest trees with their fingers. The sun set over a pass in Ben Lomond Mountain, turning day into sudden night with no sunset.

38.

Buying an Airplane to get its Parking Space

As Seagate grew, Gordon's group grew with it. He had learned an important management lesson: no motivation was as powerful as an idea an employee believed was his own. Gordon learned to give away credit for his ideas. He put some of his ego into his airplane flying. He trained for a commercial pilot license although he had no interest in becoming an airline pilot. Flying skills were enjoyable to learn and studying for written tests had always been easy. Commercial pilot flight training involved mild acrobatic maneuvers: lazy eights and chandelles. These maneuvers involved complex turns, climbs, and descents, never very steep nor upside down.

He explained this one day to Susan, the magnetics lady with the sexual chemistry, who worked at the Lanx Company. "I just got my own pilot license," she said. "I'd like to come along on one of your practice flights."

"Sure. Meet me at the shade shelters at San Jose Airport tomorrow morning."

As they stepped into the plane, Gordon said, "I hope you don't get airsick."

"Cast iron stomach, Gordon." Gordon leveled off at 5000 feet and made several sloppy chandelles. Susan's nearness and well-endowed figure made it difficult to focus.

"How'd you get this parking shelter, Gordon? There must be a long waiting list," she asked.

Gordon had long wanted to move his airplane from its unsheltered tie down parking spot at Finis' San Jose Airport airplane service business, and he had been finally able to get a shade shelter parking spot by finding a way to bypass the city's 20-year waiting list. He had seen an ad: "Airplane and shelter tie down for sale at San Jose." Calling the seller, he arranged to meet him at his shelter to look at his airplane for sale.

As Gordon drove up he saw an older Mooney airplane with a "For Sale" sign, parked in a shelter in the most desirable end tie down. A man was standing near it next to a funeral hearse and wearing a beret.

"I'm John," the man said. They shook hands. "You're probably wondering why the hearse."

"Well, yes," Gordon replied, unwittingly setting himself up for the first of John's many yarns.

"I'm the funeral director at a mortuary I own in the Bay Area. To survive in a small business like mine, you've got to make money any way you can. So I run a limousine service as well, which lets me make money off the hearses between funerals." Gordon thought using hearses as limousines was weird, but it was a great story. He later learned that John's hearses and his limousines were totally different vehicles.

"John, I've got a question I've wondered about, waiting for an expert like you to come along. As a flying mortician you must know how to scatter ashes from an airplane. Let me tell you about my pilot friend Ted who was given a shoe box containing ashes to scatter at sea. He flew out over the sea, opened his pilot's window, held the box outside, opened its lid, and then..."

"Stop!" John cried. "I'll tell you what happened. When Ted opened the box, ashes filled his airplane cabin with a grey cloud. Ted couldn't even see the instrument panel to fly for the next minute. And I bet when he turns the instrument switches and knobs in that plane today, they make a gritty sound."

"That's exactly what happened, John! So how should Ted have scattered the ashes?" Gordon was unwittingly walking into another of John's yarns.

"Ted should have put the shoe box in a paper shopping bag, rolled up its top, and dropped the bag out the window."

"But that's not scattering at sea," Gordon objected.

"Who's looking?" John replied, closing his trap. They both laughed. "The bag and box dissolve in the sea soon enough, so it comes to the same thing as scattering. Let me show you something else." They walked over to John's Mooney and he pointed at a dent on the left horizontal tail, with the paint scarred.

"John! Ted's plane has a dent like that in its left tail! How come?"

"Because there are small bone fragments in the ashes and when they fly out the pilot's window they blow back and hit the tail. They weigh enough to make those dents." Gordon was imagining a shoe box of ashes held by a pilot in one hand, who had to use his other hand to hold the window open. *I wonder how heavy human ashes are.*

"About twelve pounds, Gordon."

"How on Earth did you know what I was thinking about, John?"

"You told me you were an engineer. I had just used the word 'weigh' and when I saw you thinking I could figure out what you were wondering about. Quantitative people like you always ask me how much cremains weigh."

Gordon negotiated a deal with John to buy the partnership that owned the plane, in order to also get its shelter. The city of San Jose didn't allow selling or trading airplane parking rights, so Gordon should not have been able to get a shelter by buying an airplane in one. But the city shelter rental records were in the name of John's partnership, not his own name. The city would see only a partnership address change.

Gordon didn't need to own two Mooneys, so he called his L.A. friends Phil and Penny. They had become interested in private flying after Gordon and Shirley flew them on vacation to Guaymas, Mexico. They had just earned their own private pilot's licenses. Gordon sold them John's Mooney for the same $18,000 he paid for it, first advertising it for sale in a newspaper so he could list it as an incidental surplus asset in the purchase of the partnership. This gave him a sales tax exemption on the purchase from John, so Penny and Phil had to pay sales tax only once. They had later flown the two Mooneys together around America, Canada, Alaska, and Mexico.

On the trip to Alaska, they had packed survival gear into the two Mooneys: axes, rifles, and three kinds of mosquito repellent. They had flown up the Alcan Highway to Alaska, stopping at World War II airports built to ferry American war planes to the northwest corner of America, for Russian pilots to fly to their front line against Nazi Germany. The Russian pilots were women who knew only two throttle settings: full power to fly and off to land. They were fearless in night air battles against the Germans and suffered great losses in the war.

A few months after Gordon had sold the second Mooney to Phil and Penny, John called with an offer to show Gordon the sailboat he had bought with his Mooney money. Gordon had found that John was a waiting list junkie. He had originally acquired the San Jose shelter by waiting the necessary 20 years, and also had his name on a boat slip rental waiting list at Pier 39 Marina in San Francisco Bay. He had sold his Mooney when his name came up at the marina, because he needed the money to buy a 60-foot ketch to tie up there.

"I'll take you and Shirley sailing on the annual San Francisco Bay Opening Day, Gordon."

They met at John's mortuary. It was a stately white building with tall columns in front, flanking a large double door. Gordon thought it looked like Scarlet O'Hara's mansion in the movie *Gone with the Wind*. He walked among the coffins John had for sale, admiring some of the expensive ones. "Make a lot of money on these, John?"

"Far less than you'd think, Gordon. State law regulates the prices and I have a personal rule to never charge to bury a small child. I've told my son not to follow me into this business."

"John, what are these unpainted plywood pieces hiding back there? They look like a do-it-yourself coffin kit."

"That's just what they are, all right. Sometimes people are angry at their departed ones. Some wives ask me to just flush their dead husband's ashes down the toilet, and I have to tell them that state law prohibits that."

"So, the plywood kit is to shame them, John? Has anyone ever actually bought a kit?"

"Yes, once. There are only four of the six sides of a casket there, and I lost money making the other two. I'm done here. Let's drive to the marina and go sailing on my boat, the Wind Song."

An hour later they were sailing on the San Francisco bay, sipping beer and enjoying a scene of water, sky, wind, and sailboats. It seemed like a still-life painting to Gordon. *Racing sailboats travel slower than airplanes taxiing on the ground.*

They sailed several hours to Angel Island, visited mostly by boaters like John. Angel had been the "Ellis Island of the West," processing West Coast U.S. immigrants, and was a detention camp for Chinese immigrants in the 1900's. World War II Japanese and German POWs had been held on the island. It had also been used as a jumping-off point for American soldiers going to and returning from the Pacific War. The island had been home to a Nike missile base in the 1950s and 1960s. Now it was a state park.

After exploring the island and having a picnic lunch, they began their sail back to San Francisco. Halfway back, they saw an overturned Hobie Cat catamaran. One of its pontoons was high in the sky, its sail and the other pontoon in the water. Its pilot was behind the boat standing on the catamaran hull in the water, trying to right the boat by pulling on an up haul line attached to the top of its mast. As they drew closer, Gordon could hear his voice and realized the bay wasn't quite the peaceful scene it appeared. The man was roundly cursing his sailboat, unwilling to admit his inability to right the craft. His voice faded in the distance as they sailed on to home.

39.

Business Booms are Followed by Busts

Seagate couldn't build drives fast enough in 1987, running 24-hour shifts in its Singapore factories, trying to build 16,000 drives per day for the IBM PC-AT. That was the good news. The bad news was that this single customer accounted for 80% of Seagate's revenue. All of it suddenly vanished the following year when IBM decided to build its own PC disc drives.

One day, Gordon returned from a two week absence to find Seagate employees acting strangely and layoff rumors circulating. Many engineers were working even longer hours than usual in foolish and forlorn hope that hard work would avert the oncoming disaster. Wiser employees stopped showing up for work, spending their time updating their resumes and interviewing for new jobs in Silicon Valley over the hill. Everyone ignored strangers that began to appear in the buildings, holding clipboards and making lists of computers and instruments that could be sold as surplus when their users were laid off.

Gordon hoped and believed that Seagate would choose the employees to be laid off by keeping only those necessary to get their next disc drive design into successful production. To survive, Seagate had to cut costs but also maintain revenue. He had worked to get his entire group on Seagate's "keeper" list.

Waiting for the inevitable, Gordon found that curiosity could overcome fear. There was little useful work to do and he found himself thinking that if he somehow returned to college for another PhD he might do his thesis on the abnormal psychology of people facing layoffs. *Maybe the pressure is getting to me too, because Marc is surely making up a layoff list for my group and has no idea who is really critical. It's maddening when I ask him about the layoff and he denies it's happening.*

The silly psychology PhD idea reminded him of a lunch with his group a few months before, at 99 Bottles of Beer in Santa Cruz. They went there for lunch every few weeks to try different brands of beer and get new punches on their 99's card. When all 99 holes were punched, a small brass plaque with your name was put on their wall, and they gave you a 99 Bottles of Beer T-shirt. At their last lunch, Gordon had challenged his group to invent improbable PhD thesis topics, and had proposed one on the "Mechanics of Food."

"After all," he had claimed, "the textures of food on your tongue play a big part in its taste. Hamburger patties have to stay in one mechanically intact piece as they cook. Bread has to cut cleanly and the slices have to stay in one piece as you make or eat a sandwich." While the others tried to think of even stupider PhD topics, Gordon suggested another one on "Predicting the Sounds of Newly Invented Machines."

"Before clothes or dish washing machines were invented, nobody could have guessed what they'd sound like. They both make quite unexpected noises."

"But the inventors couldn't have cared less," Rob retorted ungrammatically. "Why does the sound matter?"

"Why does any PhD thesis topic matter?" Gordon replied. "Most PhD topics are sillier and less fun than these. I bet you couldn't find any scientific theory that could predict the sound of thunder, even knowing lightning existed as a natural phenomenon."

Kermit chimed in, "I bet I'll finish my beer before you chin waggers do and get my 99's plaque first." That shut everyone up and the contest ended, everyone attacking their hamburgers.

In Doug's next weekly engineering meeting, Gordon noticed Doug's hair was getting grayer and his face was looking gaunt. Gordon thought the loss of the IBM business and the impending layoff must be a great strain on him. Having to fire so many of his engineers must be a terrible burden for such a decent man.

Carter stopped by Gordon's office the next afternoon, as Gordon struggled to do productive work while waiting for the big layoff. Carter had become Gordon's network contact in Marketing. This informal network included Seagate individuals from every department, people who wanted Seagate and its products to succeed. They often met at Malone's Bar, and sometimes included Al, Tom, or Doug. Such unofficial networks were common in successful companies. They weren't documented in any official company organizational chart but upper management people often quietly participated. It was a way for people to communicate around the distortions of truth that pass up any chain of command. Managers favorably twist facts as they pass them on to their bosses, and bad news sometimes doesn't get to the top for action. Managers know that information is power and are tempted to not keep their workers fully informed. Bureaucratic companies and governments ignore or punish such informal people networks.

"Let's go play croquet on the city hall lawn," Carter suggested. It was the middle of a busy morning in late 1988, and the idea hit Gordon as bizarre. Thinking for a moment, he realized that Carter was indirectly warning him that the big layoff would happen tomorrow. Carter's marketing department was in Al's headquarters building and Carter was cozy with the ladies that worked there. No doubt they were typing up the layoff notices. Useful work was impossible in the situation and Carter somehow knew he would be laid off too. "I've got the croquet equipment. Let's go."

They met across the street with Camille and several other doomed friends in their network. It was a lovely late fall day in Scotts Valley, breezes carrying down the fragrance of the redwood forests covering the surrounding mountains. They joked easily with each other as they enjoyed the game in spite of the impending doom, each content with the work they had done to help Seagate succeed. It didn't seem to matter who scored, who fouled, or who won the game.

"Camille, it's been an adventure working with you," Gordon said, aiming his mallet so his ball would knock hers into a hedge.

Camille smiled. "It was good for me too, Gordon honey." He stumbled and his ball missed, bouncing into the hedge he had intended for hers.

The next morning was December 1, 1988. Layoffs are always worst close to Christmas.

Gordon arrived at work to find a new security guard sitting at a card table in his building lobby, holding a clipboard with a list of names.

"Please hand me your badge," the guard said.

He looked at Gordon's badge, found his name on the list, and handed the badge back. Gordon walked toward the lobby door that led to his office. He heard the voice of an engineer who had arrived just behind him.

"Aren't you going to give me back my badge?"

The rent-a-cop guard is letting the man figure out for himself that he's no longer an employee.

A thousand employees had been laid off. Gordon's group had dropped from 21 people to 9.

Gordon soon learned that Marc had fired Stern. *Seagate should have fired Marc. Stern's an exceptional recording head technologist that helped Seagate's products benefit the world; Marc's only concern is benefiting himself.*

Camille and Carter had both been sacked.

Rob walked in Gordon's office door. "I heard all the Scotts Valley production workers were fired without notice and they're not being allowed into the buildings to retrieve their belongings from their lockers. There's been rioting in front of Building 5."

"Look out my window over at the headquarters building, Rob. See that huddle of people standing in the parking lot in front of it? There was a phone call threatening to bomb their building, and those people streamed out for safety."

Tom's marketing vice president that had called from Korea with the booming voice was also fired, along with the entire marketing department of highly paid men.

Later that morning Gordon discovered a San Jose newspaper reporter who had somehow gotten into the building and was wandering around interviewing people. A small attack squad of surviving employees was also roaming the building, seizing PCs from empty offices. After determining that they were not stealing them for personal use, and after escorting the reporter over to the headquarters building, Gordon found working was impossible and left the building. *The depressing mood here is driving me nuts. I'll go get a haircut...*

He drove down Scotts Valley Boulevard to BJ's Classic Hair Salon. His secretary had arranged Gordon's first visit to BJ's after Gordon had complained about the poor haircuts he got at regular Scotts Valley men's barber shops. He had been nervous during his first visit. The salon was full of women and was just as raunchy as male barber shops. The only difference was that the pictures of scantly clad people on the walls were of men instead of women. Gordon saw a copy of Al's restaurant cookbook *Fandango* on BJ's waiting area table.

"So, BJ, you know Al?"

"Sure. He comes here once a month for a haircut, just like you." They laughed.

Gordon didn't want to return to Seagate after he left BJ's, so he stopped to look at a truck parked in a vacant lot. Its driver had an assortment of machine tools laid out on a canvas spread over the dirt. Gordon bought a drill press and a vise, paying with a check after noticing that the canvas covered the truck license plate. *The banks are closed now and I can stop the check tomorrow morning if the drill press doesn't work.* The man also had routers and band saws, but Gordon had learned long ago that his safety level in motorized tools ended at drill press. Some people that used band saws and routers had only eight or nine fingers.

When Gordon got home he told Shirley about the big layoff. "That's terrible!" Shirley said. "Firing so many Santa Cruz people and so close to Christmas!"

Within a week nearly all of the personnel employees that handled the layoff were themselves laid off.

This was Gordon's introduction to the modern corporate world with its limited gratitude for employee loyalty. Xerox had given Gordon eighteen months pay when it closed his PARC lab. He had always thought that California employment law required at least two weeks notice or pay upon job termination. The layoff taught him that California law didn't require any severance pay at all. Draconian layoffs like this weren't uncommon in 1980's Silicon Valley companies and are the norm today in many U.S. industries.

Alice cancelled Seagate's Scotts Valley rental building leases as fast as possible; then Marc fired her without notice. Alice had been invaluable to Seagate and she was surprised and outraged that her reward was to be fired. "Tough luck, Alice," Marc had said with a smile.

Seagate soon rehired some of the fired assembly women to replace the marketing men, including the unsinkable Camille. The ladies turned out to be exceptional in working with Seagate's customers because they were smart people who knew disc drive technology first hand. They had learned it on the drive assembly line. The ladies used charm and token rewards to get Seagate engineers to come to customer technical meetings on time. On-time arrivers got chocolate chip cookies. Latecomers found a room full of cookie eaters but no cookie plate.

Seagate's stock price collapsed below its book value after the business bust, and all stock options of the remaining employees went underwater, becoming worthless. Rumors of a hostile takeover of the company began circulating and Seagate's Board of Directors voted to adopt a "poison pill" defense. SEC regulations required anyone buying up more than 5% of Seagate's public stock to disclose the purchase, which would trigger the poison pill that authorized Seagate to give each of its other shareholders ten shares for every one they held. This made hostile takeover attempts ten times more costly and impractical.

Al apologized for the poison pill at the next employee meeting a few months later. "We found it distasteful but necessary. Seagate's low stock price could be exploited by a raider who could borrow money to buy up a majority of our shares using Seagate's net worth as collateral for an investment bank loan of the stick purchase money; then bleeding money out of the company sales revenue and assets. They would take millions of dollars and Seagate would be left paying off the heavy debt with the money that used to be profits."

40.

Seagate Women

Nancy was one of several female Seagate design engineers. Bright, attractive, and lively, she got along famously with the male engineers by kidding and bantering with them on their own level. She acted like one of the guys and was well respected as an engineer. Gordon thought she had the tomboy female skills often learned by girls that grew up with brothers.

One Friday Nancy stuck her head into Gordon's office. "Why are you wearing your ordinary white shirt and dress slacks today?"

"I always wear white shirt and slacks. What's special about today?" he replied.

"Today is dress-down casual Friday."

"Did you just invent that?"

With an impish smile, she replied, "Everyone knows about casual Friday and we don't want you left out!"

"Well, I guess I know about it now," he said thinking it was a great idea. After she left, he drove down Scotts Valley to a clothing store. The loudest shirt they had was a mild Hawaiian motif, so he drove to 99 Bottles of Beer. They had T-shirts embossed with their motto "Only Beer can make Thirst so Wonderful." He bought one and wore it the rest of the day.

The next Friday, Gordon was wearing a T-shirt from Loreto, Mexico with a picture of a large green Toucan parrot. He was sitting at his credenza looking out his office window at the overgrown Tree Circus, and at a recording design calculation for a new disc drive that his Sun Sparc computer workstation was agreeably running. The program used a self-consistent magnetic recording math analysis he had developed and programmed at his former Xerox job.

The VAX computer terminal next to his desk behind him was also busy, showing progress on a head flight design the minicomputer down the hall was dutifully running. Gordon was about to sign a $150,000 purchase order for a Fourier transform infrared spectrophotometer instrument that Peter wanted for the science analysis lab.

Gordon sensed a presence at the office door behind his back and felt a potent sexual aura through the Common Sense. It was Camille, the striking blond. Gordon stood up with some difficulty because his legs had turned to Jell-O as usual. Tom had rehired Camille and promoted her to a senior position in marketing after the marketing men were fired.

"You're the best scientist at Seagate and I want to ask you a question about my platform in running for Scotts Valley City Council," she said.

"Have a seat," Gordon said, trying to get control of his legs. "Would you like some coffee?"

"Sure." They walked down the hall to the coffee room, poured their coffee, and returned to sit at his conference table. Gordon required his secretary to only get coffee for Seagate visitors, not employees. She frequently asked if she could get Gordon some coffee, anyway.

"You're running for a council seat?" *She can't have much of a chance of being elected to office in Scotts Valley if Al was overruled by the City Council on a simple request to make his headquarters address "#1 Disc Drive."*

"I'm running for public office because I want to do something in my life that posterity will remember. Don't you feel the same way?"

"Well, Andy Warhol said everyone will be famous for 15 minutes. I think I may have already had my fame accidentally with Alluvial O. Fansome."

"Who or what is Alluvial O. Fansome?"

"He was born a half-century ago when I was a student at Cal Tech. I wanted to mail away for a Rosicrucian booklet called *Mastery of Life* that I saw in an advertisement in *Popular Mechanics* magazine. The ad said I would learn secrets of the ancient Templar Crusader Knights, the Holy Grail, and Freemasonry. I didn't want to use my real name because my classmates would laugh at me when they saw the Rosicrucian booklet in my mailbox. An alluvial fan is an Earth feature I had just learned about in geology class.

"Alluvial is famous at Cal Tech today, fifty years later. He has a wife, a driver's license, gets junk mail, and has a web site at MySpace.com/alfansome."

Camille decided to ignore this claim to fame. "I'm running for the council on an 'unlimited water' platform so new businesses can be started in Scotts Valley."

"How can that work, since Scotts Valley is entirely dependent on well water and the ground water levels have been dropping for years? That's why the city banned new businesses."

"A professor at Santa Clara University told me that water from the Sierra Nevada snow pack comes to Scotts Valley through an underground aquifer. The locals here don't know about that."

"Sierra mountain runoff water does flow into the California Central Valley, but then it would have to flow uphill over the Temblor Range on the west side of the valley, then down into the Santa Clara Valley, and finally uphill again over the Santa Cruz mountains to Scotts Valley." As he said this it was dawning on him that if he didn't stop talking this dazzling lady would leave.

"That's hundreds of miles for the water to travel, and might seem unlikely except for another discovery at Santa Clara University," he quickly added. "On their campus near the Faculty Club is a monument for the first airplane flight."

"You mean by the Wright brothers?" she asked.

"No, I mean by John J. Montgomery, who flew a glider across that whole distance from the Sierra Nevada to Santa Clara. And if someone could glide that far over those mountains without an engine, water should be able to go that far too," Gordon fibbed. By then, he had collected some of his wits and wasn't about to tell her that Montgomery had actually only bailed out in a hang glider from a hot air balloon floating over Santa Clara University, and that his determined but inaccurate wife put up the monument after his death.

Camille paused, thought for a few seconds, and finally nodded. "Please let me ask you another question. As a scientist," she said hesitatingly, "may I ask if you believe in God?"

Gordon wondered how to answer this without distorting the truth. She thought she was asking a question in the context of her ordinary human space-time experience, but she was actually asking about the deeper reality it arose from.

"I'm a very ordinary engineer and scientist," he slowly replied, "but I happen to be excellent at applying the scientific method. I'm able to disregard the assumptions that people are taught from birth, as the scientific method requires on a question like you're asking. My answer to you is that I don't fight truth. God is as real and present here and now, as the sky above and the Earth below."

This seemed to surprise her, and she again hesitated. "But if God is here, how can He allow evil, murder, and death?"

Gordon pondered how to answer truthfully and it occurred to him to use a parable. He smiled, remembering that Jesus often spoke in parables in the Bible. "Imagine a mother watching her small children playing outside in her yard. She's working in her kitchen and keeping her eye on them through a window. They're playing Cops and Robbers.

"'Bang! Bang!' shouts her son. Her daughter holds her hands to her chest, falls down on the lawn, and lies still. The mother smiles, knowing her daughter will soon rise up again and be well."

He saw recognition start to come into her eyes.

"Camille, think and see: *there is no death*.

"Why do people like horror movies? Why aren't they evil? We enjoy them because we know all the evil will vanish when we leave the movie theater. Even though we know the movie isn't real we still live it and are totally absorbed by it while it runs. Our lives on Earth are just a different kind of movie show, so entertaining, so complex, so real and so perfect that it resists disbelief. You can accept the idea that the infinite power of God could easily create and run such a movie, right? When we die we leave our space-time movie and return home to God; we end our pretense that God was somewhere else during the movie. The movie is for our enjoyment and there're no restrictions on the amount of good or evil anyone can do in it."

Camille dropped her head in her hands, and was still for a moment. Finally, she looked up at Gordon with tears glistening in her eyes. "I don't know what made me ask you about God, but thank you. My grandmother is dying and your words comfort my fears."

41.

Eclipse over Mexico!

A total solar eclipse was predicted for July 1989 and Gordon's aviation friend James invited him to watch it at Rancho Las Cruces, a private club near the southern tip of Baja California, Mexico. The club was created after World War II by a wealthy Mexican and his Hollywood friends John Wayne, Bing Crosby, Desi Arnez, and Clark Gable. It had a beautiful tropical setting in a palm tree oasis.

In Mexican land ownership, American gringos should only be minority partners. When Bing asked if his Las Cruces home could be sold for cash, he was told that land ownership was restricted to Mexican citizens, but his family could use the house in perpetuity. There was a long history of Americans believing they could own Mexican land in places like Ensenada, Puerto Vallarta, and Alamos. Many of them ultimately learned the hard way that foreign ownership could be only a temporary right in Mexico. When gringo land developments became valuable, Mexican citizens sometimes attempted to take them over. The only safe property title had majority ownership by a Mexican citizen having important friends in Mexico City. One early major takeover came after the American development of Mexican oil fields in the 1930's. The Mexican government seized the oil industry from its U.S. investors and nationalized it, forming their country's oil monopoly Pemex.

Gordon and Shirley planned to fly their Mooney to see the eclipse, with Penny and Phil flying their own Mooney. The club was near the Baja tip 700 air miles south of the U.S. and took 3.5 hours to fly from the U.S. to Loreto to go through Mexican customs, then another 40 minutes to fly to the dirt airstrip at Las Cruces. The Mexican authorities feared a tidal wave of private planes would overwhelm the small Baja airports and they wouldn't have enough aviation gas. The rumor was that Mexico would either close all airports at the Baja tip or impose a $65 landing fee.

The day before the eclipse, the two planes flew to Mulege halfway down the Baja gulf coast, the closest place they could get rooms for the night. Gordon flew at low power which gave him a 1400 mile range at 150 mph. He carried an extra five gallon can of gas, enough to make the round trip down and back without refueling. But Mulege had plenty of gas when they arrived and they filled up. By that afternoon there were 35 small airplanes parked in every possible spot, blocking the Mulege airstrip. Aircraft arriving later were unable to land and had to turn back.

At a Mulege bar that night, Gordon spread a rumor that the eclipse would be total at Mulege as well as at the Baja tip, downing several killer margaritas in the line of duty. However, his rumor failed and planes began taking off for points south at 5am on the next day, for the noon eclipse.

Gordon, Shirley, Penny, and Phil piled into one Mooney and they headed south, listening to increasingly funny radio traffic. Some pilots feared the Mexican authorities' landing fee and landed at Villa Constitution, well north of the eclipse centerline which meant they would miss totality. Other planes went into Punta Colorado, Punta Pescadero, and Punta Arenas, filling up those small airstrips until there was no room for more planes to land. Dozens of people had advance reservations for lunch at Punta Pescadero, but once its airstrip filled up, their planes couldn't land and their reservations were useless.

Gordon landed at the Las Cruces dirt strip at 9:45am, taking its last parking spot. James had already arrived in his twin engine Beech aircraft and was waiting to greet them. They walked to the club patio and saw a row of small houses facing a beach. Dolphins swam and jumped offshore. A lovely green island lay shimmering in the distance, beyond the club's blue swimming pool. The tropic scene was wonderfully beautiful, reminding Gordon of the movie *South Pacific*. Gordon set up his telescope on the patio, the portable Questar he had bought with Seagate stock option money. The sun was directly overhead for ideal viewing, without a cloud in the sky to obscure the eclipse. As they waited for the eclipse to begin, a homebuilt ultralight aircraft took off and circled overhead.

The eclipse began just after noon with an edge of the moon kissing the sun. Shadow bands raced towards them, down Baja hills from the west. The sun's disc was slowly consumed by the moon passing before it and daylight took on a surreal quality when only a knife edge of sun remained. Gordon noticed that every leaf on a nearby tree was casting a tiny shadow of the thin crescent moon. Totality arrived at 12:50 as sudden night shut down the sky, leaving only a dim sunset far distant in every direction. An immense solar corona sprang into view, broad pointed rays of white stretching far away from the sun. Twin red prominences blazed from the sun's left and right sides, scarlet arcs of gas traveling from one sunspot to another.

Mercury, Venus, Jupiter, and Mars emerged in the dark sky. A bright ring of Bailey's beads encircled the dark moon, each bead a ray of sunlight peeking through a lunar canyon. Six and a half minutes of eclipse darkness totality passed, nearly the longest possible in the solar system.

Birds began to sing as daylight returned, as if it was dawn. Dolphins swam close to shore, perhaps to huddle nearer to the humans in the unnatural experience. Gordon heard the motorized lawn mower sound of the ultralight aircraft overhead. He spoke to its pilot and his son after the eclipse. They had flown the motor glider airplane across the Atlantic Ocean from Salzburg, Germany, at 100 mph on one 27 gallon tank of gas. They told him they had wanted to watch the eclipse from the air to be closer to the sun. *Hmm, 93 million miles from the sun minus a thousand feet is still 93,000,000 miles.*

42.

Seeing Red Dots

A year after the big layoff, Seagate sales were again booming as IBM PC clones became popular. When IBM had first begun selling its PCs, major U.S. companies began seriously accepting them. Executives everywhere knew the saying, "No one ever got fired for buying IBM computers." Companies like Dell and Compaq began selling IBM PC clones at prices lower than IBM. IBM started buying Seagate drives again, after finding that the cost to build their own drives was higher than just buying them from Seagate. They were squeezed for profits because they had to lower their IBM PC prices to compete against the clone companies.

Computing uses blossomed a few years after companies began allowing their employees to buy PCs, producing more corporate value than the older mainframe IBM computers companies were accustomed to. Clone PC Intel hardware and Microsoft Windows software quickly became ubiquitous.

The disruption of mainframe and minicomputer computer technology by PCs was in full bloom.

Gordon hired new engineers to handle his group's growing workload, but he hired one engineer too quickly. Following the advice of a friend, he hired an engineer without his usual detailed interview, technology design quiz, and background check. He soon had to ask the man to leave after his incompetence became undeniable. Gordon gave him a month's pay to ease his departure, signing his timecards in advance.

A week later Rob told Gordon the man was copying company confidential drive design documents to take with him, so Gordon asked him to keep the pay but no longer come to work.

Seagate's finance people called Gordon a month later, to tell him the engineer was demanding Seagate let him exercise his stock option to buy Seagate shares. The man's option agreement had a standard legal clause requiring Seagate to notify him if his option was cancelled, within a month of his leaving the company. It had been over a month since he left, but when they examined his timecards they found only three weeks had passed from his last paycheck date. Gordon thought the man was a little too greedy stealing design information and not waiting a few more weeks after he left. He called him at his home and gave him the news. "When you update your resume to look for a new job, you'll have to account for your time here at Seagate. If they call me for a reference I'll explain that company policy allows me only to verify your employment here. That's the best I can do to help you continue your career. I hope you'll take my advice about engineering professionalism."

"The drive yield on our Singapore production line has dropped from 98% to 50% over a one month period." Tom was talking to Ken, who ran Seagate's Quality Department. "Fly to Singapore, find the problem, and fix it in three days or less."

Ken stepped off the plane in Singapore a day later, refreshed from his first class flight, although it was 1:00am when he arrived. He was soon at the Singapore plant talking to Joe, its production manager. Joe was Chinese, as were almost all of the Singapore employees. Seagate's U.S. people gave them American nicknames if their Chinese names were hard to pronounce, and most liked their nicknames. It seemed they favored fictitious names for cultural reasons, and favored inside offices without window views, where they couldn't be seen from outside the building. Some Americans thought this had to do with them not wanting to be visible to mythical Chinese devils. Others thought it had to do with feng shui.

This was early in the history of high-tech electronics manufacturing in Asia, and Americans were ignorant of Asian cultures and languages.

"Joe, what's causing the drives to fail?"

"It's bad stepper motors." These motors moved the recording heads from track to track over a disc.

"What's the yield of good stepper motors?" Ken asked.

Joe seemed reluctant to answer, but finally spoke. "Only 50% of the motors work in drives. The rest cause drives to fail their final test."

"Please let me see the production records for the last month, Joe." Again, Joe seemed strangely reluctant, but slowly complied. "So, the WIP, the Work in Process, is about 1000 drives per day. Can I see the inventory records of the incoming motors and their quality inspection records?"

These were silently produced. Ken became certain that something was not being said. "Joe, is there something you want to tell me?"

Another long pause. "I am shamed by our failure to produce good drives," Joe replied.

Ken was aware of Chinese cultural embarrassment in admitting error. "Joe, the only important question is what's wrong and how to fix it. There may not be a question of fault at all, just how to change the assembly process to raise the yield back up."

Ken checked the incoming inspection records on the stepper motors and found their quality was very good. Baffled, he flipped through pages until a number caught his eye. "Joe, you're starting 1000 drives per day, but only 500 are being shipped. These inventory records say that only 500 new motors arrived per day last month. How can the plant run at 1000 drives per day with only half that number of motors coming in? Joe silently dropped his head.

It began to dawn on Ken that an explanation was that the 500 good drives had the 500 new motors, and that the other 500 drives might be 500 bad motors going round and round in assembly line circles inside the plant. Ken knew the production line had a rework cycle that tried to salvage motors that made drives fail final test. The motor was removed and an Avery red dot label was stuck on it. The motor was then returned to the assembly line for another try in a different drive. Frequently, that motor and drive worked together. It was a matter of whether the tolerances of the drive and the motor happened to match well together or not, sort of like a couple on a blind date. If a motor with a red dot failed in another drive it got a second red dot. A motor was scrapped if it got three dots.

Ken and Joe put on white bunny suits and walked through the factory. Ken checked the manufacturing stations involved in the red dot rework cycle. Each station had its process instructions clipped to a wall. He found the paper instructions at one station looker newer than the others. It should have read, "Send motor with three red dots to scrap," but now read, "Remove three dots from motor and return motor to assembly line."

"Joe, so no motors are being scrapped at all? The drive yield collapsed because the WIP became saturated with bad motors?" This seemed crazy, but Ken knew the Asians were smart people and there would be an explanation. Seagate's startup cowboy culture still persevered.

Ken and Joe left the factory floor, took off their bunny suits, walked to the cafeteria, and sat down with cups of coffee. "O.K., Joe. Please just tell me the straight story. Believe me, that's what Tom wants to hear."

Without further hesitation, Joe gave a very direct American-style answer.

"The finance department in Seagate's U.S. headquarters insisted we increase the drive production rate. Finance measures the rate by how many drives go into final test each day. We knew this was wrong and we asked them to only count actual shipments of good drives to customers. They said that would make their quarterly financial accounting numbers look bad. We ordered more new motors but they weren't arriving fast enough. They insisted we increase the final test rate, and we did what we were told."

Ken was stunned. "We need to immediately fix this and call Tom." Ken knew that even if the accounting numbers were looking good, revenues were going to quickly collapse if the company wasn't shipping enough good drives. He and Joe restored the scrap station instructions and the two calculated how many times bad motors had been deliberately assembled into drives.

It was late afternoon when they went to Joe's office to call Tom in Scotts Valley, where it was early morning of the previous day.

"Tom, you're not going to believe the drive yield collapsed in Singapore because of Seagate's finance people in the U.S."

"Try me," Tom answered levelly. Tom listened to the story, hung up, thought a minute, and called the head of accounting. "Be in my office within five minutes." The man showed up in three.

"Financial accounting tricks don't ship drives that bring in sales revenue," Tom told him. I'm ordering you and your people to immediately end this crap. You will count only actual drive shipments accepted by customers. All of you will take the Seagate Institute of Technology course and learn hands-on that our company revenue comes from assembling and selling drives that work. If any of you haven't passed the course two weeks from now you should look for new jobs. Do you understand me? Thank you." The man's hands were trembling badly. As he left, Tom made a note on his calendar.

By the end of another week Tom had magically doubled the number of new motors arriving in Singapore, and they were now shipping 1000 good drives per day.

A week later he called the accounting manager. "I checked with the SIT instructors and two of your people didn't take the final exam."

"I'm sorry, Tom. They said the course was too difficult. I'll talk with them." His voice was trembling.

"Indeed you will. You'll tell them that ignoring their president's order is a termination offense. Fire them both immediately. You should have called me about this. Instead I had to check with SIT myself and call you. I suggest you do not make me personally verify tomorrow that you have fired those two today. Make another mistake like that and I'll fire you too."

Ken was promoted to Vice President of Quality with a title bestowed by Tom, "The man with the Kiss of Quality." Ken was actually the second the Quality VP to be given this title. The first one had been sent to Asia to resolve a similar quality problem but had allowed himself to be diverted by the Seagate manufacturing people there to travel to Phuket Island south of Bangkok, a lush vacation island where he wouldn't interfere with their production numbers. He was no longer employed at Seagate, having failed to ask himself "What would Al say?"

Ken's normal job in Quality was to test new product drives for reliability. These tests were run on a few thousand drives over several months, giving each drive a total of about a thousand drive test hours. One important reason so many drives were sacrificed in testing was to uncover latent design flaws, often in the parts drive makers bought from suppliers rather than in their own drive design.

Disc drive manufacturers advertised that they tested to a million drive-hours, justifying the claim by multiplying the thousand of drives tested times the thousand test hours. Their customers logically concluded that drives they bought should last a million hours on average, even though its design had only been tested for several months. A million hours is more than 100 years and disc drives have never been expected nor advertised to operate longer than five years, over the entire half-century that drives have been made and sold.

Reliability claims were easy to exaggerate because they were hard to prove. Drive performance specifications could be verified in minutes, but reliability verification took many years and the products became obsolete in less than a single year. The first drive company that claimed million hour reliability forced all other drive companies to follow suit, to remain competitive. Wise drive customers assessed reliability based on manufacturer guaranteed warranty periods, typically three to five years.

There's about a 1% chance of a disc drive failing in its first year of operation. Failure rates can increase to over 5% or even more a few years later, depending on how drives are treated.

43.

Sue if You Can't Sell Drives

"Seagate is being sued by Atasi over the voice coil actuator motor in our new IBM PC-AT drives," Doug announced in one of his weekly management staff meetings. Atasi was a drive manufacturer that had failed to successfully compete against Seagate. It had ceased drive manufacturing and was using its remaining cash to fund lawsuits, hoping to survive on settlement money. "I know you engineers think lawyers are a curse on humanity, but the company asks you to cooperate fully in defending us.

"Moving on, I want you all to know that my advisor Roy collapsed from a heart attack just before this meeting. He's on his way to the hospital now."

Gordon had been sitting in Doug's outer office with Roy minutes earlier, waiting for this meeting to start. Doug had somehow detected Roy's face going pale and had turned to his assistant Betty.

"Give Roy one of the aspirins you keep in your desk, immediately. Call 911 and tell them he's having a major heart attack. Don't let them delay a minute in sending an ambulance." Doug had then risen from his chair and proceeded into his conference room for this weekly engineering staff meeting. Gordon had marveled at how he could calmly run the meeting.

It took a week for the patent lawyers to get around to Gordon. Two men sat on one side of the table in Gordon's conference room, with a young woman they introduced as Phyllis, a paralegal. The men wore expensive English suits and didn't smile. Phyllis was short, plain, and wore thick glasses.

Gordon figured that when visitors sat at random chairs around a table the discussion would usually be amicable. This one would be adversarial because the visitors were all sitting on one side of the table with Gordon on the other. It would be one side versus the other.

Gordon had heard that the lawyers had copied mountains of documents from other Seagate engineers, and he figured Phyllis' job was to sit up all night sifting through them, looking for the proverbial "smoking gun" lawyers always talked about.

"Dr. Gordon, what documentation do you have on Seagate disc drive model ST-4026?"

Gordon figured he should answer as simply as possible. "None," he replied.

There was a pause while the lawyers hunted for a "magic phrase" that might get them the answers they wanted. "Don't you have *any* documentation on the drive?"

"All ST-4026 documents are downstairs in the Engineering Documentation Library."

"We heard you issue documents called minispecs—what are they?"

Damn, somebody must have blabbed! "They're unofficial recording design numbers, condensed into a single page for each drive. They're for engineering use and aren't official specifications, which are downstairs as I said."

"We'll need copies of all minispecs."

"O.K." Gordon knew better than to argue with people who could bill $500 for every hour they chose to spend.

Later that day he sat down in his office at the Apple Macintosh computer he kept minispecs on. One nice feature of a Mac was it took only a minute to tell the machine to print them all out, though the printing itself took hours. The next day he handed a four-inch thick pile of minispecs to Phyllis.

He pointed out to her that each one had a "Seagate Confidential Information" notice at the bottom.

"These contain proprietary Seagate information and you may be personally liable if any of them become public." He didn't try to explain the recording physics that the numbers on the pages represented or that minispecs contained no information at all about voice coil actuator motors.

She looked confused so he added, "Look them over carefully. As Shakespeare said, 'there's divinity in odd numbers.'" Gordon walked off, annoyed by his wasted time, fighting off any feelings of sympathy for her.

Gordon walked to Doug's office to tell him about the minispecs the lawyers had demanded.

"You know, Doug, President Thomas Jefferson would be dismayed to see what's happened to the U.S. patent system he set up so carefully. Small inventors have little chance against infringers with money to pay lawyers, and the U.S. Patent Office actually encourages lawsuits like this one by issuing patents in doubtful cases. If Seagate was a small company we wouldn't have a chance of winning against those packs of lawyers.

"Inventors would be better served if the Patent Office adopted a peer review system. It should circulate applications to qualified people for review before issuing a patent, like technical papers are confidentially reviewed by an author's peers before publication. Far fewer bad patents would be issued, the same way fewer bad papers are published."

"Gordon, you and I can't change the way things are. It's unfortunately true that if one party in a lawsuit has slim financial resources, the other party with deeper pockets usually wins. Corporations like ours budget five to twenty million dollars to fight lawsuits like Atasi's. If we weren't prepared to spend that money, lawyers would bleed us dry."

In the end, the question of the legitimacy of Atasi's patents was never settled in court. Seagate proved Atasi had taken its motor design from older motors patented earlier by other drive companies. Such "prior art" legally invalidated Atasi's later patents, and showed that they should never have been granted. Atasi was legally required to list all such earlier patents in their applications but had not. When confronted with these earlier patents, Atasi's lawyers offered to cancel their suit if Seagate would pay their legal fees. Al flatly refused to pay the lawyers a single dime.

As Gordon walked into Malone's bar that evening, he noticed a new sign behind the bar, announcing that Malone's was "Seagate Building 16." Seagate's expansion in Scotts Valley had ended with 15 buildings.

Doug explained the Atasi outcome.

"Gordon, even though we proved to them that Atasi's patents were invalid, they threatened to continue their law suit against us anyway. Atasi couldn't make money selling their disc drives against competitors like us, so they had to give up manufacturing drives. Their only hope of survival was getting money from lawsuit settlements. If they had gotten money from us, they would have used it to sue other drive companies to get more and more. As you said, Jefferson invented the patent system to help American enterprise, not hurt it. But it often works the opposite way today. Our attorneys tell us the Atasi lawyers committed ethical misconduct in this suit. They're asking the state bar to bring action against Atasi's law firm."

"That's a real crappy situation, Doug. Most disagreements in the world are settled by the people directly involved, using ordinary social and ethical rules. The Hippocratic Oath has guided doctors since 400 B.C. to help patients and not hurt them. Engineering professional ethics keeps buildings and bridges from collapsing, airplanes from crashing, and our ethics make our disc drives reliable.

"To me, it's immoral that laws schools and bar associations allow unethical behavior by lawyers. Do you realize that law schools teach their students that disagreements should be settled in court for money? Cheat someone, or drive drunk and run over a child, or steal an old person's savings, and law professors teach that it's only a question of monetary penalties, with lawyers entitled to secretly take a quarter of the cash. Trial judges legally bless the cash; they make the cash secret from the public whose taxes pay for the courts; and judges even enforce payment of the cash to the lawyers without the court hearing required of any other creditor."

Doug smiled tolerantly, letting Gordon vent his feelings.

"Law leaders say bad doctors should be punished by malpractice lawsuits, but lawyers don't sue to revoke doctor's medical licenses. That wouldn't produce cash for them. Instead, they sue malpractice insurance companies to get big settlements that all medical patients ultimately pay for. Law professors advise TV producers to show TV attorneys fighting for justice and honesty, at the same time they're teaching law students that justice means lawyers getting money!"

"It's not as quite as hopeless as you're making out, Gordon. The problem's that the legal profession has always been run by men, the naturally competitive sex. But law is a social occupation, natural for women because they tend to work cooperatively. There are an increasing percentage of women lawyers and judges and so there's hope for future fairness, decency, and honesty in the practice of law.

"And America does have some ethical lawyers that do help their clients receive fair treatment and justice, lawyers who disregard the amoral lessons of their teachers. Those are the exceptionally intelligent lawyers, the small percentage able to make a living from the honest practice of law. There are some honorable law leaders as well."

Gordon nodded silently, smiled ruefully, finished off his beer, and left for home.

44.

Kermit's Poison Mushrooms

Gordon was sitting at his desk a week after the Atasi lawyer hassle. His phone rang. It was Rob.

"Kermit's in the Santa Cruz hospital, in the intensive care unit. He ate some mushrooms he found on one of his forest walks last Sunday. It's a deadly poisonous variety and the doctors in the small Santa Cruz hospital don't know how to cure him. Kermit didn't want me to call you because he thinks you already have enough problems to worry about."

Gordon knew that Kermit had taken a university course on mushroom identification and enjoyed picking them on his solitary weekend hikes through the San Lorenzo Valley forests, to take back to his apartment to cook.

"Thanks, Rob. I'll go see him." Gordon hung up the phone deeply shaken. He profoundly liked and respected his friend Kermit. *I brought him here to Santa Cruz and showed him the forests I knew he would love. Now they may kill him. And last year Sam died after his motorcycle accident. Some car driver they never caught ran him off Empire Grade Road into a tree.* Gordon took off his glasses, dropped his head and covered his eyes with his hands.

After a while he hauled himself onto his feet and left for the hospital. Half an hour later he found a pale Kermit in the intensive care unit with IV tubes plugged into both arms.

"What happened, Kermit? How can I help? I thought you took a mushroom safety course at the university."

Kermit smiled wanly and spoke softly. "There's bad news, good, bad, and good."

Gordon knew Kermit very well and as sick as he was he was being technologist precise. He meant there were exactly four news items.

Gordon smiled. "Tell me the four in that order."

"The course I took made me think I could tell whether any forest mushroom was edible. I was wrong: bad news. But after I ate the mushroom I knew from the course that the symptoms in my gut meant it was poisonous. Knowing that I was poisoned was good news, because I knew to call 911. I looked the mushroom up in the course textbook and found its poison is fatal without treatment because the liver can't eliminate it from the body. The poison circulates in the blood until death: bad news. So I phoned the professor in San Francisco who taught my mushroom course. He came to this hospital an hour ago and told the doctors how to get the poison out of my system. I should fully recover in a few days: good news."

Gordon felt a wave of relief wash over him. "I'm thankful you'll recover."

He knew that was about all the emotion Kermit would accept. Kermit smiled as Gordon handed him a small green animal he had found in the hospital gift shop, a stuffed Kermit the Frog from the Sesame Street TV show. Gordon sat and chatted with Kermit for an hour, until Kermit looked ready for sleep.

45.

Grenex's "Million Dollar Disc" — NOT!

"Gentlemen, I'm going to show you outstanding results from your investment in us at Grenex." Jim was speaking as Grenex Technology VP at a meeting with the TVC venture capital people. Al, Doug, and Gordon were also present. The TVC men were wearing expensive looking suits. Al wore his usual sports shirt.

Jim placed a transparency on the 3M projector. "Here are recording technical measurements on a disc we recently made. We call it our 'Million Dollar Disc.'"

Gordon winced. *I asked Jim to go easy on Grenex's test claims, and especially not mention their so-called Million Dollar Disc. I hadn't had the heart to tell Grenex that disc was junk. But Jim acted like a new father and wouldn't listen to my test results on that terrible disc.*

Jim concluded his presentation. "This Million Dollar Disc shows we're ready to go into full scale disc production."

TVC had brought a disc technology consultant to the meeting, an engineer Gordon had worked with at Xerox. The man raised his hand. "Your data is measured at a bit density no higher than on Seagate's oxide discs. You need to store twice as many bits per disc as oxide for your cobalt disc to be economically successful. That's required by the TVC contract. Can you show us data taken at double density?" Jim hadn't expected this question, looked baffled, and had no reply.

"Gordon, show them your Seagate test data," Doug said. *Damn, I should have given Jim a clearer warning about that disc.*

Rising to put his own foil on the projector, Gordon said, "Here's our results on that same disc." The projector screen lit up with orderly rows of dozens of numbers identified by obscure acronyms, like EHF: 450 uv, RES: 30%, OW: 22 dB, BER: -2 and OTC: 0%. Kermit had programmed his spin stand tester to automatically make these recording measurements and print them out on a single page, using a H.P. lab computer with a Seagate disc drive. "They're encouraging, but they also show that problems still remain, especially contamination particles in the Grenex sputtering process."

"Gordon, we'd like to retest our 'Million Dollar Disc' at Grenex," Jim said, "to see why our results differ so greatly."

Double damn! He's leaving me no way to get out of this.

"Jim, contamination particles on that disc made its surface act like sandpaper. We had only tens of seconds to measure the test data I'm showing, before the disc chewed up our recording head and crashed it. Here's a photograph of that disc after the test."

Gordon projected another foil showing a disc with a rough ground-up metal circular trench where the test head had flown and crashed, a circle of grey surrounded by shiny mirror-like cobalt surface where the head hadn't flown.

"My test engineer has a ritual she uses for testing Grenex discs. She cleans each disc with a three step process she invented, and then gets Kermit's test computer ready to take instant measurements before she loads her test head onto the spinning disc. She usually has 10 to 20 seconds before the disc crashes her test head. She thinks the stress is giving her an ulcer."

Turning to the consultant, Gordon continued, "I don't have double-density data to show you either. That would require double-density heads, which need to fly at half the height of these standard heads. The contamination won't allow that. We've fabricated and tested double-density heads and they crashed in mere seconds, before any measurements could be made."

There was total silence in the room until Al rose. "Looks like Grenex needs to do more development work."

As Gordon walked out with the Seagate group, Doug said to him, "Please stop by my office tomorrow." Jim and the Grenex people were sitting alone in the room, looking crushed. Gordon was in a blue funk. *Jim's thinking I set him up, no doubt. What a disaster.*

The TVC people walked out with them and asked Al and Doug to accompany them to their car. They closed the car doors for privacy. "What do you suggest we do about Grenex's Phase Two financing, Al?" Phase Two was to demonstrate Grenex readiness for production of thousands of discs per day, at acceptable cost and yield.

Al and Doug knew this question meant TVC wanted to negotiate. They weren't ready to cut Grenex off completely and lose their entire investment, but they didn't want to fund the $15,000,000 Grenex second round deal either. There seemed to be too much risk after the "Million Dollar Disc" disaster.

After a short negotiation TVC offered to provide $5,000,000 additional cash and $2,000,000 in additional equipment leases, if Seagate contributed an equal amount of lease money and also agreed to give TVC majority ownership in Grenex. Venture capital companies often demanded a bigger percentage of the stock when a startup company got in trouble, and they often got it because the company principals and other backers didn't want to give up either.

"Gentlemen, I've got a different proposal," Al said. "Seagate doesn't want to dilute its Grenex stock shares."

Gordon was on his way to see Doug the next day. Marc saw him walking by his office and motioned him in, closing the door. Marc's office was a junkyard of tall piles of paper in every possible place, including the chair that a visitor might wish to sit on. Gordon saw a framed aerial photograph of Scotts Valley partly hiding behind a paper stack sitting on the floor and reaching nearly to the ceiling. "Possible future Seagate building sites" was marked on the photo, including the site of the former Scotts Valley Airport. Marc was nervously playing with his tobacco stained hands. He was a heavy smoker and the city fathers had forbidden smoking inside all Scotts Valley buildings. Marc was having withdrawal symptoms.

"Gordon, I want you to know that you'll be held responsible if Grenex fails. I'll personally see that Seagate fires you and I'll spread the word to every other disc drive company. No company will hire you and your career will be over." Gordon was speechless in stunned silence, eyes wide. *He's even smiling as he makes his threats.*

He stumbled out of Marc's office, blindly walking down the hall. In his daze Gordon slowly realized that Marc was setting him up as scapegoat to take the blame if Grenex failed. Marc was a master at backstabbing office politics. Gordon had neither time nor inclination to fight back. His time was consumed by disc drive technology designs and alligator emergencies. *Marc has no real responsibilities here, giving him all the scheming time he needs.*

As he walked to Doug's office, an unfamiliar emotion washed over Gordon, a feeling he had never experienced in his entire life. He had always kept himself a little detached from normal social life. Now he had been dragged by the scruff of his neck into direct confrontation with life.

He slowly realized this strange feeling was hate. He now deeply hated another human being for the first time in his life. Dazed by the wave of emotion, he blindly staggered against a nearby door sill. It was Stan's office. Stan looked up from his desk and saw him teetering.

"Gordon! Are you O.K.? Come in and sit down." Gordon took a step into the office. "Just sit down. I'll get you a cup of coffee."

Ten minutes later Gordon finished telling Stan about Marc. "I have to deal with Marc's threat myself, without asking for help from Doug or Al. Marc would turn any request for help against me. He's a master of office politics, I'm not. So I haven't told anybody about this. Except now I've told you."

Stan sat back in his chair, rubbing his chin. "Gordon, you're doing an excellent job for Seagate and I'm sure you and the Grenex people will succeed with the double-density cobalt disc. Just keep on doing that and don't worry about Marc. Doug, Al, and I are perfectly aware of everything that goes on. Please stop worrying."

"Thanks, Stan." Gordon felt less alone as he left Stan's office to walk to Doug's.

He was still dizzy when he arrived at Doug's office and he sat down in its anteroom to collect his wits. After a minute his head seemed to be spinning less and he looked up to see Doug standing patiently and silently in his office door, looking down at him. Gordon came out of his daze when he saw a twinkle in Doug's eye. "Come in and sit in my office."

"Gordon, when we got into the car with the TVC venture capital people yesterday, we discussed Grenex's next financing round. Al didn't want to dilute Seagate's percentage of Grenex ownership by giving more to TVC. Al has always wanted to own Grenex in the end and make it a Seagate division. So Al offered to buy out TVC by giving them back the money they invested in Grenex. They were happy to get out without a loss and agreed. Seagate now owns Grenex. We're making it a Seagate division immediately.

"But we need to quickly fix Grenex's disc development problems. Jim's 'Million Dollar Disc' disaster got us a better deal from TVC, but Grenex's dollar burn rate is now Seagate's problem instead of TVC's.

"Can you and the Grenex people drop the TVC advanced cobalt disc development, get your 'mystery' cobalt disc into volume production, and give us the double-density drives you told me about when all this started years ago?"

Gordon hastily recalled the Grenex backup plan he had made with Jim.

"Let me think a minute, Doug." Gordon let his mind's eye expand until he could visualize the entire Grenex production process, its remaining problems, and what might change when they switched to the mystery cobalt alloy. His best talent was this ability to wordlessly see an entire concept in an encompassing gestalt. He saw a number of risks ahead for Grenex. *I can deal with them. Marc's scheming I can't.*

"O.K., Doug. I'll guarantee that in three months Grenex will be above 85% yield using the mystery alloy. Grenex and my group will get you production disc quantities for a new double-density ST-251 disc drive, by replacing the oxide discs in our ST-225 drives. I also guarantee that drives using the mystery discs will have high production yield. They'll also write and read bits at 10 megabits per second, twice the ST-225 rate."

"Gordon, you don't need to give me guarantees. If you see Grenex cobalt production discs working in ST-251 drives, I know it'll happen. Concentrate on that and don't worry about anything else." With that last sentence, Doug was looking Gordon straight in the eye. Gordon suddenly realized that Doug was quite aware of Marc's schemes. *Doug may be able to keep Marc collared, but maybe Marc can still fool Al.*

Doug continued, "Federal securities law requires that in purchasing Grenex, all its stock options have to be cancelled. Your and your group's Grenex stock options will be replaced by options for an equal number of Seagate shares."

"Wow, Doug, that's incredibly generous! Seagate shares are worth $35 today, but Grenex shares would be worthless until after they get into successful production."

"That's Al's doing. Our financial people handling the Grenex purchase suggested one Seagate share for every 500 Grenex shares, but Al insisted on one-to-one. I want you to also know that although Seagate owns Grenex shares, Al doesn't personally own any. He's doing this out of fairness to you and the Grenex people."

"Doug, can I make a request, now that Grenex's becoming a Seagate division?"

Doug's eyebrows rose questioningly.

"Please rename Grenex 'Seagate Magnetics.' That'll help their people fully join our Seagate team."

"They're going to want to keep the Grenex name. Does the name really matter?"

"It really does matter. We need them to become full Seagate team members."

A week later there was a new sign in front of the Grenex building renaming it, "Seagate Magnetics."

A year earlier, Gordon and Jim had decided Grenex disc R&D was essentially complete and a tough, experienced manufacturing man was required to get disc yields above 85%. Grenex needed patient and meticulous attention to hundreds of manufacturing details. Especially critical were cleanliness and smoothness at the atomic level, in polishing the nickel plated aluminum platters; in cleaning them of all microscopic contamination; and in coating them with defect-free cobalt magnetic films four millionths of an inch thick. Grenex had been manufacturing hundreds of discs per day but only a handful had been usable in drives, and those wouldn't record bits at double density.

At the time, Gordon had told Doug, "Grenex is just a bunch of research lab people who aren't production minded. The only way to get good discs in volume out of Grenex is to put a manufacturing man in charge, a 'kick-ass' man tough enough to make the Grenex people listen to him."

Grenex had been trying to stop the crashes by putting a fatty acid lubricant layer on the disc surfaces, having learned that a Seagate competitor was shipping drives with fatty acid lubed cobalt discs. This was an organic chemical that left a microscopically thin lubricant film on the disc. Grenex had given up on the fatty acid after the competitor's drives began crashing in customer computers with "white worms" on their discs. The thin layer of fatty acid on the discs was rolling up into microscopic tubular "worms" as drive heads landed and took off multiple times. When the worms grew to 20 millionths of an inch thick, heads could no longer fly over them, began hitting them every disc revolution, and finally crashed. The competitor's president told his customers that the white worms were "as harmless as white clouds in the sky," but his company went bankrupt when its customers fled to buy Seagate drives with brown paint discs.

Seagate had hired Thom, a big man whose hobby was weight lifting. Jim and Gordon had immediately demonstrated to Thom that the crashes were caused by microscopic disc contamination, and Thom had set out to clean up the Grenex process.

On the first day of Thom's watch as the new Grenex Vice President of Manufacturing, he had found a lady in the disc production clean room not wearing the face mask of her white bunny suit. This was a common Grenex discipline problem.

Thom had instantly assembled all the Grenex employees, fired both her and her supervisor in front of them, and then told them all, "Any violation of clean room discipline and the bunny suit rules will result in immediate termination for any of you other employees as well.

"The rules are mandatory and necessary. If you leave a single dust particle on a disc platter going into the cobalt sputtering machine, that disc will crash any head that flies on it. Even microscopic dust particles you can't see are far too large to fit between a flying head and disc. They'll scratch the head and cause a crash. That's the major problem our discs have. We're all going to work together to stop those crashes by cleaning up the disk production process; together we're going to find and fix every one of the causes."

Although the Grenex workers had instantly learned to fear Thom's temper, they also came to respect and soon to admire him. Day by day Thom personally toiled inside the disc production clean room, looking like a polar bear in his extra-extra-large bunny suit. He worked on hundreds of cleaning, polishing, and sputtering details, until Grenex finally achieved a clean manufacturing process. In a year of work, Thom had finally gotten disc production to high volume at good yield.

Thom had replaced Earl in daily operations. Earl's R&D contributions were complete and he would ultimately make a tidy sum off his stock options. The original Grenex employees Earl had hired would also receive handsome financial rewards, even his disc polishing technician whom Earl had fired for having an affair with Eve, his electrochemist. Eve was Grenex's expert on their electrochemical baths that nickel plated the aluminum platters so they could be polished atomically smooth. Earl had discovered that the two frequently disappeared together for several hours in the middle of the day.

Eve was kept on after her lover was fired because of her amazing discovery that adding urea from animal manure into the electroplating baths stopped the discs from crashing Gordon's test heads. Eve had told only Earl about her urea discovery, and was using it only on small test batches of mystery alloy discs, waiting to see if Gordon's engineers found new mystery discs were no longer crashing. Earl had warned her that the TVC contract made this necessary.

Although Thom had gotten their process to high volume at good yield, their glide yield wasn't quite high enough to reach the goal Tom set at Seagate: double density cobalt discs at the same low cost of brown paint discs. The major remaining disc problem was that Seagate heads and electronics weren't able to record any more magnetic bits on advanced cobalt discs than on the ordinary brown paint discs, just as Gordon and

Jim had predicted several years earlier. Ordinary discs cost less to make because paint spraying equipment was far less expensive than vacuum sputtering machines. Tom would never allow more expensive discs into Seagate drive manufacturing unless they stored twice as much data. Even then he would insist they rapidly drive their cost lower than oxide, using the economics of high volume production.

This was the situation when Seagate bought Grenex.

The day Doug told Gordon that Seagate had bought TVC's share of Grenex, Gordon immediately drove over the hill to Silicon Valley to meet with Jim and Thom. Gordon found to his relief that Jim didn't blame him for the TVC meeting disaster over the "Million Dollar Disc."

Gordon related his conversation with Doug, about shifting to the mystery disc cobalt alloy.

"The TVC venture capital people bailed out just as we're nearing production capability. TVC panicked over the crashes, and because advanced cobalt film discs didn't allow any higher bit density than brown paint discs.

"I talked to their drive consultant, the guy that came to the Phase Two meeting, about switching to our mystery cobalt alloy recording discs to get double density discs. He told me TVC thinks we're desperate to keep getting their money and we'll just keep frittering it away. TVC feels burned by *all* cobalt disc technology; they didn't want to even hear about our mystery cobalt alloy."

Gordon and Jim looked at each other, and both started to smile, each knowing what the other was thinking: non-technical business people shouldn't make technology decisions, but often do.

Thom looked surprised at the smiles, and then he smiled as well. He was a production man, willing to make any product that worked, that customers wanted to buy.

Gordon continued, "I designed double density heads that Stern makes for me in our head lab, and we've been using them recently, to test your mystery alloy discs. I've brought you a batch of these heads, for you to use as test heads here."

He handed Jim a flat plastic sealed box, with a dozen heads inside.

"But you pointed out at the TVC meeting that our discs will immediately crash them," Jim objected.

"That's the amazing thing, Jim. Something seems to have changed in your production process, but only for the mystery discs, not your advanced TVC discs. Kermit has been able to test your latest mystery alloy discs at double density using these heads, without any crashes. The heads fly at 9 microinches, half the fly height of standard heads, and your discs don't crash them! We glide tested these discs at 6 microinches, and they pass! Their double-density recording tests look encouraging as well!"

All three smiled, and relief washed over Thom and Jim's faces. They both knew that becoming a Seagate division would immediately subject them to Tom's demands for high production at low cost.

Gordon asked, "What do you think about Al's renaming Grenex as Seagate Magnetics? We can call it SeaMag for short."

"We're happy to join the family!" Thom and Jim said in unison.

They immediately called a meeting of all their technology people, to find out why the mystery discs were gliding so much better. Gordon showed them his disc test data, proving they were smoother and free of the asperity bumps that had been hitting and crashing standard density heads.

Gordon asked if anyone knew why the discs had stopped crashing. He looked around the table. Every face was blank except Eve's. Seeing her shy smile, Gordon raised his eyebrows inquisitively.

"It's because I've been adding urea, from animal fertilizer," Eve said quietly. Total bewilderment spread through the room. Everyone's eyes widened, turned, and became riveted on Eve, who was normally silent and invisible in meetings. They were all stunned into silence and could only wait for her to continue.

"I changed the electroplating process," she slowly continued. "I add liquid urea to my experimental plating tank before I make a small batch of mystery disc platters. Urea stops the nickel plating process from growing asperity bumps," she said with a diffident smile.

Confused faces turned to astonishment. "Give that lady a cigar!" Gordon cried. "Double her stock option!" After the commotion, cheering, and laughter died down, Gordon asked her, "Eve, I know successful electroplating experts have 'black magic' tricks, but how on Earth did you ever even think of using animal piss?"

She answered with an air of mystery. "I can't say, and I don't know why it works. I tried dozens of ideas in my small experimental plating tank to stop the crashes, until this one finally seemed to work. Urea acts as a leveling agent, smoothing the nickel-plated surfaces. I was sure all of you would laugh at using urea, but the discs were crashing anyway, so I decided to start using it for the mystery disc batches without saying anything. I didn't change the production plating baths for the advanced discs, because the TVC contract specified they had to approve any major production change. I was afraid everyone would say I was crazy, and stop me from trying my idea."

Gordon had observed this mysterious act of invention before, in the rare people having the talent. Inventors seemed alike, from Thomas Edison to the Wright brothers. They shared a love of painstaking experimentation in search of solutions to practical problems. Rarely could they explain where their unusual ideas came from. When their invention led to commercial success, scientists would study why it worked; publish papers that sometimes didn't properly acknowledge the actual inventors; and sometimes take credit for the invention.

SeaMag switched to the mystery cobalt alloy sputtering alloy, added urea to the production plating baths, and began making the cobalt discs that Jim and Gordon had quietly developed. There was no real mystery involved, just sound engineering in designing a longitudinal magnetic recording disc compatible with Seagate's longitudinal recording heads and electronics. The disc yield was high, and they were getting close to mass production of discs able to store twice as much data as brown paint discs.

They struggled and won a final technology struggle: understanding and controlling residual gasses in their sputtering systems, to grow cobalt films on discs in the proper atomic crystal structure. Their double-density recording performance became excellent.

For the upcoming Las Vegas Comdex show, Doug asked Gordon to build double-density demonstration drives to show to customers visiting the Seagate executive suite in the Golden Nugget Hotel. Gordon's group installed SeaMag discs and double density heads that Stern made in his head lab, into standard Seagate ST-225 20-megabyte production drives. They modified their electronics to write and read bits at twice Seagate's standard speed of 5 megabits per second, turning them into 40 megabyte ST-251 drives. They hooked up an oscilloscope to demonstrate bit playback waveforms and another instrument to show bit reading error rate. Any customer with disc drive recording experience would be able to see the drives were operating properly at double bit density.

Carefully packing all the equipment into padded cardboard boxes, Gordon drove to his Mooney at San Jose Airport. The experimental electronics were far too delicate to ship commercially. The boxes filled up the airplane baggage compartment and the back seat, with one box left over. He set that box just outside the airplane door, got into the pilot's seat, squeezed the box into the right front passenger seat, and fastened its seat belt over it.

Landing in Las Vegas, Gordon got a van and made his way to the Golden Nugget and the executive penthouse where Al, Tom, and Doug were staying.

"Al, you can tell drive customers that this is just the beginning. In a few years, drives with thousands of megabytes will be built, all using cobalt discs."

That evening Gordon went to Seagate's annual customer celebration at the Jubilation Club. Finis reserved this entire nightclub every Comdex for their best drive customers. In the packed crowd, Gordon sampled an endless buffet of shrimp, ribs, and cocktails. After a sit-down dinner the floorshow began, topless showgirls singing popular old songs. Vegas knew its older customers had the most money and knew exactly which songs and how much skin they enjoyed.

Gordon found the Cow Ware Company in their usual booth at Comdex the next day, selling their dairy cow management PCs with Seagate drives. They told him they needed larger capacity drives. He said, "We'll be selling 40 megabyte drives soon, and at about the same price as the 20 megabyte drives you buy now."

Loading his plane to fly home was easier then coming to Vegas. He had left the drives and instruments in the Seagate suite. Doug would bring them back in Al's Learjet after Comdex.

46.

Candy-Ass Towns

Stern stepped into Gordon's office one morning. "Gordon, fly us to Ojai tomorrow. There's a company there making a ceramic grinding machine we might buy for the head lab."

"O.K., Stern. We'll be taking John the funeral director along. He wants to look at a build-it-yourself kit airplane they sell at Santa Paula and that's the closest airport to Ojai. I'll give him a call."

Stern asked, "He's the guy who sold you your second Mooney and parking shelter at San Jose Airport?"

"Yes, he's thinking of getting back into flying. Buying a kit airplane is a less expensive way to get a plane. It can take years to build one, but John has a notion about getting a plane assembled in the Philippines."

The three flew to Santa Paula Airport the next day. John walked off to find the kit airplane factory, and Stern and Gordon waited at the airport for the grinding machine company manager to pick them up.

"Look at all these antique airplanes, Gordon! That one's a World War I biplane, and there's a Beech Staggerwing."

Gordon smiled and said, "Stern, I didn't know you were an antique airplane buff as well as a steam locomotive buff. A lot of the planes here are antiques, kept as hobbies by Hollywood movie stars."

A car drove up. It was the grinding machine company manager, and they got in to drive to Ojai.

Gordon said to the manager, "I'm surprised machine tool manufacturing is allowed in Ojai. Herb Caen called Ojai one of the 'candy ass' towns along with Aspen and Solvang, in his newspaper column in the *San Francisco Chronicle*. He said these towns are too artsy-fartsy for real people to live there."

"There's truth in that," the manager replied. "We're having to move the plant out of town to avoid city fines for the noise we make inside Ojai town limits."

They spent the next several hours at the plant checking out their ceramic grinding machines. They were computer controlled ten-ton steel machines, nearly as big as a compact car.

"Forgive my ignorance," Gordon said, "but our recording heads are only a 1/4 of an inch in size and weigh only a fraction of an ounce. Why do we need a grinder as big and heavy as a tank?"

"So it'll be absolutely mechanically stable to allow grinding accuracy to millionths of an inch," the manager replied.

"Stern, do you think the Seagate building floor is strong enough to bear this weight? We may have the same floor loading problems we had with the four-ton electromagnet."

But Stern had already decided against buying one of the machines. They weren't accurate enough for him.

They found John waiting for them back at Santa Paula Airport. "Hope you weren't bored too long," Gordon said.

"Nope. I took a nap for the last two hours. I finished with the kit airplane company pretty fast, so I walked down the street to a motel and made them a deal: a room for a few hours at a quarter of the normal price. They did make a point of saying it was a *single* room." They all laughed.

"I decided against buying the kit airplane. They're moving the factory to Oregon and don't have any completed planes here to test fly. They said California is too difficult to do business in. The town just raised their airport rent to more than twice what Oregon will charge them for twice the space."

47.

Disc Drives and Toy Trains

"What's that smell, Kermit?" Gordon was sniffing an odor of hot shellac wafting into his office. "Let's go look. Wait, let me stow away this disc track motor magnet." The magnet made a clanging sound as it stuck to the back of one of the 8-inch square steel earthquake beams that diagonally crisscrossed his office walls.

The two followed the odor downstairs and found a 4x8 foot plywood sheet with hundreds of tiny copper coils tacked onto it, all wired together and being fed current from a power supply. The electrical current was heating the coils and vaporizing the uncured shellac that the coils had been dipped in to make them hold their shape.

"What's up, Steve?" Gordon asked an engineer standing by the plywood sheet, a friend who was starting a moonlight business painting airplanes at nearby Watsonville Airport. He was one of Stan's engineers, a bachelor who usually wore clashing clothes, like blue shirt, red pants, black socks and brown shoes. Gordon kidded him about getting married, so he could have a fashion advisor.

"Manufacturing changed to a new vendor for track motor coils, which turned out to be a coil maker for toy electric train motors. Nobody told him that shellac gassing out from hot coils inside a disc drive would make heads stick to discs and stop them from spinning. Seagate purchasing ordered a million of these coils. Engineering is trying to see if they can be made usable by this outgassing technique."

Gordon laughed. "I suppose Seagate will make the toy train coil vendor use this technique if it works, and only pay them a penny more for the additional labor it requires."

"Not even a penny," Steve replied. "A penny would raise his price 100%."

Gordon looked closely at Steve to see if he was serious. "I suppose the coil vendor will have to agree because he probably already spent a lot of money tooling up to fill the order for a million coils."

Steve nodded agreement.

"So when can you start painting my Mooney airplane, Steve?" Gordon asked. He was helping Steve get his airport paint shop business started.

"I'll begin bead blasting on Monday," Steve replied.

"What's that?"

"That's how we strip off the old paint. We can't use chemical strippers because California environmental laws now forbid them. Instead we use plastic beads shot from an air gun, to blast off the old paint."

This seemed too new a method for Gordon to accept. "How many airplanes have you used it on?"

"A bunch, even a Lear 35 jet we just painted." Gordon had been at Steve's shop a week earlier, when the Lear owner asked him the same questions. Steve had told the owner he had painted many jets using the bead blaster, but after the man left Steve admitted he had never painted anything larger than a single engine Cessna.

"You've got to be a little creative to survive when running a small business, Gordon."

Why does this remind me of John the funeral director?

After Gordon's plane was painted, every mechanic who looked inside its tail cone would ask him why there were piles of plastic beads inside the fuselage.

48.

Inventor of the Integrated Circuit
and Advisor to the British Crown

"We've hired a Chief Scientist," Doug announced at one of his weekly staff meetings. "His name is Sydney. He's the inventor of the integrated circuit memory chip and technology advisor to the British Crown."

This surprised Gordon. *Hmm, Americans invented the memory chip, not an Englishman.*

Gordon noticed that Doug's beard was getting tinges of white. *The insane business cycle of this industry is getting to him.* This reminded Gordon of a beard he used to have that had turned white. During a ski trip to Steamboat Springs, a friend in their cabin had said, "Gordon, if you cut off your beard you'd look ten years younger."

"Come with me," Gordon had replied, pulling him into the bathroom and handing him scissors and razor.

As snipping began, Shirley called from the living room, "What are you two doing in there?"

"Cutting off my beard—and things I can't say out loud," echoed off the bathroom tiles.

"But I don't know if I'll still like you without the beard." The only reply was continued sounds of snipping and scraping.

Doug continued the meeting. "Our patent attorney tells me that we're not submitting patent applications on the technology we invent."

"But we're all up to our necks in alligators just trying to make the technology work," one engineer insisted. A chorus of others chimed agreement.

Doug calmly continued. "Seagate's been sued by a patent attorney named Harry who claims to have invented the cobalt disc we're manufacturing. He wants five dollars royalty per disc, more than it costs us to manufacture one."

"Doug," Gordon said, "I've looked at Harry's patent and it's completely fraudulent! He has a friend who consulted for SeaMag, and he heard about every disc improvement we invented. Harry kept rewriting his patent applications until they covered all possible technologies to make cobalt alloy discs, even though his company didn't invent any of them. He illegally patented technology already in public use, like electroplating. He patented nickel plating the aluminum platters, carbon overcoats for head crash resistance, even the diameter of the recording discs. Harry named himself as inventor on the patents even though he doesn't have the slightest iota of technical knowledge. He knows nothing about the disc technology he patented; he's only an attorney. He kept his patents pending and secret, modifying their claims to include every innovation he heard of through his consultant grapevine. He repeatedly refiled his patents, updating them to include our new inventions. Somehow he got the U.S. Patent Office to let him keep his original patent filing date even after his revisions, so he could claim he was first. He ought to be put in jail for making fraudulent patent applications!"

"Gordon," Doug calmly replied, "the U.S. Patent Office regards attorneys as 'officers of the court' and presumes everything they say is truthful."

The meeting ended with a roomful of heads shaking silently in disgust.

In following weeks, the new Chief Scientist Sydney was seen driving a shining white Lamborghini around Scotts Valley and wearing expensive clothes that looked similar to Doug's. They didn't look quite as well on Sydney, who was rather rotund. He didn't comb his hair, which stuck out in every direction and gave him a mad scientist look. He apparently liked the look.

Doug's Italian tailor had made several expensive suits for Sydney but had not been paid. After a month, the tailor sent his Sicilian brother to stand guard outside Sydney's hotel room at the Pasatiempo Inn near Seagate. The Mafia-looking brother terrified Sydney and he called the police.

A policeman came to Sydney's motel room and brought the man standing outside into the room. "Has this man told you why he's here? Do you know him? Has he threatened or attacked you?"

"Well, he hasn't actually threatened me. But I'm afraid to talk to him and I'm afraid he *might* attack me. I have no idea who he is."

The policeman turned to the other man. "Sir, what's your story?"

"My brother custom tailors Italian suits. This guy Sydney cheated him out of several thousand dollars for suits he made for him. I'm here to make sure this crook doesn't skip town without paying. When I got here I knocked on his hotel door. When he peeked out I told him why I was here, but he wouldn't open the door. I'm not leaving until he talks to me. Here's the invoice for the suits he ordered, with his signature."

The policeman looked at the paperwork. "Does your brother want to press fraud charges against this man?"

"Yes."

"O.K., have him come to the Santa Cruz jail today. Sydney, I'm taking you to jail for questioning."

Several hours later the tailor had finished filing charges at the Santa Cruz jail and he stopped by Seagate to see Doug. "That man you referred to me is in jail for not paying me. I thought you'd want to know. And did you like the last suits I made for you?"

"Thanks for stopping by and telling me," Doug answered. "The suits are fine."

That evening, Doug was talking to Al and Gordon at Malone's Bar. "Seagate advanced Sydney salary money and he also has the Lamborghini we got for him."

Gordon remarked, "Doug, the DRAM memory chip was invented and patented at IBM. I believe Sydney is a fraud and a pathological liar."

"Let me handle this," Al replied. "I'll put a lawyer on it first thing tomorrow." Seagate did not actually employ any lawyers. Al detested their kind and preferred to rent them when he had to. He kept a lawyer doll on his desk so he could periodically snap its head off.

Al filed fraud charges the next day and Sydney's lawyer called Al to plea bargain.

"Sydney will pay back Seagate's money and return the Lamborghini if he can avoid prison," the lawyer said.

"No deal," Al told him.

Sydney was convicted of fraud. This put Seagate's name in the national news and the heads of several major U.S. companies called Al to congratulate him on his courage in prosecuting Sydney. They admitted they had fallen for similar Sydney frauds but had been too embarrassed to prosecute. Sydney apparently counted on such sheepishness but had not known of Al's strict ethics.

Seagate paid the Italian tailor and Seagate vice presidents took turns driving Sydney's white Lamborghini until its six-month lease expired.

When Gordon went to the next Seagate Magnetics meeting, Earl told him, "Gordon, the national notoriety that Seagate is getting over Sydney is very embarrassing."

"Earl, let me try to convince you that this is Silicon Valley cowboy company culture at its finest flower. Personally, I believe in Al's idea that a little fun and craziness takes the edge off the hard work and long hours."

49.

Up the Colorado River and into the Grand Canyon

Seagate had been running smoothly for a while and Gordon took a week off to boat up the Colorado River into the Grand Canyon with his Xerox friend Ted. Ted's wife Alice was a dental hygienist and a tolerant but strict mother who managed to bring up her two kids drug free and with college degrees.

As they drove their two power boat trailers over Boulder Dam they saw that Lake Mead was completely full and overflowing. They parked and walked to the edge of the dam. Torrents of water were booming over the twin dam spillways, roaring turbulent water that nearly filled the two immense tunnels bored seventy years earlier through the rock walls of Black Canyon.

They continued driving east into Arizona, turned north half way to Kingman, finally driving past the isolated town of Meadview to a launch ramp in upper Lake Mead. They arrived at the launch ramp and put on their bathing suits. Shirley put on her hot pink bikini, Gordon's favorite because it clung enticingly to the curves of her body. They launched their boats, tied them to the dock, and began packing them with camping gear from their cars. The boats were soon piled above deck level with camping stoves, gas lanterns, ice chests, water buckets, beach chairs, blowup rubber rafts, five gallon cans of spare gas, and cases of beer.

Gordon looked askance at the untidy heap piled in Ted's boat. "If your son was here he would say your boat looks like the Joad migrant farming family moving to California in John Steinbeck's novel *The Grapes of Wrath.*" Ted ignored the comment.

They cast off in the two boats and ran up Lake Mead at 35 mph, soon crossing the thermocline where dark green cold Colorado River water dove under warm blue lake water. The low desert hills surrounding the lake disappeared as they passed through the Grand Wash cliffs marking the end of the Grand Canyon. These cliffs were the southwest end of a massive uplift block that included much of north Arizona and south Colorado. This enormous plateau had slowly risen a mile in altitude over a 65 million year period, forcing the Colorado River to cut the Grand Canyon a mile deep and nearly 300 miles long.

Warm winds brought the scent of riverbank grasses and flowers as their boats ran up the canyon, and occasional cold breezes came sinking down side canyons. They passed Quartermaster Canyon with its sheer red and gold cliffs sitting far back from the river. They passed these side canyons on the opposite side of the river, knowing that immense thunderstorms occasionally flooded them and brought torrents of gravel and rocks into the main river channel, forming underwater rock bars hidden beneath the water.

They passed the bat caves, where a river-edge airstrip and a million-dollar cargo-carrying cable tramway across the canyon, had been built in the late 1950's. Guano fertilizer was mined from the caves and taken to a tram tower at the river's edge to be carried up the tramway to another tower high up on the west canyon rim. A military jet hit the cable a year after it was built and brought it down. The local Hualapai Indians had built a tourist center near the abandoned top tower so visitors from Las Vegas could look at the Grand Canyon below.

Forty miles up the river and an hour and a half later, Gordon and Ted were slowly put-putting up Surprise, a flooded narrow side canyon off the main river. It had a grove of cottonwood trees growing next to the water and a short way up the canyon, beyond where the river water ended. The green grove contrasted starkly with the arid desert sand and rock farther up the canyon.

Gordon remembered this was the spot where Ted's boat had broken down a few years earlier. A snap ring in his drive shaft universal joint had rusted and finally broken, from years of water exposure. Ted's boat engine had clunked to a sudden and final halt.

Gordon steered closer to Ted until their two boats were slowly running side by side.

"Ted, do you realize that for a boat engine to run, dozens of mechanical parts inside have to cooperate in a synchronized dance, an intricate metallic ballet of whirling harmony? And if a single mechanical dancer falls out of step..."

"Stop, Gordon, stop!" Ted cried, remembering his boat breakdown. It had taken him more than a day to float with the river current back to Lake Mead, and hours more paddling with his single oar until he found a park ranger boat to help him.

After another hour they were thirty miles further up the main canyon. They stopped when they saw a park ranger boat speeding down the river towards them, suddenly turning on its red flashing lights. The boat pulled alongside and everyone held their breath waiting to hear their sins.

"Let me do the talking," said Alice. "I'll handle that Ranger Rick in his Bobby Boat."

The ranger looked dubiously at their overloaded piles of camping gear, impossible to miss.

"Are you intending to camp up in the canyon?"

"Why, yes we are," Alice replied sweetly.

"Federal regulations require you to carry a portable toilet to use in the canyon. Please show me yours."

Alice held up a cardboard box for the ranger to see, with a picture of a portable toilet. Gordon saw she was carefully holding it so the ranger couldn't see that it was only the lid of the box a portable toilet had come in.

The ranger nodded and quickly sped off downstream. Alice put the lid away. "We didn't have room for the toilet itself so I left it in the car. But the box lid fit so I brought it along."

Gordon gave her a round of applause.

Shirley remarked, "I wonder why Ranger Rick seemed in such a hurry to get downstream."

Starting upstream again, they rounded a bend in the canyon and immediately saw why Ranger Rick had been in such a hurry. A thunderstorm filled the entire canyon in front of them, a dark gray cloud stretching from one canyon wall to the opposite. Lightning began striking the canyon rock walls, accompanied by booming thunder.

They stopped to put their boat rain covers on and then slowly continued upriver. Clouds and pouring rain dropped the visibility to where they could barely see the canyon walls. Thunder echoed off the rocks, sounding like gods bowling. They were pelted by intense rain driven by fierce winds. Their boats had no windshield wipers and they could barely see the river ahead. Gordon watched Ted's boat frequently, careful to keep his distance.

Ten tense minutes later they passed out of the thunderstorm and then sped to their favorite camping sandbar. It was now sunny, hot, and calm as they made camp and raised a shade canopy over what would be their kitchen area. They sat down in the shade in their beach chairs and opened ice-cold beers from an ice chest.

An hour later, Shirley looked up from her book. "I see another thunderstorm coming towards us." A few minutes later, sudden wind gusts snatched at their canvas shade shelter and four pairs of hands could barely hold it. Minutes passed as they struggled; then the thunderstorm dissipated as quickly as it had arrived, the wet canyon walls taking on deep red hues as the sun returned.

"Look up!" Gordon cried. Dozens of waterfalls were pouring off the cliff tops far above, roaring as the water hit the canyon floor below. A rainbow arched across the entire canyon, like a natural bridge. The four sat back in their beach chairs watching the waterfalls on the red canyon wall across the river, glowing in the afternoon sun. Towering white cumulous clouds decorated the sky. In ten minutes the waterfalls ended and the only remaining sounds were the green river lapping at the sandbar, and an occasional songbird.

Alice began rapping with Gordon about badly engineered consumer products. Her side of conversations could often be heard from considerable distances.

"Today's products like toasters and bicycles are over-engineered!" she loudly proclaimed. "There hasn't been a decent toaster that doesn't burn or only warm the bread since the Sunbeam Toaster back when we were kids! I had a fat tire bicycle when I was a kid, with gears inside its rear wheel hub, protected from dirt and water. Now we have 21-speed bikes with narrow tires that fall into sidewalk cracks, their gears hang out in the open to rust, and their high and low gears have no more speed range than my old three speed gearshift!"

Gordon shouted back, "YOU'RE ABSOLUTELY RIGHT ON, ALICE!"

Alice paused to take a breath, and a mixed chorus of Alice and Gordon voices echoed back off far canyon walls.

"Disc drive designers over-engineer too," Gordon said. "They became engineers because they liked to design stuff, so they redesign parts that worked in their last disc drive even though the old parts would still work in their new drive design. Manufacturing people get stuck with dozens of variations of parts like the recording head air sliders and flexure springs, when three or four versions would be adequate and far less expensive to manufacture and inventory."

Alice nodded her agreement. "And here's another thing. Wasn't Linus Pauling a professor at Cal Tech when you went there?"

"Sure, Alice. He was one of the most charismatic professors at Cal Tech, besides being a double Nobel Prize laureate. We were all in awe of him."

"I think he's daffy! He lectured on the medical benefits of Vitamin C a year ago at a dental hygienist association meeting I went to. We were all skeptical of his vitamin claims, and when he finished his talk one hygienist asked him what other medicines he took. He read off a long list of prescription drugs and paused. Then he peered at us over the tops of his bifocal glasses and said, 'those are actually the medicines my wife takes. She's in ill health. We've been married for 60 years and we're very close. So I also take her medicines as well.'

"That's crazy!" Alice exclaimed.

"Alice," Gordon said with a smile, "Let me tell you about Linus Pauling the showman, who makes remarks like that to keep the attention of his audience. I could tell you similar stories about another charismatic Cal Tech professor, Richard Feynman."

Finished with her shout at Gordon, Alice turned to Shirley. "You manage your commercial real estate by yourself. How'd you learn how?"

"That wasn't difficult, Alice," Shirley told her. "If I have a question I talk to my real estate agent, or my accountant, or my lawyer. It's a lot of time and work, but why do you think it's so hard to learn?"

"Well, Shirley, I thought about managing real estate too and I took a night school course on it. The legal problems alone seemed too complex to manage."

"Ha! I never took those courses so I never knew it was supposed to be hard!"

The next morning, Gordon and Shirley decided to take their boat and explore farther up the canyon. Water flow into the river was below normal, from Glen Canyon dam far upstream above the Grand Canyon. Together with the high level of Lake Mead, the river was unusually tranquil.

Gordon and Shirley started upstream. Separation rapid was completely washed out and calm. It had been named for two men who left Major John Wesley Powell's pioneering expedition down the canyon after the U.S. Civil War, only to be killed by Indians while they were hiking out.

After a few river bends they came to the first serious rapid, Mile 234. They had always stopped below it in earlier years because continuing in hard hull boats meant serious risk of sinking in one of the larger rapids upstream. Ted had sunk a boat in one of these rapids years before, had become stranded on a river sand bar overnight, and ridden a log downstream for a day to get back to Lake Mead.

Gordon and Shirley encountered only small river riffles in Mile 234 and decided to continue on. They passed Travertine Falls, a lovely dark violet spring seeping down a canyon wall.

A mile ahead of them they saw the canyon making a sharp bend and they began to hear the sound of turbulent rushing water coming from around the corner. The river still ran smoothly so they kept going. The noise grew louder.

The canyon was wide in this area and the river ran smoothly. Gordon could see the canyon was narrowing ahead of them, where the bend started. He leaned down to check the gauges in the twin gas tanks that ran along the sides of the boat. *The one we're running on is rather low but it should have another twenty minutes of gas.* They continued on.

"Hey! Look, Shirley! We're passing Diamond Creek where our last rubber raft trip down the Grand Canyon rapids ended." This was the home of the Hualapai Indians, whose reservation covered the western shore of the lower Grand Canyon. Tourist helicopter flights from Las Vegas visited their villages and made lunch flights down to the river's edge. At the moment, their beach was deserted.

In a few minutes more they were rounding the canyon bend, and found themselves in a faster running narrower river, imprisoned between vertical rock walls. The canyon was closing in, confining the river and speeding its flow. The instant they finished rounding the bend they saw the source of the noise.

In front of them towered an immense rapid. Its rushing water rose to a higher river level upstream in a staircase of three successive whirlpools. The noise of the turbulent water reflected off the rock walls of the narrow canyon and was nearly deafening. White pony tails danced in the sun, in the wave farthest upstream where the rapid began. Gordon remembered the times he and Shirley had run the canyon from Glen Canyon Dam in rubber rafts, thrilled when pony tails were spotted ahead, marking the next rapid to run.

Gordon held just enough power on his engine to keep the boat pointed upstream, matching the river velocity. It seemed suicidal to go any closer to this rapid in a hard hull powerboat. *Maybe this is the rapid that sank Ted's boat years ago.*

Suddenly a big black rubber raft swept through the pony tail wave, its dozen passengers hanging on to ropes and whooping with excitement. Their yells were drowned out by the roar of the rapid as their raft plunged into the upper whirlpool. A boatman stood on the rear of the rubber raft, his hand on an outboard motor, steering through the whirlpools. The nose of the rubber raft bent sharply as it fell into the upper whirlpool and the raft accelerated rapidly towards Gordon and Shirley's boat.

"We have to get out of this narrow canyon, Shirley. There's not enough room for two boats here!"

Gordon's boat was at a dead stop in the water. *I've only seconds to get it moving and escape.* Jamming his throttle to full power, he began a quick turn to head back downstream. But as his boat turned halfway around, its engine sputtered to a halt. The boat was now broadside to the river flow and about to ram into the rock canyon wall.

He shouted to Shirley over the roar, "Hand me the sounding pole," and jumped over the windshield onto the bow of the boat. Stretching back and grabbing the aluminum pole, he swung it forward and stabbed its tip at the black wall to keep the bow from smashing into the rock wall. The pole bent sharply as he fended the boat off, pushing its rubber tip against the wall as hard as he could. He glimpsed the black raft flashing by, mere feet behind them.

The river current now seized their boat and began to carry them at high speed downstream, very close to the wall. A river vortex swirled the boat around, throwing its stern and propeller towards the wall. Gordon jumped back over the windshield into the boat, carrying the sounding pole to the stern.

He jammed the pole against the wall again to keep the propeller from hitting rock. "I hope there aren't any underwater rock spurs! Switch gas tanks and get the engine started, Shirley!"

Finally, another river swirl carried them back to the center of the river as he heard Shirley start up the engine. She was now in the pilot's seat, steering the boat downstream. He put the pole down and sat down where Shirley had been.

"Did you see the look on the boatman's face, Gordon? His eyes were as big as saucers!"

"He was probably completely surprised to see a power boat at all."

Gordon took the pilot's seat and sped up the boat. "I think there was just a little gas left in that tank and it sloshed back away from the gas line when I gunned the motor that quickly."

They ran downstream, caught up with the rubber raft, and stopped to talk to its boatman. "Sorry about the excitement back there. I'm sure you didn't expect to see a power boat this far up the river."

The boatman grinned. "There was no way I could have moved this rubber barge out of your way fast enough. You were smart to hug the wall instead of trying to run downstream ahead of me."

Gordon smiled back, reluctant to admit how out of control he had been, and handed the man a beer from his ice chest. "Here, have an ice cold beer. I've run the river in rubber rafts like yours, drinking beer cooled in river bags. It's good on a hot day but the river doesn't make the beer quite cold enough."

He started his boat up again and they sped back downstream to where the river widened and slowed. He shut the engine off to float with the river current back to camp. Shirley put up a shade umbrella and picked up a book to read. Gordon laid back to watch the moving spectacle of sunlit canyon walls high above black gneiss rock at river level. The gneiss had been polished by millennia of river flow into shapes that looked like folds of robes on black marble statues from ancient Greece. On the opposite side of the river, a sculptured wall of polished black schist rock passed by. Bright spider webs shot through it, pinkish white granite intrusions radiating through linear cracks in the schist.

River eddies and swirls gently turned them in circles, first one way and then the other. Swirls gently slapped against the canyon walls, making lapping sounds against the folded black walls. For 65 million years, canyon uplifting had forced the river down a steep course, flowing too fast to run smoothly. The river was carrying them along at nearly 8 mph. The black raft was in view far up the river, also floating without power. Its boatman was passing out cool beer from his river bag.

Back at camp an hour later, the four read books or napped, the canyon wall across the river slowly turning to deeper shades of gold as the sun behind them made its afternoon fall from the sky.

Gordon saw motion out of the corner of his eye and looked up. Suddenly, a cliff in the opposite canyon wall fell, as centuries of daily heating and cooling finally freed a massive rock slab a thousand feet high. A dust cloud enveloped the wall, quickly followed by the roar of falling rock. They sat stunned and mute for several minutes as the dust settled and the scene slowly returned to normal, the Grand Canyon now wider.

Five minutes later another large rubber raft floated by, carrying river runners down the route that Major Powell had pioneered a century and a half before in his wooden boats. Modern rafts carried steaks for dinner and volleyballs for play in the sandbar camps, in stark contrast to Powell's Spartan food and coffee.

"They missed the rock fall entirely and have no idea what just happened," Ted said.

The next day, they floated down the river back to Lake Mead and trailered the boats back home.

50.

To Ancient China and Minneapolis

Stern, Jack, and Gordon were summoned to Doug's office on a rainy day in 1989. Looking out Doug's window, Gordon saw tall sequoia trees waving their branches wildly in the heavy downpour.

"I want you to go to Hong Kong and inspect a factory that manufactures recording heads. It was built by a Chinese entrepreneur who also built a head assembly plant in his nearby home town inside China. The man has vanished and both plants are being sold. This may be Seagate's opportunity to make our own heads instead of buying them from the Japanese."

The three landed in Hong Kong two days later. The plant manager picked them up at the airport and took them to a small factory in a second-story floor of a warehouse. They climbed a stairway past a dozen small Chinese shops on the ground floor, selling dubious looking groceries and home goods.

After the man gave them a plant tour, Gordon took Stern aside. "This looks like the same Winchester head grinding and polishing processes that we use in our Seagate head lab. There's no future technology here, and the production volume here is too small for Seagate."

They walked back to the general manager who said, "The finished heads from this plant are sent to the entrepreneur's plant in Doungguan, China, to be assembled into head assemblies. We'll go there tomorrow."

The next day the man took them in a taxi to a Hong Kong luxury hotel. They walked through its large well-appointed lobby and down an elevator to its basement, emerging onto an ancient dock on Hong Kong Bay. There they boarded a ferry boat that proceeded across the bay and up into the Pearl River. An hour or so steaming up the river inside China took them to a landing where Chinese guards carefully examined their passports.

The manager whispered, "They're strict because of the Tiananmen Square Massacre in Beijing a while ago. The government jailed all the demonstrators it could find. Some of them tried to escape from China on this ferry to Hong Kong."

A car drove them up a dirt road into the country and they were suddenly in ancient China, driving past farmers working in rice paddies with wooden farm tools and oxen, just as they had since 5000 B.C.

A single modern building stood at the end of the road, a concrete walled factory anomalous in the ancient countryside. They got out of the car and went inside.

"The entrepreneur built this factory to employ people in his home town near here. The plant assembles recording heads to sell to disc drive companies in Asia and the U.S. It's a godsend to these impoverished people, but he ran afoul of the Communist authorities who closely control all enterprise in China. I hear he's now living in Seattle."

They entered the plant and saw dozens of teenage girls sitting on workbenches, peering through microscopes to see tiny copper wire coils they were winding onto black ferrite heads. Other girls dabbed epoxy on the backs of heads to epoxy them to flexure springs.

"These head assemblers are unmarried girls from poor families," the plant manager told them. "They work here for a couple of years earning money for their dowry, and then quit to get married and have the single child the Chinese government allows."

Gordon asked, "This plant doesn't seem to follow the same environmental rules as the U.S. I smell solvent for the flexure adhesive they're using."

"Yes. Unfortunately some become sick from the chemicals and have to quit before they earn their dowry."

After the tour they returned to the Pearl River ferry, which carried them back to Hong Kong.

Later that evening, Gordon and Jack were walking down a Hong Kong street. "I feel like we just escaped from prison," Gordon said. They passed street vendors with arms covered with dozens of fake Rolex watches, sparkling silver from wrist to shoulder. "Jack, many younger Seagate engineers that come to Seagate's Asian plants return home with watches like those. They're easily seen as fakes because Rolex second hands move smoothly and fake second hands moved in jumps."

Returning to Seagate two days later, they delivered their report to Doug. Gordon noticed that he looked tired and a little grayer. Doug had just spent a week with Seagate's largest customer, repeatedly raked over the coals for Seagate's engineering delays in designing a drive with a new voice coil track motor. Tom had committed the company to deliver faster drives using the new motor, without consulting Doug.

"That Chinese head operation is too small for Seagate, Doug. It's only today's technology with no R&D capability for tomorrow."

"Well, we'll have to find a different way to get our own head technology and production."

"Also, most or all of their manufacturing tooling appears to belong to the Imprimis drive company in Minneapolis."

"That's quite interesting, Gordon." Doug was smiling inscrutably.

Gordon learned the reason for the smile a few months later in October 1989, when Seagate bought Imprimis, a disc drive company in Minneapolis. Imprimis had been a division of Control Data, a struggling Minneapolis mainframe computer company losing the battle of mainframes against minicomputers and personal computer workstations. This struggle made Imprimis also unprofitable. Al wanted their high-end drive division which manufactured highly profitable 5.25-inch drives for workstations. Seagate already had the lion's share of the personal computer disc drive business. Imprimis also had an internal recording head design and manufacturing division which Seagate could manage back into profitability and high volume production.

Doug asked Gordon to fly to Minneapolis, examine Imprimis operations, advise him on redesigning the Imprimis head production lines for Seagate drives, and on new technology projects they were running.

Gordon flew to Minneapolis and met first with Norm, their senior technology vice president. Doug had told Gordon that Norm could help with Imprimis' upper management priorities. Gordon was hoping that Imprimis had good technology and only needed intelligent execution of a fast production ramp to make heads for Seagate drives. The critical steps would be to get their management's "go ahead," and to find engineers and production people that knew their technology capabilities in detail.

Norm and Gordon poured themselves cups of coffee, bland but free like most office coffee, and sat down in Norm's office. "Norm, all of us want to get your ferrite head plant into high volume production for Seagate's drives. You've surely heard that Seagate is a Silicon Valley cowboy company, and Al, Tom, and Doug will be expecting quick results. Can you assign us your best ferrite head engineering and manufacturing people and give us carte blanche to work through the engineering details as quickly as possible?"

An engineer at heart, Gordon believed that technology was all about its details, not its paperwork. But he knew Imprimis management might think otherwise. He was asking Norm to clear the way for the Seagate and Imprimis engineers.

Norm knew Seagate ran its company by letting its technical people independently decide how to get their jobs done. He had started as an engineer himself. He had also heard the stories about Tom and knew he didn't ever want to directly confront him.

"Gordon, normally when we start a project like this we hold a series of management meetings to carefully work up plans. But we should try this Seagate's way. Please tell me something else first. Why do you want to ramp ferrite head production instead of our new thin film head technology? We think ferrite heads are obsolete."

"Norm, the time for thin film heads will come soon for Seagate's future drive designs, but not for our present generation of drive products. Your people will have to get the cost of your thin film heads lower for Tom, and you'll also need to do R&D to further miniaturize your head technology into nanotechnology heads. In the meantime, ferrite heads will work just as well in our products and will make Tom more money. Your ferrite production machines will have been completely written off the Imprimis financial books by now, making the heads considerably lower cost."

Norm was looking thoughtful and Gordon smiled. *He's a technologist at heart like me, not a bottom line businessman like Tom.*

Norm made up his mind. "I'm going to introduce you to Brian, who manages our ferrite head production engineering. He's also our best ferrite technologist. If he agrees to your cowboy company plan after you two talk, I'll get you carte blanche here. Brian's office is in the northeast corner of this building. Let's go see him."

They began walking from Norm's office in the southwest corner of the Imprimis building. Norm's eyes were now twinkling a bit, Gordon noticed. They started down a long hall, walking past glass-walled labs and factory areas. After fifteen minutes they turned left and started walking up another endless seeming hall.

"Just how big is this building, Norm?" Gordon asked.

"This main corridor we're in now is over a half mile long. The building is so big it lies in two Minneapolis counties, Normandale and Edina. They have different property tax laws and we sometimes install labs and machines in the county with the lower taxes. There's even a creek running beneath the building."

They passed a sign hanging from the ceiling of the hall: "Leaving Normandale County. Welcome to Edina."

Finally they made several short turns and arrived at Brian's office. *I wonder if I'll be able to find my own way back.* Norm introduced Gordon to Brian. "I'll leave you two alone. Brian, please stop by my office after you're done."

Brian gave Gordon a tour of the ferrite head factory. They discussed details of the accuracy and speeds of the Imprimis ceramic grinding machines that shaped the individual heads and their air sliders, they examined the epoxy bonding line where women wearing bunny suits and vapor masks epoxied stainless steel flexure springs to the backs of air sliders, and the final test area where each head was mounted on a spin stand and tested for bit writing and reading performance.

They returned to Brian's office and Gordon pulled engineering drawings of Seagate' heads out of his briefcase.

"We're going to start detailed engineering and production design work right now?" Brian asked.

"Why not?" Gordon replied. In the tour he had seen that Imprimis was manufacturing the same current technology ferrite heads that Seagate was buying from Japanese companies.

"O.K.! Let's go for it!" Brian answered. He was a talented engineer who thoroughly distained the management games and layoffs that had preceded Seagate's purchase of Imprimis.

The two went over technical details, comparing Seagate's Japanese head specifications to Imprimis' technology, looking for differences.

"Brian, your lapping blend process for the slider skis is different from the way the Japanese do it, which will change how Seagate's heads fly. But let's leave your process as is. It would take too long to change it to match the Japanese process, and that would carry too much risk of failing to meet Tom's production schedules."

Lapping blends smoothed the sharp slider corners, where ground ceramic edges met at right angles.

"But the heads won't fly at the correct height, Gordon. How'll we fix that?"

"I'll take your slider lap blend process documents back to Scotts Valley and run them through the head flight design program on my VAX computer. I'll adjust the width of the slider skis to get the same fly height as the Japanese heads. When I get that correct, I'll run the program on the maximum tolerance variations your process allows in head and lap dimensions, to see if your blends are controlled tightly enough to keep their fly heights within our tolerances."

Brian was impressed and pleased. Customers for his heads were too often stubborn engineers and managers who made arbitrary demands on his heads without understanding Imprimis' manufacturing capabilities and limitations. It was the "pecking order" problem: the customer was always right. Brian was coming to realize that Seagate was quite aware that good engineering paid attention to manufacturing cost, yield, and time to volume. Inventing technology was only part of designing a product for mass production, and sometimes the easiest part.

"It's quite clear to me that we can do this correctly and quickly, Brian," Gordon said. "I'll call you after I run the design parameters. You keep these Seagate drawings and specifications, and call me when you find any other concerns. Start making engineering qualification head samples for us now, but leave the head ski widths and flexure load mount point open until I check the flying design and call you. Right now, I'm going to go look at some of the Imprimis research projects."

Brian looked disinterested. Research was boring to his practical "get things done" mindset.

"Can you give me a map of this building? I'm afraid I'll get lost and wander around forever."

They laughed and Brian said, "Let me walk you to your next visit."

"No, I'm not going to stop you from doing real work to make you into a hall guide."

They parted and Gordon went to the research main office using Brian's guide and a magnetic compass he kept in his Italian men's handbag. Meeting with the Imprimis research director, he quickly learned that Imprimis was running several impractical projects that had no hope of leading to profitable products. One was on holographic memory research.

Gordon met with the holographic memory research leader. The man spent half an hour describing his project and asked, "What do you think?"

"I'm going to recommended that Seagate cancel the project."

The man looked completely bewildered. "But someday all memory will be holographic," he objected. "It's the wave of the future. We must continue our research so our company won't be left behind."

"Have you thought how to miniaturize that eight foot long optical bench you do your holographic research on, into the size and cost of a memory product? Or how to get the $150,000 cost of that 500-pound research setup down to $20 and 2 pounds in a usable and sellable product? Or how such a product could be used in computers?"

The man looked insulted. "I'm a research scientist, not a mere engineer."

Gordon sighed patiently. "Any new memory product like holography will have to commercially start out by using existing computer interfaces for magnetic disc drives. Computer manufacturers aren't going to design new peripheral interfaces for holography unless and until you're selling large volumes of product that make money. I can tell what a holography product would be like from the physics of what you're proposing. Even if Seagate did design a commercial holographic storage product, its storage capacity would be far too large to be of practical use in a computer. Disc data speeds aren't fast enough to efficiently access so much data in a single box. Computers needing that much storage capacity use many magnetic disc drives, running in parallel to get ultra high data access speeds."

The man opened his mouth, closed it, and then stopped in bewilderment, realizing that Seagate wasn't going to accept the fuzzy reasoning tolerated by his former Imprimis management.

Meanwhile, Brian had made the long walk to Norm's office. "Seagate's the best thing to ever happen to us, Norm! Gordon and I get along perfectly! He expects only excellence from us in technology engineering, manufacturing cost, and time into volume production. The best thing is that he simply assumes we're smart enough to do it! That makes me feel pretty good, Norm."

"Thanks, Brian. That's what I figured you might say."

Over the following months, Seagate's "smartest person wins" culture allowed its engineers to easily get along with their Imprimis counterparts, who were more than happy to accommodate increased production demands instead of more layoffs. Seagate switched its drive production to use Imprimis heads and renamed the division "Seagate Recording Head Operations."

RHO was soon successful, and its managers called a meeting with Al, Tom, Doug, and Gordon. "We propose that Seagate switch from ferrite heads to our new technology thin film heads. We batch fabricate them on wafers containing thousands of heads with their air sliders, just like semiconductor chips on silicon wafers. That makes them so inexpensive that their cost will only be a little higher than our ferrite heads, and thin film technology allows more bits to be stored on each disc." Gordon smiled. *I did warn them of Seagate's primary rule, Tom's mantra that parts costs only go down, never up.*

Tom raised his eyes and the man stopped in mid-sentence. "Inexpensive means lower cost," Tom said plainly. "Parts costs can never be increased in our disc drive business. I am the Seagate expert on the business of manufacturing, and I can tell you exactly what the yielded cost of your ferrite production heads in our drives is. Do you people know that cost?"

One of the men responded, "About three dollars, Tom, for the cost of our ferrite heads out the door."

"Their cost is exactly $3.8865 as of today, including the cost of heads scrapped when they fail in drives in our production line. If we treated the head price as casually as you do our company would quickly be out of business." Tom paused, looking around the room with a pleasant expression that fooled no one. The room remained silent.

"I challenge you to get your thin film head costs lower than your ferrite heads. Seagate Magnetics did that on their cobalt discs. They store twice as much data and are now less expensive than the brown paint discs they replaced. High volume manufacturing is your path, just as it was for SeaMag. Work with our engineering people like Gordon and don't come to me again until you're ready with higher bit density heads at lower cost."

A week later back at Scotts Valley, Gordon got a call from the holographic memory project manager protesting its cancellation.

"But holography is the wave of the future. How can you cancel a project with such a future?"

Gordon replied mildly, "Holography has been the wave of the future since it was invented four decades ago, and it may always be the wave of the future. I ask you again, what will be holographic performance specifications? How much faster, cheaper, and higher capacity will they be than the magnetic disc drives that Seagate sells?"

After a moment the man said, "I told you we're researchers not engineers. We expect you to figure that out."

"And so I have. I recommended that you and your people be reassigned to thin film head nanotechnology research."

"But we were told that Seagate won't use our current thin film heads. Why would you recommend we do R&D on the future of thin film head technology when you won't use it now?"

"Your next generation of nanotech thin film heads will be the beginning of Seagate's future."

51.

Earthquake!

"There's been an earthquake in San Francisco," the bartender said as he set a beer down in front of Gordon. He was in the bar of a Minneapolis hotel the evening of October 17, 1989, following day-long meetings at Seagate's recording head division. A week earlier he had complained over the phone about their late delivery of new engineering test heads to Scotts Valley. They had told him a tornado was headed for their Minneapolis plant and everyone was bailing out for safety. When he told them he was flying to their plant to get his heads, they had warned him the Minneapolis temperature was -40°.

Gordon had come anyway, to find out the facts for himself. *They're not going to fool me. I'm going to find where my heads are.* It had turned out to be a balmy 35 degrees in Minneapolis with no thunderstorms.

He was scheduled to pick up the heads at their factory the next afternoon, and fly home the day after that.

"What earthquake? Where? Was there damage in Santa Cruz? "

"Don't know," replied the bartender. "It's on the TV."

Gordon left the bar and went up to his hotel room to turn on his TV and phone home. He got only busy signals, as he kept redialing and watching the room TV. It was showing San Francisco area pictures of a fallen section of the Bay Bridge and a collapsed Oakland freeway. Crushed cars could be seen between two collapsed freeway decks. *I bet none of those drivers knew to get outside their car and huddle next to them.*

Like all native-born Californians, Gordon had been taught in grammar school to get beneath a desk or in a doorway in an earthquake. This wasn't good science because the weight of a collapsing building could easily crush any desk, table, or doorway. Earthquake experts had later found that building structures did not completely flatten when they collapsed. Triangular spaces were created next to crushed walls and tables. They had seen grim evidence in collapsed school buildings, all the students obediently under their desks, crushed and dead, with triangular open spaces next to the desks. It was safer to crouch next to a desk or table, or next to an outside wall, but this "triangle rule" was little taught.

Like many other discoveries, present day "experts" would have to retire before new truths could be accepted. Decades had passed after Darwin's *Origin of Species* was published, before his generation of biologists retired and the Theory of Evolution could become widely accepted.

Gordon's hotel room phone rang between two of his dialing attempts. It was his secretary Elizabeth calling from California. "I thought you might be in your room trying to call home," she said. "The news says all incoming phone lines are saturated with outside calls from families and friends. I figured I might be able to call out and reach you. I just talked to Shirley in Boulder Creek, and she and your home are O.K. She told me she was out on the deck when it happened. She was ignoring it as a typical California earthquake until the back and forth shaking became intense. She ran off the deck onto your driveway, and watched the trees swing and your neighborhood chimneys fall onto roofs. She said your cat Winchester was smart enough to follow her!"

"That's a relief. Thanks for calling both of us."

"We still have power in Scotts Valley, but there's none in Boulder Creek, and there's great damage in Santa Cruz." Gordon remembered the old unreinforced brick buildings in Santa Cruz and feared the worst. "Shirley was able to start your emergency generator, and your elderly neighbors Joe and Eva are staying at your house. Their chimney collapsed into their living room, throwing bricks everywhere. Their refrigerator threw its contents all over their kitchen and there's broken glass everywhere."

Gordon thanked her again and called Northwest Airlines to get a flight home. They were happy to reschedule Gordon's flight home, adding $500 to his fare because they had a near monopoly on Minneapolis flights.

He flew back to San Jose Airport the day after the earthquake and began his drive home. His car was stopped by a police barricade at the point where Highway 17 began its southwesterly climb over the Santa Cruz Mountains. Gordon could see immense boulders that had rolled onto the highway.

"Take it slow and watch for road collapses," a policeman said after he checked Gordon's driver's license to verify he lived in Boulder Creek. "Bear Creek is the only passable route to Boulder Creek."

Gordon drove slowly up the highway, turning onto tortuous Bear Creek Road. As dangerous as Highway 17 was, it was four lanes wide and far straighter than the Bear Creek two-lane mountain road, which gave him little room to dodge fallen boulders and trees. Santa Cruz mountain roads were rough enough in normal times and he finally arrived home an hour later than the 45 minutes the drive normally took. He saw Eva and Joe as he walked in and kissed Shirley. "I'm so sorry about your home," he said to Eva.

"We've been camping here for three days, with no water except what's in the water heater and toilet tanks, and no power in the neighborhood except our generator," Shirley said.

"Living in Boulder Creek is always an adventure" he replied. "If it isn't a power outage, then it's a forest service helicopter looking for the marijuana gardens of hippies living in the woods. Or it's a forest fire. Remember last year when a town fire truck came up our driveway and parked for hours with its motor and lights on, protecting our home from a forest fire above our cliff?"

Gordon wondered what earthquake damage he would find at Seagate the next morning. He envisioned a scene of total collapse, thousands of disc drives buried in earthquake rubble. He hoped he wouldn't see buried people.

When he arrived at Seagate he found the buildings were still standing, but they had been badly shaken and everything loose had fallen off shelves and been scattered across floors. His group was all there, and everyone's home was still standing, though many were damaged.

Rob introduced Gordon to Phil, a new employee Tom had just hired, who had flown to San Jose Airport on the day of the quake for his job interview. Phil shook his hand and said, "Every road into Santa Cruz was closed by landslides except the coast highway. I spent the earthquake evening on a foggy, slow drive south down Highway 1 and when I passed through the dark ruins of Santa Cruz, it looked like a deserted ghost town. I had to sleep in my rental car. Early the next morning, I found Tom camping out in his headquarters office with a gas lantern and camp stove."

"I can tell from the fact that you actually made it in for the job interview that you're our type," Tom had said, hiring him on the spot.

The earthquake caused major damage to businesses and homes in Santa Cruz County, where its intensity was greater than at its Loma Prieta epicenter. Scientists put the earthquake intensity at Boulder Creek at magnitude 8.1, nearly matching the intensity of the great 1906 earthquake that had destroyed San Francisco by fire.

Most of the earthquake recovery forces were concentrated in the San Francisco Bay area. Santa Cruz County was considered just a rural backwater. It took over a week before power and water were restored to small towns like Boulder Creek.

The Santa Cruz City Council rarely agreed on any issue and they squabbled for a decade over rebuilding the city. Many wanted improved public safety for future quakes but others demanded historical architectural accuracy. The town was finally rebuilt, eliminating many of the unreinforced brick buildings that caused so much damage and several deaths.

52.

Communist Disc Drives

A few months after they returned from China, Gordon and Jack were back in Doug's office. "This time I want you to go to Russia with Sandy, who's looking into setting up a sales office in Moscow for Tom, so we can sell drives there. They'll ask us to build a drive factory in Russia and to use their technology. See what they have."

Sandy was Seagate's V.P. of manufacturing, having taken over the post after Tom was promoted to President. After talking to Sandy, Gordon and Jack realized that opening a Russian office would be a difficult task. Russia didn't allow electronic document transmissions by email or even by fax. All communications had to be monitored by Russian authorities. The only electronic means allowed was Telex, a forerunner to fax machines that no longer existed in the West. Seagate would have to find and set up a Telex machine in Scotts Valley, to talk to another in Moscow. Sandy had also learned that hours of advance notice would be required for each Telex, for the Russian monitors to get prepared. Gordon nominated Marc to head the Moscow office.

They landed in Moscow two days later. The city looked bleak and dreary as a taxi drove them to their hotel rooms at the Armand Hammer Center. They passed a massive American Embassy complex, empty and dark.

"It's never been occupied," Sandy said. "The U.S. State Department contracted with Russians to build it without overseeing their work. The Russians installed bugging devices in the walls. The Americans discovered many of the bugs but couldn't be certain all had been found. The embassy building was left unoccupied and abandoned."

Looking around their hotel they found a restaurant and a gift shop, both displaying signs announcing that they accepted hard currency only. That meant American dollars were O.K., Russian rubles not. Gordon bought a set of Matrioska nesting dolls for Shirley. He said to the store clerk, "What are rubles worth? Should I get some rubles to spend in Moscow?"

"Rubles aren't worth much and they don't pay us very many of them. But we don't work very hard either."

When Gordon tried to shave the next morning he found his electric razor had somehow turned itself on while traveling and its battery was dead. It took days to find a disposable manual razor for sale in the city.

The next morning a limousine from the State Committee for Informatics drove them to visit a factory in the suburbs of western Moscow. The limo had a radio telephone but its wires were torn and disconnected. They were met by the plant director and a Russian engineer. The engineer took Gordon to a private meeting room.

When they were alone he immediately asked, "How do I buy Seagate drives?"

Gordon replied, "What size and what capacity drives do you need?"

"I'll take any kind of drive that doesn't crash like the filthy drives the Bulgarians sell us." He suddenly shut up and looked around the meeting room. Gordon guessed he was thinking of bugs.

The Russian engineer continued in a lower voice, "Magnetic recording technology here in the East won't look very modern to you, but if you understood the conditions we work in..."

They talked for several minutes until the plant manager came to invite them to join the others for a factory tour. On the tour Gordon saw their disc drive technology was more than thirty years old. Apparently some U.S. drive manufacturer had long ago built a plant in Sofia, Bulgaria, which they ran until the Cold War Iron Curtain closed around Eastern Europe. The Bulgarian plant had continued on with its frozen technology.

The tour ended with the plant manager taking the group outdoors to inspect an outer wall of the factory. "These bullet holes mark Hitler's closest approach to Moscow during World War II, in November 1941. The workers in this factory fought the Germans off with their hunting rifles. Not far from here is the cottage Napoleon stayed in during his 1812 occupation of the city. Both armies were destroyed by our Russian people and by our Russian winters."

That evening they were taken to a farewell banquet hosted by the Director of the State Committee for Informatics. Gordon survived the first two toasts of straight vodka, but with the third he began pouring the jiggers into a nearby potted plant. *The plant looks dead anyway.* The Russians grew more and more exuberant, telling increasingly loud

World War II stories about their courage as generals. Jack matched their voluminous toasts.

At breakfast the next day Jack said, "I talked to a scientist from their top secret Russian institute in Izhevsk. Do you know what they did there?"

"Nope."

"That's where they developed their hydrogen bomb. He told me Russia isn't very careful with radioactive materials and most of the workers have come down with cancer, including him."

They had a day to sightsee before their return flight. At Red Square they saw St. Basil's Cathedral and the 40-ton Tsar Cannon, the largest bore in the world with one ton cannon balls.

Jack said, "Do you think this giant gun was ever fired, Gordon?"

"No, that bore would explode the first time it was fired. Cast iron of that day wasn't very strong. In fact, iron still wasn't very strong when the British built the Titanic steamship."

As they entered the Moscow airport the next day, Gordon saw a soldier interrogating a Russian woman carrying packages she wanted to take onto a plane. When they all boarded the same plane half an hour later, he saw she had only half of her packages.

As the British Airlines jet took off, Gordon sighed with relief. "It feels the same as when we left China, Jack, like escaping from a prison."

53.

Success Means Change

As Seagate grew to 80,000 employees worldwide, its original cowboy culture became increasingly incompatible with its maturing business. Seagate's priority of low-cost mass production needed to evolve into an equal priority for developing new technology. The company increasingly failed to be the first manufacturer of higher capacity disc drives. As the second manufacturer of a new drive model, its profit margins were strained even with its low factory costs. The first manufacturer enjoyed high prices and profits, but when competition began between two companies, prices and profits immediately fell for both. Gordon and other Seagate managers struggled to change this corporate culture but the original low-cost manufacturing culture was hard to displace.

As the company grew, large corporation rules inevitably arrived. Newly hired managers gave priority to less essential tasks, like mandatory employee meetings on topics like workplace violence, sexual harassment, and corporate ethics. Many of the engineers Al and Doug had originally hired hated the meetings, thinking the subject matter obvious, the time wasted, and the value to the company contribution nil, except for a little protection against lawsuits.

At one such meeting on corporate ethics, a woman from human resources addressed a roomful of engineers. "Let's discuss using the company xerox machines for personal copying. Suppose you need a copy of your driver's license. You could use a company xerox or you could spend an hour of Seagate's time driving to Kinko's. Makes sense to just use the company copier, doesn't it?" She looked around at the stone faced audience.

"Now suppose you want to make 90 copies of an invitation to a party at your house. What's the ethical choice in that case?" She looked around at the room full of engineers; some yawning, others trying to hide their boredom, a few doing engineering paperwork. Gordon sat in the rear doing email on his laptop computer.

Mike, one of the senior engineering managers spoke up. "I don't believe that question has any relevance at Seagate." The woman looked baffled.

"We work 70 hour weeks. I'm home so little that my wife just divorced me. Where and how would I make friends with 90 people to invite to a party I wouldn't have time to attend anyway?" The room erupted in laughter, including the lecturer.

"Let's move on to another subject: Seagate itself. What do you like and dislike about the company today?"

Mike answered. "The good things are the company is changing for the better, we all trust Al, we managers are free to do our jobs, everyone wants success, and the pay and benefits are fair. What's bad is that we have little job security with these draconian layoffs, no chance of job advancement, company communication is weak except for Al himself, and the original 'open information' Seagate seems to be vanishing."

Gordon spoke up. "These problems come naturally in a rapidly expanding company, and our culture has to evolve if we're to continue to succeed. We have to keep the open company spirit and begin to value technology innovation as well as manufacturing muscle. And it's we managers who have to champion that, not somebody else."

Seagate did begin to advance in drive technology, but the process would take a few years. Acquisition of the Minneapolis head and high-end drive business greatly helped Seagate evolve into high-tech R&D. Al also bought Finis' Longmont drive company, which brought sophisticated design management to the company. Its CTO John required his engineers to use standardized parts as far as possible, designing new parts to be adaptable for future drives as well as the current one in design.

Buying Longmont was Al's solution to the type of disruptive technology problem that had doomed DEC. Seagate had failed to sell its own 3.5-inch drives, but Finis had succeeded in establishing a market for them. Al could see that 3.5-inch drives were the future. By buying Longmont, Al avoided the trap that DEC fell into.

Al also knew that bringing Finis' fist-class drive design and management team into Seagate would greatly enhance Seagate's R&D ability.

Gordon became freed from most engineering panics and he turned to R&D. When asked to give public talks he no longer chose purely technical topics. In one talk he told people that global technology manufacturing benefited the world's people more than past political diplomacy. His "world peace through high-tech manufacturing" was an overstatement of course, but technology globalization did greatly benefit the lives and well being of ordinary people worldwide.

"Those living in poor nations untouched by technology have few material possessions to lose, making violence and war common. People tend to avoid violence when they have possessions to lose. Asians in Singapore and Thailand have become increasingly better off, and China will follow. Asian employee pay was initially lower than in richer nations, but rose rapidly over time. Also, the world should adopt global free trade laws to help people put out of work by lower foreign wages, to help them find new jobs at living wages.

"The futurist Robert Sawyer predicted that technology will one day be able to record a person's entire life. Every act, every conversation, everything learned and every event experienced will be recorded, a life record for every person on Earth. All records will be private and confidential unless the person is suspected of committing a crime. Then, if he agreed, a panel of judges will inspect his life record, which will conclusively prove guilt or innocence. Nearly all crime will cease and only the brightest honest lawyers will have work.

"Of course, new technologies can be used for evil as well as good. If life records of the future could be read without a person's permission, privacy would vanish. Without privacy, new businesses, new products, trade secrets, and inventions would cease to exist. Perhaps courtship and marriage would vanish as well.

"These life records will be stored on future disc drives the size of a quarter with giga-giga-gigabytes of storage capacity."

He showed a cartoon of a future scene of a man kneeling on a carpet, inspecting it inch by inch.

Its caption read, "I just upgraded my life-record disc drive to 100 exabyte capacity but I dropped it somewhere in this carpet. Please watch where you step."

"An exabyte is a thousand petabytes," he said, "each petabyte is a thousand terabytes, each terabyte is a thousand gigabytes, and each gigabyte stores a billion alphabetic characters."

54·

Diversifying the Storage Business

Doug was the next Seagate founder to leave the company. He resigned as CTO to begin a long-awaited deep water voyage in a large sailboat he had designed and had built in Delaware. He planned to sail it down the East Coast, through the Panama Canal, and back to California.

Stan was made CTO after Doug left, and took on Seagate's struggle to become technology-first and market-first with new drives.

Al decided to stabilize the company's boom and bust business cycles by diversifying into different parts of the computer data storage business. He interviewed Steve, an executive from a semiconductor company.

"Al, flash memory is a type of semiconductor memory that doesn't require power to keep stored data intact, unlike normal computer memory DRAM chips. Flash is electrically programmable memory originally developed to store small programs for special purpose devices like calculators and credit card readers. Flash chips today store only a few megabytes and cost a hundred times more per megabyte than Seagate's magnetic disc drives. But Intel and other chip companies are scaling flash chips up so one will store 128 megabytes.

"If Seagate sold flash drives in volume the chip price would drop below $30 and we'd quickly be selling high-volume removable flash storage devices. The competition isn't Seagate's non-removable hard drives that store tens of gigabytes. It's the 3.5-inch floppy disc drive which has been stuck at 1.4 megabytes for years. Low cost flash drives will kill floppies. They could also take the small-capacity low-end disc market, the smallest diameter single-disc drives. But mass storage will stay magnetic.

"I also have another suggestion for diversification. Let's develop data backup software for the enterprise computer systems that big companies like airlines and banks have. The backup products they use today were developed for old mainframe computer systems, and they depend on having an overnight 'backup window' after business hours. But that overnight window is gone today with the Internet and 24-hour a day worldwide business.

"Those enterprise computers have always backed up to tape drives which are slow and cumbersome. Backup systems will soon replace tape drives with disc drives because Seagate is making discs so inexpensive. In a few years a tape cartridge will cost more than a disc drive with the same storage capacity. The disc backup systems I'm describing will use hundreds of high capacity, slower, cheaper PC disc drives, much less expensive than the fast on-line drives that today's big storage systems use, the drives your Minneapolis drive division builds. Those drives will still be used for fast on-line storage. The new near-line backup drives don't need to have fast track access and disc rotation speeds, just fast serial data storage and retrieval speeds."

"Seagate can develop and sell backup software that fills that opportunity, and can also build and sell the high-capacity near-line PC disc drives. Our backup software will still recognize and allow use of the old tape drives these large customers use today for backup. They'll want to continue using their old tape drives until they see the future I'm describing, where tape backups will be used only for disaster protection, for offsite data backup storage in remote tape vaults."

Al thought a moment and replied, "Steve, your two new product lines have several additional advantages besides diversifying our drive business. First, we won't be directly competing with our own drive customers. If we did that they'd retaliate by buying their drives from our competitors. Second, we'll make money selling the backup drives. Third, both businesses are within Seagate's core competency, computer data storage. I've watched too many businesses expand into product lines they don't understand and ultimately fail in.

"So I agree," Al decided. "Let's start both businesses. Join us at Seagate and we'll start a new division with you as head. We'll call it 'Seagate Software.'"

Al was quite willing to simultaneously start two new businesses. He knew to make big bets when he had winning cards.

55.

Epilogue

Twenty years after Seagate invented the PC hard disc drive, the company replaced IBM as the drive industry leader. Seagate's magnetic disc drives progressed from their initial five megabytes capacity to hundreds of thousands of megabytes. Al drove prices so low that drives began appearing in consumer products like automobile GPS route finders, video cameras, portable music players, and automatic TV video recorders.

Billions of disc drives are in use today; they store the world's information and empower the Internet.

Magnetic drives outran challengers like optical disc drives, holography, and flash memory chips, by offering hundreds of times higher storage capacity at lower prices. Flash did reach gigabyte chip capacity, years later than Boris had predicted at the Arrowhead Workshop, but at a cost three times lower than Boris' estimated. Like many engineers, he underestimated the pricing power of mass markets. The smallest diameter 0.85-inch and 1-inch drives have competition from flash today, but large capacity drives do not.

Seagate's flash memory investment became SanDisk, which Seagate prematurely sold before it became one of the world's largest flash manufacturers.

Holographic memory is still pursued today by a few companies, nearly two decades after Seagate closed Imprimis holographic research. Holography remains "the wave of the future" and may always remain so.

High-tech maturity finally arrived when Seagate consolidated its drive engineering design centers into Longmont, Colorado, and into Minneapolis, and started a research division in Pittsburgh. Today, Seagate's design and manufacturing technology is world class and it is the leader in its industry.

Seagate makes more drives than any other company, in the worldwide drive market that will soon exceed one billion drives each year. It continues to grow its business through advances in technology and manufacturing, and buying other drive makers. It drove many other disc drive companies to sell out or consolidate, including IBM which sold its drive business to Hitachi.

Seagate became the first drive company to successfully produce and use sputtered thin film cobalt discs in high volume. Today, about a billion discs are made each year world-wide, all sputtered with cobalt alloy films like the mystery disc. Its longitudinal magnetic orientation is finally being displaced by the advanced perpendicular orientation that TVC demanded, two decades before its time.

Seagate today is the most vertically integrated disc drive company in the world, making its own heads and discs. They are less expensive and frequently superior to the components its competitors have to buy from outside suppliers. Seagate's Asian divisions grew from Singapore into Thailand and today into China.

The Seagate recording head division in Minneapolis met Tom's demand for lower cost thin film heads. They reduced the head and air slider size so many more thousands of heads could fit on a larger wafer. That dropped the cost per head, just as semiconductor chip cost drops by putting a larger number of smaller chips on larger Silicon wafers. Seagate's recording heads now fly above its cobalt discs at only a fraction of one millionth of an inch.

Seagate abandoned the old ferrite head technology, having successfully harvested its last profits, and continued its path to high technology at low cost. The company adopted the Minneapolis thin film head technology and evolved it into today's nanotechnology magnetoresistive heads, which operate by quantum mechanics principles. Minneapolis head manufacturing boomed with success, requiring it to expand its building. Its half mile long corridor became nearly a full mile long.

The Seagate Software business that Al and Steve started became enormously successful and Seagate spun its backup software off as an independent business named Veritas. Its stock became worth more than Seagate's own stock, in the dot-com boom before 2000. Seagate sold its shares in Veritas and used the money to take itself private in a multi-billion dollar stock transaction, thereby capturing several billion dollars of the dot-com boom before it would be lost in the bust. Cowboy company yet! Seagate is today a public company again.

The establishment of the Center for Magnetic Recording research at the University of California at San Diego, and another center at Carnegie Mellon University in Pittsburgh, led to computer data storage research centers being established in universities all over America, then spreading around the world, to Japan, to Singapore, and to Thailand. Soon they will spread to China.

Al finally left Seagate in 1998 over a difference with Seagate's board of directors, which earlier had begged him to stay, promising him 150,000 shares of company stock if he remained as CEO five more years. Two years after their promise, the Board suddenly became desperate for him to leave. Gordon thought Al might have been protecting his 1980 engineering team responsible for Seagate's original success, by refusing Board cost-cutting demands to shut down his Scotts Valley engineering design center. The Board wanted to consolidate all Seagate's PC drive design engineering into Finis' 3.5-inch drive Colorado plant that Seagate had bought. California had become unfriendly to employers and Seagate wanted to move engineering to Colorado and Minnesota, and manufacturing to Asia. That happened after Al left. Three Seagate drive design centers in California were closed, in a major layoff of engineers.

Longmont was the correct decision for Seagate's future PC drives. Only Seagate's headquarters remained in California, white collar jobs with no manufacturing and far smaller California taxes.

Marc was also fired in the layoff, to Gordon's complete and utter satisfaction. Stan called Gordon a week after Marc left. "Stop by my office. You'll want to see what the custodial crew found in Marc's desk while they were cleaning out his office for its new occupant." Gordon walked over to see Stan, now in Doug's old office.

"Hi Gordon, come on in. They found several items that'll interest you. Here's the first one." Stan handed Gordon a Seagate purchase order request form, stapled to a memo.

"Stan, that's a P.O. request I wrote for a gas chromatograph instrument that I bought several years ago for our science analysis lab. That memo is my justification analysis. My first P.O. request vanished after I submitted it, and Marc claimed he never saw it. We wrote a second P.O and took it directly to Doug to get it signed. I figured Marc somehow grabbed and hid the first one but I never could prove it. Here it is!"

"They found more of them in his desk." Stan handed Gordon a thick pile of purchase order requests, all signed by Gordon but no one else.

"You can't know how utterly elated I was to see him fired, Stan."

"There's one more thing," Stan said, handing Gordon a small plastic box. Inside it was a lapel pin with a Seagate logo. "That's your five year pin, Gordon. Marc was supposed to have Doug award it to you at an engineering meeting nine years ago. I can't believe the petty maliciousness of the man and I'm glad he's gone too."

Marc was unable to find another job after Seagate fired him, and his alcoholism worsened over the following years, until he lost his house and finally took his own life. He was the first and only person Gordon ever hated.

After Al left Seagate he founded his own startup company incubator firm in Santa Cruz, "Al Shugart International." Al was made a member of the U.S National Academy of Engineering in 1997. The Institute of Electronic and Electrical Engineers gave Al its Rey Johnson IEEE Award in 1997 for his advancement of information storage technology, and Al was made a Fellow of the IEEE in 2005 for his lifelong contributions to the creation of the modern disc drive industry. In 2005 he was made a Fellow of the Computer History Museum in Sunnyvale, California. Al won the CEO of the Year Award from Financial World Magazine and was Data Storage Magazine's most admired executive from 1993 to 1997. In 2007, Seagate was named "Company of the Year" by Forbes Magazine.

Al died in December 2006 of complications following a heart operation.

Doug's sailboat was constructed at a Delaware boatyard at a cost of $4,000,000, and he took it on an Atlantic blue water voyage down the East Coast. His journey ended in Fort Lauderdale, Florida, where he bought a condo on the Intracoastal Waterway, near his boat. He remained there, mysteriously breaking contact with his West Coast friends; his wife remaining in their San Lorenzo Valley home. Doug owned a Learjet 35 by that time, which he ran as a charter business at San Jose Airport. He left his Lear based on the West Coast as well.

A year after Doug left Seagate, Gordon ran across him in Boulder Creek. He looked gaunter. Gordon asked, "Don't you miss the excitement of a Silicon Valley technology company?"

"Technology," Doug replied, "What's that? I'm only here for a Federal tax audit on my Learjet expenses."

Doug died in 2004 of pneumonia, alone in his Fort Lauderdale condo. His Scotts Valley Seagate friends held a wake at Malone's Bar. Doug would have approved.

Kermit left Seagate, telling Gordon he was going to retire in Costa Rica. Ron "Mr. Clean" had told him there were lots of women and easy living there. Gordon thought that Kermit may have had a problem common to older engineers. Integrated circuit chips were getting too small to see without youthful eyesight, and resistors and capacitors couldn't be soldered into circuits without using special micro machines. Kermit could no longer manually solder together his 3D rats-nest experimental electronic circuits.

Kermit set out southward in his old car, after Gordon had advised him to at least have its oil changed. Rumor said his car broke down east of Los Angeles in Yucca Valley, and Kermit simply bought the first house he found, retiring there. *That would fit with how he bought that car before we hired him at Xerox. I wonder if he's playing chess again, day after day, winning contests.*

Ron "Mr. Clean" was last seen heading east to Hilton Head, North Carolina, in his resale-red sports car with its three-inch ground clearance and the few personal goods it was able to carry.

Stern returned to his native Germany and became a noted university professor. He kept his Santa Cruz home for visits to the California sun he loved.

Jim contracted Multiple Sclerosis and faced life in a wheelchair with grace and courage.

Gordon flew to his last Las Vegas Comdex show many years after his first trip in 1983 to meet Al, and he parked his Mooney on the same ramp where only Bugsy Siegel's modest Flamingo Hotel sign had been visible. Now he saw the stunning panoramic view that had replaced the aging motels and gaudy wedding chapels of the old Las Vegas Strip, today's schizophrenic clash of architectures. New York's Empire State building was crammed next to the Chrysler Building, Statue of Liberty, Brooklyn Bridge, Eiffel Tower, and the Great Pyramid of Cairo, together looking like gigantic toys carelessly scattered by the children of giants.

Sydney, "the inventor of the integrated circuit memory chip and technology advisor to the British Crown," faded into obscurity in prison but resurfaced a decade later. Gordon's fondness for foolishness and offbeat adventures like Baja airstrips, Bugs Bunny cartoons, and cowboy disc drive companies, attracted him to a UFO program on the Discovery TV channel. Shirley especially liked UFO stories, and frowned when Gordon suggested that if a flying saucer ever landed nearby he would quickly hide his wallet. The announcer in the UFO program interviewed "Sydney, the famous Roswell UFO expert."

"Well, well," Gordon said, "Sydney is alive and well and up to another hoax. What would Al say?"

During Gordon's 14 years at Seagate, his group had to rebuild its clean rooms two more times; once after Scotts Valley Engineering was closed and they were moved to Silicon Valley; and then again when they had to move to the main Seagate Magnetics building in Fremont. Gordon's commute from home in Boulder Creek grew to an hour and a half each direction.

After riding the Silicon Valley boom-and-bust roller coaster through a final business cycle, Gordon left Seagate in 1997 to join the University of California at San Diego, becoming Associate Director of the CMRR research and education center he had helped found fourteen years earlier. What goes around comes around. The dot-com bubble was in its final boom as Gordon left, and foolish startup companies were popping up with no hope of profitability. Gordon was happy to avoid the inevitable consequences in store for a volatile technology company like Seagate.

The IEEE made Gordon a Fellow for his work on cobalt discs. He now studies designing intelligent computing features into disc drives, looking towards the future when the immutable laws of physics end today's commercial race of marketing new drives that put more gigabytes on each disc, sooner than competitors can. Physics won't allow bit sizes smaller than a few hundred individual cobalt atoms, and bits are now approaching this limit.

After living 14 years in Boulder Creek with its single good restaurant and single hardware store, Gordon and Shirley were happy to move to San Diego with its potpourri of restaurants, theaters, and multiple Costco and Home Depot stores. They knew they could only move in a southerly direction from Boulder Creek. Going north would mean gloomy rainy winters without Santa Cruz sunny spells between storms. L.A was too overcrowded to return to and San Diego seemed ideal.

Shirley found a San Diego home with a sunny view. It was single story like all her houses, again between 7 to 15 miles from the California coast. They sold their Boulder Creek house to a cautious Silicon Valley engineer from Delaware, who had worked for a San Jose solar power company for five years before he decided the job was stable enough to sell his house in Delaware. His mortgage bank required a septic tank inspection and Gordon asked Jack to bring his big truck over to pull out the Juniper bushes from the front yard. Gordon's coat hanger dousing rods told him the septic tank was buried under the bushes. It took several broken chains and a septic tank company with a honey bucket truck, to find and inspect the septic tanks. Gordon had warned the buyer it was unwise to disturb the septic monster living down below, and the inspection left the house front yard a mess. But it was no longer Gordon's concern. The man's Silicon Valley job lasted only a few years more, and he wound up commuting weekly between Boulder Creek and Pasadena, the closest place he could find work.

Gordon flew their Mooney to San Diego and Shirley flew her Cessna. Winchester cat came in the Mooney, and enjoyed the airplane ride more than the drive to San Jose Airport. They found new parking places at an excellent small airport named Montgomery Field. The field was named for the same John J. Montgomery of Santa Clara glider fame, who had also started hang gliding at San Diego's Torrey Pines seaside cliffs. Gordon's long-time San Diego flying friend James got him a hanger at Montgomery, avoiding another long waiting list. Montgomery was also the home of Shirley's original flight instructor Bill, who was now conveniently nearby for recurrent flight training in their Mooney and Cessna.

Their friends came to visit them often in San Diego, unlike Boulder Creek where they came only once to marvel at the sequoia trees and the Brookdale Lodge with its dining room creek, then leaving never to return.

Flying to Scotts Valley a final time to help Seagate with patent questions, Gordon worked with Karl, one of California's best patent attorneys. Karl was helping Seagate contest Harry's cobalt disc patent, and he had gathered several people together from early Grenex. They went on a field hunt for old evidence that might help prove that Seagate invented the sputtered cobalt disc before the phony dates on Harry's fraudulent submarine patents.

They hunted through SeaMag like private detectives. It was like a TV lawyer show where attorneys did real investigative work. They found that Harry had put several incorrect technical details in his patent conflicting with the historical Grenex documents. Karl said, "That'll be enough to invalidate Harry's patents."

After finishing with Karl, Gordon visited the Scotts Valley engineering building and the big office he had spent so many turbulent years in. The building halls were now filled with attractive software ladies instead of male drive engineers. Gordon's old labs were junkyards full of abandoned equipment and trash. Scavengers had picked over them and taken everything of value.

He was surprised to feel a sense of closure and finality instead of loss. He thought over his past battles and victories and knew that Seagate had been the ultimate technology adventure of his lifetime.

A final word: the U.S. Minuteman ICBM fleet has remained operational in its underground missile launch silos for four decades now, at Air Force bases in Wyoming, Montana, and North Dakota. Their inertial platform gyros still spin ceaselessly in the underground darkness, and their nose cone computers endlessly perform operational readiness checks.

This ICBM fleet perpetually waits for anyone to start World War III. Twenty minutes after the missiles launch, many of the world's major cities will burn and turn into radioactive dust clouds. The clouds will spread throughout Earth's atmosphere and bring global nuclear winter. Few people will survive.

ICBM arms reduction treaties have resulted in the deactivation of only 500 missiles of the original 1000. The oldest obsolete Minuteman I and II maintenance-hog missiles were scrapped, Gordon's hydraulic leakers included. Today's warheads remain overkill, having the explosive force of 1,800,000,000 tons of TNT.

Many Americans today are oblivious to the continued existence of this ICBM fleet, some thinking the name refers to an anti-illegal immigration group.

The world needs to remember this Cold War ICBM fleet still exists and that it remains the most potent weapon of mass destruction on Earth.

The home computer is as common as the telephone these days, but have you ever wondered who to thank (or blame) for the revolutionary hard disc drive that you depend on? Welcome to the high pressure world of Silicon Valley and the startup company Seagate Technology. Author Gordon Hughes was there in the beginning (he's the former Senior Director of Recording Technology) and his fictionalized memoir of the times and travails of this Silicon Valley startup is both gripping, amusing, and so fascinatingly told that it's as addictive as a brand new computer game.

From his days studying with Richard Feynman and Linus Pauling at Cal Tech to his first heady days in the world of computers, Gordon Hughes tells a riveting tale of the early days of an industry that has changed the way we live. A brilliant raconteur, Hughes writes like a dream, infusing the scientific world with grace and adventure and telling personal stories of his marriage and friends with aplomb. There are also lively accounts of Hughes piloting private planes and using a dowser to test his lawn for a septic system. He's also put magnetic sensors into solid rocket fuel to protect space shuttles for NASA, and his company's technology soon goes global, making its way to Russia and China.

But part of the magic of the book is that it isn't just a tale of technology. Indeed, during the course of his life Hughes experiences a sudden spiritual enlightenment, becoming aware of a Central Light. A true scientist, he uses the scientific method to explore and sort out the truth of what he has seen, coming to the startling conclusion that he has touched God.

Hard Drive! As the Disc Turns is a smart, thrilling read that's not just for computer experts but for anyone who has ever pushed a power button.

- New York Times best selling author Ellen Tanner Marsh